The 7th Wife of Henry the 8th

Betty Younis

ISBN: 1523479981
ISBN-13: 978-1523479986

Familiae Meae

Chapter One

April 2, 1502

She sat by the fire, warming her feet. Were the winters becoming harsher, she wondered idly, or did her advancing years just make them seem so. She shivered and drew her shawl closer round her small, bent shoulders. The wimple she habitually wore accentuated her sharp, birdlike features - her small narrow eyes, her thin lips and aquiline nose. The movement caught the eye of Joan, one of the women seated near her.

"My lady, are you cold?" Joan stood quickly, nodding to yet another woman who immediately disappeared into the shadows of the deep and cavernous room in which they sat, only to reappear moments later with a young boy in tow. As he added logs to the fire and fanned it to a hotter burn, Joan bustled round the old woman, placing another shawl across her legs. A dry smile of gratitude creased the old woman's face, and her eyes strayed to the diamond-paned and leaded window nearby. The scene beyond confirmed her thoughts.

Barely had the trees budded, surrounding their dark and arching branches with only an ephemeral, ghostly hint of green which could be sensed but not yet seen. They began as single specimens standing mightily and alone on the great lawn, each with limbs too numerous to count but each with a natural symmetry that was wondrous to behold. Gradually, they increased in number as they fell away towards the great stone wall which formed the initial perimeter of the palace grounds until at last a large copse of ancient heritage all but hid the massive structure. Beyond that still, the rising hills of the park shimmered in the morning's cold mist. She looked out a long time, remembering she knew not what, but praying for yet another year, another season in this life. Sighing while crossing herself, she returned to her work.

Her hands, gnarled with age and arthritis, carefully picked tiny stitches on the linen stretched tight in her embroidery hoop. Only the occasional crackling of a log in the fire broke the silence of the dreary day; only its leaping flames lent life to the stillness of the scene. Suddenly, a loud thudding of footsteps beyond the heavy oaken door of the chamber announced a visitor. She looked up and waited, a faint smile playing round her lips. As she had hoped, a young man blew into the room.

He was tall for his age, and too thin to carry such height. His auburn hair, cut bluntly across his forehead and shoulders, glinted in the firelight as he advanced and knelt at her feet. As she touched him gently on the shoulder, his deep gray blue eyes met hers and he rose.

"Where are you off to, my lord?"

The words were imperious, and he paused in deference to their demanding tone. Smiling inwardly, he composed his delicate features into a serious, yet innocent mask as he spoke.

"My lady, we are riding in the park today, as I believe you know. A fine stag has been seen recently, near the Thames' edge. We shall bring him down."

Before he could continue, a much older, much taller youth strode confidently into the room. His light brown hair, cut in the same manner as his friend's, fell forward with a flourish as he doffed his cap and bowed so deeply that it almost swept the floor. The youth waited to rise until the woman again spoke.

"Oh, rise, young Brandon," she said, smiling at his exaggerated courtesy. "So you are taking my grandson on the hunt today, are you? And shall you teach him courage and stealth as part of the day's lesson?"

"Madame Beaufort, your grandson has the courage of his father and the stealth of his ancestors. He needs no teaching in these areas. He already outshines me, and I can only hope to learn from my most noble friend."

"Indeed," Lady Beaufort confirmed. "Indeed." After a moment, she continued.

"Be gone, both of you. And see to it that you take care in the hunt and come back before the sun sets."

The young men bowed again and backed slowly out of the room. The guard at the door pulled it behind them.

*****

"So, Henry, shall I teach you stealth today?" laughed Charles as they cleared the cloistered hallway and stepped onto the graveled surface of the drive. Two horses reared and snorted while the groomsmen struggled to keep them under control. With quick silky moves the youths mounted their chargers, took the reins in hand and adjusted their grips.

"No, I have it already, as evidenced by the cross tucked safely in my vest," replied his friend with an equal laugh. "And yourself? Did you get it?"

From within his jacket, Charles produced a burgundy bag which clearly held something rectangular in shape. They nodded knowingly at one another and with a yelp galloped away towards a tall, narrow gatehouse situated within the wall which defined Greenwich's innermost grounds. The guardsmen saw them coming from across the sweeping expanse of lawn and trees and opened the gates. Dressed in bright red and black Tudor livery, they stood at attention as the young prince and his companion thundered through and on towards the outer gatehouse. This massive, heavy edifice was more pedestrian and restrained in its decorative elements, and sat low to the ground relative to the arching one through which they had just passed. It boasted symmetrical turrets which projected from battlements on either side of its outer entryway, but was asymmetrical at ground level, with a pedestrian entry to the side of that intended for horses and wagons. Just as the inner gatehouse spoke of a noble and artistic appreciation for architecture with its soaring and finely carved stone, so the outer one spoke of ancient and entrenched power. Its heavy lines arose from a thick, fortified limestone wall which reached nine feet in depth and was taller than two men. On its exterior side lay the great road to London from the estuary of the Thames at Woolwich.

Henry slowed as they approached to give the guardsmen time to halt traffic on the road so that he and Charles could pass over and into the Greenwich Park, the King's own hunting grounds. As he did so, he shouted over his shoulder to his companion.

"We did not lie to my grandmother about our intended destination, for we are going to the park. We just shan't be stopping there."

Another laugh ensued, and with a nod to the guardsmen at the far side of the road, they cleared it and disappeared into the forest.

The wood was dark and damp with the early spring. Signs of awakening life were still few, and the heavy black limbs of the primordial oaks still played a solitary tune twixt heaven and earth. The ground was ripe and smelled of dirt and leaves and death and life. The hooves of their galloping mounts shook the stillness of the place, but registered only a distant thunder in the moldy undergrowth over which they flew. Henry took the lead, but he barely touched the reins; Governatore, his favorite bay, knew the way well. Charles beat a steady second close behind. On and on they went until finally, breaking free of the forest, they entered an open meadow and turned abruptly towards the river, racing along the path which defined its shore. Already the spring rains had begun to erode its banks, and they frequently had to slow and pick their way through the undergrowth which rambled along the path's other side. Their youth and excitement were evident in the ebullience which surrounded their every movement, their every shout, with an almost palpable joie de vivre. After a short while, a thin stream of smoke could be seen in the distance, rising from some as yet invisible hearth. They were almost there.

Up ahead the river drew a sharp turn, forcing the path on which they rode to do the same. As though on signal, Henry slowed and shouted over his shoulder.

"Where?" He pulled up abruptly and waited for his friend.

With no answer, Charles surged ahead before pulling his own mount to a sudden halt and jumping off. He threw the reins over a nearby bush. Henry followed. Together, they plunged into the thick undergrowth but this time Charles led the way. He seemed to know where he was going and after a short moment bent low, feeling beneath the umbrel arches of a spirea.

"Ha!" He yelled as he hoisted a dark and bulky bundle upwards. "Ha - it's still here!"

"Where else would it be, you nit?" asked Henry with a laugh. "Of course it's still there. These are royal lands - no one else dares trod within them."

Both began to pull frantically at their clothing. Jackets, boots, stockings and undershirts all came off and landed in a heap between the two. Just as quickly, Henry opened the bundle Charles had produced and began sorting the clothing within.

"Here - this is yours. This is mine. This is...yours, and these are my silk stockings." On and on he went until the last piece had been divvied out.

They dressed quickly, pulling on their boots at the last. Charles bundled their riding clothes back into the sack, and returned it to its hiding place beneath the brush. Henry backed away and struck a pose, silently questioning his companion. Charles looked critically at his friend before striding over and adjusting the gay peacock feathers which adorned Henry's hat. He stood back and smiled.

Henry had donned a pale linen chemise and used the drawstring to pull it close about his neck. Over that thin garment a deep and rich burgundy velvet doublet over which he buckled a fawn-colored leather jerkin completed the formal look.

His upper hose, also of burgundy, were full and gathered at mid-thigh. Finally, a fine pair of buckskin boots reached to his knees while nether hose met with their upper counterpart. He smiled back at Charles, acknowledging his satisfaction.

"And you, too, my friend - you look as splendid as, as…"

Charles laughed and bowed.

"I look as splendid as needs be, although I think the blue of my slashes do not suit me. But never mind. Let us go."

"Yes," agreed Henry, glancing at the sun as it rose in the sodden sky. "I told her we would be there by noon."

"We've missed that, your Highness," shouted Charles. "But never mind – 'tis good to keep a maid waiting."

Chapter Two

She waited anxiously by the half-open window. Softly her servant spoke.

"Elizabeth, he will come. That is not the worry."

The young woman beside her turned and as always, Agnes was struck by the beauty and intelligence of her charge's face. Long rather than round, it was complemented by a high forehead. But just as the onlooker might begin to think that the forehead was not just high, but perhaps too high, his gaze would inevitably be drawn to her pert nose which offset the forehead to perfection. Her upper lip was slightly short, giving a glimpse of white, even teeth. But all of those features, even if they had not conspired to produce a charming and sweet visage, were naught when set against her eyes. Dark and almond-shaped, they were large and hauntingly beautiful, seeming to draw everyone and everything into their purpose and gaze. No pale skin could compare to her darker complexion and cascading chestnut hair. A simple wreath of wild flowers, picked by her that very morning, adorned her head, and when she smiled, sunlight seemed to fill the room.

"What is the worry, then, dear Agnes?"

Old hands reached out to caress the young face which stared at her intently.

"Elizabeth, you are very young. You have not yet reached womanhood, and yet you do this. I promised your mother I would protect you and love and nurture you. I am not certain of what you are about to do."

"You are my mother," Elizabeth replied kindly. "My mother died giving birth to me, but she left me with yet another. Do not worry, dearest and kindest soul, I know my heart."

A sudden cacophony of magpie caws filled the air. A mighty flock of crows, disturbed by the break in the stillness, rose majestically, circling ever higher until they vanished in the distance.

Elizabeth felt her heart beat faster.

"He comes! My dress, Agnes, my dress – 'tis good?"

She stood and smoothed the wrinkles from the simple, velvet frock she wore. A pale blue bodice, laced tightly beneath her breasts, revealed a finely woven linen underdress. A full skirt of the same blue was intercut with light velvet ivory panels, each adorned with intricately stitched bouquets of pale wild flowers. Agnes smiled.

"Elizabeth, only a blind monk could not love you, child."

A man appeared in the doorway of the great room and moved to join them at the window. As he limped across the stone floor which was covered in deep and rich carpets, Elizabeth watched him tenderly. She knew of his exploits at Bosworth Field, knew in detail how he had plunged his horse in front of their King, Henry VII, in order to save that man's life. He had done this, yes, but at his own peril: it was true that he had survived, but the crushing weight of his steed as they fell together that fateful day had rendered his right leg useless, and only with the help of a stout cane could he walk at all. The sword which had pierced his chest ensured a lifelong shortness of breath. He had been rendered useless even as Henry had been rendered great.

But the House of Tudor did not forget their own. In recognition of the sacrifice and loyalty displayed by her father that day, and in the many fitful days and months of the new reign which followed, Henry raised him from his relatively low standing as a knight of the court. Hence forward, declared the new king, Thomas de Grey would be Baron of Coudenoure. In honor of his service, he would receive a small annuity from the crown. A hunting lodge on the edge of Greenwich Park, originally built in the 13th century as a monastery and long since out of use, was ordered refurbished and appropriate lands assigned to the new barony from the crown's own property of Greenwich Park. It was here that Elizabeth had grown up, just as Henry had come of age at the nearby grand palace and park known collectively as Greenwich.

A loud thundering interrupted Elizabeth's reverie, and all three looked out the window. Galloping at a mad pace up the long, straight drive of the manor house came Henry and Charles.

"Child of mine, you are certain?" asked Thomas of his daughter.

She nodded.

"Father, I shall never love anyone else."

"Come then, let us greet our guests."

The horses reared and snorted as Thomas and Elizabeth moved out to greet them, bowing low on the sweeping gravel scape as the two dismounted.

A warm embrace between Henry and Baron Coudenoure followed. Elizabeth hung back shyly, waiting.

Henry tossed his reins to the servant as Agnes bowed and stood by the wych elm double doors.

Above their gnarled and polished exterior a heavy marble lintel proclaimed the family's heraldic motto in huge block letters:

XXII AUGUSTI MCDLXXXV

REGI PATRIAEQUE OMNIA

"Come," said Henry to Thomas, "We will talk as men." Thomas smiled and led the small party back into the manor. Henry never looked at Elizabeth, nor she at him.

"Elizabeth, my child, take Lord Brandon into the great hall. Agnes will see to your needs. Henry and I have business to discuss in the library."

Elizabeth did as she was told, and Brandon followed behind her. The old man limped slowly down the arching hallway, waving away Henry's offer of assistance.

"Young man, you will be delighted with what I am about to show you," he declared as he shuffled along. "Do you recall your last visit here?"

"Indeed," replied Henry, uncertain where the conversation was going.

"And do you remember that your father, His Royal Highness, had very kindly remembered me when he was offered the contents of that treacherous beast Lord Ritland's library as part of the settlement for his disloyalty and overwhelming hubris?"

They passed beneath the heavy limestone lintel, a remnant of the original 10th century monastery which marked the entry into Coudenoure's library. Henry attempted to reply to the question but Thomas kept talking, oblivious of the younger man's eager attempt to join the conversation.

"Well," he continued without waiting for Henry to reply, "Your father graciously sent to me yesterday…" he sat suddenly, almost violently, on a chair of deep repose, gasping for breath. Henry quickly moved to his side.

"Thomas, my lord, you are not well."

A twinkle and a kind and knowing smirk met his concern. Henry laughed, but before he could take the chair next to the old man, Thomas waved his cane vigorously.

"I need no help to fall into a chair, young Henry, but there, yes - you see the crate? Yes, drag it over here and open it. I have been waiting since yesterday to open it."

"You waited for me?" Henry was deeply touched.

"You are doubly dear to me, my son," replied Thomas. "As the son of my prince, and as the son I never had nor will have till you marry my Elizabeth." He looked down suddenly and his tone shifted as he clumsily wiped at his eyes.

"Now, open the damned crate!"

Henry stood for a moment, amazed at the open affection the old man felt for him. It was true that all during his childhood, lord Thomas and his daughter, Elizabeth, had provided a constant and nurturing second home for him. When his father was distant, when his mother was too busy with other children and the crown's many households, when his domineering and demanding grandmother, Lady Margaret Beaufort was too much to bear, Henry had always been able to escape to a loving place of peace and warmth - Coudenoure Manor.

Nevertheless, Thomas' overt display caught him off guard, and made him realize how lucky he was to have such unconditional love from such a loyal and intelligent subject. Coupled with his own love for Elizabeth, it made for a perfect future - he could not envision a happier place to be.

"Well, my lord, we shall open this trove and see what treasure my dearest father has bestowed upon you!"

After much cursing and hunting for tools to pry the heavy lid off the box, it finally stood open, positioned between Henry, sweating at the exertion, and the old man faint of breath with anticipation. With youthful impatience, Henry tossed aside the clean hay which had been used for packing. Both peered in.

"Oh may God have mercy upon my soul." The old man crossed himself as Henry pulled a heavy tome from the wooden crate. It was bound in plain calfskin crackled with age. Henry passed the book-sized collection of bound parchment sheets to the old man. With shaking fingers, he opened it to the first page. Both stared in wonder.

"Livres des merveilles du monde," breathed Thomas reverently, "The book of the marvels of the world."

"Indeed," exclaimed Henry. "My word, I do not know of anyone who owns such a manuscript. Tell me, did this Marco Polo write it himself?"

"No, no, young Henry," explained Thomas, "The story was dictated by him to his cellmate, Rustichello, while he was in prison once he returned home. Now when was this particular copy made..."

They both searched until Henry finally pointed excitedly to a passage buried deep within a prologue.

"Thirteen hundred. 'Twas published in the year of our Lord 1300 - holy mother, it is some 200 years old!"

The old man sat stunned and thrilled at his sudden acquisition of one of the rarest books in England. He drifted further and further from the moment, lost in the worn pages of the work by Marco Polo. Henry sat nearby and waited, pleased that the old man was pleased. But he was keenly aware of the time and of his original purpose. With a polite cough, he drew Thomas back from his wandering thoughts.

"Yes, yes, of course," he said. "You wish to discuss the business at hand, do you not?"

"My lord," Henry launched into his prepared speech, "I am the son of the King, albeit the second son. When Arthur comes to the throne, I shall support him and enjoy a full life at court. I will, of course, have my own lands and castles and estates, and shall strive to be good man, a learned, just and compassionate man, in all I undertake."

Thomas nodded.

"Go on," he said.

"Your daughter, Elizabeth, has ensorcelled me. I love her deeply and truly as my only love. When we were children on our neighboring lands, she and I played at childhood games as though we were brother and sister. You know this, as does my father. We know each other as only those who have grown up together can do. Now that we are older, we have come to realize that we share a great many passions - for books and music, for science, for home and the House of Tudor. I know myself, and I know that my heart will forever be hers."

Henry stopped, bowed low before Thomas, and on bended knee finished his speech.

"I therefore beseech you, Thomas de Grey, Baron of Coudenoure, to grant me thy daughter's hand in a pre-contract of marriage. This pre-contract, in recognition of the law of the land and the law of my father's will, shall be binding, and will be followed in due time by marriage proper."

Henry bowed his head, then stood.

Thomas looked at him lovingly and long before replying.

"Henry, my son, nothing will please me more as you know. But your father? What are his thoughts?"

Henry shifted uneasily on his feet.

"I have determined to do this, Baron, and so I shall. My father will be pleased but it is best to tell him only after Arthur and Catherine have announced an impending birth - an heir to the House of Tudor."

Thomas nodded and smiled.

"I see your point," he said. "With the line secure, your father may be willing to consider a marriage for you born of love rather than continental politics. You will be free, or freer, at any rate, to marry within the kingdom. And to marry as your heart dictates."

Henry nodded.

"Exactly. My father knows and respects you, sire. He is mindful of your sacrifice for him, and also of Elizabeth being your only heir. He will be pleased, I am certain."

"Elizabeth is not only my sole heir, Lord Henry," Thomas countered. "She is my only family, the last of my line. Mind you treat her well."

"My lord, you know me to be chivalrous to all ladies - have no worries on that score. I swear to you, by my father's throne, by my heart, and by all the gold and riches I shall ever own, that I shall be faithful to Elizabeth to my dying day."

"She is learned, Lord Henry, as are you. She is a mere woman, but she is keenly interested in all that books may have to offer the humbler sex. You must promise that she shall always have access to this library, to my books. Even though 'tis a strange proclivity in a woman, 'tis harmless in her case."

Henry nodded in agreement. Thomas reciprocated and rose.

"Come then, let us go and tell her. I suspect she is fully aware of what we are discussing and will be impatient to know my decision."

Charles Brandon and Elizabeth sat opposite one another in a seldom used room across the stone hallway from the library. Agnes sat nearby, fiddling with her embroidery but not actually embroidering. Charles' intermittent attempts at conversation had fallen flat and he had finally given up and joined them in their silence. All stood as Henry and Thomas entered the chamber. Thomas clumped to his daughter's side.

"Tell me, daughter, do you love this young ruffian?" He smiled playfully at Henry.

Elizabeth's eyes shown with a love so powerful as to be almost frightening. She flushed as she answered.

"Yes, father, I love him more than life itself." Her answer was to her father, but her eyes never left Henry's face.

"There is no formal ceremony necessary, just witnesses," Thomas began.

"I am here as a witness for my friend and liege," Charles took a step forward as though to confirm his words with actions.

"Excellent, young Lord. And you, Lady Agnes, are here as my child's surrogate mother."

"I am, sire, and I shall bear witness to all that is said," came her solemn reply.

"Then, Henry, Lord, Duke of York, Warden of the Scottish Marches, and Elizabeth, Lady of Coudenoure, tell me your pre-contract."

Henry took Elizabeth's small hands in his. His manner changed and he looked into her clear eyes, realizing again how happy he was in her presence. He spoke the words he had rehearsed so often in the days since she had agreed to be betrothed to him through pre-contract. His voice, initially small and almost quiet, gained strength as he spoke.

""I, Henry, take thee Elizabeth to my wedded wife. In witness of this contract, unto thee I plight my troth. You shall have my heart forever and a day, and I shall yet marry thee when the day cometh."

He looked upon the young girl in whom he had so much faith, and whom he loved more than anything.

"In honor of the privilege you grant me by your love, I ask you to accept these gifts, small tokens, of the great love I have for you."

Charles stepped forward and first produced the necklace Henry had hidden away in his clothing that morning. A gold cross, inlaid with rubies, hung heavily from a thin gold chain. Elizabeth bowed her head while Henry gently placed it around her neck. Next, Charles produced the velvet wrapped rectangular object which he himself had secured from Greenwich Palace that morning at Henry's request. Henry placed it in Elizabeth's hands. Without looking up, she loosened the drawstring and pulled from within a bound volume. Reading the cover, she gasped.

"Galfridus Monumetensis - Geoffrey of Monmouth!" Only two copies were known to exist - she knew this from her father.

"What?" Her father stepped forward and Elizabeth continued reading.

"Historia Brittonum." She passed the volume to him. He took it from her as gently as a mother swaddles her babe and his eyes gleamed with a passion only a bibliophile could understand. Tears welled up in his aged eyes, and he looked at Henry.

"This is a 12th century manuscript - My son, what gifts! This is beyond anything I have ever known!"

He looked down and dashed the tears away with his free hand. Henry smiled, knowing he had done a kindness that the old man would never forget. He looked at Elizabeth, her face shining with love.

After a moment, she spoke, mirroring the words he had murmured only moments before.

"In honor of the privilege you grant me by your love, I ask you to accept this gift, a small token, of the great love I have for you."

Agnes stepped forward and gave Elizabeth a small pair of needlework scissors. Without meeting Henry's eyes, Elizabeth separated a lock of hair and snipped it, holding it out to him.

He was overwhelmed at the simplicity and beauty of the gift. A young girl with nothing, and he with everything – tears welled in his eyes at the thought of how much she loved and trusted him. He made a silent vow to himself never to allow any hurt to befall her or her father. They relied totally on him and his chivalrous nature responded to such humble adoration with a surge of protective masculinity.

She looked up at him and their gaze locked for a long moment. Finally she spoke.

""I, Elizabeth, take thee Henry to my wedded husband. In witness of this contract, unto thee I plight my troth. You shall have my heart forever and a day, and I shall yet marry thee when the day cometh."

The room grew suddenly still. As if a sudden cloud had obscured the sun, the light within the great hall changed instantly from the brightness of a bold spring day to the darkening gloom of a winter's eve. Agnes shuddered uneasily. But no sooner had the light diminished than it appeared again, and as on cue, Thomas clapped his hands as an end to the small, informal ceremony.

"Now, let us eat and be merry, for I am to have a son and my daughter is happy! What more could I ever want?"

The group turned to congratulations and a happy chatter enveloped them. Only Agnes stood back, and on impulse, moved to the window and looked out. The sky was a cloudless blue. So where had the change in light come from, she wondered? What had caused the momentary darkening over her dear Elizabeth's pre-nuptials? She crossed herself vehemently, saying a prayer as she did so. She checked again but no, she saw no clouds at all or any other visible cause for the disturbance. A chill set upon her, and she hurried to catch up with the others.

Chapter Three

The simple layout of Coudenoure's rooms reflected their original ecclesiastical purposes: the ground floor was set off all round by a high clerestory which gave light and vertical depth to its stone walls. The current library, with its wide hearth and arched ceiling, had once served as the refectory for the devout greyfriars of an early order of Franciscans. The room extended along the west wing of the manor and save for the most northerly portion of it served entirely as a repository for Thomas' beloved books. One and a half centuries earlier, a fire had swept through the small community of brothers, leaving only the charred ruins of its adjacent sanctuary. Accordingly, the north end of the refectory, now the library, had been retrofitted as a small oratory for worship and meditation. This arrangement proved insufficient for the needs of the monks, however, and the king had ordered their relocation to Cambridge. Across the massive hallway which now served as a foyer lay two rooms. One looked out over the wide lawn which graced the front of Coudenoure, and was referred to by all as the great room. It sole use was for formal occasions and special events. Smaller than the library and square in shape, it too reflected its medieval origins with heavy stone floors and walls, and a clerestory. The back room on the east side served as the main kitchen for the manor as it had for centuries. Its two great hearths and a large double door which opened onto the rear yard of Coudenoure had been part of the original buildings.

Agnes joined the family in the great room. The long table, hewn from a single oak, was positioned near the hearth against the far wall. Thomas sat prominently in the middle chair, with Henry and Elizabeth decking him on either side. A short Latin prayer was in progress as Agnes joined them.

"Lady Agnes!" Charles spoke in an exaggerated manner as each crossed himself at prayer's end, "...You have outdone yourself!" He looked out over the laden table and rubbed his hands together in anticipation. Agnes smiled and inspected the fruits of her staff's work that morning in the kitchen. A platter of civet of hare took center place. On one side of it, a fat swan had been marinated with cloves and garlic and placed in a pastry coffin. On the other sat a large boar's head, stripped and stuffed with apples and raisins. As the eye travelled outward from these delicacies, sweetmeats and sugared plums, tarts and wine soaked fruit provided the secondary dishes. Yes, Agnes thought, it was a meal fit for a high holiday, or the pre-contract celebrations for Lady Elizabeth.

Henry and Charles, hungry from their long ride earlier that day set upon the meal with a gusto seldom shown at normal meal time. Elizabeth, too, with the appetite of extreme youth and excitement, tucked into the feast. The servants, hidden away in the far recesses of the grand hall, smiled as they waited upon the party, knowing full well that the leftovers would soon come their way. As appetites were satisfied, Charles turned to Agnes.

"So, Lady Agnes, perhaps you will be next at the marriage altar."

Agnes ignored him, pretending not to have heard until he made another attempt at one of his favorite topics for humor.

"I say, Lady Agnes, even at your advanced age perhaps..."

"I heard you the first time, young Charles. And tell me, what makes you think that I am of an advanced age? Um?"

Charles laughed aloud.

"Touché," he rejoined, "Indeed, you do not look a day over..."

"Yes?"

"Fifteen."

The table roared with laughter - Agnes' hair was salt and pepper and a comfortable middle-aged waistline was one of her more pronounced attributes.

The conversation rolled on in an intermittent fashion until Henry rose and called for his lute. As he strummed it lovingly, Thomas sang a ballad while Charles and Agnes danced.

"The couple!" Thomas cried as Henry and he finished. "Now the happy couple!"

No one else knew how to play the lute, but Henry twirled Elizabeth to the sound of Thomas clarion baritone and the stomping and clapping of Charles and Agnes. Even the servants watched with lighthearted abandon and added their tapping and clapping to the festivities. After all, their mistress was marrying royalty - it could only bode well for the household's fortunes and thus for theirs. It was a golden day, and they knew it. It would not be forgotten.

Finally, as the light began to wane, Thomas rose and stamped his cane upon the floor, signaling an end to the festivities. Henry suddenly realized that they had long since missed the deadline for leaving in order to meet Lady Margaret's timetable.

It was later still by the time good-byes and well wishes were heard and said. As they stood in the gathering eve, Henry impulsively pulled Elizabeth aside, out of earshot of the others and around the corner of the manor house. Ignoring the hoots and whistles from Charles, he took both her hands in his as he kissed her sweet lips.

"My love, we had no time today to talk just ourselves."

"'Tis well, Henry. We have the rest of our lives to talk."

"And to do other things." His look brought a deep blush to her cheeks, but she held his gaze steadily.

"My lord, I know not about these things, but I know that I love you, and that I am yours in every way."

Henry kissed her again.

"My darling, when you are old enough, and my brother has sired an heir, then we shall be husband and wife. We shall know the full glory of physical love and it will be the rightful and joyful consummation of what our hearts already know."

Henry backed slowly away, and then turned quickly towards the front of the house. Elizabeth watched him go, her hand to her lips. They were still warm from his gentle kiss, and closing her eyes she smiled, completely overwhelmed by joy and happiness.

Charles was waiting impatiently on his mount.

"Come, man! I promised your grandmother we would be back by sundown!"

With a gallant bow to Thomas, Henry sprang lightly into his saddle, and gave full rein to Governatore. They galloped down the drive and Henry gave a loud happy, "Whoop!" It was done. Elizabeth heard and laughed aloud.

Beyond the drive they turned and retraced their path along the river, racing along betwixt the damp banks of the flowing water and the brambled discord of growth opposite it. Charles slowed at the bend where hours earlier, they had changed their riding gear for more formal and festive attire. Henry continued on at a gallop, shouting at Charles over his shoulder.

"Forget it! We are too late and will never clear Greenwich wood before dark even now."

"Lady Margaret will want to know why we are suddenly attired so differently, Henry. You cannot slip past the old crone."

"Leave it to me," said Henry. "We'll enter by the front gate and stay close to the tree line. There is a back door by the scullery and the servant there will help – I know him."

As the night drew on they rode hard, entering the wood well past the hour of darkness. They were forced to slow their mounts and ride at a steady trot in the gloom of the deserted forest. The damp smell of the hot lathered horses, the rot of fallen leaves and vegetation, and the evening mist brought powerful memories to Henry's mind. He had grown up here, in this virgin land. The kings of England had always owned this wood, and it had lain as it had for centuries, for millennia, repeating the cycles of life over and over and over. His childhood had been played out among these trees and copses and he could not smell the scents of the wood without it conjuring up powerful images of his past. His thoughts ran to Elizabeth, and the events of the day. Her childhood had been spent as his had, outside in the meadows and glades of Greenwich, and frequently with Henry as they invented and played children's games and roamed the land together. He remembered her dress, her hair, the faint scent of lavender clinging round her at their small ceremony that morning. He had never wanted for anything, but now, knowing that he would spend his life with the woman he loved more than anything, he knew that regardless of his material wealth, his prior existence had been incomplete. But no more.

The road which separated Greenwich Palace proper from its associated grounds loomed before them and Charles pulled his horse in sharply.

"Do not be a fool, Charles," Henry taunted, "It is the dead of night - there will be no traffic to beware of."

"'Tis not the traffic that worries me. 'Tis your grandmother," Charles shot back as they slowed their horses to a walk and crossed the muddy way. Henry took the lead and they clung to the tree line, still walking their mounts lest the sound of their approach alert the household to their presence. The lawn was wide and deep and it was some time before they approached a small door entering into a back wing of the palace.

A shout from a guard met them as they entered the pool of light cast by several torches mounted securely in iron fittings on the palace walls near the entrance. Henry jumped from Governatore and threw his reins to the man.

"My lord." He bowed deeply as Henry and Charles passed into a long dimly lit hallway.

"Luke, see that my grandmother does not find out about this, do you understand? You know nothing about our movements this evening. And get our horses to the stables quickly."

Another bow greeted his words and with the stealth of lions on the hunt the two young men made their way through the back hallways of the great palace clinging to walls and avoiding the servants. Finally, though, they hit an impasse and Henry turned to Charles.

"See that servant?" he whispered.

Charles nodded.

"He is in my grandmother's hire."

"They are all in your grandmother's hire, my friend."

Henry smirked.

"Indeed, but I know *which* ones she pays extra and *what* she pays them extra to keep up with my movements and report back to her. 'Tis a simple matter to pay more."

"Then how do we pass?" Charles nodded at the guard who still stood stiffly at attention at the great door which would give them access to the grand foyer and to the stairwell and thus to their rooms on the second floor.

"Like this."

Henry produced a small coin from a belt at his waist and boldly approached the guard, holding it out as he did so.

"We passed this way several hours ago, do you understand?"

The guard winked and pocketed the money. Charles and Henry opened the door and looked shiftily about. The man rubbed the coin in his hand and stood at the door warily. He watched them take the stairs three at a time and disappear into the dim recesses of the floor above. When they had gone, he strode through the great foyer and with a knock entered the room Henry and Charles had stood in that same morning. Rising from a deep bow, he spoke to the old lady who sat in the shadows of the fire.

"They are home, Lady Margaret."

"It is late, is it not? Did young Henry say where he had been?"

"No, but they were well dressed so I daresay he was not out with unsavory types. And Lord Charles will always protect him."

The old lady sat up sharply and pinned her eyes on the man.

"Dressed well did you say?"

"Yes, madam. Both of them. Very well indeed." He described their attire.

Lady Margaret Beaufort stared into the fire, listening to his words and remembering the simple hunting gear her grandson and his compatriot had been wearing that morning. When he had finished, she smiled and nodded at one of the nearby women. The woman promptly produced a small coin and gave it to the guard.

"Well, well," the old woman said to herself. "So he has outwitted me. But has he actually done it? Surely he would not pre-contract with that silly girl without telling the King."

But then she remembered.

"Mary! Yes, you. Did you find my ruby cross? Three days it has been missing!"

"No, m'lady, and I have questioned everyone. No one has seen the piece."

A deep flush crossed Lady Margaret's face.

"So perhaps after all he has betrothed himself. And young Charles will never betray him."

She mindlessly fingered the embroidery piece in her lap mumbling to herself as she did so.

"I shall have to counter. Yes…yes. But 'tis a small matter. A very small matter indeed."

Chapter Four

A great thundering noise woke Charles from a deep sleep. He lay on the soft feather bed staring at the tapestry which hung across its top canopy, wondering if he had dreamed the disturbance or if it were real. But no time elapsed before the thundering turned to a great clatter in the hall below. He jumped up and dressed, shouting through the door which stood open near his bed.

"Henry! Henry, wake! There is something afoot!"

"What say you?" called his friend sleepily from the adjoining room. Charles raced in.

"There are men here, for God's sake. I know not why. Now dress quickly, my liege. Quickly!"

He continued to whisper urgently to Henry as he looked out the window.

"What is it? My father? Is the King here?"

"I know not. Come!"

Both men grabbed their swords and ran through the hallway towards the great stairs. Only the night candles, those left burning to provide minimal illumination while the household slept, lit their way. The shadows danced and played upon the great stone walls providing an eerie surreal backdrop to their pell-mell race down the stairs. The heavy torches carried by the men who waited for them there did nothing to dispel the sense of ominous import which enveloped them all. From the darkened recesses of the huge hall came shouts and orders.

"Light the candles, oaf!" yelled a man in back. "I tell you light them all!"

Like ants emerging from an anthill, servants began swarming out of the doorways and back hallways. Candles were lit but no words were spoken by the men who now confronted Henry and Charles. Recognizing one of them, Henry strode forward. As he did so, they all bowed deeply, remaining in obeisance until he spoke.

"Rise, men. What brings you here at this hour?"

Lady Margaret appeared at the top of the stairs with a line of women behind her, all of them fidgeting with their clothing as though they had dressed as they ran down the hallway. Leaning heavily on the two closest to her, she sang out sharply.

"Silence!" The room fell again into a deathly hush, and as the men bowed anew as Lady Margaret descended the stairs.

Slowly and majestically she approached the Earl of Oxford, John de Vere, the man Henry had recognized.

"Upon my son the King's honor, what brings you here? News of some sort?"

He nodded, fearful of what he was about to say.

"Well, then?"

Henry moved closer to his grandmother.

"Lady Margaret, you must sit."

The candles now blazed, and the room was well-delineated from the shadows which still obscured its deeper recesses. Adjacent rooms shone forth as well, and Henry and Charles led her into the small sitting area off the main hall which she preferred and which she used constantly. She sat quietly while the servant stoked the fire knowing that something awful had befallen her family. Otherwise why would Arthur's godfather have ridden to Greenwich from Ludlow Castle where she knew he had been with Catherine and Arthur? What had happened to cause such a wild midnight ride? Why did they insist she sit for the news? Servants flitted in the shadows, and Charles bade them leave. Only the handful of lords - earls and dukes each - stayed in the room. When the last servant pulled the door behind him, John de Vere finally spoke.

"Lady Margaret, the sweating sickness came to Shropshire."

"I know this," she replied. "I knew two days ago, for a messenger brought word. There was deep concern for His Highness and his most noble wife, Catherine, as you surely know. But the sickness was in the marches, but not at Ludlow Castle itself."

De Vere waited, letting the silence speak before he did.

"My lady, your grandson Arthur, the heir to the throne, was taken ill this morning."

Margaret's face paled. Henry stared at the man, knowing but not knowing what he was about to say. Charles caught a deep and ragged breath. Behind them, the men who had ridden with de Vere pulled themselves closer together as though seeking strength and solace in their sheer number.

"How is our Lord Arthur?" Henry asked in a strangely husky voice.

De Vere bowed his head for a moment. His gray locks, wet with perspiration and rain from the long and wearying ride from Shropshire, hung in sad ringlets about his wrinkled face. Finally, looking up, he spoke in a solemn and low voice.

"My lady, Lord Henry, our great Arthur died today at Ludlow Castle."

Henry took a step backwards rubbing his hand across his forehead.

"What?" he cried. "It cannot be!"

Charles' eyes grew huge and without a moment's hesitation, he fell before Henry.

"I pledge my service to thee, Lord Henry. And to your father, and to the House of Tudor."

The others in the room followed his example. Only Margaret remained as she had been.

"And Catherine?" she asked after a moment, the men still upon bended knee.

"She, too, has the sickness, but she lives yet. There is hope for her."

Henry stood dumbfounded, uncertain of his own emotions. Happiness? Fear? Anxiety? Sadness? He did not know. He could not speak and a few moments later found himself in a chair with the audience of men and Margaret and her ladies before him. Still he said nothing.

"And King Henry?" Lady Margaret spoke sharply. "He is tonight at Richmond, with Queen Elizabeth. He has been told?"

De Vere rose and shook his head in denial.

"My lady, I fear to tell the King the news. I am telling you first, and also I tell you that his heir, Lord Henry…" he nodded at Henry as he spoke, "…must be secured from harm before the king is told. Otherwise, he will fear the worst. We must make certain young Henry is safe from the sweating sickness and I have heard a rumor that it has reared its terrible head at Kingstowne in Surrey."

A man moved forward and coughed. Henry recognized him as Thomas Howard, the Earl of Surrey.

"'Tis true, Madame," he stuttered as he spoke, "My son has told me of it this very day."

Margaret nodded, thinking quickly. Despite her grief, she recognized the opportunity she had been waiting for to remove Henry from Greenwich and Coudenoure Manor with its temptations and intrigues. Without hesitation she spoke.

"Henry will ride with you to Richmond. He will be safe there and his father will need to see him to reassure himself of his sole remaining heir's safety. You will all rest here till the dawn, and then ride."

She turned to the woman closest to her.

"Lady Colleen, see that these men are fed, and that fresh horses are provided them for the morrow."

Henry rose heavily from his chair.

"My brother is dead? You are certain? How can that be?" He simply could not take it in. Margaret rose, too, and gently took him by the arm.

"You will warm yourself here by the fire, young Henry. Dawn is almost upon us, and the King needs you."

All shuffled out, all but Charles. He sat near Henry in silence waiting for his friend to speak.

"Charles, you must go to Coudenoure."

Charles shook his head vehemently.

"No, Henry, I shall come with you - you may need a trusted man and I will see you through whatever is about to come."

Henry stretched out his hands towards the fire thinking of Elizabeth and the vows they had exchanged only hours earlier.

"You will join me as you must for I need your council, but first you must ride to Elizabeth and Thomas. You must tell them the news, and let Elizabeth know that I am safe and all is well. I will send a letter with you."

"Ach!" exclaimed Charles. "I had completely forgotten about your pre-nuptial today! Good Lord, what will you do?"

Henry looked at him.

"Just this, Charles. You will leave with me and the men who have come. My grandmother must think you are riding with me to Richmond. But when we have cleared the gate and entered the road, you will part from us, and ride to Coudenoure. Thomas will want to know the details, and you must consult with him. For after your counsel, I value his the most. He will know how to handle the pre-nuptial arrangement and what to do about telling my father. Until then, no word of my pre-contract must be known. It must be kept secret, and when you have finished at the Manor, you will come to me in Richmond. Only then will we discuss our thoughts and decide our path. What think you?"

Charles nodded in agreement.

"Agreed, your Highness," Charles stared at the fire and absently prodded the burning logs with a nearby poker before continuing. Henry knew his friend, his predilection for thoroughness in his thoughts before speaking, and so waited. After a moment, he went on.

"It has the advantage of keeping your grandmother at bay. She cannot question me, and her eternal suspicions about you and Elizabeth will be quieted by your being away. We will see what the good Baron Thomas has to say. Yes, 'tis a good plan."

They sat together until a servant appeared with a steaming plate of bread and roasted beef. They ate in silence, contemplating the unexpected turn of events which had just befallen Henry.

"You there in the shadows." Henry clicked his fingers at a nearby servant. "See that this fire burns hot for my friend - he has a difficult and long journey ahead." With that, he strode out and ran lightly up the stairs. Once in his room, he moved quickly to a desk near the window. The candles were burning, and he sat down to begin his difficult task.

Margaret had returned to her bedroom and paced before the fire. Her ladies waited, thinking that grief was working its way into their mistress' bones, and that sadness would be in her voice when she spoke. Instead, her pace quickened and she mumbled to herself in a frantic tone. Suddenly, she looked up. Only deep satisfaction played across her features as she dismissed them all.

"But mind you come to me before the men leave for Richmond," she directed as they pulled the door behind them.

Smiling to herself, she too sat at a desk positioned near the window. But her task was very different from that of her grandson. Deeply satisfied, she knew she had countered effectively, temporarily at least, her grandson's plans to marry Elizabeth. She was sad for Arthur, but relieved for Henry. And Henry had always been the more robust of her two grandsons, better able to wear the crown. Yes, events had turned her way. Now she must find a future for Elizabeth and her father that would take them far from Henry. She smiled as she took up her pen, and thought of the victory which was almost within her reach.

Dawn was spilling across the great lawn as she finished her work, and carefully folded it and sealed it with her own bright red wax, stamping it with her own insignia. A knock on the door and the sound of horses being brought round from the stables told her it was time to see the men off.

There was solemn chaos in the chill air as the men mounted and prepared to ride. Before Lord John de Vere could do so, however, Margaret pulled him aside.

"This is for the King, and only for the King, do you understand?" she looked at him sternly and produced her epistle from within the folds of her shawl. They turned their backs towards the others. Lord John took the letter and placed it within his shirt while nodding.

"All is well?" his brow furrowed - he wanted no surprises from the old lady.

"Aye, but we must move quickly to help young Henry avoid the clutches of a local woman," she replied knowingly.

"He is but a child!" John was shocked. "And his destiny is to rule England. What is it - some pre-contract between young lovers?"

She nodded.

"What is your plan?" he asked.

"Her father is a local baron," she confided, "And both he and his daughter lust for books. We shall have the King send them on a papal embassy to Rome. They may ask for indulgences for our fair Arthur, and review the Vatican's collection for manuscripts for our own kingdom. You know my son's penchant for books - he will agree I am certain."

John laughed at the old woman's craftiness.

"Indeed, they could be years at the task," he chuckled slyly. "Manuscripts must be copied. And one must find the scribes to do so. Years."

"Indeed," came the response. "Now go, and get the King's signature on all we need to send them to Rome. He will be overcome with grief and will not care about such a minor matter. And see to it that he provides a stipend from the Crown's purse lest they try and beseech him on the matter of money."

John bowed deeply as he replied.

"It shall be done," he exclaimed.

Henry had watched the exchange uneasily from his horse. Lord John, seeing the young heir's face, moved quickly to quell any suspicions he might have. He called loudly to Lady Margaret.

"Your Ladyship, we shall be especially mindful of the King's wife in her grief, and will send her to you here at Greenwich so that you may watch over her. It will be done as you wish."

Henry's face relaxed. His grandmother's scheming related to the tragedy of his brother's death, not his own happiness. En masse, the group turned as like a ship caught by a mighty wind and galloped towards the great limestone gate. Lady Margaret watched, then turned back to the palace with a smile upon her lips.

As they cleared the gate, Charles fell back, and with no notice disappeared quickly into the wood on the far side of the road. Henry rode on.

Chapter Five

Elizabeth slept late and Agnes had let her, knowing that the excitement of her pre-contract with Lord Henry had exhausted the woman child. Her sleep was deep, and she did not hear Charles as he rode wearily to the front door of Coudenoure. Agnes let him in.

"Lord Charles, where is Lord Henry? Why are you here?" Her senses were heightened by the unusual appearance of Henry's devoted friend: he was still wearing his finery from the previous day. He had a lost look about him which did nothing to dispel her mounting alarm. She did not wait for his response.

"I shall fetch the baron." She disappeared up the stairs.

Charles sat quietly in the manor's foyer, and noticed for the first time its high arches supported by ancient timbers. On either side of the main doors stained glass, simple yet richly colored and heavily leaded, depicted scenes clearly medieval in nature:

peasants bowing before the throne of God, or the King - Charles was too tired to figure out which. A servant appeared with hot cider, and after a bit, Thomas was helped down the stairs by Lady Agnes. She saw them comfortably situated in the library before taking her leave and pulling the door behind her. It seemed she suddenly had no curiosity as to the matter which had brought Charles out on such an early morning ride to Coudenoure. Her demeanor clearly said she had better things to do with her time. But once outside the room, she began to run her hand along the limestone and mortar wall purposefully. A rough piece of mortar told her where to stop. Pulling it gently out from between the two stones, she pressed her ear firmly to the opening. The voices of Thomas and Charles could be heard quite clearly.

"So Henry will be King." Thomas' voice held surprise, and more.

"Aye, for Arthur is gone," responded Charles. "And what that will do to him we do not know."

Thomas nodded, his blue eyes suddenly sad.

"He could have been a great scholar," he said. "He has an almost reverent feel for books and learning. I fear that will be lost, for there is no time for it with a great kingdom to oversee. Good God, what a turn! And on yesterday of all days. Is it a sign? And Elizabeth?"

Charles did not answer and so they sat quietly, both thinking of Elizabeth.

"Henry wanted your advice," Charles began cautiously. "It is true that he and Elizabeth are now pre-contracted, but who could see this dire event? And on the very day of their happiness."

Thomas said nothing.

"My Lord Thomas, I am certain that Henry loves your daughter, and I am certain of her love for him. But I fear that whereas yesterday, our good king's benevolence and well wishes could be had for the arrangement, today there is no such assurance. We need a plan, one that will ensure..." he trailed off.

Still Thomas said nothing. Charles begin to babble.

"We must think of what is best for Henry and England, and I know that he loves your daughter and she loves him and that as long as he lives he will love her and she will..."

"For the sake of all that is holy, boy, be quiet and let me think."

Charles was only too happy to oblige.

An eternity passed before Thomas spoke. Charles had begun to fear the old man had fallen asleep or worse, but the stamp of his cane upon the floor told him otherwise.

"We must protect Henry at all costs, for the House of Tudor rests upon him," he began.

Charles leaned forward, listening intently.

"We must also protect Elizabeth, for she is yet a child who will not understand. All she knows is her heart and what it tells her."

His companion nodded.

"We must let her youth and her purity of heart be her shield against this matter."

Charles was uncertain of the old man's meaning, and said so.

"Yesterday, the second son of the king was to marry the daughter of a baron. 'Tis fine. 'Tis good. But today, the heir to the Tudor kingdom, to all of England, France, Wales and Ireland, is to marry the daughter of a baron. 'Tis not fine, and 'tis not good. There are international considerations in Henry's future now. And there are those who will try and use him, or use Elizabeth, to achieve their own ends. And some of those will not hesitate to use them cruelly, even unto their utter destruction."

Charles began to follow Thomas' thoughts.

"We will tell no one of the pre-contract. Agnes is true to Elizabeth, and would protect her with her life. You are equally true to Henry. And as for me, well, they are my world."

"What shall I tell Henry?" Charles asked.

"Tell him that Baron Thomas de Grey, of the Manor of Coudenoure and his daughter, Elizabeth, stand beside him in all that he must face in the coming days and years. Tell him that God has chosen him for the throne of England, and that while we stand with him, and that while he may count upon us for his very life, yet we know that his future has changed. Tell him we wait, and we know that in time, with greater age and experience, he will know what to do. And until then, it is a secret we would rather die than reveal."

"And Elizabeth?"

Thomas looked Charles squarely in the eye.

"We must pray for a distraction, for my daughter truly loves him. Her youth and her purity will shield her as I said, but they will also play against her, for they will also shield her from a mature understanding. Yea, we must pray."

Agnes replaced the mortar, and went slowly, heavily, up the stairs to wake Elizabeth.

*****

It was late in the afternoon, and Elizabeth sat on the far side of her favorite meadow, under her favorite elm. The groundsmen had never pruned the tree's lower branches, and as a result the stately limbs began almost at ground level. Its roots were rounded above the ground, and the effect, of the branch cover overhead and the roots upon which to sit, provided a comfortable and cozy niche from which to view the world around. Henry and Elizabeth had played beneath the tree countless times, thinking they were in their own private world, never realizing that Agnes, from a high window in Coudenoure, kept a watchful eye on them always. The field which separated the great elm from the house sloped upwards as it left the neatly manicured lawn of Coudenoure, and as if struck by an afterthought, leveled out upon a high hill only after its great rise. Between the elm and the manor lay a carpet of spring wildflowers. Snake's head fritillaria bent their checkered petals towards the earth. The tall and stately spires of foxglove were beginning to open their throaty little gloves, some white with purple spots, others a deep lavender bespeckled with white. Wild daisies were budding and everywhere, a cover of bright orange crocuses lay across the landscape and created a breathtaking backdrop. The floral colors, the vernal light, the lime of the newly budded leaves on the gray and black gnarled branches of the heavy trees - all danced to a cool and gentle spring breeze, creating an ethereal space quite isolated from things as ordinary as time and circumstance.

Elizabeth was adult enough to run to a place she felt secure when she was upset, yet still child enough that that place was the aged elm across the great meadow. Agnes was always kind to her, but that morning she had been particularly so. When she went to her father in the library he, too, had been overly gentle. She was beginning to put it down to the old pair realizing what her pre-contract the previous day would mean for them, namely, that one day she would leave them to follow her husband. But then Charles appeared in the library door with Agnes, and she knew something fateful had occurred. She listened attentively as they broke the news to her, and she took the letter Henry had penned in the early hours before dawn to her and placed it in her bosom. She sat without speaking.

"Elizabeth," Thomas continued the thread of the conversation, "His Royal Highness Prince Henry will have many things on his mind this day."

"Where is he now?" she asked.

Charles supplied the answer.

"He has been taken to the king at Richmond Palace. His father will need to see him for reassurance of the Tudor line, and he had to be got away from here due to reports of the sweating sickness nearby."

"And when will he return?"

Agnes, Thomas and Charles all three shifted uneasily. Finally, Agnes spoke.

"Elizabeth, we cannot dwell on his return for it may be some time. We must busy ourselves so that the days pass quickly. Lord Thomas and I spoke earlier and we have agreed that you will have a new tutor, one who will engage you not just in languages, but also in science and philosophy and numbers as you have so often requested. You will have no time to grieve."

Elizabeth understood immediately but she asked the question anyway.

"Why would I grieve, unless this new circumstance shall end my contract with Henry?"

"Ahh," she spoke slowly as she looked round at them, "That is not given to us to know, is it? For my Henry may not be as free as he was as a second son. 'Tis like you, father. When your brother was alive, you were destined for the priesthood, and had been schooled in its rigors since an early age. Indeed, the beginnings of our great library was bequeathed to you by your priestly tutor. But when David fell, your destiny changed, did it not? You became a warrior, a man of the world and not of God."

"I am both," Thomas declared, "But you are right. I took up my sword when David died. 'Tis only because of my fate at Bosworth that I am once again a man of learning and letters. As it was with me, so now Henry's fate has changed. But he is destined to a great future, Elizabeth, one in which the entire country will need him and look to him for safety, for sustenance, for law and justice. I fear we may no longer be able to call him our own - England has need of him."

She had left them then, needing to be alone. The afternoon had been spent looking out across the meadow at Coudenoure. Henry and she had trained a small chipmunk to come to them for food under the elm, had even named it, laughing that the small and happy yet demanding creature was good training for the day they would be blessed with children. For they had known forever of their need for one another, of their future together.

"Bucephalus," she called and passed an acorn she had picked up on her way up the meadow into its small, furry paws. She laughed aloud at the name - Henry said that such a small, inconsequential creature should surely have some greatness about it, even if it only resided in its grand and historic name. From then on, even when they suspected that the first Bucephalus would be quite ancient if he were still alive and that they likely were feeding his great, great grandson, the game had continued. She closed her eyes and lived in the past for that afternoon.

But Elizabeth was a practical woman, and she knew that her current situation required a practical solution. Suddenly, she remembered the letter she had tucked in her dress earlier. She pulled it out, fussing at herself for such forgetfulness - the past two days had taken a definite toll on her. She unfolded it and began to read.

"My dearest Elizabeth,

How I ache to hold you! I must hear your voice once again telling me not to worry, not to fret as all things work for the good as God intends. I need your sweet countenance, your soft brown eyes, your lips, your gentle touch.

Since you are reading this, you know that God has decreed my future shall not be that of a second son. I am saddened by the loss of my dearest brother, by what I know my father and mother are about to suffer, and by the intrusion of events, nay the world, into our private affairs (for now new considerations shall surely fall upon me). I remember the king often telling Arthur that when he was crowned, he would have no private business but that England would be his home, his wife, his love and his passion. There would be no room for selfish and individual needs – he and Catherine were simply God's vessels fulfilling divine purpose.

But yet I need you, Elizabeth.

I humbly beseech you to be patient, my love. Let us see how fate unfolds itself over the next few weeks. Only then can we calculate a plan based on certainty and not on wishfulness.

Hold tight to your love for me. Above all else, remember I love you, Elizabeth, and that you are my own as surely as the sun will rise tomorrow.

Charles has been instructed to wait for your reply before he joins me in Richmond. Pray write to me, dearest. I shall wait impatiently to hear Charles' voice for I know it will be the harbinger of a letter from my lady love.

Henry"

She read the letter many times before looking up. The sun was low in the sky as she pulled a small pouch from beside her and took from it a blank page, a small bottle of ink, and a quill. Her face was different now. It had a determined set to it which Henry would never have seen before. She began to write.

"My darling Henry,

Bucephalus sends his love, which I deeply suspect is tied up with his love of acorns, but perhaps I malign him. I do not know why I open with nonsense. Perhaps I am afraid of what is left should I sweep the silliness away.

My father, Agnes, and Charles believe it would be deadly to announce or even tell anyone of our pre-contract. You are our future king, my love, and none of us will have the situation manipulated to gain governance or place over you. You shall be a mighty ruler, one that all of England will love, but you must not be weighed down by an event that happened only yesterday (only yesterday)."

She paused in her writing, thinking of the past 24 hours. After a moment, she dipped her quill and began again.

> *"My love for you is constant, and will burn as brightly a thousand years from now as it does this afternoon. It is independent of time, circumstance, place or even life itself. I sit under our elm as I write, thinking of what is best for you. I believe that our threesome are correct, and that our pre-contract must not be bruited about. We must wait, for we know not what God intends, only that you, my future king, shall rule a mighty kingdom one day.*
>
> *Until then, I am yours. Even now, when I close my eyes, I can feel yesterday, your lips upon mine, my hands in yours. Keep that memory safe, my love, for whatever else comes, we will always have it.*
>
> *Your loving,*
>
> *Elizabeth"*

She folded the epistle carefully and replaced her writing implements in the pouch before beginning the walk across the meadow back to Coudenoure.

Chapter Six

April 15, 1502

"Elizabeth, come, have a bite to eat. You are looking pale, my child and 'tis no look for a maid."

It had been Lady Agnes' chant for almost two weeks. In true motherly fashion, the older woman had fussed and nearly coddled Elizabeth out of her mind since word of Arthur's death and Henry's future accession to the throne had come to them two weeks earlier. For Elizabeth, there was no respite. Agnes followed her from room to room, intent on lessening the younger woman's burden. Endless chatter about weather, seasons, servants, and neighbors flowed forth from her like a mighty wave upon a smooth and beaten beach. Embroidery hoops and books had been surreptitiously placed in all of Elizabeth's favorite nooks, and each time they came upon one Agnes feigned surprise before suggesting that Elizabeth take up the piece and continue on with it.

But it was not just Agnes with whom Elizabeth had to contend. The very servants who had clapped and celebrated on the day of her pre-contract now whispered quietly together in corners, shooting her uneasy and sympathetic looks whenever she passed. They had heard the news of Arthur's passing as had the whole country, but for them, the uncertainty which always arose when the throne came into play was compounded by their fears for their own futures. They were stiff and jumpy when waiting on the family and responses were slow to questions and requests. It was as if they were waiting for her to do something, waiting for some *thing* to happen, but it did not. She began to feel oppressed by the very environment in which she had always taken comfort.

Her father was moody and withdrawn, keeping his thoughts to himself when she most needed to hear them. Just as Agnes attempted to lighten *her* burden, so she attempted to lighten that of her father. She pulled his favorite incunabula and vellum manuscripts from the shelves of their library. But he refused to move to his desk and study them as was his usual habit. Instead, he sat before the great hearth in that room, listening to her and Agnes' endless prattle, never adding his own nor even really engaging in the days as they flew past. Her efforts to rouse him were the very definition of pointless – he remained in his own world. Elizabeth felt as if she were floating on the wind as she went mindlessly about the manor. She glided here, she glided there, but she was no more part of it all than if she were a thousand miles thence. She counted each hour of the day, longing for the moment she could retire to her room and be alone with no one to remind her of what she knew all too well. A cloud hung over Coudenoure, but no one would call it by its proper name: Henry. She had received no response to her letter from Henry.

She thought back to Charles' promise that day he had broken the news to her. She remembered his promise and his words to her.

"He loves you much, Elizabeth, but it may be some time before he can see you here at Coudenoure again. There is much to be done about Arthur's death, and the King will have need of Henry. There may be unrest and we will have to address it quickly. Be patient…" Charles had paused and looked at the ancient stones of Coudenoure with its diamond-leaded panes and turrets. He looked out over the great lawn, and then back at Elizabeth before continuing.

"…He loves this place, you know. You and your father have been the family he never knew. And this great heap of a bygone monastery is his favorite place."

That was all she had, and as the days had passed, she found herself listening for the familiar thundering of hooves which announced Henry's visits. It never came. Finally, exasperated for no reason and with enough frustration to flame a fire, she escaped out of doors. It was here that she and Henry had found themselves and their love for one another as they had played and romped from one end of Coudenoure to the other. There was no place they had not investigated, no nook they had not discovered. It comforted her now to revisit those places.

She wandered about the estate aimlessly for several days, retracing their steps and their thoughts. As they had grown older, Henry had begun to focus not so much on play but on the layout of the grounds, always wanting to bring order out of the chaos of the jumbled mix of buildings, trees, mud and weeds. As she walked endlessly through the mess of it all, a sudden idea took hold. She halted where she stood, following the notion through. After a moment, she all but skipped lightly to the rear of the grounds and looked around, assessing the randomness of the yard. There was the fine stable with its pitched roof and wide doors. Beyond that was a long, low building, divided by stone firewalls into individual stalls, each with a specific purpose. The washhouse was first in the row, followed by the bakery and brew house. A smithy banged noisily on his anvil in front of the next stall, while the last one was almost hidden by the great kiln which stood before it. Over a low rise was the dairy building and farther yet the slaughter house.

On the side of Coudenoure was an orchard of pears and apples. The scene was medieval in its complexity and chaos. The layout had grown organically without thought of plan or esthetic. Between each building was dirt which turned quickly to mud when it rained. There was no surrounding wall or moat, for the monastery had not been cloistered. That lack of a defining wall had always given Henry and Elizabeth the sense that the estate simply faded away into the surrounding fields with no beginning and no end. Coudenoure sprang suddenly from the earth and then evaporated slowly over the wide horizons of the vast pasturage and wood which lay beyond it.

"Of course! That's it!" Elizabeth mumbled to herself. "We shall bring order and beauty out of the ordinary. Henry will love it."

She ran back into the library so quickly that Agnes rose and Thomas awoke from his slumber in front of the fire. Seeing their alarm, she moved to calm them.

"I have decided what I shall do while I wait for Henry!" she exclaimed.

They stared at her, not sure what to expect.

I will lay out a great garden for Coudenoure. I will take the country round about and make it beautiful."

"Lady Elizabeth, it already is beautiful, as God made all of nature to be." For the first time in two weeks, Agnes' sounded stern. Her father looked at her keenly.

"What have you in mind?" he asked.

"We shall use mathematics!"

Thomas laughed at his daughter, happy to see her happy, but uncertain of what she meant. She continued.

"Father, you and I shall lay out gardens in precise designs. We shall fill them with unusual plants. We will collect seeds as we now collect books – I have heard of such things from the reports of the New World."

Thomas stood while she continued.

"The chaos of the outbuildings will be replaced with an ordered structure. We will make it so."

"'Tis interesting, child, but would be a massive undertaking."

She waited.

"But t'would be a grand undertaking. Coudenoure is small enough that we could manage it." He nodded his head as he spoke.

Agnes looked at them both, pleased to see them once again communicating and collaborating, but unsure of their plan.

"Lady Elizabeth, maids do not do such things."

Thomas interrupted in support of his daughter.

"They also do not study Greek and Latin and Italian. They do not read books and talk about them, either. 'Tis a harmless pastime for my daughter, Lady Agnes. Nothing will come of it but delight for our little manor."

He stomped his cane upon the stone floor and a servant came running from the shadows.

"Stoke the fire, you nit. Lady Agnes, will you join the Lady Elizabeth and I as we peruse the grounds of Coudenoure?"

Agnes laughed.

"I think not, sire. Instead, I shall have prepared an evening meal at which you can share your findings with me."

The cloud seemed to lift a bit from Coudenoure.

Chapter Seven

It was May before the sound of hooves upon the long drive once again disturbed Coudenoure. But it was not Govenatore with Henry astride. Nor was it Charles. It was someone else entirely, and Lady Agnes ran pell-mell through the manor and out the back to find Elizabeth and Thomas.

"You must come immediately," she gasped, bent over to catch her breath.

"Henry? Is it Henry?" Elizabeth threw the large sheet of paper she held to the ground and began to run.

"No!" Agnes shouted between gasps. "Come back child!"

She turned to Thomas.

"It is Lady Margaret Beaufort."

"The King's mother?" Thomas began to limp hurriedly toward the main house. "Why is she here?"

"I do not know, but I am uneasy, sire," Agnes walked with him. Elizabeth followed behind.

"One of her escort came ahead so that we can make ready for her."

"'Tis as it should be," Thomas declared. "The King's mother! But why does she visit us?"

Agnes stopped, forcing Thomas to do the same.

"I do not want Elizabeth to meet her. She can stay here, or we can hide her away in her room."

Thomas looked at her with concern.

"I do not know why we need to do this, but we do," Agnes continued. Thomas waved her silent.

"Hush, woman, we will all honor the King by serving his mother."

They walked on into the great hall. Elizabeth listened in silence, knowing that Agnes was almost never wrong in her intuition, but also knowing that her father would not be moved. It would be an interesting afternoon.

Lady Margaret's steed appeared at the end of the drive, being led slowly and majestically while the woman herself sat stiffly upright in the elaborate saddle. Thomas and Elizabeth bowed deeply as she was helped out and escorted into the central hall and through to the library. Agnes clung to the shadows but before closing the library door, Thomas motioned silently to her.

"Go to your listening post," he began. Agnes interrupted him.

"I have no idea, my lord, about which you speak." She was unsuccessful in the lie. Thomas ignored her.

"If you hear anything that might put our Elizabeth in danger, or should Elizabeth herself say anything that might give Her Highness cause for concern, you must interrupt at once. And remember, she knows nothing of the pre-contract."

Agnes nodded and Thomas pulled the door behind him.

Lady Margaret Beaufort sat in front of the great fire in the same pose she had held on her horse. Elizabeth had heard tales of her from Henry: she had secretly died and her limbs and countenance had been arranged into her never changing pose and dire expression; she possessed an eerie sense of his goings-on, particularly when she did not approve; she was a viper in a wimple; family was everything and the individual nothing.

The servants brought fresh fruit and cider, and when they left Thomas finally spoke.

"My Lady Margaret, what brings you to Coudenoure?"

Margaret spoke with incisive decision.

"An order from our King, my son," she said.

Thomas waited.

"He asks after you, and sends his regards to you and your daughter." She looked directly at Elizabeth for the first time. Yes, she thought, I understand the allure this girl has for my Henry. She was not fair and her dark chestnut hair gave her complexion a darker hue than was usual, setting her apart from the common maid. But it was her eyes – Margaret found herself staring into deep recesses of intelligence, dark pools of knowledge that maids did not normally possess. She shook off the sense that the young woman knew why she was visiting Coudenoure, indeed, knew everything about her. She was bewitching, for certain, but Henry must not be allowed to marry so far beneath him. A king with this woman? Never. She turned her gaze back to Thomas, and snapped her fingers at her faithful Joan who stood nearby. The lady-in-waiting produced a rolled sheet of parchment and passed it to Margaret, who silently handed it on to Thomas. In turn, he unrolled it and read silently for some moments.

"I will do as my king desires," he declared. "But tell me, how did he settle upon this plan? I know naught of the Papal Court."

"He wishes indulgences said for dear Arthur," Margaret said imperiously. "He trusts you and knows that you will do as he bids."

Thomas bowed his head in affirmation.

"And the manuscripts?"

"That is a pleasure for you, sire, apparently," she nodded at the shelves bulging with all manner of books and codices. "I believe King Henry has chosen you because of your knowledge of all matters contained therein. He knows you will choose carefully."

Thomas stroked his chin thoughtfully.

"And my household? My daughter is barely a woman and I cannot leave her alone with her lady's maid, Lady Agnes. T'would not be seemly nor wise."

Margaret knowing it had come to the critical point, proceeded slowly.

"Tell me about this young woman, this daughter of yours. Does she belong at court?"

"No!" Elizabeth barged into the conversation involuntarily. Aghast at her own outburst, she quickly tried to make amends. "My father and I are the last of our line. I must look after him for he is lame, as you can see."

No one spoke and Elizabeth kept her eyes on her folded hands in her lap.

"Child," Lady Margaret spoke with the thinnest veil of sympathy, "Your father is to travel to Rome in the service of my son our great king. You have just heard that you cannot be left to your own devices, and I agree. The only alternative would be for you to accompany him on his journey."

A strange sound, like falling mortar, interrupted their conversation. Margaret looked sharply at the interior wall of the library. Thomas pretended he had heard nothing. Elizabeth spoke.

"Me? To travel to Italy?" It was such a strange notion she did not know what to think.

"It would be odd, certainly. But tell me child, have you any interest in languages or reading?" Margaret already knew the answer - the trap was beginning to close.

"My lady, I have great interest in books and manuscripts and knowledge of all kinds."

"And Italian?"

Elizabeth blushed.

"I do speak it and read it," she said softly. Thomas intervened.

"'Tis a simple pastime for my Elizabeth," he said sternly. "There can be no harm in a maid filling her hours with such harmless pursuits."

"You miss the point, my Lord Thomas. You see, if she speaks Italian, she may well prove invaluable to you on your journey. Not only would this course solve the problem of what to do with her while providing you with the comfort of family, but also give you someone to help with the language."

"But the language of the court is Latin," Thomas countered, suddenly seeing where the old lady was headed. But too late. In her excitement, Elizabeth did not see the dark turn of the path ahead and chimed in.

"But I read and speak Latin as well, so I could assist you, father."

The innocence of the girl was remarkable, thought Margaret.

"Then it is settled. Your household will go with you, including your daughter. She will never marry beyond her station, so 'tis no thing if she should travel and pursue learning with you. 'Tis a harmless pastime, as you yourself have said."

It was almost finished.

"But Madam," Thomas rose as he spoke, "I am only a baron with a small manor. I have not the funds to mount such an undertaking."

"Read again my son's instructions," Margaret demanded. Thomas sat and read again, realizing that even that eventuality was covered. Once again Joan produced what was necessary. This time, it was a small purse which clinked heavily as Margaret passed it to Thomas.

"This is funding for your journey. As you read, the king has allotted you court funding for your manuscript purchases and living expenses and indulgences. You will receive disbursements periodically while in Rome. You will be fine."

She rose.

"My barge will be here two days hence to take you down the Thames to port. From there, I have arranged passage on a galleon. A member of the Spanish ambassador's retinue, a nobleman and his family, are travelling on the same ship, so the accommodations should be fine."

Joan once again produced a document sealed with the king's own imprint.

"When you arrive, these are your papers for Pope Alexander VI. Under duress, you may use them in your travels to protect you and your family, should you need to do so."

Without another word, lady Beaufort walked to the front door. After being assisted in remounting her horse, she looked down from her perch and felt a moment's pity for the old man and his daughter. Whether the sea voyage did them in, whether brigands on their journey to Rome beset them, or whether they arrived safely at the Pontiff's court, it did not matter. She was certain she would not see them again in this life. She had saved young Henry from a disastrous match and in doing so had saved the Tudor line. She nodded to them and was escorted slowly back down the drive to the river where her barge awaited her.

*****

"And *you*, sire! Did it not occur to you that the old bat was manipulating you? That it would serve her purposes quite well for our Elizabeth to be taken to the ends of the earth and quite likely never heard from again? Um? What say you, old man?"

Elizabeth had shooed the servants from the main hall and was at Agnes' favorite post along the outer library wall. She wondered why the stone floor beneath the loose mortar had not been worn away, so frequently was it occupied. Nevertheless, she listened breathlessly while her father took a verbal beating from Agnes.

"Did I not say no good would come from her visit? You laugh, I know, at my prescient nature, but by all that is holy I was right and she means

Elizabeth harm. A maid, a young maid, to travel to *Italy*? And why stop there? Why not the lands beyond Italy of the Moors, my lord, and on to Cathay as well? My *word*! What is that but nonsense and yet you let her speak it. You let it happen."

On and on she went, the torrent of words like a raging river. Thomas never spoke, not out of courtesy - letting her finish her diatribe - but because he was absorbed by the wording in the King's decree. What a strange turn of events. Strange, strange indeed. Agnes finally paused for breath and Elizabeth decided to rescue her father. She hurriedly replaced the mortar and entered the room. Both Agnes and Thomas demanded that she leave, but for once, she withstood their heat and stayed in the room.

"So, father, what is this? I know not what to think about it all."

Thomas nodded. "Child, Agnes and I have been discussing it. 'Tis strange indeed."

"Not strange," Agnes almost shouted. "The old bird knows of the pre-contract. She must, and she is intent on it not happening. She is the one who has hatched this plan."

But Elizabeth shook her head in disagreement.

"Agnes, she cannot know. No one knows but us three, Charles and Henry."

"And further," Thomas added, "This decree is signed by King Henry himself – did she involve him as well?" His tone was sarcastic. "I think not, Agnes. The king would never allow himself to be talked into such a plan, especially by a woman and all to negate a pre-contract? No, she knows nothing."

"You are wrong, Thomas," Agnes was still breathing fire, "And what exactly does the decree say?"

Thomas read it slowly, paraphrasing as he did so.

"It is King Henry's wish that indulgences and prayers be said for his beloved Arthur at the Holy See itself. He wishes for Rome to hold masses and remember the kind and gentle youth who would have been king. It is not enough that all of England do so. The Pope himself must remember and pray for Arthur's soul as well."

Thomas paused and added his own thoughts. "I cannot imagine our King's grief at so great a loss. It must make him mad with sorrow." After a moment, he continued interpreting the decree.

"In addition, and in recognition of my, Thomas', love of manuscripts and learning of all kind, he has directed that I purchase, or, in cases where that is impossible, I should have copied, manuscripts of all sorts: geography, holy books, literature, philosophy, whatever I find that would enhance my library and that of the King, and therefore England's pool of knowledge."

"It is a strange combination of pursuits in the service of my king. To seek prayers for our beloved Arthur and yet seek out manuscripts – 'tis odd."

"'Tis *bait*," Agnes spat the words out. "She knows of your love of books and added this delight to blind your eyes lest you resist the siren song she sings."

Thomas nodded slowly.

"Lady Agnes, I believe there may be some truth in what you say."

Agnes had the wherewithal to hold her tongue.

"But how did she involve the king? I know my Liege well, and he would not stoop to such devious means to end a pre-contract. Not at all. He would send for me and we would talk as men talk, and decide what was proper betwixt ourselves. His own mother would not be involved."

Elizabeth remained silent, stunned by all she heard. This was no conversation about what she had done that day or how her latest embroidery piece coming along. It was the first time she had ever been allowed to participate in a conversation about anything other than the mundane or the sacred, literature or language. She had always been protected from the harshness of life decisions and the despicable nature of those who frequently stood above her. She was shocked at the thoughts being expressed, but something more - she was comfortable with them, and she spoke.

"We must think carefully," she began, and the older two looked at her more in curiosity than in seriousness, "For Henry's well-being, and ours, may depend upon it. I have heard what you say, and Agnes is right. It is too much to believe that Lady Margaret knows nothing of the pre-contract. We may safely assume that somehow she has ferreted that information out. Given that, and given the lengths she is obviously willing to travel to deny Henry and me our happiness, then we must assume that if she fails in this, her opening gambit, she will resort to more drastic measures to achieve her goals. Correct?"

She had their attention now. This was no child speaking, but an intelligent woman laying out a factual analysis of their situation.

"The answer is clear: we must go to Rome. It will allay Lady Margaret's fears, make her feel successful in her scheming. Meanwhile, Henry has much to learn and accomplish in the coming months. Remember, he was a second son, never tutored in international politics, in law, in the myriad issues a king must know and deal with - King Henry only ever tutored Arthur in those subjects. Our Henry has much catching up to do, and the near future is overfull for him now. We will not be yet another burden for my love. We will do as his grandmother wishes, but we will return at the first opportune moment. And in the meantime…"

"Yes?" they asked in unison.

"In the meantime, we must find a safe conduit to Henry, for he will need to know that we have gone to seek indulgences and manuscripts, and that we will soon return. We need a conduit for my letters to him, and his to me."

Thomas nodded his head in agreement, realizing the wisdom of Elizabeth's words. Even Agnes recognized the danger of their situation and understood the need to outwit the old woman by doing exactly as she wished. They watched as Thomas opened the purse given them by Lady Margaret and counted the gold coins within. After a moment, he looked up.

"We have much to do," he began, "And the first consideration is to decide who will manage Coudenoure in our absence. Then, we must consider how one prepares for such a thing as travel to Rome."

As though in answer to his questions there was a heavy knock upon the front door of the manor.

After a moment, two people were shown into the library by a servant. They were an older couple, clearly not peasants but also not of highly ranked or station. The woman wore a faded frock of a brown but fine material, gathered at the waist. The sleeves were long and frayed near the wrist. Her partner, also in brown, wore a simple shirt with a vest whose buttons had disappeared. His pants were almost threadbare at the knees. Neither had a coat. The look was familiar to Thomas, Agnes and Elizabeth, for when their own clothes became too worn and faded for continued use, they passed them along to their servants and others. Clearly that was the provenance of the outfits of the couple who stood before them. The old man took off his hat, bowed and spoke, confirming Thomas' thoughts.

"S-s-s sire," he stuttered, "We are from Greenwich Palace, where we serve Lady Margaret Beaufort."

"Indeed," muttered Agnes.

"We have been i-i-instructed to look after Coudenoure in ye're a-aab-absence."

Thomas nodded and the old woman took up the narrative.

"And sire, Lady Margaret has graciously sent her packaging cases so that your wardrobes and the items you will need for your journey may be safely stored until you reach your destination."

Yes, thought Agnes, the old witch had thought of everything.

"And your wages?" asked Elizabeth. The old man and woman looked at her in disbelief.

"Young maid, we are not accustomed to speaking of such matters with such a young -"

Elizabeth cut the woman off mid-sentence.

"I am sure, and 'tis no concern of ours. I repeat my question - your wages? We have no money to pay you." She ignored the pile of gold coins in Thomas' lap - they would need it all on their voyage.

"Lady, Lady Margaret has generously agreed to pay our wages. You needn't worry your head about that."

"I had no intention of doing so," Elizabeth replied tartly. "Now, bring the packing cases into the house and have Cook prepare you a meal. When we are ready for your services, we will call you."

With that, they were shown out and Thomas, Agnes and Elizabeth began the hard task of planning a journey for which they had no desire to a place they had never known in pursuit of items yet to be dreamed of.

Chapter Eight

Elizabeth had never been beyond Greenwich. Her physical world consisted of Coudenoure Manor and its grounds, Greenwich Wood and its associated meadowlands, and the path along the Thames which ran at the foot of the estate. Her childhood had been that of any gentlewoman of noble birth: restricted and male-dominated. She had never really considered travel beyond her small sphere for the simple reason that it was not offered nor was it considered even possible. She had been content with what the estate and the surrounding woods and fields had to offer. But the ordinariness of her rural life, her utter lack of first-hand knowledge of the world, stood in sharp contrast to the one she inhabited intellectually. She was fluent in four languages, had read the Classics, and could discuss politics and international law with a confidence of thought and articulation that was almost unheard of in a woman. Her abilities, honed as they were by conversations with her father and the reading of the many volumes in their library, had moved from those of an amateur scholar to what, under any other circumstances, would have been considered formidable - a rare thing, even among men of the nobility.

Her father and Agnes had never forced segregation of class among the few children who lived on and around the estate, and as a result, Elizabeth was conversant with widely divergent cultural mores. She slipped easily and naturally between the vernacular of the servants and the Latin of English bishops and Primates. Concomitantly, the childhood games she knew stretched from those which required fine steeds and finer upbringing still, to those played by the ragtag band of ruffians who ran about the estate on which their parents served. Even Henry, taught to strictly to observe class boundaries, had been known to romp with them. But among all of these children, even among those closest to her, Elizabeth stood out. It was a matter of aloofness, they said, a matter of her holding herself apart. As years passed, it was put down to her education, and was much cited as an object lesson in why women should not be educated. But the truth was far more complicated.

Elizabeth preferred the company of books. Her father's avocation, combined with her own naturally curious nature and her unorthodox upbringing, had produced a rare creature, one who could choose which world to inhabit. Did she want to be a child today and play with the others, or did she want to visit her friends who lived in the books and manuscripts she read? Almost always, Elizabeth chose the latter. She had never known anything beyond Coudenoure and so did not realize the oddness of her situation, the sheer audacity of the intellectual world in which she lived. Unconsciously, she assumed that everyone lived in a similar manner.

There had been no time to conjecture about the trip to the Vatican. So sudden was the order from the King that the small household had been thrown into chaos. Two days! Again and again Elizabeth circled back to the suddenness of the directive, but no sooner did she begin to feel she understood it and the complexity it engendered than a servant, or Agnes, or Thomas, burst into the room demanding her attention to this detail or that one concerning the impending voyage. But it was only impending for a day. The second day, the day of their departure, arrived in the form of a brusque knock upon the manor door in the early morning. It was Lady Margaret's groomsmen, arrived with a small army of porters, to manage their departure from the estate and onto her river barge. The low-keeled, decadent Thames' transport would take them down river where other servants of Lady Margaret's would assist them onto the ship.

"She is quite resourceful, is she not?" mused the old man. Agnes could barely contain her disapproval as one crate after another disappeared out the front door and down the drive towards the river. "You should know, Lord Thomas, this is on your head!"

Thomas ignored her as did Elizabeth. Despite the desperately hasty arrangements, and the invidious nature of the event, they both found themselves looking forward rather than backward. It was done, this thing, and both father and daughter became more and more excited about it as the day passed. When the barge finally pulled away from the small dock which had serviced it, only Agnes was looking back towards Coudenoure. Thomas was deep in discussion with the ferryman who steered their passage. Elizabeth felt the fresh breeze coming from the direction of the port. She already missed Henry, but there was naught she could do. She stood and faced towards the sea.

*****

The rays of the late afternoon sun cut a low arc across the small, Kentish village of Woolwich. Situated on the banks of the Thames, it hosted minor sea traffic as a southern port for London. International merchants frequently preferred to load and unload from Woolwich rather than London. Wharf workers were cheaper to come by, and the trip on up river into the heart of the commercial district could be left to the middlemen, those who bought in bulk and sold in singles. Passage in and out of the tiny port was easier than navigating the busy shipping lanes of the Thames further north, and the facility of access to the great North Sea further enhanced its appeal. It was here that Lady Margaret Beaufort had directed her pilot to drop anchor.

Elizabeth, Agnes and Thomas watched in amazement as their possessions were unloaded from the barge onto a cart for the short trip to a galleon anchored nearby. At dock in Coudenoure, Lady Margaret's river-craft had seemed enormous. None of the three could swim, and anxious moments had ensued as they had carefully boarded the boat as it rocked and swayed with the river's tide. Now, however, they saw that experience and the barge itself in truer perspective. It was dwarfed by the three ships which were in port that day, especially the one which they saw was accepting their luggage. Another wagon appeared and they were helped onto it.

"Holy Mary, Mother of God," began Agnes when she realized where they were being taken. She crossed herself repeatedly. Even Thomas, who had more world experience than Elizabeth and Agnes combined, paled at the sight before him. The sails of a great three-masted vessel picked up the fading western light and reflected it onto the muddy waters of the Thames. Pennants sporting the heraldic Tudor rose, red with a white center, flapped merrily from the tops of its sails and its bow and stern. Its long beak extended far beyond its bow and was wrapped in Tudor colors. As if that were not enough to impress, a wooden maiden extended from the end of the ship's beak, clothed in Tudor colors as well. A rickety gangplank stretching from the ship's center section to the dock was swarming with laborers laden with all manner of sacks, crates, bags and barrels. Mixed with the oleo of cargo was the family's own baggage.

"How do we board that beast, pray tell?" Agnes asked, aghast as the answer dawned upon her. "By that? That narrow piece of wood? Never! I say to you, Lord Thomas, this is on your head!"

Thomas nodded with his mouth open in consternation. Elizabeth was simply agog and soon lost the power of speech altogether. The day had been so full of strange sights and sounds and people that she still had not collected herself, but was at this point floating along barely tethered to the earth, absorbing it all. Thomas had to be carried up the gangplank, and Agnes insisted on being carried as well. Only Elizabeth, confident but overwhelmed by the day, walked up the swaying contraption under her own power, in silent awe of what was happening to her and her family. Almost as soon as her feet were firmly upon the ship's deck the captain began calling orders.

"Clear the dock and pull up the plank!"

His command was echoed down the ship, across the gangplank and onto the wharf by porters and sailors alike.

"Set the sails! Weigh anchor and we are gone from this place!"

A wild scurrying took hold and made the previous chaos seem like that of a child's nursery room. Thomas and Elizabeth clung to the railing of the deck as the ship began a slow lurch into deeper water. Agnes threw up. Elizabeth felt her heartbeat rise as the dock grew further and further distant. Activity continued up and down the wharf from which they had just departed. Men with heavy packs on their backs still scurried about with their loads, distant, rough shouting and commands could still be heard, dories still plied the shallow wayside of the dock. Each movement and shout seemed choreographed to the time and place, random and yet not random in a ballet of intricate precision, played out against the river and the tide and the village with the sure monotony of eternal practice. Elizabeth watched it all in a trancelike state, feeling the ebb and surge of the current beginning to take her away, gradually ever farther from the scene ashore.

Suddenly, the pattern of activity on the dock was visibly interrupted. Elizabeth strained her eyes against the last of the fading light to discern the cause of the disruption.

"Father - what is happening there, back on the dock? And there?" She pointed as she spoke.

"Yes, child, I noticed too, but I cannot make it out. It is too distant now for me to see clearly in this light. What do you see?"

"There are horses but we are much too far now to hear any shouting. I can see two men, yes, there are two. They are, they are…father, I can no longer tell. It looks like one of them has waded into the river with his arms raised aloft, but that would be most strange. No doubt the gathering darkness is playing tricks."

"Aye," agreed Thomas. "Indeed. Well, daughter, 'tis of no interest to us now. Take Agnes by the hand and let us see what accommodations this ship and its captain will offer us."

They made their way back to the center deck where the captain awaited them.

Chapter Nine

Henry woke from a fitful sleep, not certain where he was. The weeks since Arthur's death were only a whirlwind of unsettled memories now, filled with a jumble of grief, of processions, of government ministers inspecting him like a prized gelding, of his mother and father clinging to him as though their very lives depended upon his existence, and of midnight rides to palaces and fortresses he had previously only known through his father's and Arthur's descriptions. In normal times, any one of those would have given rise to deep consideration and a plan rooted in the context each engendered. But that was impossible in the swirl of events which Arthur's death unleashed. The only unifying theme which motivated great and small alike was young Henry's safety, for if the Tudor line had no successor, civil war would undoubtedly come again. It had been less than a generation since Bosworth Field had put an end to the great feud between the clans of the Lancasters and the Yorks. Their war had split England asunder, bringing grief and famine and chaos to all of England. The War of the Roses? Thought Henry. Laughable how such a poetic name could be used to describe such a godless conflict.

And so Henry had gone on an endless progress from estate to estate, passed from noble hand to noble hand, so each might make a display of loyalty to him and his ancestors. From one to another he had ridden with a faithful cadre of his father's men, always on the move lest the dreaded plague, or the terrifying sweating sickness, catch up to him. Fear of insurrection infused every conversation at every great estate with fear and disquiet. Some reacted well to the stress of a change in the succession and the Tudor line from England's land; others did not. Exhaustion had long since set in, and his father's command - that he stay on the move until the risk of an uprising or disease passed - had been his only imperative. He had been denied the right to attend his brother's funeral. The fears regarding his safety precluded any natural expressions of grief from young Henry, and the constant eyes upon him meant he dared not show weakness through tears.

As Henry lay in bed and sleepily watched the breeze rippling the leaves on the tree just beyond, he realized he was finally back at Greenwich in his mind, and he knew he still had not adjusted to the strain of being next in line to the throne, to the constant adulation and attention now showered upon him. As a second son, he had known rights reserved only for those of the highest rank. He knew deference, indeed, had always routinely practiced it in the presence of Arthur and their father the king, and had been shown the same by those whose rank was below his. But this, this was different. Men and women alike now bowed deeply upon his entry to a room. Every word he spoke seemed to be taken seriously and was repeated throughout whatever the venue happened to be at the moment, even by men three times his age. Young maids who three months earlier would have laughed at the spindly, awkwardness of his youth now blushed attractively and smiled invitingly when they happened to catch his eye. Their mothers displayed a willingness to put their daughters on show for Henry and whispered invitations in his ear that would have embarrassed a common pimp. Fathers managed to work their daughters' names into almost any conversation, and at palace after palace, manor house after manor house, he was waited upon by women in their best clothing, displayed to their best advantage.

It was strange to consider that he would be king. Never in his life had he imagined such a thing. He had dreamed of chivalric wars and rescuing desperate damsels, but always in the role of a nobleman battling for King and country, never as the king himself. His upbringing had reinforced this notion, for King Henry had envisioned a smooth succession of the Tudor dynasty to Arthur – he wanted no talk of rival claims or fractured clans and families. Young Henry's vision of his future had been one filled with adventure and feats of derring-do, but at the end of each fantasy which played through his head on occasion he had gone home to a country manor where his wife would be waiting for him, and he would spend his time devising architecture, writing music and studying philosophy and such. And there was always another critical element at the end of each of his fantasies. Elizabeth.

She was the wife who would be waiting for him at the end of a long and wearying crusade; it was she who would bathe his wounds and assuage his tired mind with her loving body and keen mind. Elizabeth would be a loving partner, warming his bed at night and his mind by day. At what moment, what age, his fantasies began ending with the cozy and familial theme he could not say. Perhaps he had always known that Elizabeth was the one person whom he trusted beyond all others and loved beyond measure. He was not sure. His need for her was simple, direct, and constant.

With a sudden kick of the eider down comforter which lay over him he jumped up and shouted for a servant. The day was well advanced and he had things to do.

"Charles!" He called to his friend in the adjoining bedroom. No answer.

"Charles, you layabout! Get up, man! A fine stag has been seen recently by the Thames' edge…"

He heard Charles laughing now.

"You will have to change your story, Henry, if you want the Lady to continue believing you. How many fine stags can there be by the Thames' edge?"

A servant appeared with ale, fruit and ham. Henry and Charles schemed while they ate.

"What about…Grandmother, we must slay several dragons today which have recently been spotted sitting by the Thames's edge?"

Henry laughed.

"Do dragons sit?"

"No, I have it…"

"No, *I* have it, Charles. Come, let us ride to see my love."

As always when he was at Greenwich, Henry raced down the stairs and went immediately to the sitting room favored by his grandmother. As always, she had heard his approach and awaited his appearance.

"So, young Henry, where are you and Lord Charles off to today? More stag hunting?" She spoke with a sarcastic tone that was unmistakable.

Charles blanched slightly at the words. Henry maintained his composure and quickly changed his line.

"No, Lady Margaret, indeed, we have grown tired of pursuing stags just now. We intend to hunt boar today."

He considered leaving it at that, but he couldn't.

"Indeed, a fine boar has recently been seen by the Thames' edge." He paused and a smile played across his thin lips.

"We shall bring it down."

Margaret nodded, impressed with young Henry's willingness to mock her knowledge of his pursuits.

"Be back by nightfall," she demanded. The two young men bowed obsequiously and left.

Margaret smiled to herself. Young Henry was in for a shock, for the servant she had stationed along the Thames had reported an hour earlier that her barge had sailed by with its curious circus of occupants and baggage. Coudenoure would be empty when he galloped up its long drive to greet his lady love.

She had considered telling him, thus saving him the bitterness of the discovery which awaited him at Coudenoure, but his anger was sure to be mighty upon finding Elizabeth's absence. The old couple she had sent to run the place had been given specific instructions as to what to tell Henry. He would need the ride back to Greenwich Palace to cool off and understand that it was the king's wish and therefore could not be ignored. By the time King Henry awoke from his grief Elizabeth and her family would be in Rome, and while he might not remember signing the decree which took them away, he would likely find use for them there. If necessary, she would see that he did…herself. In the meantime, she could deny any knowledge of events. It would be years before they returned, if ever, and there was no one else who dared override her authority and tell young Henry the truth. Yes, a fine plan. She had only to feign ignorance upon his return that evening, and to appear sincere in her condolences that he had spent his day in pursuit of game that had eluded him.

*****

As Henry and Charles reached the familiar bend in the river which signaled that Coudenoure was close, Governatore snorted and surged forward in a wild gallop. Henry's routine was well-known to him and fresh oats awaited him at the end of the long drive. But as they turned onto the gravel way, Henry pulled up short. Charles' horse reared as he reined it in and shouted to his friend.

"What is it?"

Henry nodded at the manor house.

"No smoke from any of the chimneys. 'Tis unusual, that is all."

"Who are those people, there, that old man and woman, in front of the door?"

Henry nudged Governatore forward at a trot.

"We shall find out," he said. "Let us pray that it is not the sweating sickness or the plague."

As they dismounted, the older man stepped forward and bowed deeply.

"Yo-yo-yer Lordship," he began. Henry pulled his riding gloves off while he listened.

"Go on, old man."

S-s-sss-sire, the Lord Thomas is not h-h-here."

"Indeed," said Henry. The old lady bowed and stepped forward.

"My Lord Henry," she began.

Henry's eyes narrowed.

"The Lord of Coudenoure, Lord Thomas de Grey, has left with his family."

Henry stood silently.

"Do tell," Charles said quietly from behind him.

"Sire, good King Henry sent him and his family to Rome to seek indulgences for our poor Arthur."

"Go-go-go-God save his soul," chimed in the old man.

"And Coudenoure? Who shall mind the manor while our Lord is in Rome?"

"Lord Thomas asked Liam," she nodded at her partner, "...and me to do so. We live round about here and 'twill be glad to see that it is well looked after till he and the Lady Elizabeth return."

Henry stood silent and still, betraying no hint of emotion.

"'Tis a strange thing, is it not?" asked Charles. "Did Lord Thomas indicate when he would return?"

"Aye, my lord," the old lady felt confident in her story now, and her voice reflected it. "He said they would be gone for many a year."

"Indeed," came the quiet reply.

Henry turned and remounted Governatore.

"Good Lady, I thank you for this news. Sir, I wish you good day."

The old woman smiled broadly.

He nodded at Charles and turned to ride back down the drive. After a short distance, Charles pulled even with Henry.

"What is this?" he asked quietly.

"How did the old woman know my name?"

Charles nodded.

"Yes, I caught that. What is afoot? Do you think Elizabeth and Thomas are in danger?"

"I do not know," replied Henry. "Let us clear the drive so that they may know nothing of our concerns. We will talk when they can no longer see us."

He clicked to Governatore and they rode in silence, clearing the gate at the end of the drive. As they turned onto the river path, the bay suddenly snorted and stopped. A small girl had stepped in front of him on the path.

"This is the King's land, my lady," Henry smiled. "What say you to that?"

"I say identify yourself, my lord."

Charles and Henry laughed.

Henry leaned forward towards the child. Her blue eyes showed fear but she stood her ground.

"I am Prince Henry," he said gently. "And you?"

"I am Elizabeth's friend and I travel on your land at her direction."

Henry and Charles quickly dismounted.

"What is it, child?" Henry knelt and the girl came forward shyly. She pulled her hand from behind her back and held it out towards Henry.

"'Tis fine, child. 'Tis fine. Is this from Elizabeth?"

The girl nodded, her eyes still wide with consternation. She seemed unwilling to let go of the small bundle she held until she finished her speech.

"My Lady Elizabeth said that the people at Coudenoure should not know what I am doing. She said to tell you that you must protect me if they find out."

"Child, no one will hurt you," Henry said. "And no one will know. Now, what is that you have there?"

She relinquished her small bundle. Charles reached into the pocket on his vest for a coin to give the child, but she shook her head violently.

"No! My Lady Elizabeth said if you paid me, it would become known. You must not!"

"Then how shall we thank you?" asked Henry.

The small girl gave the question serious thought.

"By bringing her home, my lord. That would suit me best."

Henry unwrapped the dirty cloth he had been handed and found a folded paper within. He quickly opened it and began reading aloud:

> *"My Darling Henry,*
>
> *If you are reading this, then you have been to Coudenoure and found me gone. I am so perplexed that I almost do not know what to write.*
>
> *Two days ago, your grandmother, the Lady Margaret Beaufort, appeared at our door with a decree for my father from our great king."*

Charles sat down on the ground while Henry continued.

> *"He is to travel to Rome for indulgences for Arthur from the Holy See and the Pope himself. While there, he is to seek out manuscripts and codices of all manner for his library, and for England."*

"What?" Charles interrupted. "What mission is this? Indulgences and manuscripts?"

> *"I am not old enough, nor wise enough, to go to court, and Lady Agnes cannot run the estate. Lady*

Margaret therefore insisted that we travel with my father to Rome."

The little girl suddenly spoke.

"My lord, my lord, there is one more thing I am to tell you. I almost forgot!"

"What is it?"

"I was to tell you that they left this very morning on the barge of your grandmother, and will sail from, from..."

Henry and Charles both breathed deeply.

"From where, child? Can you remember?"

The little girl closed her eyes as though remembering Elizabeth speaking in her mind.

"She said they were going to Woolwich, sire. Yes! That is it! Woolwich. And that your grandmother gave them quite a bit of coin."

"My lord, I know not what to do so I go with my father. The worst that can come of this is that we are apart for months, possibly a year. I pray no longer!

My Love, know that I think of you endlessly. Please for the love of my father look after our library and Coudenoure.

I am, your loving,

Elizabeth

The little girl bowed prettily, then disappeared into the underbrush as quickly as she had appeared.

Charles looked at his friend and shuddered. He had never seen Henry so upset.

"So the old woman knew all along of our trips, I suspect. Henry?"

Henry nodded, his face darkening with anger.

"'Tis true, I believe," he responded. "And she must have knowledge of the pre-contract. Otherwise why send my Elizabeth on such an impossible journey?"

"It can only be to keep the two of you apart," rejoined Charles.

Henry looked up at the sun in the sky, gauging the time. Charles knew his thoughts and spoke them for him.

"We must fly to Woolwich," he said and jumped into his saddle.

Henry did the same.

"I will deal with my grandmother later," he shouted.

But even as they rode, the barge made Woolwich. But even as they thundered past the usual turn for the woods, continuing to follow the river instead, the baggage loaned to Elizabeth, Thomas and Agnes by Lady Margaret was being loaded onto the ship. And even as they cleared Woolwich village itself and rode hard for the dock, the mighty galleon had weighed anchor and sailed nearly out of sight. The sun had almost set.

Henry threw himself from Governatore, shouting at any and all.

"Come back!" he screamed. "Hear me! Come back!"

But his only answer was the wind in the billowing sails of a nearby ship.

He waded into the river, shouting and waving his arms.

"Elizabeth! Come back! Elizabeth!"

Chapter Ten

Henry awoke the next morning and as was his habit at Greenwich lay for a long time watching the breeze ripple the leaves just beyond his bedroom window. Charles and he ate breakfast in silence and made their way slowly down the grand stairs of the palace. They knocked on the sitting room door of Lady Margaret and bowed as they entered. Margaret stiffened, expecting the worst.

"Good morning, grandmother," Henry said pleasantly.

Charles bowed low and echoed his friend's sentiment.

Margaret watched them with hooded eyes, trying to ascertain the direction of the attack of anger she knew must soon be forthcoming. Henry might not know of her role in the affair, but he could not, would not, express anger against the king. That left her as the target for his hurt and fury.

"Where are you off to today, young Henry?"

Henry looked at her without blinking.

"My lady, we are riding in the park today. A fine stag has been seen recently, near the Thames' edge. We shall bring him down."

For once, Margaret was speechless. She had no inkling as to how to proceed.

"Indeed, Madame," said Charles, "It should be fine hunting today. Fine indeed."

They bowed, turned and left the room.

Margaret was stunned. She had expected fury, tears, raging words and violent actions. But this? She knew from the old man and woman themselves, through her network of spies, that Henry and Charles had been to Coudenoure yesterday, had been told of the departure of Elizabeth and her father and Agnes, and had been told that their return would be months, perhaps years in the future. And now this? What was she missing? What game was young Henry playing at?

The guards at the palace gate which fronted onto Greenwich Road saw them coming. Stepping out into road itself, they halted the wagons and horses making their way into London with their wares for the urban market. All dismounted and waited reverently for a glimpse of whatever royal was about to cross their path. A murmur went round that it was Prince Henry himself, the young man who would be their king, who was leaving the palace. Within seconds, he and Charles appeared at the gate and walked their mounts in a stately fashion across the road. But before they could enter the woods on the far side, a spontaneous cheer arose.

Henry pulled his steed up short and waved at the men and women who were bowing now. A weak smile almost lit his features. As he rode on and disappeared into the woods with Charles behind him, they gathered in knots in the road, discussing his demeanor, his clothes, his horse, his companion. Once in the woods, Charles called out to his friend.

"My lord, what a prince you have become! I believe they would follow you even to the ends of the earth if you asked them to."

"But I shan't," came Henry's angry yet doleful reply, "For they have no way of bringing Elizabeth back to me, do they my friend."

The ride was silent and slow, and it was not until they reached the meadow which gave access to the path along the bank of the Thames that they spoke again. A group of men, liveried in his father's colors, were waiting beside their horses for Henry to appear. Charles saw them in the distance.

"So the word was received," he said in low tones as they clicked to their mounts and hastened to meet them. "And do you think they shall give trouble?"

"No," replied Henry, "For what I want costs no one anything and I am the first prince of the realm. There will be no issues, and they will present it to my father as I wish."

Thomas Howard, Earl of Surrey, bowed to his knees as Henry approached. His guardsmen followed suit and behind them two other noblemen did the same. But Henry barely saw the men before him. He had surveyed the group and settled his gaze on the two people who only yesterday had lied to his face about his grandmother's involvement. He strode to them oblivious of all around him. The old man, Liam, and his wife wore the same, tired garments they had worn a day earlier. But the confidence they had shown on the steps of Coudenoure as they had glibly ignored his grandmother's role in the entire debacle had disappeared. In its place was abject fear. Like a mare with blinders on he continued to stare at them in open anger, ignoring Charles' cough and hand on his shoulder. For the first time in his life, he understood rage. He had been denied the one thing, the *only* thing he truly needed in this life and in his mind, Liam and his wife were to blame almost as much as his grandmother, for if they had not engaged him in idle conversation the previous day, he might have made Woolwich in time. His hand moved to his sword and played with the gilded hilt while he continued staring at them with a hostile smile. A look of extreme fear crossed the old woman's face and she threw herself on the ground, face down in abject obeisance. Liam continued kneeling but terror shook his entire frame, for the look on their prince's face was barely human. Henry enjoyed playing with them, letting them think he might loose his rage upon them. It was a strange, malignant feeling that took hold of him, one which, if he had not been bound by servitude to his father the king and therefore restrained, he would surely have acted on. After a moment, he shook the feeling off, returning to his own self. After all, what would his love, Elizabeth, say to him? He could hear her now, "...You must always be kind, Henry, to those beneath you. It is God's plan and His provenance for us all as we seek grace."

He turned away from the pair, wondering briefly if this was what it felt like to be king. All his life he had known that as the king's son he held power in his hands. He had understood from an early age that those around him were more wont to do his bidding than the bidding of his companions. But there had always been limits. There had always been voices and dictates from above which imposed sanctions upon his actions should they fall beyond the bounds of chivalry. But now? He wondered.

Henry nodded to the Earl and they walked some ways off from the group before speaking.

"My Prince, they will never set foot at Coudenour again."

Henry nodded his head while the Earl continued.

"We have done as you asked: the estate shall be managed by my own servants. My mother, God rest her soul, died last month, and her manor at Guildford shall be closed, for I have no need of it presently. The staff who served her there under my direction shall serve you at Coudenoure. Francis is a man I trust with my life, sire, and his wife Bess is a good woman. They ran my mother's estate well and are grateful to serve you in any capacity that you may desire. They are discreet, and totally loyal to His Highness the King."

"And not His Highness' mother, Lady Margaret?"

The Earl coughed politely.

"They understand to whom they owe their allegiance, my liege. It will not be an issue I can assure you."

Henry kicked at the ground for a moment, thinking through the points he had put in the letter he had sent the previous evening to the Earl.

"And how shall I get my letters to my love, Elizabeth?" he asked.

"It is arranged, sire. Bess has a sister who is in service to the sister of England's ambassador to the Papal Court in Rome. You shall give your letters to Bess. Francis and Bess have a son who shall serve you at Coudenoure as well, my lord, and he shall get them to his aunt whenever the need arises. From there, they shall be sent with other mail directly in the care of the Ambassador himself, Lord Gallingbrook. I have already posted a note to him this very morning. He is my friend and there will be no problems."

Henry sighed, feeling as though a weight were beginning to lift from his shoulders.

"And money? My father our great King Henry has been known to squeeze coin."

The Earl laughed.

"Indeed he has, and we all know it. But again, 'twill be no issue."

"But it will," responded Henry, "For I am certain that my grandmother will see to it that the coin they travel with is all they will receive. You see, my father comes by his thrift naturally."

"Aye, but an allowance will be sent from my own purse, your Highness, through the same channels as the letters."

Henry looked at the older man with relief clearly written across his features.

"I shall not forget this kindness you have done me, Lord Thomas. It will be to your benefit and to that of your family."

The Earl bowed deeply.

"We owe all we are and have to the Tudors. It is an honor to serve you, my lord."

Henry pulled two rolls of heavy paper from within his vest. Each was sealed with high grain wax and stamped with Henry's initials. He passed one of them to the Earl.

"This is for my father," Henry instructed him. "It states that I, too, am concerned with the rumors of plague and sweating sickness, and that I will pass the next few weeks at Coudenoure. Its isolation shall be my talisman against those evil diseases, and I wish to have privacy in which to mourn my brother."

"As you wish."

"It also states my desire to follow his wishes for my future, and begin to enhance my understanding of coming duties. As such, I have sent for the terms of the Perpetual Peace which I intend to study, and with his grace's consent, I wish to ride north for James' ratification."

Again, the Earl nodded. Henry then gave him the second roll, sealed in the same manner as the previous one.

"I ask you to deliver this to Sir Robert Janyns. He is the architect for my father's new chapel at Westminster, and I wish to review the plans with him."

"As you wish. Sire, the king's glazier might also have plans you wish to view. He is responsible for the great stained glass work which shall be part of the finished design."

Henry nodded affirmatively. They stood for a moment, each trying to make certain that all necessary points for all arrangements had been adequately covered. Finally Thomas spoke.

"Prince Henry, we serve your father and after him we serve you. And only the two of you. Should you need additional help or should you wish additional information on anything: matters of state, funding, politics - you need only speak the words."

"These matters shall keep me busy while at Coudenoure," Henry stated, "...and that will be enough for now."

With that, they returned to the group. The old woman still lay prostrate. Liam could not bring himself to make eye contact, staring hard at the ground while Henry made small talk with the other nobles. Finally, having satisfied himself with the arrangements, Henry and Charles left for Coudenoure.

It was odd not to take the bend in the river at a wild gallop. Governatore strained at the bit and pranced sideways in his efforts to begin the final run to the front door of the manor. Instead, Henry and Charles took the short distance at a walk, pausing at the end of the long gravel drive. Coudenoure looked strangely deserted. It was clear that the Earl of Surrey's servants had not yet arrived, for there was no one to hear the steady beat of hooves on the drive and therefore no one at the door to meet them. No smoke rose from the chimney; no groundsmen worked the yard. As they pulled closer Charles gave a great cry announcing their arrival. After a moment, the great heavy door opened and Cook appeared there. She was middle-aged and portly with a clean white apron and a small white cap to indicate her status in the kitchen. She bowed deeply, waiting for permission to speak. Charles nodded and a torrent of words came forth.

"My Prince Henry, oh thanks be to our good Lord in heaven! There is no one here! I beseech you to help us all for we know not what to do."

Henry moved towards her and helped her to her feet. Tears were in her eyes as she continued.

"They took them away, my lord! Yesterday, Elizabeth, Thomas and Agnes were taken away on a barge to sail on a ship to the good Lord knows where. Oh my heavens!! We cried and begged but 'twas no use - the Lady Elizabeth said it had been ordained by the Lady Margaret, the King's own mother. Ach!! What are we to do, my lord?"

The sound of wheels on gravel interrupted her and they all turned. At the end of the drive a large wagon had appeared drawn by two solid plough horses. On the rough seat were a man and a woman dressed in dark simple clothes. The man was clean shaven and narrow faced, while the woman was round and cheerful looking despite the oddness of the moment. As the huge horses pulled to a halt, they both jumped down.

"My lord? We are seeking Prince Henry…" The man spoke as they both bowed.

"I am Prince Henry, and you?"

"Francis, your Highness, and this is my wife, Bess. We are come to assist you in any way we can."

"Aye," Henry nodded. "You will run this estate while its owner, the good Baron of Coudenoure, is away on the King's own business. The Earl of Surrey speaks highly of your service to his mother."

The woman blushed and smiled.

"We are happy to serve." Her eyes met those of Cook and the two women seemed to hold an entire dialogue in the silence which followed. Cook spoke first.

"Come. I will show you your quarters, and Raphael…where is that boy? Raphael!" she shouted and a young boy appeared around the corner of the manor.

"Raphael, take the baggage of these good people and afterwards bring them to me in the kitchen. Do you understand?"

A slender boy with face besmudged held out his hand and looked plaintively up at Cook. From within the voluminous pockets on the apron, she produced a sweet tidbit and gave it to him with a scowl he ignored. In turn, he bowed and smiled before disappearing around the wagon.

"And the groomsman? Where is he?" Charles demanded. "Henry, I shall rouse the stable folk." He took the reins of both horses and began a brisk walk to the back of the manor.

All assembled bowed and disappeared, happier now that Henry had arrived and order was being restored. For his part, Henry had never felt so alone. On a sudden impulse, he struck out across the yard. The neatly trimmed grass soon gave way onto the meadow, still blooming with the wild flowers Elizabeth loved so much. Normally, he would have picked the finer ones as he and Elizabeth walked to present them to her when they had settled beneath their tree. But there was no point in that today, and his hands only swept gently over the tops of the grasses and the flowers, feeling their textures and releasing their perfumes. The seed heads and leaves caught at his stockings as he walked and brushed against his vest. He sat beneath their elm and closed his eyes tiredly, recalling better days. A sharp tweet caught his ear.

"Bucephalus, you old man! I have nothing for you today." The chipmunk waited patiently, not believing the words.

"'Tis true, you and I are without luck it seems. Now move on."

But the small animal stood its ground and after a while, seeing that Henry truly had arrived bare-handed, went about its small business, collecting bits of grass and seed for its tiny lair beneath the gnarled roots. Henry sighed.

He watched idly as the manor below him slowly came to life. Charles had lit a fire under those in the yard who might have chosen to see the day as one in which no work need be done. From around the corner came gardeners, small children and groomsmen for the wagon and the horses. The sound of smithing reached his ears soon afterward, the clang of the anvil on the nearly molten metal. Smoke began to rise from the chimneys, and after that, the faint smell of baking bread and meat wafted over the meadow on the breeze. The curtains in the great hall and the library were opened and Henry could see servants scurrying about in the library, setting things to right for when he would choose to return.

He was exhausted. His brother's death, his sudden accession, his pre-contract, his grandmother's scheme and Elizabeth' and Thomas' departure; the long rides from castle to castle; his father's men and their adulation of him - yes, it had all worn him out. He sat beneath the tree and felt the stress and tension of it all in his muscles, in the very fiber of his soul. This was the right thing, coming here. Coudenoure was his home, and he needed it desperately at this moment. He would set it to rights for the day Elizabeth returned. He was almost asleep when he spied a large piece of paper blowing through the meadow. He watched it settle only to be picked up again when the wind blew. It skipped merrily along the breeze and Henry wondered what it could be. Henry ran down and grabbed the paper leaf before it could escape, then settled himself back under the elm to examine it. His heart caught in his throat.

It was a geometric drawing in Elizabeth's hand. He turned it to try and puzzle out its purpose and in doing so realized that it was Coudenoure and its grounds. She had drawn it as the hub of a web of gardens and buildings. But rather than the scattered layout which the estate currently possessed, she had brought order to it all. The great front lawn remained, but the drive was marked by four great statues: two as it left the river and began its straight course to the house; the other two to mark the narrowing of the drive by parterres. As one moved closer to the manor itself, the expanse was broken up by these two parterres, one on each side of the gravel way. They were complex and Henry laughed aloud when he realized that the interior of each was in the pattern of a series of stylized Tudor Roses.

She had left the orchard on the immediate west side of the manor, but its trees no longer grew willy-nilly. Instead, Elizabeth had clearly marked them to serve as a colonnade through which long strolls could be enjoyed, particularly in the spring when they would flower. Henry nodded absently in agreement with the plan. But it was the grounds behind Coudenoure which she had attacked with vigor. Here, the out buildings were pushed farther from the house. They would face each other across a broad, cobbled avenue which would reduce the mud and dust which continually surrounded the current situation. Beyond them the avenue would give way to the neat, cultivated rows of crops on which the life of the manor depended. A low stone fence with a wide gate, set off with stone pillars, would provide scenic demarcation and an attractive view of the entire tableau.

Henry's mind's eye gladly filled in the details. Where the out buildings had once stood immediately behind the manor house there would be a series of garden rooms, each with a designated purpose and geometric design. There would be Cook's potager and a small glass house in which to grow greens for winter treats. There would be a garden of their favorite flowers, made private by a tall, yew hedge trimmed neatly round the perimeter. A room of roses beyond that, and finally, a green room to celebrate form in summer and winter. Henry felt a wave of happiness wash over him. She had planned for their life together at Coudenoure and he loved every aspect of what she had dreamt. He dozed under the elm for a long time before finally rolling the paper and tripping through the meadow back to Coudenoure.

Chapter Eleven

There was no member of the Spanish ambassador's retinue returning home on the galleon. That, too, had been a fiction, like so much else of Margaret's story. In fact, their little party of three constituted the entire number of those voyaging aboard the "Phobos" who were not employed to do so. To Thomas' surprise, the captain was English.

"I married a dark lass, you see," the man offered as explanation. "Isabella, may God rest her soul." He would have continued but two children, both dressed in dirty breeches and loose overshirts, swarmed up from the bowels of the great vessel, screaming and chasing each other around his legs. He attempted to ignore them but got nowhere.

"Papa, papa, who these?" they squealed in pidgin English.

"This fine lord and his ladies are sailing to Rome with us," their father explained. One of the children shyly reached out to touch the satin skirt of Elizabeth's dress. She rubbed the fabric gently with her tiny hand, obviously impressed. Agnes tumbled to the fact that the child was in fact a girl and was appalled.

"Good Sir!" she exclaimed, "And do you let your daughter dress thus? And what are children doing on this wretched craft at all? Eh?"

The little girl now rubbed the fabric of Agnes' dress, and Agnes held her protectively against her legs. She continued without regard for the captain's attempts to speak.

"Little one, you are to come with me. Is that your brother? Hmm? Old man, what think you, bringing such tiny ones here?"

The captain smiled a flirtatious smile at Agnes before bowing.

"Might I be allowed to speak?" he cut in.

"Good luck if that is thy plan," Thomas said drily.

"M'lady, these are my children, 'tis true. But Isabella died, and I have no family in Spain. I brought them to England to live with my brother and his wife but they hid away until I consented to take them back home with me. What am I to do?"

"Not this, 'tis clear." Agnes was firm now. She had enough maternal instinct for fifty women and worrying about her new charges, as she thought of them, took her mind off the dreadful fact that she was on the high sea, aboard a galleon surely doomed to shipwreck where all aboard would be lost. Agnes did not have an optimistic soul.

"Good Sir, do we have quarters below deck?" Thomas changed the subject. Despite the wildly entertaining circumstance of the day, he was exhausted and could no longer keep up, no matter the excitement. The captain sensed this and without missing a beat called out to some of his crew.

"By the by, I am Captain Ransdell," he said to Thomas. "You will be sharing my quarters – 'tis all we have on the Phobos." He indicated the stern of the ship which was squared off and rose partially above the main deck. As they began to make their way there, Agnes spoke loudly to him.

"I expect hot water immediately to wash these children. Do you understand? And I will need clean rags and they will need clean clothing…" Her voice continued but trailed off as she made her way below deck still talking.

It was very late by the time they finished their initial tour of the ship and sat down to a light supper, and all three ate almost nothing though for different reasons: Thomas was too tired, Agnes did not trust the cooking, and Elizabeth was still lost in a dream world, caught between what her life had been a mere twelve hours earlier, and what it was now. The tallow candles provided dim and smoky light, and each dish on the table was heavily weighted at its base to retard its sliding to and fro with the rocking of the ship. Ransdell poured wine for the adults, and after a sip, Elizabeth pulled herself together enough to steal looks at him and the cabin. He was not as old as she had first thought. It was only the scruff of beard seeded with gray which made him seem so. His eyes were the palest green she had ever seen, and she compared their color mentally to that of the small, jade statue which sat in Agnes' bedroom at Coudenoure. His brow was heavy, but his countenance was kind, even more so when he looked at his children. The quarters he called home while aboard the Phobos were small but Elizabeth was impressed with their cleanliness and order. Clearly, he was a tidy person – his clothes were clean, well-mended and neat – but one whose children ran circles around him when it came to discipline. His comments confirmed her thoughts.

"'Tis a good thing you travel with us, and I am grateful. My children speak only a smattering of English though they be English. I wish them to be educated, to be able to read and speak their mother tongue..." He broke off to speak sternly to them as they ran about the small space. The difference between their earlier attire and lack of cleanliness compared to their current state was remarkable. Agnes had ignored their screaming as she bathed them, continued to ignore it while she combed their hair, and refused to hear it while she found clean clothes for them. As a result, *they* had refused to give up their names, even when she pointed to herself and said, "Agnes", to Elizabeth and said "Elizabeth" and had then gestured to them with a questioning look. Elizabeth spoke for the first time and asked Ransdell their names.

"My son is Roberto," said Ransdell. "And my lovely daughter is Consuelo. Lady Agnes, what a difference your ministrations have made to them this evening! I recognize them now as my own!"

In the dim light, Elizabeth was almost certain she saw Agnes blush.

As the conversation began to lag, they retired to their respective corners of the captain's cramped but adequate quarters. It was decided that the children, Agnes, and Elizabeth would sleep in the captain's tiny bedroom, while the captain and Thomas would make do in the outer chamber which doubled as a daily room and dining room as well. When they had finally closed the door to that outer chamber, Elizabeth stripped to her cotton shirt which reached nearly to the floor. She crawled tiredly into the tiny bunk allocated to her. Without waiting for an invitation, Roberto and Consuelo piled into bed with Agnes, and like a mother hen settling her wings protectively over her brood, Agnes pulled the covers round them all. Elizabeth blew out the candle and lay alone in the darkness, wishing she were younger and could curl up beside Agnes as well.

It was hard to marshal her thoughts into a coherent narrative of the day's events. In the coming years, when she looked back upon that day, some of it she wanted to forget, some of it she wanted to remember, but all of it was accessed through color and smell and touch. She had memories of it, certainly. But like all memories they were flat, and naturally filtered through the years which followed. But a mere scent or an unexpected flash of color could trip not just the memory of the event, but a complete expression of it. Even in later years, the sudden smell of lilac in the spring, when the wind rustled through the gray green stalks and rattled the perfume from the cool purple blossoms would always trigger complete recall of the ride on the wagon from the doors of Coudenoure to the dowager's barge. Not just the memory but the sounds of the horses' hoofs on the damp gravel, the creaking of the wagon boards, her father's teary eyes and Agnes' face in almost total panic: all carried through time by a single burst of lilac. Similarly, the smell of a wharf – that fishy, watery, seaweed damp air and cool salty mist always took her to the first time she saw the great Phobos with its gay flags bobbing on the Thames, water lapping against its hulk with each tidal rush.
Unconsciously, her hand beneath the rough blanket which covered her rubbed the soft undershirt she wore, and instantly, then and always, the eyes of Consuelo as she had gently reached out and rubbed the blue satin of Elizabeth's dress would be upon her.

Her thoughts turned now to Henry, and she wondered where he was. Had her message gotten through? Had the child understood what she, Elizabeth, had needed that morning in their rushed and whispered conversation? She did not know, but there were so many things now she realized she did not know. The library at Coudenoure had given her an education, but in twelve short hours, that education had been expanded upon exponentially by experience. She drifted to sleep entwining the thoughts passed on to her in books with those she'd had herself that day. It was a process that would only end when she breathed her last.

*****

As the weeks passed aboard the Phobos, Thomas, Agnes, and Elizabeth all gained their sea-legs and fell into a comfortable routine. Thomas was fascinated by the navigation of the ship - charts, lore, stars and coastlines all came into play as they made their way slowly down the coast of France. The majority of the crew had worked for Ransdell for years, and considered him and each other almost as family. They were all Spaniards, and unless Ransdell spoke English, it was impossible to isolate his Spanish as that of a non-native speaker. If this strange little band of English people were his friends, as they quickly became, then they were also the friends of the crew, and a kindly conspiracy ensued to make certain that they were well-treated. This meant that the older man's constant prying and questions piled on top of more questions were always answered respectfully. Elizabeth had come by her linguistic abilities naturally, and within a few days, Thomas had already picked up enough of the sailors' patois to begin conversing with them in short staccato statements. In turn, they loved his eagerness to learn and were constantly supplying him with new words and phrases.

At Coudenoure, Thomas had settled into a happy albeit restricted rhythm of daily life: his library, his great comfortable chair, and Agnes and Elizabeth to bring him news of what he liked to think of as the far flung corners of his empire. It had been a sedentary existence, and his physical limitations had justified such inactivity. But the Phobos did not permit such a life, and Thomas felt as if he had been awakened from a long and restful slumber.

His shortness of breath improved. His mind became quicker. Initially, the tapping of his cane as he made his way here and there aboard the ship had been tentative and slow. As the weeks had passed, however, it became a quick and purposeful rapping upon the decks. A sailor had initially been assigned to him each day to make certain that the old man neither fell nor washed overboard. It had been considered tedious duty, but was now a prized assignment. Thomas eagerly picked the brains of whoever was assigned to him, giving them the chance to show off their knowledge of the sea and what it meant to be a sailor.

Agnes spent her days happily arguing with Captain Ransdell about everything she considered inappropriate on his ship and in his life. There was a cyclical nature to their daily interactions.

"Tell me, Captain…" Her opening gambit never varied nor did Ransdell's.

"Yes, Lady Agnes, and what may I educate you about today?"

From there, the conversation would launch into one of a thousand possible avenues.

"And what have you done about Roberto's and Consuelo's upbringing?"

"Be specific, Madame."

"You have already stated that they know nothing of England."

"No madame, I did not state that. What I said was that they had learned about their home country in Spanish for they speak little English."

From there, it went to how to raise children generally, how to run a ship appropriately, what must his house look like, what was he an Englishman doing in Spain anyway, what was a proper diet for children, and on and on. In turn, Ransdell took his turns at what he termed Agnes' limited life experience.

"And tell me again, Madame…you never married?" was a frequent beginning.

"I have no need of a man," was her tried and true response.

"And you know this how, pray tell?"

Here, Agnes would always blush, turn to him, say something about his manners, and walk away.

They had come to enjoy these conversations, and in time, they managed to stop throwing barbs and actually talk. Agnes was enthralled, terrified and horrified at where she found herself, but slowly came to appreciate the freedom of the open sea, the feel of the fresh salt air upon her skin, and her newfound and self-imposed responsibilities for Roberto and Consuelo. When she was not arguing with Ransdell or fussing around the children she could be found in the galley, supervising the cook. The cook ignored her, thus ensuring the necessity of continued visits.

It was Elizabeth, however, who underwent the most profound change amongst the three of them. Somewhere in the days and weeks as they sailed south, she left her childhood behind. She began to blossom physically, and Agnes screeched at any sailor who happened to give the young woman a second glance. The sea air gave her skin a healthy glow and her dark eyes turned to ebony against the warm honey color of her complexion. At first,

Agnes had been frantic about Elizabeth and how she would manage such a monumental change. But Elizabeth surprised them all. She instituted morning classes for the children and in the afternoons, worked on her Spanish by talking to the riggers and sailors who worked above deck. These conversations drove Agnes almost insane and furnished the afternoon portion of her and Ransdell's cycle of conversation.

"My dear Captain, you *must* tell your men not to speak to Lady Elizabeth," she demanded daily. "'Tis not proper."

"Aye, well, there is proper, Madame, and then there is practical. She will speak to them and they will speak to her and there is naught we can do about that unless we lock her in the captain's cabin all day."

"I have been thinking about that," Agnes always replied. Ransdell always laughed.

"I have instructed my men appropriately," he would assure her. "Sailing with me is sure employment for them and a living for their families. They will not jeopardize that by trifling with a maid."

And always, just for fun, "...and an English maid at that – 'tis no problem for them to restrain themselves, I assure you."

At which point Agnes would once again begin berating him and the cycle would begin anew.

It was one such afternoon, as Elizabeth spoke earnestly with a sailor who was busy patching a large canvas sail, that she and Agnes chanced to speak.

"You there, sew! Coser! Coser!"

Elizabeth smiled.

"Cosen, Agnes, it's cosen."

"Yes, well, cosen you nit and stay away from Lady Elizabeth!" The sailor shook his head and continued at his task.

Agnes grabbed Elizabeth by the arm and tugged her to the railing.

"My lady, you simply cannot speak to the men aboard this dreadful ship. What will people think?"

Elizabeth laughed.

"Who, dear Agnes? What will *who* think? Do not worry so much. You forget that I am pre-contracted to marry my Henry."

Agnes and she both leaned on the rail and looked out at the wake the Phobos left in the gray blue waters.

"Look, it is the same color as his eyes, do you not think so?"

"Lady Elizabeth, he is far from us now," Agnes began gently, "And we know not what will happen tomorrow, let alone next year."

"I do," Elizabeth murmured, "I shall marry my betrothed and we will all live happily at Coudenoure."

Agnes sighed and left her there. Elizabeth continued to watch the sea foam as it churned up and then faded away into the distance, but her words rang curiously strange even in her ears. Coudenoure seemed as far away as the moon in the night sky. She thought of Henry constantly. Even as she became more comfortable with the journey they were now on she yearned for home. What was her love doing, thinking, praying? Each morning, when all had cleared the captain's quarters, she began the children's English lessons. From there, she would transition to Latin, and perhaps history or geography and the New World. They had become entranced with their young teacher and vied to outshine each other in their work. But at each midday, when the lessons ended and she sent the children off to see Agnes and have dinner, she wrote to her beloved, telling him of life on the ship, of how much her heart ached for him. Sometimes she would tell him of the sailors and their talk of their children and wives; sometimes she told him of how the ship was navigated past rocky shoals or outcroppings, always steering into the south; sometimes she worked assiduously on patterns which entwined her initials with his. It became ritual, and after signing each letter, she would place it carefully on top of the ones she had written previously. A small pink ribbon, pulled from one of her frocks, tied the small bundle neatly and she placed it always beneath her pillow. Each night, she dreamt the same dream - Henry, on the day of their betrothal, his lips upon hers, her hands in his. But each morning, she was awakened by the gentle rocking of the ship upon the waves, and she knew that her wait was far from over.

She heard a familiar rapping on the deck and without turning spoke aloud to her father.

"Father! Do they not have need of you in the navigation room?" she teased.

"Aye, child, they do, but I needed a breath of fresh air," he smiled as he spoke. "But I tell you they say we will reach the Pillars of Hercules in the early hours of the morn."

"Ah, that will be a sight I never thought to see," she said. "And what comes afterwards? The children tell me we enter Mare Nostrum as we pass below the Pillars and will soon be in Malaga, their home."

"Aye, Ransdell says the same. He says we will stop there for a shore visit – the sailors will see their families and collect the first part of their pay."

"How long do you think we will tarry?" Elizabeth asked.

"Oh, child, I know not. Perhaps a week? Two weeks? I believe the captain intends to leave his children in the hands of his neighbors since he was unsuccessful in his bid to leave them in England."

"But where is Isabel's family? Surely they will take them?"

"He is strangely quiet about that," Thomas rejoined. "I believe they may have disowned her for marrying an Englishman."

Elizabeth laughed.

"And an English family would no doubt disown her if she were English and married a Spaniard."

Thomas smiled and nodded.

"We are none of us good enough for the rest," he laughed.

They stood together looking out over the ocean and enjoying the sunset. It was vivid orange more often than not, and Elizabeth never tired of the fiery sight.

"Tell me, father, have you noticed a difference in the scent of the air in the past day?"

He looked at her sharply.

"I have not, but the sailors have," he acknowledged. "They say 'tis a harbinger of the *khamsin.*"

"The khamsin?" It was Captain Ransdell. He had overheard the word and joined them.

"The khamsin - an Arabic word for a southerly wind which sometimes blows from across Mare Nostrum."

Thomas knew he was hiding something.

"Aye, the sailors say 'tis treacherous, and that the scent on the wind is an omen of bad luck."

"'Tis nonsense!" laughed Ransdell. "Now come, I have been sent to collect you by the master of us all, Lady Agnes. She says supper is on the table and she will not have us set a bad example for Roberto and Consuelo by arriving late."

Chapter Twelve

As promised, Agnes had lit the evening candles and supper was already laid out. Consuelo and Roberto were waiting impatiently to begin.

"Papa, por que…" Ransdell cut them off.

"No! English only, remember?"

Roberto recalibrated and began again.

"*Captain* Ransdell…" the table exploded with laughter - Roberto had pitched his voice to mimic that of Agnes. His efforts earned him a playful cuff across the top of his head as they settled in and Ransdell poured the wine. One week earlier, as the Phobos had begun cruising past the Spanish coastline, Ransdell had given his crew a choice. The ship could put in for food supplies one last time, or they could settle for the salt pork and potatoes that were still in the ship's larder and make landfall at Malaga that much earlier. The choice for a quicker return had been unanimous. The decision did not matter to Thomas' family, for Ransdell did not allow him or his children to leave the vessel during these brief port visits: he claimed, rightly so, that all three had the habit of wandering wherever their eyes might take them. As for Elizabeth, Agnes always locked the two of them in the captain's quarters mumbling about foreigners and maids until they were once again under sail.

Tonight's meal was the same one they had eaten for the past four days. No one minded, however, for suppers had become deeply familial and routine, a time they all looked forward to. Elizabeth was unaccustomed to the wild give and take that dining with small children entailed but threw herself into the happy chaos regardless. Weeks earlier, Agnes had given up on all but "English at the table, please", and despite her shows of consternation enjoyed their common dining immensely. Consuelo and Roberto talked incessantly now of what they would do upon arriving in Malaga, and Thomas had to shout to be overheard as he questioned Ransdell about crossing beneath the famous Pillars of Hercules. Elizabeth was the only one who seemed to sense the change in pattern in the rolling of the Phobos upon the deep oceanic waters.

"Captain Ransdell, do you not feel the difference in the rhythm of our rocking?" she asked innocently during a rare interlude in the conversation. "Does it not feel more rapid?"

Agnes gripped the table with both hands.

"Mother of God, child, you are right! Captain, what is this?"

Ransdell laughed as he smiled at her.

"I will go and check with the navigation crew," he said, "But..."

He was interrupted by Thomas rising and claiming that he would most certainly assist.

"But you have nothing to worry about. The waters always become a bit choppier as we draw closer to the great Pillars."

With that, he and Thomas left them. Agnes continued to grip the table as she barked a command at Roberto and his sister.

"We are done here, children. Take yourselves off to the bed and I will join you shortly."

They knew the tone and did not question. As they left, Agnes spoke in low tones to Elizabeth.

"What does it mean? Do you think we are in trouble?"

"Not at all," Elizabeth reassured her. "But if it will make you feel better, I will go myself to the upper deck and see what the wind is doing. That way, I can tell you with certainty what I already know. Put the children to bed and I will be there in a thrice."

She left the room, pulling the door behind her, knowing that she had miscalled the change she felt in the ship's rocking. It was not the increased rapidity of the oscillations that had caught her attention, but their depth. The rolling was growing more noticeable now as she made her way along the narrow passage from the door to the stairs that led to the upper deck, she was unable to walk a straight path. Instead, she went from one wall to the other as the Phobos rolled in the deep. Once on the upper deck, she breathed in the salty night air and made her way to her favorite position at the bow where she could look out upon the waters. It was difficult tonight, however, for there was no moon. The night sky was devoid of all but faint starlight, and the vacuum it left behind was filled only with the sound of the great waters and the steady cadence of the Phobos' movement. She was happy to finally feel the ship's rail beneath her hands.

The scent in the air was that of a dry dust, and she wondered how that could be. Surprisingly, Ransdell joined her at the bow.

"Good evening, Lady Elizabeth," he said gravely. She nodded.

"Captain, what is that scent? 'Tis like the smell of coming rain in a dry season, of an arid and sere air running before an approaching storm."

"My lady, you are correct as was my crew earlier. This is the first sure sign of the khamsin."

As if to confirm his words, a sudden gust of spray blew across the deck.

"So we shall have a storm then?"

"Aye, maid, but not just a storm. These winds come from Africa. They blow the hot air from that desolate place across the great sea to Spain. These are mighty winds and they are to be most feared."

Elizabeth thought for a moment.

"And the Pillars of Hercules? Does the roiling of the sea there contribute to this storm?"

Ransdell looked at her and as many times before was taken aback at her intelligence.

"Yes, my lady, it does. I have just left my crew. We are too close to the Pillars to turn our sails and too far from land to make port. We must try to thread the Pillars and make for Malaga on the other side. 'Tis our best chance."

"Our best chance?" Her question was sharp.

"Aye, our best chance."

He waited for the words to sink in.

"Sir, how shall I protect my father, the children and Agnes? What must I do? Tell me."

He appreciated the practical nature of the question and turned his thoughts thus.

"You must keep them below deck for the seas will shortly begin to wash over even where we now stand."

She nodded.

"And you must listen to the timbers."

"I do not understand."

"Elizabeth."

He had never called her by her maiden name before.

"Elizabeth, you must hear carefully the creaking of the bones of the ship, the cries of the timbers of her spine. Accustom yourself to their pace and pitch. Do you understand, lass?"

She nodded and he continued.

"Against that you must, you *must*, measure the depth of the roll. Should it become necessary, bring Roberto and Consuelo, Agnes and your father to this deck."

"But how will I know?" she cried out as yet another spray drenched the deck.

But Ransdell had disappeared into the cold wet

darkness, and only the sound of him and his men screaming above the rising wind provided her an answer. She slipped into the hold and made for the captain's quarters.

Agnes had put the children to bed and sat at the supper table with Thomas. Fear was evident on their faces.

"Elizabeth, Captain Ransdell says we are flying into the face of a storm," began Thomas. She felt for his hand as she answered.

"Aye, father, he told me the same." Seeing the look on their faces, she could not bear to tell them the rest of her conversation with Ransdell. "He says we are in for a rough night but that we shall make landfall at Malaga by dinner time tomorrow."

She looked at Agnes.

"He laughed, dear Agnes, and said that you will finally get to see if he has been raising his children in a pig's sty, or if he has been telling the truth about his habits of cleanliness."

Agnes seemed to relax a bit, and spoke for the first time.

"I shall join the children, then, and try and get some sleep."

"Do," enjoined Elizabeth. "'Tis likely to become very rough, but by dawn we shall see landfall."

Agnes disappeared into the small quarters where she and Elizabeth slept with the children, but left the door open.

Elizabeth laughed at her as she spoke.

"Agnes, I will roll out of my tiny bunk should I try to sleep there," she said. "I will sit with father for a bit."

With that she pulled the door tight. Turning to her father, she let him read the concern which now colored her countenance.

"So 'tis bad, is it, child?"

Elizabeth said nothing but listened to the ship. Thomas crossed himself and began praying.

Chapter Thirteen

"Agnes. Agnes!" Elizabeth was screaming. "Get the children!"

As the ship pitched and rolled and the timbers groaned, Agnes sat up. Elizabeth was amazed that the woman had slept during the past six hours. She had somehow braced herself against the wooden lip which ran along the outer edge of the bunk. Her right foot was securely hooked through a beam which supported the back of it while her left arm hung around its counterpoint on the opposite end. The children were nestled between her and the cabin wall. Elizabeth ran out of the cabin to help her father. Another wave hit the Phobos and Agnes stumbled from the bedchamber with a child under each arm. The roar of the storm could now be heard unfiltered by the deck and the window. Each time the ship pitched, the dip of the room towards the sea below became deeper and deeper. It was like taking a cup and turning it on its side again and again. It was only a question of time before the great salt sea began pouring in over the rim.

The storm had come upon them slowly. Initially, Elizabeth had sat and listened intently but soon realized that the rhythm and the depth of the pitches were fairly constant. She had reassured herself and her father with this knowledge, and Thomas had lain down to try and sleep. The sailors must have misjudged the severity of the storm, she told herself. After a bit, she begin to hear an occasional "pop" of the joists. At first, she almost jumped out of her skin and was halfway to the door of the bedroom when she realized that these noises were simply the ship adjusting to the unusually frequency of the high rolls. But in the space of half an hour, all that had changed.

Without warning, a great splintering sound followed by a huge thud and a shaking of the very fiber of the ship had jolted her out of the shallow comfort provided by the steady noises she now recognized. Her father sat up and clutched his cane. Elizabeth threw open the bedchamber door and screamed for Agnes and the children.

An unholy rush of water hit the ship and burst through the windows of the cabin. Agnes appeared with a child under each arm. As the wave ebbed from waist level to their ankles, Elizabeth and Thomas forced the door to the outer hallway open against the water which now secured it. With a great rush, they ran for the stairs. Elizabeth saw that her father was on his way up and turned for Agnes and the children. The cabin door stood open, and another wave hit the ship and swept through the hallway, almost knocking her off her feet. Someone shouted at her from above and a hand reached down the stairwell to help her as yet another great shock rocked the ship.

Above deck was a chaos she had never dreamed could exist. The ship was being torn asunder with each crash of every new wave. Elizabeth watched in horror as the deck at the bow suddenly split open, and the huddle of men who had been standing upon it disappeared into the darkness below. She turned and found Agnes clutching the children. Her father had disappeared.

"Roberto, Consuelo, you have told me you know how to swim," she screamed above the din of the storm.

They nodded, their eyes wide with fright.

Elizabeth grabbed their hands and placed them tightly on a piece of mast which floated past with the crash of another wave.

"Agnes! Hold tight to them and this! It will carry you…"

But another wave hit and Elizabeth was carried free of the ship and into the frigid waters. All manner of cargo and flotsam and jetsam whirled about her as she struggled for air. She threw herself over a passing barrel only to have it roll from beneath her. She went under again, spluttering. As she rose with the next wave, she grabbed a piece of timber which floated on the water. Again and again she slipped under but she held tight to the stave, for it always rose back up to the surface. But her strength and breath soon ebbed, and each time she rose for air her breath choked in her throat. A passing piece of timber caught her unawares and hit her full across the back.

"Henry," she screamed. "Henry!"

As she sank beneath the waves, she clutched desperately at the ruby cross which hung always about her neck.

*****

Half a world away, he woke in the pre-dawn hours in a cold sweat. A great fear rose around him and took hold of his soul, and he stumbled from the bed to shake off his sleep. Embers still burned in the fire and without waiting for a servant he threw kindling and wood upon them and blew until he saw a small flame rise. He was shaking and sat heavily in the chair facing the great mantel, waiting for the fire to catch hold.

What had he dreamed? He closed his eyes and tried to remember, but all he knew was that the nightmare had involved Elizabeth, and that she was taken from him. He rose and moved to his writing desk and picked up his quill but the words refused to come. Instead, he worked assiduously on patterns which entwined her initials with his, the E and the H eternally linked by an uncommon love.

Chapter Fourteen

July 10, 1503

Henry guided Governatore across the Greenwich Road. There was no traffic for the guards to halt that morning, for the spring rains had turned the entire thoroughfare into a sea of mud for miles in either direction. Wagons and horses had long since been caught in the quagmire which led onto this particular section of the road by the palace, and so Henry crossed it as he had left Greenwich: alone.

He had needed a moment to himself, time to take in the past year. But where to begin? As always, when the demands of his position began to encircle him too closely and he felt the need to reflect, he turned to Coudenoure. Once he entered the wood, he relaxed his grip on the reins. Governatore knew the way and picked carefully through the muddy undergrowth of the forest. He was in no hurry and neither was Henry - it was that kind of morning. The light filtered through the new green leaves and picked up their color, casting a cool, sublime hue throughout the forest. Regardless of what was on his mind, it was always at this point in his journey to Coudenoure that he began to feel a decompression take hold of his muscles and thoughts. This sense of relaxation would inevitably increase until finally, reaching the meadow which separated the wood from the mighty Thames, he would break free of the bonds that for the past year had held him without mercy.

Governatore seemed to enjoy the sun which now shone directly overhead, and Henry paid no heed as the great bay meandered and nibbled the fresh grasses. His attention was taken up by the stately form of a distant oak rising in solitude amidst the new growth upon the meadow. The faintest hint of green encircled the great branches, providing an almost mystical cloud of ethereal color around its dark branches. It provided a surreal point of focus for him as he continued on across the meadow towards the muddy path beside the Thames. But by the time he reached it, his thoughts had turned against his will and once again to the administrative matters of the kingdom. As Governatore plodded on, Henry turned back to the past year.

Without a doubt, a blow was struck to his equilibrium by the death of his beloved mother. He had never been close to Arthur, and while his brother's death changed his circumstances, Henry could not honestly say that his mourning was more than skin deep. His affection for Arthur had never penetrated his heart, nor did his grief when he died.

But his mother. Even now he teared up as Governatore ambled along. It had been sudden – first the child died at birth, and then, barely a week later, his mother succumbed to death as well. For the kingdom, the news was devastating. Elizabeth of York was known far and wide for her charity and kindness. The bells of St. Paul's tolled the sad news and their somber message was picked up by churches all across England. And while the death of Arthur had been a blow to his father, he at least had Henry, whom many believed, with his vitality was better suited to the throne. But now the King had no one, for his marriage to Elizabeth had been a love match. Their wedding had united the great houses of Lancaster and York, it was true, but by a happy and serendipitous turn they had discovered true love for one another.

But it was not just King Henry who felt he had lost everything. Young Henry had only known true and abiding love from two women, Elizabeth and his mother. He unconsciously compared all other women to them in what sometimes seemed to him a desperate and needy search for unconditional acceptance, for true family. The king was as cold and detached in his dealings with his children as he was in matters of state, and Margaret Beaufort, his grandmother, was overtly scheming, too manipulative to be nurturing and far more interested in outcomes than in individuals. Henry was left with only his sisters, Mary and Margaret, but they, too, fell short of the virtues he so loved. When he had arrived at Coudenure that fateful day and found Elizabeth gone, he had assured himself that at least his mother would be there to see him through until his lady love returned from Rome. But suddenly, like a passing breeze which blew from nowhere and disappeared just as quickly, she was taken from him as well.

Such a sad year. And so much change! Henry's world began long after the societal upheavals which ended at Bosworth Field. The patterns of his childhood had gradually become the patterns of his youth. These, in turn, were set against the never-changing background of an agrarian world still filled with the last remnants of the medieval age. But now, the woman he loved had travelled to a far away court, and his mother had left him as well.

So many details to manage now. There had been Arthur's funeral, and even though he had not been involved in that somber state ceremony, there had been corollary duties to be performed along with it - processions had been held throughout London and the kingdom declaring Prince Henry the successor to Henry VII, and on such occasions, Henry's presence was required. These weighed heavily on Henry, for he had been brought up as a second son, one whose role was necessarily not in the limelight to such an extent.

King Henry's fear of losing his sole remaining heir had abated somewhat, but even as his grief diminished his concern for young Henry increased. For the first time, he looked upon his son not just as a pawn to be played in the great game of marriage, but as the future ruler of the kingdom for which so much blood had been shed. It was jolting to realize that Henry, whom he was now busily proclaiming heir apparent, had no particular education in matters of governance, of state, or international politics. This omission had been deliberate on the old king's part, for he decried familial battles for kingship. His generation had been torn asunder by the civil wars between the great houses of the Plantagenet line – the Lancasters and the Yorks. He had therefore sought to instill in Henry a love of art, of music, of sculpture and painting and architecture. Henry could champion these cultural niceties, in hopes of giving England some preeminence in the arts. At the same time, he could marry according to his father's wishes but hopefully in accord with his own, thus helping cement a social fabric that would not easily be ripped apart by rival claims to the throne.

All that had changed, however, with Arthur's death. Henry smiled ruefully to himself. Before the past year, he had certainly known of the Chancery – that great arm of government which served as the secretariat for administrative matters. But he had known it in what turned out to be extraordinarily limited capacities. He certainly knew that the right of kingship of the Tudor line could be found in the genealogical records maintained by the Chancery; he was aware that the oblata rolls, or the fine rolls as they were commonly called, contained the records of gifts of land, of estates, jewels and other valuable resources to the crown. Henry was aware that minor local officials such as sheriffs and escheators held office through appointment calendars maintained by the Chancery, and that no contract was binding unless recorded by writ kept in the Chancery. But that was where his knowledge ended.

The exact mechanism for transferring property to the crown? Henry was oblivious. The method of insuring that the goods and services contracted for by the crown were actually received? Oblivious. There were the Parliament Rolls with their endless petitions and answers and bills, and the Statute Rolls for all acts which pertained to the kingdom at large. Of course there were the Patent Rolls with their recording of inventions, of land grants and licenses for widows to remarry, for wardships, pardons and charters for various causes and groups, and the Liberate Rolls for payout of crown pensions, stipends and salaries. There were the Originalia Rolls for payments of fines and Scutage Rolls for tracking those who wished to pay their way free of military service. In his mind, all the esoterica of government seemed endless, but the real problem for Henry came not in memorizing the names of the various rolls, their functions and functionaries, but in actually administering a huge and cumbersome state system. And that was only the Chancery!

The Exchequer, responsible for all of the financial dealings of the state both within the kingdom and beyond, interacted with the Chancery and the

Crown in ways that Henry simply did not understand and truth be told did not want to understand. The Great Roll - the record of all royal financial transactions, was kept by the Exchequer, but no account was closed until the Barons of the Exchequer received proof of royal receipt. Henry crossed himself as he rode silently on towards Coudenoure and thought of all the gibberish he had learned thus far as the future King of England.

In the future, he must govern. That much had sunk in over the past twelve months. How he would go about that - the details of the machinations of government, he did not know. Administration was a talent that he had not been born with and a necessity in which he had not been schooled. That was to be Arthur's job, not Henry's. Henry's job was to marry well and support the arts. His wife, Elizabeth, would look after their various estates, and Henry would look after culture within the kingdom.

The first time King Henry had taken the young prince to court with him and sat him beside the throne as he dealt with administrative issues of the kingdom, Prince Henry had thought he might possibly go mad. The droning of the petitioners, the strident voices of the ministers, the hubbub and milling of hundreds wanting access to the king morning, noon and night was not something he was interested in - it was as simple as that. That afternoon, Henry had dozed and fallen off his chair.

It was at that moment the king knew he had a problem.

And so for the remainder of the year, young Henry had been ripped from the tilting yards and tennis courts of his extreme youth and taken to the court of his father the king. More change. There would be no more gamboling adventures in the countryside with other young noblemen. No. No more hunting. No. No more youthful schemes. No. He would remain at his father's side. There, his mornings were to be filled with interminable lessons from the King's treasurer himself, Lord Hubert de Burgh. The great lord was patience personified, but not in a virtuous way Henry had decided. Rather, he would pose a financial query to Prince Henry, and then, with the patience of a dull-witted sheep, wait for an answer. He would sharpen his quill while Henry thought. He would rise and look out the window while Henry fidgeted. He would tap his yellowing nails upon the old wooden table at which he always conducted these lessons. Most every afternoon Henry found himself examining de Burgh's head, the strange medieval cut of his hair as a border of brownish gray around a shiny circular pate. Sometimes Henry eventually stumbled upon the answer, and at other times de Burgh graciously helped him find it. But regardless of how the answer was reached, or when, there was no respite for the young Henry.

His afternoons were taken up with the politics of the great houses of Europe and England. After an early supper, he frequently found himself looking into the wages of various tradesmen who worked for the king. Easter, Whitsun and Christmas were holidays for everyone, but there were so many days recognizing so many saints that it was not feasible to allow time off for all of them. A system had been worked out whereby workmen received every other feast day off as a holiday, but this was simpler said than done, much to Henry's sorrow. As King Henry informed him, he would not in the future be paying his workmen directly, but he must needs know the mechanism through which it was achieved.

That, and a thousand other issues which mirrored it in distressing detail had been his lot. As he turned onto the long drive of Coudenoure, however, he prided himself on having maintained a hold, albeit a slippery one, on matters close to his heart. A distant bell rang, a quaint notice to the staff of the manor that the prince was arriving. After the pomp and hoopla of the past year, it was more than enough. As he dismounted Governatore, Francis and Bess appeared. Both bowed deeply and the stable boy ran from behind the manor to take his reins.

"Good day," he began, "What news have you?"

"Good day, Prince Henry," Francis spoke. "We have quite a bit of news from hereabouts, but none, sire, from the Lady Elizabeth."

"And her father? Her Lady Agnes?"

Francis shook his head. Henry's words belied the disappointment written across his face.

"'Tis no matter," he said, "The Lady Elizabeth will in God's time tell us of her circumstances."

"I am certain, my lord," chimed in Bess. "Shall we prepare a dinner? Have you eaten?"

Henry smiled inwardly at the older woman's maternal attitude towards him. No one beyond Coudenoure would dare speak to him with such familiarity, but here, somehow, things were different. The moment he turned onto the great drive, he was home, and while treated with the utmost respect as his rank required, he nevertheless was made to feel that his presence was genuinely appreciated. It was as though he were a member of a family and had just returned home from a long and arduous journey. Beyond the respect, there lay open affection for the young prince. Henry felt it now as he always had when Thomas and Elizabeth ran out to greet him. It was both comforting and soothing, particularly after being hostage to King Henry's ministers and their interminable lectures for most of the past year.

"Aye, my lady, kindly have Cook prepare something. And I shall be staying a fortnight. Others will be joining me for I will leave from here for my sister's wedding."

Bess bowed again and disappeared through the great doors of the central hall.

"Walk with me, Francis. I wish to see the improvements I have ordered."

Henry paused before adding, "I shall want to see the receipts that will be provided to Lord de Burgh as proof of the work. Is Master John of Gloucester responsible for the masonry?"

"Aye, my Prince, and Master Alexander of Westminster is his carpenter."

Henry nodded.

"And of course, I shall need to view the estate's tax roll and the workers' pay schedules."

He felt positively administrative. De Burgh would have been proud.

From the end of the drive a great noise of hooves sounded and Henry waved as Charles pulled in his reins so tightly that his majestic steed reared in protest. Charles flung himself off the horse and after bowing to Henry, hugged him tightly. Henry laughed and pounded his friend on the back.

"Well, well, my prince," said Charles stroking his chin, "And can you tell me what the tariff rate is for silk from Cathay? Or alternatively tell me the wages for thirty-one cutters for diverse piece-works, eh?"

Henry laughed as Charles continued on.

"Or perhaps you would rather discuss the wages owed to Master Henry who worked upon the chimney for one month or the cost of marble and limestone for Westminster?"

Henry cuffed him about the head, and after a moment, they turned to Francis.

"Lead on, kind sir," Henry laughed, "And ignore this fool."

Francis began the tour by walking twenty feet down the drive. He stopped, allowing Henry and Charles to inspect the shallow trenches which had been cut from the sod on either side. An intricate, scrolled pattern, each side a mirror of the other, was cut out in fine detail on either side of the drive. The dark earth of the trenches stood starkly against the green of the spring grass.

"And what shall be the plants for these parterres?" Henry asked.

"Sire, I believe boxwood with an infilling of lavender but best to speak with Master Gerald of Henley on the Thames. He will best know but his wife is giving birth and he has left us for these three days."

Francis turned and led them towards the rear of the manor house where the sounds of hammering and the shouts of men at work could clearly be heard.

As they rounded the corner, even Charles gasped at the change which had occurred since their last visit. The empty fields which had previously delineated the space between the manor house and its farmlands were now a wide and cobbled way. On either side foundation of heavy limestone were set in an ordered manner. All activity had stopped as they realized who was surveying their work and a collective bow washed over the workers. A large man wearing black robes and black stockings hurried towards them. A black scarf was draped round his neck, and he doffed his black hat as he realized to whom he was speaking.

"Prince Henry, Prince Henry!" he exclaimed in a high squeaky voice.

Henry acknowledged him and turned to Charles.

"May I present Charles Brandon."

The man bowed.

"Lord Charles, this is Sir Robert Janyns, the architect responsible for my father's chapel at Westminster. He is overseeing the work I am having done here at Coudenoure as well."

"Yes, well," the architect launched himself into a diatribe before anyone could speak. "My Prince, 'tis very difficult to acquire the limestone needed for this project. I have to tell you that I am fraught with anger at that blacksmith…" he paused, pointed and shouted at a man twenty yards away, "…Yes, you, you whopstraw…" He caught his breath.

"And there is no end to the problems with dreadnoughts," he continued.

Charles interrupted.

"What dreadnoughts?"

"The roof tiles, my lord." The sound of Janyns' voice contained volumes of disapproval at the ignorance thus displayed. "The clay tiles." The last fairly dripped with attitude. Henry interrupted before Charles could respond.

"Then do not pay the man if his work is unsatisfactory! Find another!"

"Here? In this, this…" "Wasteland" was the word he had been searching for, but the look on Henry's face made him think twice.

"He shall do, my Prince, but he must be watched."

As they strolled towards the newly cobbled avenue and the foundation stones on each side of it, Francis returned to the house and Janyns harangued each workman in turn as they passed by them. Henry sighed, knowing that the price one paid for

Sir Robert Janyns' brilliance was more than just coin.

"And these foundations? What are they for?" he asked.

"Those will be the workshops and cottages which now you see behind you." Janyns turned back towards the house and nodded at the hodgepodge of outbuildings situated between them and the manor.

Henry was delighted.

"Aye, look Charles, these buildings will be made of the same stone as the manor. It shall be pleasing indeed to the eye."

Janyns smiled for the first time and nodded.

"Unity of materials is important, as is order and repetition. But look there."

They walked on down the avenue towards the empty area at which Janyns was pointing.

"This shall be an orchard garden," he declared.

"I thought the orchard was to stay on the side of the house," Charles interrupted.

Janyns sighed and looked heavenward, as though seeking assistance in dealing with Charles. The look was not lost on either of the young men, but Henry chose to ignore it and therefore Charles followed suite.

"There shall be two orchards," he explained with a world-weariness in his voice. "This one shall be a most attractive allée at the end of which shall be a small but exquisite rose garden with a great statue to honor our good Prince Henry. It shall lead on to the farmlands."

Henry nodded his excitement. Charles gave Janyns a sour look. They turned back and made their way to the work area. From beneath his robes the architect produced a tightly rolled sheath of papers. Henry waved them away.

"No, no, not here," he declared. "Let us go in and set them proper upon a table."

Janyns bowed in agreement and Charles led the way back around the manor and into the great hall. From there, they entered Henry's most beloved room, the library. A nearby table was quickly cleared of books by the servants and Janyns spread his plans out on the dark oak surface. Candlesticks on each corner kept the ends from spiraling back inwards. Henry's breath was taken away by the simplistic grandeur of the architect's design for the gardens. Janyns let his client take in each detail before he spoke.

"I see you understand my plan," he said when Henry finally looked up.

"I see the order you bring out of chaos, good sir, and the beauty you bring to even simple things," Henry complimented him. Janyns' face went pink with pleasure.

"And did you see this, my prince?" He pointed to an area on the orchard-side of the manor in which he had drawn a rectangular space which was empty. The rectangle joined with another which ran across the back of the library.

"This shall be an outdoor observation area, wherein you and the Lady Elizabeth may sit and enjoy the gardens and the orchards of your estate."

Henry nodded, as Janyns continued to walk him through, step by step, the planned gardens, stables and grounds.

Charles watched, and for the first time felt pity for his friend. This was what he loved: music, architecture, books. How much, he wondered, would he be able to take with him into the future that now awaited him? Was it possible for him to remain the same or would the weight of state affairs and responsibility for an entire nation bleed him dry of any vocation he might have beyond administration and warfare and politics? Any humanity? Charles sighed and shook off the mood. It was for him, Charles Brandon, to ensure that whatever happened in the future, Henry would have a youth to look back on with joy and relish, one that even on the darkest days might infuse his life and his decisions with a sense of order and serenity.

Chapter Fifteen

As Henry and the architect continued discussing the project, Charles slipped out and found Bess. She was in the yard, demonstrating to a young girl how to throw grain properly for the chickens which ran about them. Charles looked at the child closely and realized it was she who had stopped them the previous year with a message from Elizabeth. Upon seeing him, a look of concern crossed the face of the young urchin. Before Bess looked up, Charles winked at the child.

"My lord?" Bess gave a short curtsey and directed the child to do the same.

"And what are we doing here?" Charles asked jovially. "Lady Bess, surely you will introduce me to your companion?"

The child clutched Bess' apron and looked shyly at Charles.

"Ahh, this is Prudence, your lordship. She is a scullery maid and is today learning to feed the chickens correctly."

"I see," said Charles, secretly marveling that there was, in fact a proper way to feed grain to chickens. "And her parents work about the estate?"

"At one time, my lord, but no more. Prudence' parents died of the sweating sickness as did her brothers. Lady Elizabeth took her in and she is learning to be a proper cook, aren't you Prudence?"

Prudence nodded shyly and Charles moved on to his purpose.

"My lady, surely Cook can provide some small tidbits before supper? I am famished and I daresay the prince is as well."

With a quick bow Bess scuttled off to the kitchen with Prudence in tow. Charles heard her barking commands at the kitchen staff and knew he wouldn't have to wait long. With any luck at all, Robert Janyns had returned to his charcoal and paper and compasses by now, and he and Henry, if the weather held bright, might get in a spot of hunting before the sun went down. His hopes were dashed.

They still sat at the table, discussing architecture. Before he could rudely interrupt them and send the architect on his way, however, Bess opened the library door and servants poured in with trays of sweetmeats, pies and fruit. Henry invited Janyns to stay for the repast. Janyns, who looked as though he never turned down an offer of food, settled comfortably in and began cutting a savory pie. At least, Charles thought mercifully, he had changed the subject.

"Tell me, my good prince," Janyns said, "What hear you from your lady love, the mistress of Coudenoure?"

Henry shook his head sadly.

"Ahhh, Sir Janyns, I hear nothing and it preys on my mind mightily."

They sat silently for a moment.

"What is the cause for Lady Elizabeth's silence, think you?"

"I am not certain," Henry replied slowly. "But surely she must be well."

Janyns nodded.

"I am sure she is, Prince Henry. But women are a fickle lot and one never knows what their small minds might be thinking."

Charles concurred.

"But not Elizabeth," Henry explained to them.

"She is beyond her sex. She has all the wonderful womanly attributes such as kindness and beauty and gentleness, but none of the viperish ones which usually accompany them."

"Like gossip and petty behavior and back-stabbing." Janyns clearly had some woman in mind as he continued.

"Their tongues can burn the bark off an elm from twenty feet, and their eyes, their beautiful blue, limpid eyes will crush you with condemnation for the smallest of indiscretions. You might never recover."

He sniffed loudly.

Charles patted him on the back, feeling a sudden kindredness of spirit. Henry, however, would have none of it.

"Not my Elizabeth. She is as true as the sun when it arcs across the sky, as beautiful as the moon shining on a dark and still night. She is wise beyond her kind, and I cannot stop thinking of her."

They all sat morosely lost in their own thoughts as Bess brought out more food. Henry closed his eyes and saw Elizabeth beneath their elm; Janyns mumbled to himself "…the *smallest* of indiscretions, *really*…" and ripped a leg off a roasted chicken; Charles thought of the kitchen maid he had known the previous evening at Greenwich where he had stopped on his way to Coudenoure and her inquiries as to when she would see him again. The mood had definitely turned sour and the three men continued to eat and drink more out of self-pity than hunger. Henry's eyes grew heavy and he stood to excuse himself.

"I seem to have eaten my way into true heartache this afternoon. Please excuse me while I rest for a bit."

With that, he disappeared upstairs to the bedroom he now called his own, and passed out on the deep down comforter which covered the bed. Charles did likewise in a room across the hall, while Janyns stretched out in Thomas' old chair in front of the fire. With his feet on the footstool, he snored loudly while the servants quietly cleared away the remains of the meal.

*****

Henry woke with a pounding headache and a sad feeling. He lay for a long time thinking of Elizabeth and wondering what might be the cause of her silence. Surely by now, he reasoned, some epistle from her should have reached him. With a sluggish mien, he roused himself and went to his writing desk.

"My Darling Elizabeth," he began,

"How the days fly by! The lessons continue at the knee of first this minister of government and then that one. All of them sound the same now, and it is only when I can escape here, to Coudenoure, that I may be myself. In all other places, I am eyed, stared upon and expected to utter great pronouncements on this and that when I know not what to say! I have learned a few phrases which seem to satisfy, such as, "Umm, speak more to me of this matter, my lord, so that I may make a more informed decision,"... or..."Pray tell, is that so?"...or..."I see, hmm indeed." Perhaps I shall build upon these and by and by have an entire catalog from which to draw.

But while the days fly by, the nights do crawl. I remember your lips, your soft, warm lips the day of our pre-nuptials. I remember your hands, as small as those of a child and how they fit within mine so well, so perfectly. Elizabeth! How I miss you!

I am at Coudenoure now and will stay until I join the progress north for Margaret's wedding. 'Tis a fine thing, and should secure the peace with Scotland. As for Coudenoure itself, my love, you will be happy with the surprise I am making for you here. In truth, it shall be our home and our sanctuary against any and all that might try and come against us.

I know not why you send no news, no letters, but I know your love for me is true. There must be some thing blocking my receipt of them. They must be getting lost before I am able to touch paper which only recently you have touched. Perhaps your scent, of lavender and roses, will still be faintly upon the page.

Oh my love, write to me. How I need you.

Yours for eternity,

Henry

He folded the page carefully and sealed it with his imprint upon the wax. Downstairs, he called for Bess.

"My lady, once again, please have your son deliver this so that my Elizabeth may know I think of her."

Bess bowed deeply and upon rising, spoke softly to Henry.

"Fear not, young Prince, for I am certain the lady loves you. How could she not love such a noble and fine prince?"

But her words did nothing to cheer him up, and the evening was spent in tired conversation with Janyns and Charles. A light supper was brought to them at ten o'clock, and by eleven, Henry had determined to put an end to the weary day. He stripped off his clothes and crawled under the covers hoping that blessed sleep would overcome him shortly. For the first time that day, a wish of his was granted, and he slept the sleep of youth.

*****

Early the next morning, a pounding upon his door awakened him.

"Yes?"

"'Tis me, Charles, and I hear there is a fine stag by the River Thames this morning."

Henry smiled at the old line.

"Well, then, order some repast and we shall make our way to the great woods."

Robert Janyns joined them as they ate ravenously of the food Bess had laid before them. He watched them with wonder as they downed one bite after another.

"'Tis youth, sheer youth, I declare," was all he said as he nursed a strong cider and pushed away the food put before him.

"Eat!" Henry ordered him.

"Prince Henry," the older man intoned in his high, squeaky voice as he stood and bowed to be dismissed, "I promise your lordship that the day will come when you, too, will pay the piper for having feasted the night before." With that solemn oath, he took his leave, walking majestically, though a bit wobbly, to the door. He dramatically flung a red scarf over the same black clothing he had worn the day before, belched, and closed the door behind him. Charles laughed.

"Why do you suppose the good Janyns wears such mournful color?"

"Well," said Henry, "'Tis slimming…"

They both giggled.

"Promise me, my friend, if ever I should begin to show paunch around my middle that you will remind me how unbecoming such a state is."

"You? Never! You are tall and a bit railish if I say so myself. You might have problems as the years roll on my prince, but that t'will never be one of them."

"I will ask him about his choice of clothing," declared Henry with a laugh, "For I meet with him to discuss the new Westminster Chapel of the King's prior to joining Princess Margaret in her progress north to meet her new husband."

As they finished and rose, Henry shared his plans for the day.

"We will go to Richmond today – I have ordered one of my father's barges to take us up river and my falconer is already there."

"Ahah, what an ideal plan! I haven't my equipment, though."

"You may borrow one of my gloves - what else do you need?"

"You are right, my lord. That should be fine. You know, of course, that Hercules disappeared last year."

"No!" Henry exclaimed. "What a fine bird he was - what happened?"

"We are not certain. I kept him at Westhorpe Hall and he chose not to return after a release last fall."

"I cannot keep any of my birds at Coudenoure. Elizabeth does not allow falconry on the grounds. She says 'tis hard enough for any living creature to eke out an existence under the best of circumstances, and bringing in falcons does not constitute such conditions."

"And yet you hear nothing from the lovely lady." Charles remarked.

As the barge embarked and was oared slowly up river, Henry poured his grief out to his friend.

"I know she loves me and I know she has the truest of hearts. I am beginning to fear that something has happened."

They both crossed themselves.

"What says the English ambassador to the Vatican? Can he not look into the matter for you?"

"I have tried that route, but he assures me that the Baron of Coudenoure and his retinue have not yet arrived at the Papal court."

"'Tis strange, I will agree," Charles said thoughtfully.

"Will you look into it for me? If I seek answers beyond the ambassador, my father may become suspicious."

Charles laughed aloud.

"My liege, do you not think that your father knows?"

A look of alarm crossed Henry's face.

"How could he?"

"I know not, but know it he does. The Earl of Surrey told it to me in the strictest confidence three months ago."

Henry was aghast. Charles continued.

"Your father does not pay heed to it, you must trust me. Apparently, he believes it to be a childish infatuation that will pass. Indeed, there are other rumors abroad about your marital future."

Henry ignored the last and trolled his hand in the lapping water beside the moving barge. So his father knew but said naught. How to interpret such a strange turn of events? Did he think so little of his son's chivalric nature that he believed Henry would engage in pre-nuptials and not follow through? Did he not even suspect the depth of the connection between Elizabeth and him to bring about such an event? The river water washing gently over his fingers took him back in time, and he closed his eyes remembering the day he and Elizabeth had hired one of the many wherries which served as public transport upon the River Thames. The small, two-seat craft were oared by pairs of rowers, and provided their passengers with cushions and awnings for the ride up river to London and beyond. Since Henry VII had moved his primary court to Richmond, situated upon the river north of the city, but yet still maintained Greenwich as a secondary residence, situated south of the city upon the river, wherries had become the most common way for courtiers and administrators to travel between the two, with frequent stops at Westminster in between.

Henry smiled as he recalled Elizabeth screaming in girlish delight as she had stepped into the wherry. As they had traversed up river towards London, she had looked behind them repeatedly, predicting dire consequences should Lady Agnes become aware of where they were. On the way back to Coudenoure, the sun was behind them, the darkening river before them. It was magical then, and the memory of it was magical now.

He remained quiet, lost in remembrances but still turning the new piece of intelligence over and about in his mind, examining it from all sides. Charles continued talking, heedless of his friend's change of mood.

"Yes, apparently, the King is well aware that you spend quite a bit of time at Coudenoure and he follows the improvements you make upon the house and the grounds with amused interest. He believes it is a healthy outlet for the artistic creativity which was initially encouraged in your youth, before your destiny became apparent. Evidently, the ministers with whom you train, the ones responsible for your education in the politics and governance of the realm, have told him that you daydream too often during the lessons. Your father feels that if you have a practical outlet for this bent of your nature, then you will be able to better focus on your lessons."

"Does he indeed?" Henry mumbled just to keep up his part of the conversation.

"I believe he has even seen the plans of your work at Coudenoure. You know, Sir Robert Janyns was never known for his discretion. Besides, the work you have engaged in at Coudenoure is grand, Henry. It is truly becoming one of the finest estates in England. Of course, 'tis very small, but over time you could enlarge it."

Henry snapped himself back into the conversation.

"Yes, one of the very finest. Although, I hear tell that Lord Giles Daubeney has done remarkable work on that derelict ruin of the Knights Hospitallers up river from Richmond - what is it called? Hampton Court. Yes, that's it. Order of St. John's of Jerusalem."

"Daubeney?" Charles tried to put a face with the vaguely familiar name. "I know him not I think."

"Chamberlain of the King's Household. Prior to that, the Lieutenant of Calais. Gray curly hair? Squinty eyes?"

Charles shook his head and Henry waved his hand in a dismissive fashion.

"'Tis no matter. But Charles, why not stay at Richmond tonight and tomorrow we will ride and see it? Yes, I am told it is quite interesting. And William Fitzwilliam is at court at Richmond already. We shall take him with us!"

A slow curve appeared in the river, and as the barge rounded a large promontory on the western bank, Westminster came into view. Henry never tired of watching London unfold itself along the ribbon of the Thames. The long façade of Westminster stretched imposingly on the east bank, with quays and docks obliterating the shoreline in its shadow. As the King's barge came into view, the frenetic activity which roiled along the embankment and the road which split it from Westminster proper slowed first to a crawl, and then ceased altogether as the merchants and seamen realized whom it was ferrying upriver. A wave of bows then cheers in honor of Henry rose spontaneously. In turn, he rested his foot upon the lip of the great barge and waved merrily back to them. It was an unrehearsed moment and one which filled both sides with glee and happiness. As Henry settled back amongst the cushions once more, Charles said nothing, but patted his friend's shoulder. He would be a great king indeed.

*****

At long last Richmond came into view, and Henry was finally able to put the matter of what his father knew or did not know about his pre-nuptial state from his mind. Clearly, the King knew nothing of the pre-contract into which he had entered with his beloved Elizabeth. Otherwise, something would have been said. He must then know only of the "infatuation" as he termed it. Prince Henry was certain he had nothing to worry about – his secret was still secure. Lord William greeted them at the small dock used for the king's personal transport.

The afternoon was spent on the great plains adjacent to the palace. Henry's companions were not at ease with one another and jousted to demonstrate superior knowledge to him of the sport of falconry.

"Ah," Charles replied after a particularly curt barb from Fitzwilliam, one which found fault with his handling of the hood each time the bird came to rest on his wrist, "I see that you take advice from a woman, and a convent prioress at that!"

"Indeed, Dame Berners has much good advice on the subject, but how would you know, since you can barely read."

It was becoming unpleasant and Henry tired of the constant jibes. Here of all places, among friends at his own father's palace, he should be able to relax instead of becoming judge and jury of which friend was the finer courtier. The constant bickering reminded him of the days in which he dutifully trailed behind his father at court, tending to administrative matters, listening to the advice of his inner council, hearing petitions. Everyone wanted to be first among the many; everyone used him in some manner to improve their own estate. An almost palpable jealousy permeated the air. Henry found it suffocating. He retired early from the field, and took dinner en suite. At dawn the next morning, he slipped quietly away to the dock, and was up river before his friends were even awake.

He smiled, imagining their faces as they read the note he had left behind.

The mist rising off the river shrouded the barge in a veil that enveloped it in solitude. Henry listened to the rhythmic strokes of the oars, waiting for the sun to break through, eager to see what had been done to yet another monastery no longer used by those called by God. A streak of sunlight on a building up ahead caught and held a gleam from a finial on a large roof. Henry realized he was looking at the chapel at Hampton Court. A letter the previous evening had alerted the tenants of his arrival, and a small party waited for him upon the quay. All bowed deeply as the barge was tied. An older man matching the description given by Henry to Charles the previous day now stepped forward.

"Welcome, my prince."

"Lord Daubeney, thank you for arranging my visit and on such short notice particularly."

"Aye, well, I wish to show Hampton Court to all those who will see it!"

He led Henry through the outer buildings - a brewhouse and a dovecote - chatting as they walked. The party had fallen away from them, and Giles Daubeney broached the subject the king had tasked all his ministers with discussing with Henry, should the opportunity ever arise.

"Young prince," he began, "The King tells me that you will be participating in the progress north for Princess Margaret's wedding to the Scottish king. 'Tis the time of year for weddings, is it not?"

"Um?" Henry suddenly remembered Charles' statement the day before: *"There are others rumors abroad about your own marital future."* He stiffened slightly but the older man did not notice.

"Lord Daubeney, it might be, but I prefer to discuss that window yon – do you have your own glazier who designed it?"

But Daubeney would not be deterred.

"No, sire, he is the King's man, but our sovereign allows him to work for me on occasion. Tell me, have you considered marriage yourself?"

"'Tis blunt, your conversation," Henry replied.

The older man smiled.

"Perhaps, but I have heard rumors that the Princess Catherine is pining for a man. They say she is ripe and lovely."

"Do they?" Henry asked. "And so soon after my brother, dear Arthur? What kind of woman would even be considering such matters directly after becoming a widow?"

Henry walked on out of earshot and Lord Daubeney skipped to catch up.

"A fine dowry attaches itself to that Spanish woman, did you know?"

Henry was fed up and turned in peevish anger.

"I believe I have seen all I desire this day, my lord. 'Tis gracious of you to be so kind to me, but now I will take my leave."

Nothing Daubeney could say or do deflected Henry from his grim walk back to the barge. The oarsmen were eating food supplied them by Daubeney's kitchen and flirting with the scullery maids who had brought it to them on the dock. As Henry appeared, they frantically left the plates where they were and took up their positions on the barge. With no ceremony and a curt nod of his head, Henry directed them to take him back to Richmond. Daubeney stood on the dock with his hat still in his hand, wondering what he would say to the King.

So that was what Charles had alluded to. His father was brewing a marriage for him, and to his own brother's widow at that! Henry's stomach turned as he thought of it. If his father so ordered, then he must so do. But he breathed deeply, reminding himself that it had not been commanded of him…yet. Henry would have to speak to his father after all and tell him of his pre-contract.

There was no other way to protect his vows to Elizabeth, for if the King arranged a marriage before knowing, only wrath would come his way, wrath with no Elizabeth in the bargain, for the King would honor his word to another king, Catherine's father, before he would that of his son's to a mere baron's waif.

But the timing of the conversation was not easy to judge. If such news were to come out now and in any way disrupt the much heralded wedding of Margaret to King James, it might prove to be to his own detriment, angering the king and predisposing him to deny Henry what he wanted most of all. He was not naïve enough to think that Lord Daubeney had brought the subject up of his own accord. No, the king must have set him about the business. Henry realized that he would have to be very careful indeed to avoid any such talk with any of the king's ministers who were accompanying Margaret on her progress north. And he would have to leave as soon as feasible after the wedding to ride back south to discuss the matter with his father. In the interim, he could only pray that King Henry had not already vouched safe his second son for Catherine. An unholy mess indeed.

The news drained all light from Henry's world, and upon arriving back at Richmond, he sent for his things from Greenwich and Coudenoure - he would remain at court until the progress began. Fitzwilliam had left early that morning, called back to Aldwarke by John Neville, the Marquis of

Montacute, who was also his father-in-law. Charles was in no better mood than Henry as they walked along the bank of the Thames, while Henry told his friend of the conversation with Giles Daubeney. As he finished, Charles spoke commandingly.

"You must, Henry, you *must* tell your father about the pre-contract. Otherwise, in his ignorance, he will betroth you to some continental princess or worse, your own brother's widow."

Henry nodded his agreement.

"But t'will be bloody difficult to avoid such conversations if my father has commanded them of his councilors. They serve him well, you know."

Charles considered for a moment.

"Who will be accompanying you northward?"

"Surrey."

"Hmm, and his wife? Mind you, his wife will be more than happy to discuss her own daughters with you, my friend. It seems you are beset about with women as far as the eye can see!"

"I can manage the earl's wife, Charles, and likely the earl himself. But Northumberland will be joining us, and he is formidable when he chooses to be."

"Have you seen his face when he is angry?"

Charles asked, clearly recalling some terrifying moment from the past.

"Indeed, I have. It was when I could not recount the lineage of some west country baron who is related to him. The lesson was quite painful that day."

They walked on in silence for some while, each scheming how to relieve Henry of any conversation involving matrimony during his sister's wedding celebration. Finally, Charles sighed.

"There is no amulet to protect you and Elizabeth, I am afraid. You must use your rank and dignity to silence them before they can launch into such speech."

Henry brightened.

"Indeed! They may serve my father, but I outrank them."

"And if all else fails," advised Charles, "Take to your bed with a cold and claim you feel sweatish."

Henry roared with laughter.

"'Tis good! Although I believe "sweatish" is not in the king's English."

"And get clear away at the earliest moment you can. You must ride hard to reach the king before they do, for if they have failed in their mission to discuss the matter with you, it will only be because you have ordained it, and they will realize it."

Henry felt better having a plan in his pocket - it was the uncertainty of what actions to take which always caused him anxiety. Now, he knew how he would handle them.

"And you?" he turned to Charles.

"Ah, more tilting and tennis for me," he laughed. "But I am due some new clothing from the continent so that will be interesting."

"Will you do something for me?" Henry asked in sudden seriousness.

Charles heard the change in tone and stopped.

"Anything, my liege and my friend. What is it?"

"I grow more fitful about my Elizabeth each day. I need to hear from my beloved. And yet all I receive is silence."

Charles patted him on the back.

"I have it, my prince. Do not worry again. By the time you return, I shall have found the weak link in the chain between the two of you and shall have repaired it."

Henry sighed with relief.

"I trust only you with this."

"Consider it done. I think I shall start at Woolwich."

"Why Woolwich?" asked Henry.

"It has troubled me for some time, my lord. How did the captain of an ocean going vessel communicate with your grandmother? She knows no such types."

Henry nodded.

"Yes, I have had the same thoughts."

"After that, I shall go where the trail leads me. What day is the wedding so that we may plan our rendezvous before you meet with the king?"

The conversation continued in quieter, conspiratorial tones. Finally, both satisfied, there was purpose in their parting.

Chapter Sixteen

The progress north was a triumph. Princess Margaret, small even for thirteen, showed no outward qualms concerning her approaching marriage to the thirty-one year old King of Scotland. Each day, entire villages turned out to cheer for the beautiful princess on her way to a fairytale life in the far north. They strained and pushed and pulled against one another to better eye the young girl. Her litter, covered in satin and lace, was open faced on all sides, and she smiled and waved shyly at the crowds. This marriage had been part of her life since the age of six, and she had been well-prepared for cleavage from her family, friends, culture and home. But there was no preparation that could overcome homesickness, no remedy for the ache she felt in her heart as she left the familiar behind and faced her future.

Behind her on liveried horses her thirteen ladies' maids followed, and beside her rode the Earl of Surrey. The train of dukes and earls, each with their own retinues and households, stretched along several miles of road, and the brightly colored pennants which waved from each one made the day bright and meaningful. A small band of drummers and lute players accompanied them as well, announcing their presence to all who could hear. It was a spectacle intended to impress, and the idolization and awe apparent on the faces of the townspeople was not lost on young Henry. A dawning of the uses of grandeur not just for propriety's sake but for the impression of power it conveyed to the people was planted firmly in his mind. Even as they crossed the Scottish border and made their way to Edinburgh, Henry continued to be amazed at what pageantry could accomplish without the raising of a single sword or giving a single command.

Charles and he had called it correctly. King Henry's men were anxious to take him aside and discuss his marital prospects. But they had to jockey with their own wives, for not being privy to the King's plan concerning Catherine, the women put their own daughters forward as potential mates. Henry found these particular conversations easy to manage. He verbally twisted, ducked, turned and dodged their various attempts to bring the conversation round to this beautiful and talented maid or that lovely and accomplished young woman. But he did so with such chivalry and such kind wit that they only redoubled their efforts. The conversations with their husbands required more direct rebuffs, and to avoid offending the King's men, Henry rode much of the way alone.

The celebrations continued in Edinburgh, where the entourage stopped for feasting and jousting.

There was no shortage of scarves and colors thrown at him each time he mounted for a joust, just as there was no lack of dance partners each evening. Despite missing Elizabeth, Henry found he enjoyed court life of this order. He had never been exposed to this side benefit of wealth and power. His father's court reflected the personality of the king himself, and King Henry had no taste for what he considered wasteful entertainments.

From Edinburgh they journeyed on to Holyrood, where Margaret was given in marriage to James. Henry watched, fascinated, dreaming of the day that he would take Elizabeth as his wife. Margaret looked small in her royal vestments, stiffened sleeves and arched wimple. Henry hoped she would be happy, but more than that, he wished for the Perpetual Peace to hold. If his father had taught him anything, it was that secure shores and borders were one of the great necessities for a secure reign.

The feasting and merriment had been drawn out into the third week before Henry found an opportunity to leave. It would have been impossible before that without offending half of Scotland, and after that, some of the King's councilors would surely have insisted on accompanying him, since they too would be leaving shortly. As the sun rose on his appointed day, Henry rose with it. He had arranged for the stable boy to meet him on the edge of the castle, beyond the gatehouse, thus ensuring that the hammering of his horse's hooves alerted no one to the departure.

He would be well away before they could join him, and James would tell them of the urgent business Henry had been called to look into at Coudenoure, something involving his young friend Charles Brandon. As part of their plan, Charles had arranged fresh horses and food at way-stops along the road back to Greenwich. Henry dressed as a commoner, for it would be impossible for him to frequent such places should his identity be known. And if he stopped at estates or castles, his father would expect him to stay until such time as it was seemly for him to leave. That could take weeks.

There was a freedom to riding alone on the open road, and Henry enjoyed it mightily. No one knew who it was that sped past them on the fine thoroughbred that towered above their field horses and wagons. Such solitude gave him time to prepare for the coming conversation he would have with his father. There was no easy way to tell the king, and the snippets which had leaked out around the edges of the many conversations he had had with his father's men in Scotland had alerted him to the truth of what Daubeney had told him at Hampton Court. But Henry was confident, and the ride home was sunny and warm. He took it as a good omen of his future with Elizabeth.

As planned, he rode first to Greenwich to confer with Charles. Lights shone in the chapel of the palace friary as the monks lit the candles to celebrate Matins. Henry handed his horse off to the waiting stable boy and gave a coin to the doorman to let him in. A quick wash was followed by a clean nightshirt but as Henry tumbled into bed, a soft knock came upon his door. It was Charles.

"Good Lord, man, I am exhausted, can you not see? Our business can wait until dawn, unless…unless…can it be that you have news of my Elizabeth? Letters?"

Henry began to chatter excitedly and danced about the room lighting the candles. He did not look at Charles.

"So how is she? Is she here? Are there letters? CHARLES! I command you! Speak!"

Henry turned to his friend and for the first time saw the look of grief written across it. Charles had been weeping, and his red swollen eyes made Henry's heart almost stop.

He sat down, still staring at Charles.

"'Tis news you have, then, is it?"

Charles nodded.

"And does it come from Woolwich?"

Charles poured himself a drink from the decanter of wine which sat nearby. He poured another for Henry and sat down beside him. This had not been part of their plan, this conversation, and he was uncertain how to proceed.

"My Prince, Woolwich was only the beginning. Lady Margaret paid her groomsman handsomely to arrange passage to Rome for the Lady Elizabeth and her family."

Henry nodded. Charles could barely speak.

"My friend, that ship, the Phobus, never made port in Rome. I traced it, through the tales of sailors at Woolwich, until its passage of the great Pillars of Hercules. At the same time, I sent urgent messages to the King's ambassadors at the Vatican and in Spain, seeking any information they might have."

Henry's blood ran cold. Charles could hold back the knowledge no longer.

"Henry, the ship was wrecked along the Spanish shores of the Mare Nostrum. There were no survivors. Elizabeth is dead."

Henry fell to the floor fists raised to heaven, screaming and crying.

"My God, my God, the one thing I wanted, the only bit of happiness I have in this world. And yet you take it? You leave me without my Elizabeth? Why, God, why?"

There was no end to Henry's grief. For days, he refused to leave his bed or his bedchamber. He refused all ministrations and company save for that of Charles; food repulsed him as did conversation.

Over and over again, he fell to his knees and cried out to God for an explanation, but the only answer was the silence of an empty world. Elizabeth was dead. What would he do?

One week later, his grandmother sent word that he was to eat per the king's command. Days later, he was told that if he did not leave his room and eat, the king would call him to court and ask for an explanation of this odd behavior. It was then that Henry realized that his father had no idea at all as to the cause of his only son's heartache. Further, he understood that his father's concern was for the crown and the Tudor dynasty, not him. There would be no miracle, neither to bring Elizabeth back nor to change his father's ice cold heart. His own heart was irretrievably broken, his grief so deep and wide that he could not see beyond it. And yet he must carry on somehow.

Chapter Seventeen

The coastal road, lonely and seldom used even at the busiest of times, was deserted. The great storm had swept across the dry plains of Africa, picking up speed as it flew across the mighty Atlas range and searing the slopes of even the towering Jebel Toubkal. Down it came into the seaward valleys, shaking loose the sands of a thousand ages and carrying them along in its hot and angry breath. As it rolled out over the vast waters of the Mare Nostrum, it picked up speed, rising higher and higher until its winds covered everything in their path. The stars were nothing against such rage, the moon a mere candle flicker in the night sky. But just as it seemed it could not sustain itself, its leading edge reached the warm air of the Spanish coastline. It fed on the warmth, obliterating all that came before it. No one could remember such a wicked gale ever gaining such momentum.

Finally, like all anger, there was nothing left to vent. But its death throes proved as terrible as its life. It whimpered and screeched and tore at the Spanish coastline, writhing in fury and dumping so much sand and water and debris that the coastal road disappeared entirely, leaving the beach in wrecked isolation.

The small village of Malaga had not escaped, and as the townspeople unlocked their shutters and set their small homesteads aright, word began to filter out of a wreck upon the coast just south of them. At first, it was dismissed. Tales of wrecks and bounty washing up upon the shore were legend in this part of the world. But when the first children raced up from the beach clutching a barrel stave and a large swath of canvas sail bearing a familiar mark, fear gripped the village – the Phobos was due back this month, and many of the townsmen had put to sea with her. More children appeared, talking of dead bodies and vast quantities of timber. People hurriedly yoked oxen to their rickety wagons, gathered up blankets and went in search of the living. Those who stayed back begin brewing broth and hot soup, warming covers by the fire for any who might have survived.

The tide was working against them that day, and for every two men they managed to pull free from the wreckage and debris another one was caught and taken by the relentless and fierce ocean waves. In an effort to save as many as possible, they began working in teams, with some running ahead and dragging the bodies to safety above the reach of the tide where they would lay until the wagons came abreast. Wagon after wagon loaded with men and debris made their way back to Malaga, where the sometimes mournful, sometimes joyous efforts of loved ones began. Slowly, the villagers picked their way up the beach, their oxen heaving the wagons over the sand-strewn road which wound along the tidal crest above them. It was a macabre business, made more so by the time lapse between the storm and their efforts - almost a full twenty-four hours. It became routine not to check for a beating heart in the swollen corpses, but to save their efforts for those who looked as if they still held a spark of life. From up the beach, a sudden cry arose. In the distance, men began waving their arms in the air to bring help. Wagons on the crest hurried to assist.

Two of the shipwrecked sailors had seen the villagers and cried out for help. They, too, had been pulling bodies from the surf in an attempt to save lives. A line of wretched souls stretched out along the sand dunes and grass which covered the line between the road and the beach proper. Some were sitting, some lying, some huddled together to try and generate warmth. As the villagers came into view, a feeble roar went up from these survivors. Help had come. The wagons arrived and the villagers began triaging the men until a sudden cry caught their attention.

"Roberto y Consuelo! Ellos viven!"

Women surged forward with blankets, knowing only too well that the call could only refer to Ransdell's two small children. They cradled and wrapped them, speaking in soothing low tones to the tiny survivors. Roberto's eyes flickered open momentarily before closing again. Consuelo barely breathed. But the strangest thing to the rescuers: the children had been found tucked into the embrace of a matronly woman. She had evidently crawled and clawed her way with them to a point just beyond the surf line, covering them with her body against the elements. As they aided her, the villagers wondering silently what a woman had been doing on this cargo ship which plied between England and Italy. No one spoke the question aloud, and she was loaded, unconscious, onto the wagon with the children.

The morning became midday which slowly bled into early evening. It had been several hours and miles of coastline since they had found any bodies or survivors. It was decided to turn for home. Those left in the search turned ocean-ward, and sent a prayer over the waves for those they would not see again. It had been a cruel day, one which had followed on the heels of the cruelest storm they could remember. They turned and began walking to the last wagon which had been set aside for them. As they crested the dune, a lone villager turned to look out one last time over the vast and mighty ocean. The sun's rays were almost gone, and he crossed himself, thinking of the power of God and how it could alter lives in an instant, as quickly as a dove might take to flight. As he turned to climb on the wagon, the glint of the last ray of light caught upon something far down the beach. He squinted, trying to determine what he had seen. Just as the last light caught the lip of the horizon and disappeared, he saw a human figure, waving weakly towards the wagon. With a cry, he ran towards it.

A few others followed on behind him carrying blankets. It was dark now, and they begin to stumble and grow fearful of the great surf. The man ran onwards, oblivious to the cries of caution from the others. He almost passed it.

A body lay crumpled in the path of the approaching surf. He screamed and clung to it as a wave washed over him, the current pulling his legs from beneath him. He choked and screamed from the roiling water, and this time his fellow villagers located him and the body he was clinging to in the gathering gloom. It took all four men to pull them from the clutches of the surf. In the darkness, they wrapped them both in blankets and began the trek back to the wagon. It was a long ride, and they were met at Malaga's outlying huts by townsmen with torches and more blankets. The doors to the sanctuary of St. Nicholas' had been thrown open and the church served as it always did as a place for the community to gather. The candles were lit and torches illuminated the shadows. Laid out all around were those who had survived the terrible wreck of the Phobos. Villagers ran to and fro attending to their needs and as the final two were carried in off the last wagon, they were placed near the great hearth that ran along the outer wall. There was great interest in the one last survivor - for those who had lost someone it was their last chance to have them back. A crowd gathered. As the soaked blankets were removed, a gasp went round the crowd.

The final survivor was another woman.

*****

She had been in the meadow for a while, now. The sky was so blue and the clouds so full and white that with the smallest effort she could reach up and touch them. She lay on her back on the soft grass and all around her were the gentle lavender blossoms, the wild daisies and fritillary of Spring. So it was Spring now! What a happy time! She really should rise and make certain Cook was at the hearth, for Henry would be here shortly. Wait! Too late! She smiled as she lay listening to the heavy thundering hooves of Governatore as he galloped up to the Manor. Henry threw himself from the saddle and embraced her with his whole being. He lay beside her in the meadow and told her of his day, of the great and many accomplishments he had wrought, all in the name of God. And of England.

He moved closer to her, and a great white light shone from behind him, illuminating his kind face like a halo.

"Drink this, my Elizabeth, you must drink this."

She frowned. Someone was pulling her away from Henry, and she did not like it. She tried to shake her head, but to no avail.

"My lady, drink." Elizabeth did as she was told, hoping that Henry had waited for her there, in the meadow where they lay. But it was late, and rather than try and find him again, she slept a deep and dark slumber, so warm and enveloping that she knew not when it might end, nor did she want it to.

*****

The sound of children laughing woke her. Sunlight flickered across a spotless stone floor and a bright fire burned merrily in a hearth nearby. Elizabeth lay motionless, taking in the scene. Agnes was not at her needlework, but was mending some garment. The children, Roberto and Consuelo, played together on the floor with small wooden figures. Agnes alternated between talking to them in broken Spanish and focusing on her work. After a moment, she rose and with a great wooden ladle stirred a huge pot simmering on the iron spider settled into the hearth near the edge of the flame. She noticed a figure in a chair drawn close to the fire and with a wince turned to inspect the person. It was her father.

Thomas seemed older somehow, his hair whiter, but his cane was beside him, and his nose was buried in a great tome bound in illuminated vellum. The image was intimately familiar to her, tied up inextricably with Coudenoure and all she held dear. If a faint scent of lavender had accompanied the scene, she might have thought she had only to open a door to be home. A faint smile crossed her lips as she listened carefully and heard the familiar snore of his afternoon nap. So perhaps it was dinnertime, she mused. That would explain the delicious aroma emanating from the pot on the fire. A small cough escaped her lips. The room burst into activity.

"Elizabeth! Can you hear me? 'Tis me - Agnes!" Agnes was by her side in an instant, and with no prompting the children who only moments earlier were playing dolls and horses pulled blankets from the warming rack near the hearth and brought them to Agnes. Elizabeth felt Agnes' worry as much as she saw it across her face. She tried to smile. In the background, a stamping noise could be heard.

"Clear a way for me! You young hoodlums, clear a way I say."

It was her father, and she felt his tears on her hand as he held it tight.

"'Tis enough, old man, the child will need food."

"Well then, you must get her a plate, and quickly." Thomas sat beside her on the makeshift bed on which she lay. He was crying openly now, patting her hand and talking quietly to her.

"I felt you would not leave me, Elizabeth. I felt it in my soul."

Elizabeth smiled and with all the strength she had squeezed his hand. His tears became sobs.

"She understands! Agnes! Quickly with the food!"

The two of them struggled as they pulled her into a sitting position and Agnes then fed her small drops of beef broth. Elizabeth had never tasted anything quite so delicious.

"My lady," she whispered, "You must compliment the cook."

It was Agnes' turn to sob. She passed the bowl and spoon to Thomas and ran to the hearth wiping her eyes with her apron.

"Quickly, children, bring me candles. We must light candles for today we have seen a miracle. Our Elizabeth has returned."

The children looked at her in confusion. Agnes put her hand to her head in frustration.

"Velas," she said finally. "Candles! Bring them to me!"

Before they were lit, Elizabeth was asleep again. But as she drifted away, she could hear as if from a great distance a happy cacophony of babbling voices, praising God and saying her name over and over.

Chapter Eighteen

On warm bright afternoons, Thomas and Elizabeth frequently sat in the sun on the narrow cobbled way just outside the door of Captain Ransdell 's small home. Here in Malaga, there were no sweeping avenues or broad walkways. No grand manors awaited beyond the privacy of hedges or woods, nor did the houses of common folk and gentry keep themselves neatly beyond the street with gates and gardens. Instead, each home sat squarely against the next, and all perched upon the lip of the street just outside their front doors. Brilliant red geraniums grown in oversized terracotta pots graced each such stoop, and on days like today, most inhabitants of Malaga dragged simple benches or chairs outside to sit and chat with their neighbors and watch what few wagons traversed the way.

Those disinclined to such idleness might pass the day in the town square. There was no official market day, and on any given afternoon, save Sundays, sellers would lay their goods out upon the ground or arrange them on their wagons to the best advantage. The city square was small but Malaga took enormous pride in it. All side streets led to the central park and the cobbled streets formed a tidy and pleasing border around the area. It was here that one might find mangoes from the peninsula, lemons or olives from further north, cured meats, simple cloth for garments, rudimentary tools or services from blacksmiths or cobblers. Fish was abundant and sold fresh or smoked or occasionally pickled. Even on off days the little open air market lent a busy, festive air to the village.

Across the square from the market was the church of St. Nicholas. In the great Reconquista of 1487, Malaga was taken by siege from the Muslims and re-established as a Christian village. Accordingly, the mosque was converted from the worship of Allah to that of the Christian God and the structure began to be called by the name of the patron saint of sailors and ships, St. Nicholas. The great pillared interior of the main sanctuary soared three stories high and still bore the intricate Moorish patterns and designs which had graced the mosque. But instead of the broad open spaces where hundreds would lay their prayer rugs and face Mecca each day, rough wooden benches now sat. A raised altar graced the far end of the long, narrow aisle and a small dais sat atop the altar. It was from here that Friar Marcos spoke each Sunday, each holiday, and on each saints' day.

Thomas had been the first to recover from the shipwreck of the Phobos. The wave which swept him overboard that fateful night had carried him to a rocky shoal. He had managed to cling to a craggy outcropping and as that wave had receded, he had inched his way gradually landward. But more waves had followed, and for every foot gained inches were lost. As the night progressed, his will and the jutting rocks had provided him purchase albeit at a heavy price - he had never been so bruised and battered. By morning, he made landfall and dragged himself shivering up the beach away from the tide. It was here that the searchers had found him, bleeding and nearly dead.

Agnes and the children had fared the best. The same fate that cast Thomas up upon the rocks had determined a safer route for them. Clinging tightly to the wood as Elizabeth had instructed, they had ridden the destructive surge all the way to shore. But before Agnes could cross herself and give thanks, another wave battered the beach and tore Consuelo's feet from beneath her. Her childish screams were swallowed by the fierce roar of the storm. Agnes had thrown herself back into the heavy surf and grabbed a tiny hand. Roberto was screaming behind her now, and with her other hand she had reached out to him. He anchored himself behind a massive boulder in the sand and held tight. The wave subsided and before the next one hit, Agnes pulled Consuelo, unconscious now, from the surf. Together, she and Roberto had tugged the small body away from the sea before collapsing. Agnes had tried desperately to bundle them together somehow and stay warm. She had placed them side by side on the sand and with the wind and rain howling about her, had draped herself over them to shield their tiny bodies as best she could from the wind and the rain.

But Elizabeth: The Morai had disagreed that evening. Should she live, or should she sink to the bottom of the sea never to rise again like so many others aboard the Phobos? Clotho had woven the shipwreck into the fabric and pattern of Elizabeth's life; but Lachesis, she who determines how long the length of the complex weave will be, chose to see what intricacies might still remain in the pattern of Elizabeth's life. At that moment, Atropos, the most abhorred of the three, lost her power for without Lachesis to determine length, Atropos could not cut the life thread which bound Elizabeth to heaven and earth. And so against all odds, she survived.

As the water battered and sucked her under, she had grasped a larger piece of debris than the one she originally clung to, and with every ounce of consciousness she held tight to it as the tidal currents and storm played with her like a cork on a fishing wire. The debris she now clung to bobbed up and down with each onslaught and she rode with it, learning to breathe deep with every ascent and pray with every descent. Her feet finally felt sand beneath them, and from then on it was a question of dragging herself further up the shore with every surge. Hours later, she was victorious, but the price was high. She had not the strength to pull herself completely out of the water. Instead, she lodged against a mighty rock and as the sound and fury finally subsided, she lay unconscious, almost buried by seaweed and debris from the Phobos. In a strange way, it was the debris which saved her in the end, for it sheltered her from the wind and insulated her against the driving ravages of the storm. The sound of workers shouting back and forth and of oxen bellowing as they strained to pull the wagons through the wet sand had finally awakened her near sunset. Throwing off the protective shield of rubbish, she had used the last of her energy to pull herself up against the rock and wave for help.

But that effort was almost her last. A hard fever set in, and for months she fought delirium and unconsciousness. A draining cough became worse, and had it not been for Agnes' gentle and determined care Elizabeth would not have survived. Once the fever past, there were months of rehabilitation to follow. She had been battered and both a leg and an arm broken in the fight against the sea that night. As a result, time had lost all meaning for her in her battle against death.

On any given day when she and her father found themselves sitting just outside the front door, Elizabeth's thoughts always followed the same patterns. She would ponder how long it had been since she had considered such mundane issues as seasons, months, days and hours. She always did this with her face turned skyward, soaking in the bright sun and letting it flow over her as the waves of the Mare Nostrum had once done. She was safe now, she had always to remind herself, and as she looked upwards, her fingers played with the flowers which sat in a nearby pot. As always, at some point in her reverie, Thomas would look at her and smile.

"So we have made it, daughter, you and me. We survived against the odds."

Elizabeth always smiled and with her free hand would reach out and rub her father's arm.

"Indeed, father, we have, as did those we love."

It was as though each of them, in their own way, needed this daily reaffirmation of their survival and depended upon their little routine for reassurance. Unconsciously, they had elevated its importance to a ritualistic level, to the point that even who pulled the chairs outdoors and placed them in the exact same spot each day (Elizabeth), who sat down first (Thomas), and who sat in what chair resonated deeply for each of them, providing a strong sense of order out of the nightmare and chaos which had engulfed them on the night of the wreck of the Phobos.

Their conversation seldom varied either, and like a church litany, Elizabeth always followed with an observation about the sadness which accompanied the wreck.

"'Tis sadness in its purest form, father, to see so many in this village brought low by the storm."

To which Thomas always gave the same, reassuring reply.

"Yes, but Ransdell is a good man, and he does what he can for Malaga."

The captain had survived as well, and in recognition of the severe losses suffered by the village, had agreed that until each dead sailor's children came of age, he would give half of all his profits from the sale of cargo towards their care. It was a generous gesture, and in turn, the village came to love the English captain and his mysterious English travelers, as the strangers were sentimentally regarded. Who was this strange man, a noble man according to Ransdell, who brought his daughter - a mere maid - on such a treacherous journey? And who was the woman who accompanied them? They were told that she was a lady to the young maid but such a tale did not make sense. The older woman was vigilant in her care of first Thomas, Consuelo, Roberto, and the Captain and then, as each completed the journey of their own recovery, solely of Elizabeth. A servant surely would not take such extreme measures. Only a family member, they reasoned, would risk her own life as she had done, and only to help others in her clan survive.

Agnes was an utter amusement to the village. Early on in their tenure in Ransdell's house, she had realized that the circumstances demanded her complete dedication if all were to survive. She grasped in a heartbeat that knowledge of sufficient Spanish to bargain, plead, understand, and cajole to get what she needed for those she now considered her family was an essential tool. There were no servants, no estate, no one to help her or them but herself. There were no ladies' gowns – her clothes and those of Elizabeth were charitable gifts from the other women in the village. There was no needlepoint to occupy her afternoons. Instead, she mended the children's clothes and did the laundry. No one asked her what evening meal should be prepared, or what she thought might please the lord of the manor and his daughter for this or that saint's day celebration. Instead, she hurried out to the market each afternoon after she hung the laundry behind the house on a rope supplied her by Ransdell. He was amused, and told her that laying the wet garments before the fire worked just as well but Agnes had insisted.

"Do you not understand the need for cleanliness?" She frequently remonstrated. "And is there anything fresher than clothing dried by the sun set in the heaven by our Almighty Father?"

Ransdell always smiled at this point. He was not a religious man, but he was deeply superstitious. Even now, he and his crewmen who had survived wondered what they had done wrong to deserve such a night as was visited upon them and on the Phobos. He himself had escaped relatively unharmed, with only minor bruising as evidence of the trauma. As had been their habit for generations, night after night, he and his fellow sailors and captains from the village met in the square an hour before sunset to discuss local news, weather patterns, cargoes and upcoming voyages. They were a tightly knit fellowship and, in the months following the wreck of the Phobos, their conversations almost always started and ended with that fateful voyage. Thomas had joined this group when he was able to walk again, and had quickly picked up more of the patois spoken by the locals. He had made inroads with the language on the ship while talking to the crew, and at this point, despite the fractured nature of his grammar and vocabulary, was able to join in the discussion.

Try as they might, however, they could not parse the disaster. There was no obvious point of blame and no noticeable causal event to explain why they had been led into the storm's path. As the months passed, the discussion turned from the wreck itself to prevention of future catastrophes. This was particularly true among the survivors. Each man who had washed ashore and lived to tell about it discussed over-arching reasons for the disaster each afternoon with the other sailors in the square. But when they were alone, when they were with grateful family or listening to a homily from Friar Marcos or preparing this or that ship for another voyage, they thought long and hard about their personal fates. Why had they survived and not their friends, their cousins their uncles or fathers? Why had destiny chosen them to carry on, but more importantly, what had they *done* to deserve to continue on? Had their talisman against death been the jacket they were wearing, borrowed on that day from a fellow sailor because their own was too torn to don and work in? Or perhaps it was the cross that their mother had told them to always keep on a chain about their necks so that God could identify them as one of his faithful - had that saved them? Before leaving on the voyage, some had kissed their children goodbye. One particular sailor remembered his wife, in an unusual gesture, playfully cupping him about the ears and rubbing his head. Perhaps that had been his salvation - after all, why had she chosen that voyage, and only that voyage, to demonstrate her love in that manner? Prayers were said and confessions given to Friar Marcos, but at the end of the day, each survivor made certain that to the extent he was able he repeated the sequence of events or clothing or peculiar send-off which had accompanied the last voyage of the Phobos.

Ransdell had come to believe that the presence of his English passengers had saved him and his children that night. What else could it be? He had agreed at the last moment to take them aboard and ferry them to Rome. Some might believe they were the cause of the wreck, but not many. Instead, they were looked upon as special for otherwise why had God singled each of them out for survival. But his appreciation of the English threesome did not stop there.

As the months passed and Malaga recovered, Ransdell had turned his mind once more to sailing. The Phobos had been his best ship but not his only one. The Deimos was the near twin of the Phobos. Both had been captured by his father during the Reconquista, and in honor of his service to the Spanish crown, he had been allowed to keep them as his own. Additionally, he had owned a much smaller vessel, the San Miguel, which had previously supplied his living before the great battle with the Moors across the sea. Ransdell the younger had inherited this fleet, as would his son Roberto. Most families in Malaga were similarly situated. It was a mariner's village and there was no family whose fortunes were not somehow tied to those of the ships anchored just off the shore in the tiny cove of Malaga.

Since the passing of his wife, the Captain had struggled to keep himself and his small children together. Initially, the villagers had stepped up and cared for them on while Ransdell was away at sea. After all, their own sons or husbands were likely crewing on those voyages and economic success for Ransdell also meant economic success for them. But as the years had passed and the children had gotten older, fewer and fewer volunteered to feed and house the rambunctious pair. Isabel's family had disowned the trio years earlier, and in desperation Ransdell had turned to England and to his own family. But they, too, were unwilling to take on the education and care of Consuelo and Roberto. At the very moment, when his heart had sunk the lowest point, he had been asked to take Thomas and his family to Rome. He had agreed to do so for money; had he realized the difference they would make in his own life, he would certainly have done so without charge.

Each time he returned from a voyage, Agnes dressed the children in their best and took them to wait for their father to be rowed ashore from his ship. They would then make their way to his house, where a warm fire burned and the aroma of a meal floated out from the hearth. Elizabeth and Thomas would be there, and a sense of happiness and family pervaded the small house. It was always spotlessly clean thanks to Agnes, and thanks to Elizabeth, the children now spoke English as well as they did Spanish.

When he was not at sea, the captain watched in admiration as Agnes and Elizabeth ran his household. Each morning, the children sat for lessons with Elizabeth. In the afternoons, they either walked along the seashore with her, looking for shells, or went to the market in search of adventure with Thomas. Elizabeth slowly incorporated herself into the work required to keep the household running, and as a result Ransdell began to understand what the concept of home truly meant. He watched Agnes at first with admiration, and then with something more. She had become his helpmate even though it was never spoken. Their relationship was one of scolding, nagging and teasing, and they both loved it.

"Tell me, you fine Captain, why is it that you never bring what I ask for? Eh? Do you think that God will drop cloth from the heavens with which to cover your offspring?"

"Well, if he did," came the inevitable reply, "'tis likely you would not use it for clothing in any case. Tell me, in England, did needlepoint truly take up all your time? You must have a tapestry there that stretches across the entire kingdom."

"And this from a man who makes not his own dinner, but thinks that I shall! Goodness! You may just have porridge for the evening, kind sir, if you keep saying such miserable things."

On and on they went, but Ransdell would always produce whatever household supplies Agnes had requested and she would always produce a delicious meal for the household. Throughout this repartee, Thomas would sit happily by the fire, sleeping or reading, while the children ran about or played in front of the hearth with the simple wooden toys Ransdell usually brought them from his travels. Elizabeth listened in amusement while she, too, read or wrote letters home. Home, to Henry.

Initially, her letters were short and stilted. So much had happened to her that she found it difficult to translate the recent past into the mold which had been her relationship with Henry. In hindsight, she realized what a simple life she had led at Coudenoure and how sheltered both she and Henry had been. He might be the son of a king, but their experience both individually and collectively had fallen within the normal patterns for those of nobility in England. Since setting foot on the Phobos, her universe had expanded exponentially. It was true that during the same time Henry's had as well, for King Henry had wasted no time in beginning young Henry's schooling for the kingship. And that was where the great divide began.

Henry deepened his knowledge of continental politics, of noble families and taxation and estates and patronage from the point of view of the ruling class. Elizabeth's perspective now included a deep understanding of everyday life for those not born with a title. There was no easy way for her to expound upon her new understanding of the world and how it was beginning to shape her identity. It was almost visceral and everyday brought profound and new insights as she unconsciously absorbed everything around her. The routine of her life with Thomas, Agnes, the children and the captain became her foundation amid such daily revelations. It was the backdrop for beginning anew after the terrible shipwreck. Her love for Henry was the sole element of her previous life which continued to shine through the days, months, and years unscathed, unchanged, and burning as brightly as it had at Coudenoure.

Her letters reflected her growing maturity and knowledge of the world, but were always laced with trivia and incidentals from her life in Malaga.

> *"And Henry, you must help Agnes and me with a mystery which has presented itself in our small household. 'Tis as follows. Most days, my father awakens early and stirs the fire for Agnes who awakens later. After that, he walks with several old men from the village around the town square. He receives breakfast from Agnes upon his return, and usually spends the day sitting outside dozing and enjoying the sun. You must understand, Henry, that in this clime, the sun shines most days – 'tis strange, indeed, but not unlikeable. As I was saying, this is his daily routine until he and Captain Ransdell walk to the town square for the late afternoon mead fest with other captains and sailors. They would not call it thus but Agnes and I have decided that such is the proper name for their gathering. But I digress.*
>
> *The mystery began many months ago, when an unusual rain came in from the sea and we spent the day indoors. Well, 'twas unusual that it rained, my dearest, but the rain itself was not unusual! My father appeared from the room he shares with Captain Ransdell and sat, as is his wont, in his chair beside the hearth. But rather than engage in conversation, he produced from*

within his robes a book! Yes, Henry, a manuscript! I must tell you, before going on with my story, that while the villagers of Malaga are as intelligent as any I have ever known, books and book learning among them does not exist. These are men of the sea and their knowledge of sailing would fill several tomes I am certain. Likewise, their women who stay home and tend the fires have a very fine and extensive knowledge of herbal medicine, of plants and crops, and of weaving. They are an intelligent lot as well. But their learning does not come from books, nor does it find its way into books. It is a learning that is gleaned from their ancestors.

As my father opened this book, we all commented upon it, as you may imagine. Where did he get it? How did he pay for it? Roberto and Consuelo scrambled into his lap to touch this fabulous treasure and to ask my father all about it. But rather than answer our questions, my dearest, he simply smiled and told us its name and some of its content. He refused to provide any detail about the transaction which must have occurred in order for him to secure it!

Now, if 'twas only one such manuscript, perhaps, in time, we would have accepted the enigma and moved on. But Henry, he has produced two more such books! And yet each time we ask him, we get the same, tired answers. We all know them by heart now so often does he speak them!

My love, I will continue to relate to you the chapters in this mystery, for Agnes and I have determined that we must know, for no other reason than knowing."

Each such letter was carefully sealed and entrusted to Ransdell before he departed on his travels. His voyages no longer included England, for he feared risking his remaining two ships in the stormy waters of the North Sea. Instead, he plied the Atlantic coasts of Spain, Portugal and France. Even though he avoided venturing as far north as England, he had maintained his Atlantic stops in those three countries and as a result, he had many trading partners with whom he transacted business and to whom he sold cargo bound for the island nation. And it was to one of these men that he always paid an additional fee to have Elizabeth's small packet of letters delivered into the hands of an emissary whom he was assured would get them to Prince Henry. Each time he delivered such a packet to his partner, he insisted that the great Lady Margaret Beaufort not be used as the conduit for delivery. And each time he was assured that this would never happen. From there he left the matter, for once having received a fellow captain's word he could not pursue an enquiry further without insult.

But as time passed, Ransdell began to wonder about the entire arrangement. He knew from Elizabeth's own lips that she had directed her prince to send his letters to her through the same channels. But each time he met with his friend and inquired about return letters to the Lady Elizabeth, the answer was a shake of the head and a shrug of the shoulders. For her part, Elizabeth was equally perplexed but continued faithfully sending her epistles with the captain. Whenever the subject came up as they all sat together at supper, she blindly ignored the doubting faces of her loved ones.

"My love is a Prince, and Princes are busy indeed. You must have faith."

"Elizabeth, 'tis not faith that we are lacking, 'tis proof that he is writing!" Agnes usually exclaimed. But Elizabeth would not stand to hear Henry's love questioned.

"You will see that I am right. Perhaps he chooses not to use Captain Ransdell's man in Woolwich! Perhaps he is sending his letters directly to Rome, where they await me at the Vatican!"

Each and every time Elizabeth mentioned Rome, conversation ceased, as she knew it would. She used this reluctance to her great advantage and kept the disbelievers at bay with the threat of pursuing such a conversation further.

Chapter Nineteen

One evening, when she and the children had joined the others from the village in a search for nocturnal crabs along the beach under a full moon, Agnes, Thomas and Ransdell set to discussing the matter of Rome.

"We have tarried here for quite some time," began Thomas.

Agnes stiffened.

"Aye, and with good reason. Elizabeth has only recently recovered, and to expose her to sea winds again so soon and the unhealthy conditions which prevail upon all ships might trigger another fever. And we shall not risk losing her again, Thomas."

He nodded silently while Ransdell spoke.

"You cannot leave," he said simply, "For the three of you are now family for Roberto, for Consuelo, and for me." He gave a meaningful look to Agnes. For once, she did not look away or busy herself at the hearth or with mending. She returned his gaze and in the flickering shadows of the fire he thought he saw her give a slight nod. He continued.

"And besides, what is all this talk of Rome? Young Prince Arthur, God rest his soul, died quite some time ago. Likely he is far beyond prayers and indulgences, even if it is Popi who is giving them out."

"How long have we been here?" asked Thomas. "Let us see - Elizabeth and Henry were precontracted in the year of Arthur's death."

"Aye," said Agnes slowly, "And 'twas two Christmases later before Elizabeth ceased having regular fevers and shivers. 'Tis God's grace the sweating sickness did not come upon the child. But she is safely beyond that now."

She crossed herself and poked the fire.

"But now 'tis the next summer," Thomas went on, "And still we tarry."

"Well, regardless of what you choose to do, 'twill be next spring before we can arrange it. The late summer storms have begun, and winter is no time to put Elizabeth on a ship."

They all agreed.

"And 'tis a dangerous time of year to sail anyway," Ransdell continued. "T'would be foolish.

No, the best time would the next season. But as I said, I cannot see you leaving. It would break a great many hearts, I am sure."

He rose and put on his cap before opening the door.

"Besides," he added, "What shall you do in Rome that you cannot do here? I am greatly saddened by this conversation. Pray think of me and my little ones. Now, I shall go see how the crab hunting is coming along."

With that, he began to pull the door behind him, then hesitated and turned his head back towards the other two.

"Agnes, I would like you to help me see how the children are faring in their hunt. Would you care to join me?"

His voice had a strange, agitated quality and Thomas turned in his chair to take a closer look. He stood almost abjectly with his cap in his hand, shuffling his feet and looking around the room as though he had never seen it before. But before he could take in Ransdell's strange behavior, a sharp movement from Agnes' chair caught his attention. She was clasping and unclasping her hands in a strange manner. She suddenly stood.

"Aye, captain, I would love to check on the children with you. Shall we?"

She picked up her shawl from a nearby chair and without another word the two of them disappeared through the door.

Thomas sat with a quizzical look on his face, his brow furrowed with the strangeness of what had just occurred. Suddenly, he laughed and clapped his hands.

"What an old fool I am!" he exclaimed as he stoked the fire and sat back down. "Of course! And yet I saw nothing of it before! Well, well, well."

He was still smiling as he made ready for bed.

"Let the others tend to the evening chores," he chuckled to himself as he crawled under the covers. "Indeed."

Chapter Twenty

Each day, she gave thanks and immediately afterwards asked for forgiveness.

Lady Margaret Beaufort had achieved her ends, but her means made her queasy when she thought about them and it was then that she would go to confessional. She had not anticipated the shipwreck and she prayed fervently for the souls who had suffered such an end, but she could not in good faith say that she was sorry about it. This paradox in her thinking was not something to which she was accustomed. In Margaret's world she always managed to avoid areas of gray. In this way she had put aside the vicious years of warfare that had been necessary for her son Henry to secure the throne. In her mind, they had been brought about by the House of York's refusal to recognize the legitimacy of the Tudor claim. Likewise, when the plague had swept through London, or the sweating sickness carried away the innocent by the thousands, she believed with her whole heart that those unfortunates must have had a dark stain upon them from the beginning. Otherwise, how to account for such horror? This system of belief was buoyed by the good fortune which had come the way of her family. Henry was king. Her grandson, young Henry, would surely follow in his footsteps. It was true that Arthur had died young, but his sibling was far better equipped for the throne in many respects. She knew her tribe to be noble, chivalrous, kind, generous and true, so the good fortune which fell to their lot was obviously further reward and proof of their worthiness from God himself.

From triumph to triumph, the Tudor line had risen ever higher in the waning years of the last century, and she took this long train of successes as God's stamp of approval upon her and her kin. Time would heal her of these feelings of uncertainty about her part in this whole affair. If she had been a different person, she would have recognized them as guilt. But she was Lady Margaret Beaufort, and guilt was for lesser beings, not for her. And so her personal priest, Friar Chauncer, spent many hours hearing her confessionals. But her whispered litany of sins was always the same, and in fact was the same one he had always heard from her - she had eaten too many sweets and worried about gluttony (even though the woman was so thin as to be almost transparent); her alms to the poor had not been adequate she feared; she had listened to the idle gossip of her ladies-in-waiting. Clearly, something was driving Lady Margaret to confessional at a pace usually reserved for thieves and murderers. Equally clearly, no one would ever know what it was. And then the thunderbolt had struck.

It arrived one bright and sunny morning in the grimy hand of a guardsman from the palace gate. She was once again staying at Greenwich, having progressed only recently from Collyweston. Her mid-morning doze was interrupted by angry and insistent voices in the grand hallway.

"What is it?" she asked Joan, her favorite among her ladies. "Do they not know that I am resting?"

Joan bowed and left the room only to return moments later.

"My lady," she began, "There is someone here to see you. He says he has been directed to deliver a gift directly to you."

"Who is it, then? Eh?"

"I believe 'tis one of the guardsmen, from the outer palace gate."

"And he has something for *me*?"

Joan began to regret not having wrested the small package from the guard.

"Yes, my lady, and he says he will give it to you and to no other than you."

"I see."

Margaret began straightening her shawl and the blanket which lay across her lap. Two ladies fluffed the pillow behind her back and stood as though at attention as Margaret nodded to Joan to bring the guard forward into the room.

He was a scruffy sort, short and rough looking, but his livery was clean and his eyes showed intelligence. He went down on one knee and remained silent.

Margaret left him there for a full minute - if he had overstepped his bounds by insisting on seeing her, that would be only the beginning of his travails. She would see to it personally. And it had nothing to do with disturbing her nap.

"Rise, young man, and tell me why you insist upon seeing me?"

"Your Highness, this morning, a small child from the village of Woolwich approached the guard house."

"I imagine they approach all the time, since they are always there seeking alms as I come and go."

"Aye, your grace is correct, but this little one pushed and shoved his way right to the front, and demanded to see the Chief Guardsman."

"Nervy. And why did he do that?" Margaret was beginning to tire of the whole business.

The guard began to fumble within the jacket of his uniform. After a moment, a small packet, tied with a bit of woman's lace, appeared in his hand. Margaret studied it intently, trying to ferret out its meaning. She stretched her hand out tentatively and the guard passed it to her. It was square, no more than three inches on each side, and wrapped in heavy, brown paper. The ribbon wrapped securely around it was pale rose, and of a quality which Lady Beaufort knew did not come from a lady of nobility. A neat bow held it secure, and as she pulled one of its ends she questioned the guard.

"You say a child from Woolwich gave you this?"

The guard nodded.

"Where is this child?"

"As soon as I promised him that I would deliver it directly to you, my lady, he melted away."

"What was his name?"

"I do not know, Madame."

"What did he look like?"

"A filthy little urchin. He smelled a bit of the sea, though, which is to reason if he is as he said he was, that being from Woolwich."

"Did he ask anything in return for delivering this?" Margaret held up the package.

Again, the guard shook his head.

"Did you find out anything at all? No? Then what am I paying you for, pray tell?"

He looked down at his folded hands and remained silent.

Margaret slowly unfolded the paper, only to find that inside were many similarly folded sheets, each tied with the same type and color of ribbon. Her ladies and the guard had unconsciously inched forward, leaning towards her trying to catch a glimpse of whatever the wrapping hid. Intuitively, she placed her hand over the entire stack.

"That will be all. Joan, see everyone out."

As the door closed behind them, Margaret picked up the first piece of folded paper from the top of the stack and tugged it free of its ribbon. She gently opened it and discovered that it was a letter written in an unknown hand. Still she could not fathom why the package had been expressly delivered to her and with care unfolded the bottom half of the paper so as to read the signature. It was then she knew her thanks had been premature and her confessions pointless. Her fingers shook as she hurriedly pulled the bow on each letter and read each signature. All the same, all the same. Looking up, she stared into the fire as her breast filled with fury. She went back to the first one and began to read.

"My darling Henry,

How I miss you! It is almost impossible to tell you all that has occurred these past months. The Phobos, upon which we sailed, was ripped asunder by a storm such as I have never seen nor ever want to see again. I survived, as did my father and Agnes.

It has taken months to recover, and we are living in a tiny village by the sea, called Malaga. The good captain of the Phobos, Ransdell, also survived as did his two children, and they have taken us in and given us succor whilst we recovered. Initially, I believe he did so in return for my Lady Agnes keeping his house and because I am teaching his children English. Now, however, he and his have become family for us, Henry. You will love them as we do should you ever meet them."

Margaret screeched.

The door flew open and Joan appeared.

"My lady! What is the matter?"

"Get out!" Margaret screamed. "Get out!"

Joan did as she was told and Margaret reached for her cane, waving it mindlessly in the air, screaming at no one and everything.

So the Baron of Coudenoure and his daughter, the Lady Elizabeth, were living with a peasant in a village and performing menial tasks for their daily bread. An English baron living thus! And the girl had the audacity, the hubris, the *unmitigated gall* to write to the Prince of England, young Henry, as though they were lovers! Her mind reeled as she struggled to take it all in. Her eyes returned to the letter still in her hand.

> *"The many letters I wrote you while at sea ('tis a strange thing, indeed, for a woman to say) are now lost forever, my dearest, but I will begin anew for my love for you survived the wreck of the Phobos, as it will always survive. I have considered how best to get them to you, and the good Captain has helped me with a plan."*

"Has he indeed!" Lady Margaret could not help herself from spitting the words aloud as she continued to read and wave her cane about.

> *"He no longer sails the Woolwich route out of fear for his remaining vessels. But he has a fellow English captain with whom he trades at the French port of St. Nazaire. To this noble man he pays a fee to ensure that my letters are safely got through to Woolwich. From there, dearest, they are to be given into the care of an agent of Charles Brandon and delivered by him directly into your hands."*

Margaret sucked in her breath and read the last sentence again. So there would be other letters. Of course there would! She should have seen that instantly. If the young tart was foolish enough to send these forth, well, she would certainly carry on doing so for there was no one to tell her what a blithering idiot she was and that she must cease immediately. She realized that she must rally her thoughts and prepare for action, for should even one such letter find its way into young Henry's hands, a mighty catastrophe would fall upon the house of Tudor. She breathed deeply and set the remaining letters aside - there would be time for those later. Instead, she called out to Joan.

"Bring the guardsman back, do you hear? Quickly now!"

She listened as her command was shouted from one servant to another. It echoed through the great hall, out the front door and down the drive from house maid to stable boy to yardsman. After what felt like a long age, a hurried scuffling sounded outside her door and the same guardsman who had delivered the package appeared. Without a word, he fell on one knee as he had done previously.

"Rise, young man, and speak to me of the urchin who demanded that this hateful package be delivered to me." She waved her cane at the small package on a nearby table. A sudden inspiration lit her mind.

"And tell me further, did he ask specifically for me?"

"My lady, he asked first for Lord Charles Brandon. I told the young lad that Lord Brandon would not be at Greenwich until two days hence."

Margaret nodded with satisfaction for him to continue.

"He went away that time."

"When was this?"

"Yesterday, Lady Margaret."

So that was how the clever maid had laid the trap. She knew that Charles was a frequent visitor at Greenwich and further that he would never give her or Henry away. The guardsman's look turned to one of concern.

"'Twas nothing, my lady, I swear. And then today, he returned only this time refusing to leave it with anyone but you. He said it was a grave matter and that he must be listened to. Given his words, I brought the letters directly to you this morning, as you know."

"I see," she said, "And I must see the captain of the guards at once." She looked at the young man and forced a smile.

"No, you nit, 'tis nothing you did. You are fine. Now get me the captain. And young man, should the urchin appear in the meantime, do not change your demeanor or treatment of him. I expect you to act towards him as you did this morning, for I want nothing to alarm the young *termite*."

He bowed again and Margaret breathed a sigh of relief. She would talk to the captain, and each time the lad returned, or any lad did for that matter, asking that some package or message be given to Charles Brandon or anyone else, it would always come to her first. If she should be away on progress, the captain must hold it until her return.

There was only one small detail remaining, and she called out sharply to Joan.

Sometime later, she ate a hearty lunch and was escorted to her chambers for a long nap; thwarting other people's plans was such tiring work.

Chapter Twenty-One

April 1, 1505

"My Darling Henry,

I write to tell you good news, my love! We are one step closer to being reunited. After much trouble, Captain Ransdell will finally let us voyage aboard his ship the Deimos to Rome. This ship supplies the bulk of his living, being the sister of the Phobos upon which we sailed from England. He frets constantly about its well being as much as though it were a child. He believes, however, that the voyage to Rome will be quick, and safe, and he may perhaps pick up interesting cargo there. There was a cholera epidemic last year which delayed us an entire season, but finally, we sail seven days thence. We are to be left there as the original plan dictated, with the English ambassador to the Vatican court. We shall seek indulgences from Pope Julius for our dear Prince Arthur. Afterwards, I shall myself assist father with his seeking out of manuscripts for the library. Do not fret my love, but be sure that there will be no time lost in doing so."

Elizabeth paused and looked out over the vast sea. She had sought a quiet place to write one last epistle to Henry and it was not to be found in the house of Ransdell that particular day. Agnes was busy turning the small abode upside down in her efforts to begin packing for the upcoming voyage. In amused frustration, Elizabeth had escaped to the sea, to a dune scattered with the tall grasses so common here. She had tucked a small phial of ink, a quill, and a folded piece of paper in one of the voluminous pockets of her apron. In the other was a small rectangular piece of wood, worn smooth on both sides. With a shawl wrapped tightly against the cool breezes which blew in from the west, she had walked the shore, enjoying the morning and seeking a good niche into which she might settle and write.

A small cargo vessel had arrived late the previous evening, and Malaga Cove was a hive of activity as dories rowed men, supplies and cargo to and fro. The ship was due to weigh anchor the next morning and had only stopped for provisions and to sell what they could of their cargo with as little passage of time as possible. The villagers were accustomed to these types of opportunities and accordingly the vendors who normally lined the town square would pack their wagons and reposition themselves as closely to the shore as was practicable. The result of this longstanding practice could be easily seen in two, wide, makeshift avenues along the boundary where the dunes turned to sandy scrubland made barren by the constant passage over generations of wagons and men. Today, these were lined with cargo from the ship arrived the previous evening, having been hastily set out upon bales of hay.

The men who crewed this particular ship were Greek, or so Elizabeth was told as she passed the area on her way to a quieter perch. She suspected this to be a convenient fabrication of the sort frequently heard in Malaga from captains who sought haven in the cove, or put in seeking supplies and crew. Their language was not Greek, and their clothing was more akin to that of a woman than a man. Long linen and cotton robes, once colorful but now bleached beige and white by the sun, were worn loosely. Occasionally, however, men with long knives tucked securely in sashes about their waists were seen. One sported a hooded hawk clinging tenaciously to his gloved hand. The scene was festive and busy, and even Friar Marcos had turned out and wandered among the wagons and the cargo.

The wind blew her dark hair loose from the ribbon which tied it. Her complexion, always dark, now matched that of the native Spaniards, and her dark eyes allowed her to pass as one of them. Unconsciously at first, she had begun to identify with the women of Malaga, and as the years had passed, the visions of England's dark forests and towering trees, of spring rains and the musty smell of autumn, of the snap of the winter's air after a frost, had all but left her. In their place were palm trees and the smell of the ocean. Her memories were now more of Malaga than of England, and when she realized her shifting orientation she had initially become concerned. After all, these things - olive groves and sitting in the sun with her father by the door, brilliantly colored bougainvillea and birds of paradise, ships and cargo bales - these would all be gone one day soon. She cautioned herself not to become attached to a way of life she knew was fleeting. But the warning came late, and she loved the place as one loves home. The paradox of being of one place but belonging to another gave her a sense of detachment, a trait which allowed her to take a long view of events, much more so than others her age.

> *"There is another bit of wonderful news, Henry, and it will make you as happy as it makes me, I am certain. My dear Agnes is married! She and the good Captain Ransdell were joined in the church of St. Nicholas some months ago. 'Twas a simple ceremony, for Friar Marcos speaks no English, and Agnes is not clever with Spanish. The ceremony was in Latin, for of the two devils as she calls them, Spanish and Latin, Latin is at least familiar to her from our church at home. And truth be told, her Spanish is quite funny, not at all suited for a ceremony such as marriage.*

She longed to be married on English soil but Ransdell and she cut a fine bargain. If she would marry him now, he promised to move his home and children to England to live with her there when we return. 'Tis a fine trade, I believe, and they are happier than even young lovers would be.

I must close this brief note, my Prince, for Agnes has need of my help as we ready ourselves for Rome. I shall write to you as soon as we are settled there, and you may be sure I will provide you with a glimpse of the machinations of that mighty city! My thoughts of you are eternal, my love.

Your Elizabeth"

It was short but it would have to suffice. Elizabeth pocketed her materials and brushed the sand from her skirt as she hurried back down the beach towards the village. A blush of pink upon the sand caught her attention and she bent to dig the conch shell out of the tidal wash. As she walked, she held it to her ear, listening to the sea it had caught in its tightly wound spirals, smiling as she went.

The sun was low in the sky by the time she reached Malaga. The last of the wagons was being loaded, and there was no more traffic between ship and shore. Elizabeth increased her pace, knowing that Agnes and her father would be worried about her after dark. But as she quietly opened the front door, there was no one at the ready to scold her. Instead, her father, Ransdell and Agnes were huddled together quietly in front of the fire. Their manner was odd, and Elizabeth said so.

"'Tis a conspiracy you are hatching?"

Agnes jumped up from her chair and Ransdell turned with a look of alarm on his face.

"My lady!" she declared, "You give us a fright with your stealthy ways!"

Elizabeth looked at her sharply.

"Indeed," she replied, "And if not a conspiracy, why are you all hunched over by the fire together like some band of miscreants?"

Silence met her question. Ransdell took Agnes by the hand and mumbled something about laundry on the back line as they disappeared. The children were nowhere to be seen.

"So father, what is this? Why are you so silent?"

Thomas turned to look at her. His sad, wise eyes had not fallen victim to time and were as softly blue and penetrating as ever. He laid his hand on hers and spoke slowly.

"My child, the ship that put into the cove this morning..."

"Yes?"

Thomas silently stared at her, patting her hand gently.

"It brought news from England, Elizabeth."

A deep sense of uneasiness roiled up within Elizabeth's chest. She looked at him tensely, expectantly. After a long moment, he spoke in a low voice.

"The news concerns our Prince Henry."

Elizabeth's hands flew to her mouth.

"No! Nothing has happened to him! I would know if it had!"

"Our prince is fine."

"Then father, what sort of game is this? What is it that you are struggling to say?"

He looked at her with the patience and love of a thousand ages, knowing full well that he was about to shatter her life. Finally, he mustered the courage to speak the words – it could no longer be put off.

"Elizabeth, he is married."

The fire crackled steadily in the hearth.

"I'm sorry, father, what did you say?"

"Prince Henry is married. The captain of the ship in the cove told us of the wedding plans."

Silence.

"He says that the young prince was to marry his brother's widow, Princess Catherine of Aragon. It will have taken place by now for the captain has been at sea some months."

Elizabeth looked at him in horror.

"What say you?" she whispered. "He cannot marry his brother's wife! 'Tis not sanctified nor allowed by the church! The captain is mistaken."

Thomas shook his head.

"King Henry went to great lengths to have Arthur's marriage annulled, for it seems Catherine is still a maid."

"*Still a maid*? She was married to Prince Arthur for..." Elizabeth thought rapidly, "She married him November and he died in April, and all that time we are to believe they did not see fit to consummate the marriage? Is that what you tell me?"

Her voice was rising in pitch and beginning to tremble. Thomas' heart broke for his only child.

"Aye, Pope Julius granted the dispensation and they are married."

"And my contract? Henry is betrothed to me, father! To me! 'Tis nonsense you are speaking!" She stood and began pacing.

"The news comes from Greenwich Palace itself," Thomas told her sorrowfully.

Silence.

"Elizabeth, sit, we have much to discuss."

"What, pray tell, would we have to discuss save my Henry being married to another? And his brother's wife at that?"

"You were very young when you and Henry pre-contracted, my child. And he was not then to be king of all the realm one day. His circumstances changed."

"You have lost your mind. Nothing has changed. Henry is my betrothed."

Thomas shook his head.

"No, he is not. Listen to the words I speak. He is someone else's husband now, and our future king. We must accept this and move on, for there is no good to be had by broadcasting such a thing as a precontract made so many years ago. We must accept, Elizabeth, and move on. He will be our king, and Catherine our queen."

She threw open the door and ran out into the night.

Chapter Twenty-Two

As dawn crept over the sparkling sea, Elizabeth quietly opened the door. Thomas and Agnes sat silently in front of the dying fire, keeping watch for her return. As she entered, Agnes ran to her and swept her up in a sobbing embrace.

"My child, my Elizabeth," she choked the words out and stroked Elizabeth's damp hair. After a moment, she led her to the fire and Thomas stood and hugged her tightly.

"'Tis a sorry thing, 'tis a sad business."

Agnes gently tried to seat Elizabeth in a chair but was brushed away.

"I am tired, father, Agnes. And father, you are mistaken. 'Tis not a sad business at all. 'Tis a great day for England, for her Prince Henry has made a brilliant match. Now, we will not speak of this matter again. We have much to do to ready ourselves for Rome."

As she lay under the bed covers, she could not shut out the sound of the sea pounding the beach with its steady tempo of crashing waves. She had walked a long journey that night upon the wet sand. But as she closed her eyes, the waves became more violent, more chaotic. She could hear nothing now but the shrieking of the timbers of the Phobos as they were torn asunder by the giant waves of frigid water. She was back on that terrible night the ship had gone down, and there was no one to help her, no one to pull her to safety. She rolled to her side, trying to block the noise and confusion in her mind, but it was pointless. There was no rhythm now to the drumbeat of engulfing waves and shrieking howling wind. It was fury in its most pure form, and the waves crashed all about her. But there was nothing to hold tight to.

A small thump on the bed tore her from her misery and she rolled over to find Consuelo cuddled beside her under the covers.

"Do not worry, my friend," the little girl whispered quietly as she wrapped herself around Elizabeth. "Papa says there is always a dawn."

A small hand patted Elizabeth's cheek as she clutched the child and broke into heaving sobs.

*****

No one in the household had any special talent for binding wounds with the tongue. Before the news of Henry, the silences which would befall the household had always been comfortable, eventually being broken by the sounds of Roberto and Consuelo with their toys, of Ransdell and Agnes with their domestic chatter, or Elizabeth and her father arguing this point or that idea found in some manuscript. There was an easy rhythm to their evenings together, one that they all cherished. Things were different now.

Each time a conversation ended, silence fell like a blade across the serenity they had once enjoyed. Each time, some one would attempt to break the tense atmosphere with a pointless remark. Each time, the result was predictable.

"Tell me, my dearest wife, how was the market today? This supper is wondrous!"

Such an utterance would be met with momentary silence, and then Agnes would respond to her husband's efforts to lighten the mood. Rather than look at him as if he was a shining example of idiocy, which formally she would have done, now she would smile brightly and reply.

"Husband of mine, the market was quite fascinating, and this beef stew has the freshest sage, brought down to market today from the Castillo estate near Madrid."

"'Tis quite delicious," Ransdell would being to flounder at this point but would continue on.

"And the market? Did you learn any new words today?"

By this time Agnes had grown weary of the exchange, and her inability to conquer Spanish was a sore spot for her in any case. While the others chattered away in the language of their temporarily adopted county, she still struggled mightily with even the simplest constructs. She would remain silent rather than add hot spice to the melancholy atmosphere.

Thomas would occasionally try to engage Elizabeth as they sat round the fire but such attempts produced nothing but nods and gentle smiles. Elizabeth was as bruised in her heart as she had been in her body after the shipwreck, and they all knew it. Even talk of Thomas' mysterious source of manuscripts did little to lift her spirits.

"So, Thomas, tell me," Ransdell began one night as they sat before the fire. Consuelo was sitting in Elizabeth's lap trying to engage her in a reading lesson but to no avail. Elizabeth sat quietly staring into the fire. Roberto had carefully placed his horsemen in two opposing rows on the stone floor and was busy plotting strategy for the winning side. Agnes silently mended the children's clothes.

"Aye?"

"We leave here in one day."

Thomas nodded.

"And yet you have never mentioned where you find the books you continuously bring into our home."

Normally, Thomas would wave his hand at this point and ignore all the questions and comments which followed. Tonight, however, he looked across at Elizabeth, his concern written on his face. She had lost considerable weight since the news of Henry, and dark circles had appeared under her eyes. She looked more waifish than womanly, and gone were the vibrancy and optimism which had always buoyed her in the past. Perhaps talk of manuscripts would cheer her.

"Well, sir, since we are leaving, I will tell you."

Even Elizabeth turned to hear what he had to say.

"Before you say, old man," Agnes interjected, "Why have you wrapped it all in such secrecy?"

"Because I get them from a gentleman, an abbot, who prefers to say not where he himself acquires them."

"A monk? A friend of Friar Marcos?"

"Umm, I think not," Thomas said evasively. "He is from a kingdom far from here, Trier, on a great river called the Moselle. He is highly educated, and travels extensively, seeking out manuscripts for his own library. His name is Johannes Trithemius."

Elizabeth had begun to listen.

"We met in the market, and fell into conversation about libraries and the difficulty in getting copies of precious books."

Ransdell rose and put more wood on the fire before Thomas continued.

"He travels not as an abbot but as a commoner hawking his wares from the wagon he uses on such occasions."

"Why?" It was the first interest Elizabeth had shown in anything in days.

"Because his country and this country do not view each other kindly," was Thomas' simple reply. "'Tis easier, when trading in such rarities, to do so under the guise of commerce."

"And how do you pay this man?"

Thomas smiled.

"I would think Agnes would know."

"What? I am not part of this," Agnes complained indignantly. "I have no notion of that which you speak."

"'Tis true," Thomas reflected before picking up his cane and moving to the wall beside the great hearth. "You know nothing of my business here, but you could write volumes about stone and mortar and how such arrangements do eventually loosen and fall apart."

Agnes watched him warily as he carefully pulled a sizable piece of mortar from between two stones and placed it on the mantel. Elizabeth thought of Coudenoure and Agnes' listening post outside the library and smiled as her father pulled a small pouch from within the wall before sitting back down. It was the same purse given to him by Lady Margaret Beaufort so long ago.

"The night of the ship wreck we lost almost everything. But before the Phobos went down, there was a moment when we gathered ourselves and made our way to the upper deck."

They all nodded in remembrance.

"I had just enough time to tie this pouch inside my shirt," he continued, "And since then, I have hidden it in yonder wall. It was given to us to purchase indulgences and manuscripts by the King's own mother, and do so we shall."

"And these manuscripts you purchase, tell me, are they stolen?"

"No, no," Thomas assured him, "They are from Abbot Trithemius' own library. Each time he visits, we discuss what it means to have a great library, what manuscripts must be had to claim such an honor. We have bonded in friendship and agreed that each time he goes home, he has copies made of those which I am lacking and brings them along on his next trip, at which time I purchase them from him. When we return to England, I shall return the favor by allowing him to peruse my library and make copies there."

"But you pay him for these manuscripts, Thomas. And you will let him make his copies gratis?"

"No, Ransdell. He will pay me in kind, in other books and fragments thereof. 'Tis an arrangement which suits us well."

"And if the Spanish authorities find you are trading with this strange abbot?" Agnes asked.

"They will not, for he is not *strange*, only foreign, and we are leaving. I have informed the good man of our impending voyage to Rome and we will meet there in future. He assures me there are many like-minded men who seek to preserve knowledge of the past in that great city."

"You mean like-minded men who lust after the written word, do you not?" Agnes laughed as she called him out on his great passion. "You are all caught in the devil's trap of a mania for books. You need to confess and do penance."

Agnes' words were serious but her tone was so sanctimonious even Elizabeth laughed.

It was the beginning of her healing.

Chapter Twenty-Three

The voyage aboard the Deimos was not long, and the sea was kind to them this time. The vessel rocked rhythmically upon the open ocean and the sails billowed gently as they skimmed along the deep blue surface of Mare Nostrum. Land was never out of sight, and a great expectation filled them all with hope. Elizabeth spent long hours at the ship's prow, looking out and wondering what Rome would bring.

The wound was deep, and would never heal. This much she understood. But she also knew that she had responsibilities to her father and now to Agnes and her family. There was no one else to be concerned for their future. Ransdell would certainly see to their material well-being, and Coudenoure would always be there. The King's annuity to Thomas was for perpetuity and so coinage would not be an issue. But there was the matter of keeping everyone together so that the sense of family they had all longed for and now finally had would not evaporate with the coming changes. That would be her task, her calling, for there would be no marriage for her.

Elizabeth had considered herself married from the day of her pre-contract. Her extreme youth had guaranteed that the event was seared like a brand upon her psyche, and every waking moment since then had been calibrated towards her life with Henry – the children they would have, the home they would make together at Coudenoure. So sudden had the news of his marriage fallen that an executioner's axe could not have done a more effective job of cleaving her life into before and after. She struggled to encapsulate all that had happened before so it could be neatly packed away in some dark and unlit room. Perhaps later, when she was well, she could take it out and examine it, as one might look at a toy from one's childhood. But it had too much power now, and she could not look at it directly for fear of its potency and the effect it might have upon her. Her weight had continued to drop and her complexion now had a sallow tinge. The sea air helped, but time was what she needed most of all now.

As they approached the port of Ostia in the pre-dawn hours, Agnes began to cluck and scurry about Roberto and Consuelo, while Ransdell and Thomas looked after their belongings. Elizabeth watched from a distance, as had become her habit. By mid-morning the wains had been rented and their household secured. Ransdell would accompany them all and stay the night before setting sail the next day. He was to return on a routine basis until plans for the voyage to England were laid down.

A narrow, rutted road led off from the dock but a mile on became a wide and cobbled way. Whether it was complete, or had started from the dock side or the city side no one knew. It had been thus forever and rough planks had been laid to ease the way of the wagons as they made the transition from sand and dirt to cobblestone. Elizabeth looked at the barren landscape, noting its similarities and differences to that of Malaga. It was hillier, and the scrub was mixed with trees. At random intervals small patches of wildflowers, here purple and pink, there white and yellow, dotted the rolling fields with snaps of bright color. The wain master called out to the bellowing oxen and all along the way pedestrians in colorful garb walked beside the roadway, sometimes bent almost double with loads upon their backs. Children ran up and down the way calling out for alms and chasing one another in the bright sunshine. Elizabeth could not help but feel cheered by the busy, bustling, colorful scene. If she squinted, she could see in the far, far distance a massive gate through which the road fed and she wondered idly what they would find on the other side.

A short while later, all traffic stopped. The sun was heating up the day, and as they began to peel off layers of robes and shawls, Thomas shouted to the man who sat patiently upon the plank which served as the wain master's seat. He was lazily switching a long withy which served as his whip for the oxen and shouted over his shoulder in return.

"It seems some artist is having a difficulty with his stone."

While the adults pondered the possible meanings of the statement, Roberto whispered to his sister. She giggled and nodded and they jumped from the wagon and began scampering up the road. No amount of screeching on Agnes' part could persuade them to come back. Elizabeth smiled, jumped down and went after them.

On and on the children ran past carts and carriages and wagons until the reason for the stoppage became evident. Elizabeth caught up and the three of them stood in wonder at what lay before them. A huge block of marble, some ten feet wide and eight feet high was being transported by multiple wagons and crews of laborers. One of the wagon wheels had left the cobblestone way, and the weight of the marble was preventing it from being brought back into line with the others. Each time the oxen snorted and tugged at their harness the angle of the wheel became less and less viable for movement. So deeply was it wedged that the laborers could make no headway. A young, tall, muscular man stood patiently watching the show from the side of the road.

Roberto and Consuelo went closer and closer to the massive marble block, each reaching out to touch its smooth, cold surface. A sudden jolt in the wagon bed caused the stone to shift slightly, and Elizabeth screamed a warning to them as she ran to snatch them from danger. But the young man beside the road was faster. Before she could reach them he had tucked one under each arm and taken them to a quiet place under an ancient pine. Elizabeth followed, breathlessly. Before she could speak, the handsome stranger had sat the children on the ground and was speaking to them in Spanish.

"What are you doing, little ones? Do you not understand danger?"

Roberto looked at the man with wide eyes.

"Is that your rock?"

The man smiled and Elizabeth noticed his eyes were kind and dark.

"'Tis my *marble,* young man. I shall use it to make a very fine likeness of Signore Capileto, a very fine *rich* patron."

Roberto nodded.

"*I* can do that."

The man looked at him in amused wonder.

"Can you now?"

Roberto nodded enthusiastically.

Elizabeth came closer before the child could continue. The man turned to her and spoke in a serious but light tone.

"Are these your charges? They could have been killed."

She was momentarily lost. His eyes were so deep and intelligent and the moment so beyond the realm of her experience that she stuttered the first thing she thought of.

"I am their mother." It fell out and she was not sure why.

"Their mother?" laughed the stranger. "And did you conceive at the age of six, madam?"

Elizabeth blushed but said nothing. Consuelo decided to explain their situation matter-of-factly.

"She is the Lady Elizabeth, and her heart is broken. 'Tis why she looks like that."

Elizabeth wanted desperately to grab the children and run, but it was too late. Consuelo and the man were engaged in a serious discussion.

"Her heart is broken, you say."

"Yes," Consuelo told him, mimicking the sorrowful tones she had heard in Agnes' voice, "And she needs a distraction but nothing seems to work."

"Si," chimed in Roberto, "Some idiot..."

"Roberto!" Elizabeth found her voice.

"Agnes says he is an idiot, and so does my father," Roberto answered and continued. "He married another and now she drags herself through life like a wounded animal."

Elizabeth glared at him palpably, but Roberto only shrugged. If the ground could have swallowed her up, she would have been grateful.

"Ah, yes, I see that," the stranger said. "I agree - what she needs is a distraction."

It was too much.

"Sir, I am right here, so you need not discuss my health with the children as though I were absent. And how am I supposed to be distracted, I ask?"

He looked at her in amusement and before she knew what was happening, her words began to trickle forth. His kindness touched her, and soon her words were tumbling over one another in a veritable symphony.

"I am surrounded by family who love me and I love them but each day is the same. I thought our trip to Rome would provide me something new to dwell upon but I was mistaken. You see, kind sir, I have been left. I am no good to anyone for my husband has left me."

"He was your pre-contracted person, not your husband and you must stop saying that." Constance was still playing the role Agnes. The child was an extraordinary mimic, even down to waving her finger just in the way Agnes always did.

Elizabeth vacillated between feeling sorry for herself, extreme embarrassment and relief at finally allowing her feelings out.

The young man looked at her thoughtfully.

"So what do you propose?"

She shot him a startled look.

"What do I propose? I am a woman!"

"Si," he spoke slowly, "But you are also an adult with choices. How will you navigate this sad ending to a bad affair?"

"I do not know, sir. If I were a man, I could sail the seas or find my fortune in a faraway land. But I am a woman."

"You have sailed the seas," responded the stranger dryly, "And you are in a strange and faraway land. Has that changed anything?"

Elizabeth felt a strange awakening.

"You are correct, sir. But the problem, my problem, is that I love the man to whom I was pre-contracted. I cannot change that."

"Yes," he agreed. "That will be difficult. But locking yourself and your feelings away is an act of self-immolation, and you are too passionate for that, I can tell."

Who was this man who spoke such wise words? Silence reigned for a long moment before he spoke again.

"Come, let us find your wain."

The traffic was once again moving along the road. The marble had not budged, but a detour had been devised on both sides of it. As they began walking down the long line of oxen, men and cargo, Consuelo once again ran ahead, this time in the direction of their wagon. Roberto held the stranger's hand and smiled up at him as they walked along.

"I am hungry!" Consuelo exclaimed as her father pulled her over the side. As the other three caught up with her, a look of caution crossed the faces of those in the wain.

Elizabeth smiled as she climbed back into the wagon. The stranger walked alongside of it with Roberto.

"Sir, I thank you for returning my wayward children," began Ransdell.

"He saved our lives."

Constance blurted out the story as she happily ate the bread and cheese handed to her by Agnes.

"'Tis true?" asked Thomas.

The stranger made a rocking motion with his hand, and all laughed.

"And I am going to carve marble." Roberto too was now using his free hand for food, but still clung tight to the stranger.

"Indeed," observed Thomas. "And how shall you do that?"

The discussion turned to the massive block they were just then passing, and Thomas became alert. The stranger spoke quietly to one of the laborers who nodded and disappeared towards Ostia.

"So, my good man, you are a sculptor?"

He nodded.

"And this is your marble?"

Again, a silent nod. Thomas looked at him waiting for more.

"Si, I just finished the David and have taken a small commission here in Rome. I needed a distraction." He looked meaningfully at Elizabeth. "As we all do from time to time."

Thomas nodded excitedly.

"I have heard of this David," he said. "Abbot Trithemius has seen it."

"'Tis in Firenze, my home."

"And my friend the abbot says it is the work of a genius, of such purity of form that it leaves one breathless."

"I agree."

Elizabeth laughed aloud.

The laborer returned and passed a small boulder to the man along with a bundle wrapped in coarse canvas. The stranger nodded and placed the two items in the cart along with Roberto.

"Now, young man, you feel you can breathe life into stone?"

Roberto nodded seriously.

"Then these are for you. This is your marble," he indicated the white gray boulder, "And these are your tools. I live and work behind the Cathedral of

St. Paul, just off the Via Doloria. When you are done, bring me your work."

As the stranger turned to leave, Thomas called out to him.

"Sir, your name? You grace us with our children's lives and gifts of marble and tools. We must know with whom we speak!"

"Michelangelo," the stranger threw his name over his shoulder and disappeared into the crowd.

Chapter Twenty-Four

Double torches lit the steps leading to the massive, single door. A heavy brass knocker rested squarely on a metal base set within the wood. Thomas knocked tentatively. No answer. Again he knocked and again, no response. A driving rain had begun as they reached the city gate late that afternoon, and their progress through the narrow, twisting streets of Rome had been slow. Night had fallen by the time the English ambassador's residence was found, and as Thomas knocked again, the wind began to blow harder. After a moment, bolts sliding and keys turning were heard. The door opened a mere two inches. The interior was dark and Thomas felt as if he were speaking into a void.

"I am Lord Thomas de Grey, Baron of Coudenoure, of the township of Greenwich, in England, and I am here to see the English ambassador, Lord Gallingbrook."

The door opened a few more inches. Thomas continued in Italian, wondering perhaps if he ought to speak English – had the ambassador brought his own servants from home?

"Do you understand? I wish to see the ambassador! I am…"

The door opened wide to reveal an older couple. The woman held a small, stubby candle while the man held the edge of the door firmly.

"There is no need to shout, signore," he said clearly if tiredly, "We heard you, but there is no English ambassador here."

Thomas looked at the paper he held in his hand.

"Is this the home of …"

"Si, signore, but again I tell you, there is no ambassador here. He has been, how do you say, recalled."

A voice from within the depths of darkness in the room beyond fed them a question. The old man nodded.

"What business have you here, Thomas de Grey of Coudenoure?"

"I am on the King's mission."

"You?" The old man and woman looked him up and down before allowing their gaze to stray to the wagon in the street behind him. Huddled together against the rain atop a wagonload of mismatched crates and bundles were small children and another man hugging a woman tightly. They presented a picture not of a nobleman seeking shelter but of a rag tag band of ruffians, Romani even, seeking opportunity.

"Si," asserted Thomas, "The King of England's own mission."

The old woman laughed.

"Oh aye, and I myself am on a mission for the Queen of Cathay." She cackled delightedly at her own joke.

The voice from behind them whispered quietly.

"Your name again, sir?"

"Thomas," Thomas said tiredly, "Thomas de Grey, Baron of Coudenoure."

Again the whispering.

"Wait." The door closed. He stood in the pounding rain hoping that someone inside would help them. Ten minutes passed before the door opened again. This time, the old man held a small purse and offered it to Thomas.

"What is this?" Thomas asked as he took it.

"'Tis what you came for. Now go!"

"No!" Thomas attempted to wedge his foot in the narrow opening. "I did not come for this, whatever "this" might be. I have come…"

The door was closed firmly in his face. More knocking produced nothing but cries from the neighboring houses. In despair, he returned to the wagon. The children slept fretfully under a canvas as he explained the situation to the others.

"There is currently no English ambassador. He has returned to England and these nits know us not."

"Then what is that they have given you?" asked Agnes.

Thomas pulled the drawstring and reached into the purse, pulling coins out and quickly counting them.

"Likely the stipend Lady Margaret told us about," he said. "But where shall we go?"

Elizabeth spoke.

"We shall go to the Via Doloria, to Michelangelo's home. He will help us."

She would brook no arguments and sometime past midnight, the tired little troupe found the address. Once again, Thomas found himself knocking upon a closed door, but this time, Elizabeth stood next to him along with Roberto.

The door opened almost at once. Before them, illuminated from behind by a great fire in a large hearth, stood Michelangelo. His jet black hair curled round his shoulders and his eyes smoldered. He had wrapped a bed cover around his waist before answering the door but his chest, muscular and viral, was bare. Elizabeth gaped. Michelangelo grinned.

"So, Roberto, you have finished already?" he laughed.

"Sir, we are desperate. The English ambassador is in England and we know no one in this place." Thomas began his entreaty.

A soft, feminine voice called quietly from the direction of the fire behind Michelangelo. He turned and spoke reassuringly to its owner before once again addressing Thomas.

"So you are beggars now, in need of a place to stay? 'Tis true?"

Thomas nodded.

Michelangelo turned his intense dark eyes upon Elizabeth.

"And tell me, my lady, is this..." he waved his hand in the air, "...enough of a distraction for you?"

She blushed and nodded, despising the stuttering giggles which accompanied her answer.

He smiled kindly, and asked for a moment. The door closed and some minutes later, he reappeared, clothed completely and with a key in hand.

"Come," he shouted to all of them, "You may stay next door. The house is mine, but I live in my studio. You may stay until such time as the English ambassador decides to reappear."

He opened the door and fumbled in the dark. After a moment, candlelight bathed him in its soft glow. One by one, he lit the nubby remnants of candles in an elegant candelabra sitting near the door.

"There are more candles near the hearth," he said hurriedly, "in there, and food in the kitchen. I have no idea as to the state of the bedrooms, but you will figure that out. Now, I must go."

"Are you working?" Roberto asked innocently.

Michelangelo laughed.

"You might say so, yes." He tousled the boy's hair and disappeared into the night leaving them alone.

At the residence of the English ambassador, a young man sat at a writing desk before a small fire. Dipping his quill in the ink well which sat nearby, he began his letter.

"Your Highness, The Inestimable Lady Margaret,

I write to inform you that this evening, the gentleman you wrote of did indeed appear at the door. I gave him the money, as you requested, but no entry, again at your direction.

Rest assured that the letters, which once arrived regularly and now come not at all, have been managed. I myself burned them all in the very fire before which I now sit.

I believe you may put your worried mind at ease, but should you require more detail, or additional services, please write me at once. I am always at your call.

Your humble servant,

William

Chapter Twenty-Five

"Up, old man! Are you planning on staying in bed all morning? I have work to do even if you do not!"

It was Agnes, more faithful than any bell or rooster could ever be. The sun was barely above the horizon.

"None of your back talk. Now, a good hot breakfast waits for you downstairs, and the artist inquires after your health."

Agnes had never recovered from the site of Michelangelo in the firelight their first night in Rome. More to the point, she had never recovered from hearing the woman's silky voice softly calling him back to the hearth.

"Siren!" she had hissed while waiting in the wagon. "What manner of Jezebel waits within?"

Instantly she had branded Michelangelo a lost heathen, one with whom they should have no truck whatsoever. The offer of a roof over their heads, however, and his continued kindnesses had mitigated her outraged disgust. Slowly, her resolution to despise such a loose man was eroded. Instead, she took the tack suggested by Ransdell - she would convert him to a faithful way of living and show him the error of his ways. In turn, Michelangelo patiently showed her that art and a creative way of thinking did not necessarily spell doom for all those who came in contact with it. The battle had been joined, and it remained to be seen who had the stronger will. Wagers were frequently placed upon their skirmishes.

Thomas entered the dining room just as Roberto came running in from the studio next door. Rome had been good for all of them, but to none of them more so than Roberto. Thomas watched him and smiled.

The child had become the gangly boy and then the man overnight, it seemed to Thomas. The clothes he had arrived in the city with had been discarded long ago, for the simple reason they no longer fit. Roberto was now a tall, muscular young man with long, slim fingers. His English heritage was evident in his sandy brown hair and blue eyes, but that was the only hint of his background. His Italian was perfect, down to the street jargon and vernacular with which he was so fond of peppering his conversation. His default tongue was Spanish and even with Elizabeth's constant tutelage his English would never be more than rudimentary.

But Roberto could not have cared less, for he had found his passion, his milieu.

True to his word that day on the long, slow journey from the Deimos into Rome, he had taken the boulder given him by Michelangelo and patiently, day after day, breathed life into it. From the natural lines of the stone he had fashioned a conch shell, complete with spiral and knob. Using the gray lines which ran like faults through the rock, he managed to suggest patterning on the outer shell. It was a rough effort, but Michelangelo had been impressed. For a boy working with only a few tools and with no guidance, he had performed a miracle. As the piece had begun to take shape, Michelangelo had offered the boy a table in the back of his workshop at which to work. There, day after day, apprentices and masters would stop and observe the child, completely absorbed in his own work, oblivious to the activity around him. They would offer suggestions and help concerning the spatial issues inherent in all sculpture. But aside from those small moments, the work was completely Roberto's. As a result, Michelangelo had offered him a unique opportunity: he could clean the shop each morning in preparation for the day's work. As pay, he would be given small stone tasks and would be allowed to sit at lessons with the apprentices. Paradise, for Roberto, was a distant second.

He began spending his off days with the apprentices, visiting other workshops and experimenting on his own with different tools and techniques. While others dabbled with painting or clay, Roberto knew that only sculpture would satisfy him. Each evening over supper he would turn the conversation to art, regardless of what was being discussed.

"And how was the market today, my lady?" Ransdell might ask Agnes.

"'Tis funny you mention that," Roberto would chime in, "Johann painted the most amazing likeness today of a peach."

"Elizabeth, how did you pass your day?" Thomas might inquire.

"You should have come with me, dearest sister, for I saw the most amazing stone today."

It was impossible not to be charmed by his passion. Consuelo, too, had found herself, but it was as far from Roberto's calling as night was from day.

Consuelo loved an orderly home. She was bound by no decree, nor any dictate to assist Agnes in her daily work. And yet this seemed to be what made her happy. She would plan each day's meals down to the smallest item, and then swing her basket merrily on her arm as she strode the market place, haggling with green grocers, smelling fish for freshness and browsing cured hams. There was no household item she did not know the price for, and she frequently bested even Agnes in bargaining with tradesmen. But her interest in hearth and home did not stop there.

On rainy afternoons, Agnes would sit patiently with the young woman, teaching her stitch after stitch of embroidery. From small samplers to larger pieces, Consuelo gradually became a master. She asked Roberto to draw patterns for her on the heavy canvas she usually stitched. Once he was done, she would take the piece to the small corner of the local market dedicated to weaving, cloth and pigments. She would carefully choose the threads herself, and then equally carefully stitch her small masterpieces to be placed over the hearth or on the wall.

In short, Consuelo was a willing apprentice to her surrogate mother, and Agnes burst with pride each time she looked at her. She would make someone a fine wife, a fine household manager one day.

Thomas had fared equally well in Rome, although his road had been more difficult. The initial plan was to stay in the holy city only a short time and to travel home to Coudenoure as soon as possible. All were agreed. During the first few weeks of their stay, raw administrative matters had taken up the bulk of his time: negotiating a short lease with Michelangelo, establishing contact with Abbot Trethemius and other manuscript collectors, seeing to the needs of his family when Ransdell had taken his leave. But once a settled feeling came upon them all, he pursued his decreed tasks in earnest. Day after day, he inquired at the English ambassador's home as to when a new ambassador might be appointed. This was critical for he found that with no letter of introduction from the King, his path to Pope Julius was all but sealed off. The righteous man had no time for English beggars with no credentials.

Week after week he knocked politely upon the door of the ambassador's residence, and made his request in scholarly Italian. But week after week, his efforts were met with shrugs, puzzled looks or outright hostility by the elderly couple who always responded. Occasionally, a small pouch would be handed to him, always containing the same amount of coinage. But that was all. His family watched as his frustration grew but there was nothing any of them could do. Finally, Thomas decided to change his approach and seek other avenues to secure the indulgences he had been asked to pray for and receive.

His daily visits to the grand home became less frequent. Instead, he spent his time composing letters and reports to King Henry. He explained his delay and begged the King's patience as he continued to collect manuscripts and seek a papal audience. Each letter was carefully sealed, set aside, and finally sent abroad in the care of Captain Ransdell. In turn, they were faithfully delivered to his contact in St. Nazaire and the small fee paid to see them safely delivered to Greenwich Palace.

From there, Elizabeth assured him, Charles Brandon would carry them safely on to the king. Confident in his King's judgment and mercy, he patiently awaited a reply. But none came.

The weeks turned into months. Seasons passed and the years began to slip by. Thomas loved his daily routine - up at dawn, cider with the small group of like-minded bibliophiles he had come to know, and the afternoon in pursuit of this or that manuscript. But he had lost a step. His eyes could still read the finest print, his mind the smallest nuance. But his knees ached each morning and evening as he went up and down the steep stairs to his bedroom. He frequently awoke from naps he had not intended to take. Worst of all, he had noticed that occasionally, Agnes let him sleep late.

It was not just age that was beginning to wear upon him. Many experience home sickness at the outset of a journey. For Thomas, it had come to him at the end. He had manuscripts enough; he wanted to go home. So sure was he of King Henry's forgiveness for not securing indulgences directly from Pope Julius that he would have thrown it all over on a moment's notice. But each time he approached leaving in his mind the same, fierce fear invaded his soul.

It had begun as a nagging suspicion eighteen months after their arrival in Rome. Each week, he went to the chamber wherein the Holy Father held audiences. Those seeking such a moment were met by a Cardinal who either passed them forward to yet another Cardinal in yet another hall, or told they would have to try another day. It was a winnowing process and only the special few were caught up by the cardinals' nets. There was no apparent system and no particular order in which they were called. As for the rest, those unfortunate enough not to have received a nod from the cardinal, they were released back into the lives from which they had come. Initially, Thomas had simply tolerated the protocol, for having no letter from King Henry meant he was treated as other commoners were. But as the weeks passed, he had noticed a pattern emerging: despite the look of randomness which seemed to envelope the entire process, each of the petitioners, if they were faithful and came each week, were eventually passed through and given an audience, albeit a brief one, with Pope Julius. Only he was repeatedly denied, month after month. On a particularly slow day, one deep in November, he approached the cardinal, with whom he was now on a familiar basis.

"Tell me, kind father, how is His Holiness today?"

"Cold, Sir Thomas, as we all are. Winters are not easy in Rome."

"Aye, neither are they easily borne in my own land."

The cardinal smiled politely and took the offered bait.

"And what land is that? I have noticed all these months that your Italian, while superb, is of the scholarly variety."

"'Tis England that I call home," Thomas responded, holding his hands out to the fire which always lit the large hearth within the great hall. "I long to go home, but I have given my word that I shall ask for prayers and indulgences from the Holy Father himself, and I cannot disappoint."

The Cardinal nodded.

"But I have noticed that of all those who pass through these holy walls, only I am continually denied."

The cardinal shifted on his feet nervously.

"Old man, we have had this conversation. 'It is not for me to determine who shall pass through to the chambers of the Holy Father."

"Oh, aye, I know that good sir, and 'tis not in my nature to blame anyone for my misfortune. And you are right - I am an old man." Here he paused and tapped his cane softly on the marble floor. "I shall likely die here, in Rome, far from my home. I shall never see my own hearth and hear my own language again. 'Tis sad, but 'tis not of your doing."

The Cardinal, a young man, looked back at Thomas and saw him for the first time for what he was, an aged, white-haired, kindly soul destined to die far from his native land. For that reason, and because he was kind, he took pity upon Thomas on that particular day. He shuffled his feet again and spoke softly in his ear.

"English sir, if you must know, I have heard such words concerning you before, from one placed blessedly close to his Holiness. There is a hold placed upon your name, such that you will never be passed along and will never come into the bright presence of Pope Julius."

Thomas realized the man was cautiously telling him something he desperately needed to understand.

"Father, why is that? Can you tell me?"

The Cardinal glanced carefully about the near empty hall, and continued in a low tone.

"They say an old woman, a crafty crone, placed a seal upon your name. She is a powerful woman."

"A witch?" Thomas crossed himself.

"No, not a witch. 'Tis the mother of a grand king who has denied you what you seek. They say she is controlling, and that you will indeed die in a foreign land, for she has decreed that you will not step into

Popi's grand presence, and she knows you must or you will never go home."

Thomas looked into the deep, soulful eyes of the young cardinal and knew he spoke the truth. He had only been wasting his time all along. After a long moment, he thanked the young man and walked slowly out into the cold.

So Margaret's reach extended even unto Rome, he reflected as he limped towards home. A cold wind blew from the sea and he pulled his worn cloak tighter around himself. Michelangelo had given him a scarf the prior Christmas and he paused in the street to wrap it tightly round his throat and face. The cardinal's confession was fraught with implications for him and his family, and he parsed its detail as he stomped along the cobbled way. Agnes and Ransdell were waiting for him when he reached home.

*****

"We were worried about you out in this cold," Agnes fussed and fretted around him as she settled him into a chair by the fire. Ransdell sat opposite, warming himself with a mug of ale. Agnes brought one for Thomas and then settled herself as well.

"Are the children out?" Thomas asked, taking a deep pull on the warm brew.

Ransdell laughed.

"Aye, but Thomas, you and I must face up to the fact that they are no longer children."

Agnes joined them and picked up the lace upon which she was working.

"And why are you asking such a question?"

Thomas sighed.

"I have been to the Holy Father today," he began.

Something in Thomas' voice, a slight catch perhaps, caused Ransdell to look at his friend sharply. Yes, he decided, the old man had suffered a severe setback of some sort.

"And discovered why I shall never see England again."

"And why is that?" he asked. "'Tis ordained by God?"

Thomas sighed.

"No, Captain, 'tis ordained by a woman."

Agnes paused in her work as she and Ransdell exchanged a knowing glance. For some months, they had wondered about Thomas' persistent bad luck in obtaining an appointment with the Holy Father.

"'Tis not usual," Agnes had whispered to Ransdell one evening as they lay together. "What think you?"

Ransdell had kissed his wife and told her not to worry, "...for if something is amiss, it will make itself known by and by."

It seemed that moment was upon them now. They listened in silence as Thomas told them of his conversation with the Cardinal earlier that day. When he had finished, they sat in silence, digesting the news while Agnes refilled their mugs. Ransdell was the first to speak.

"'Tis bad news, Thomas, for who can go against the mother of a king, and King Henry at that? 'Tis unwise at best and highly dangerous to even think of it. For a woman who goes to such great lengths to protect her grandson will stop at nothing, do you not agree?"

Thomas nodded, rested his head on the back of his chair, closed his eyes and sighed.

"My friends, I fear that I must make a dreadful choice." The despair in his voice was evident and increasing. "We all want to return home, I know this."

"No, no, Thomas," Ransdell interjected, "The "children" as you call them seem are happy indeed here in Rome."

"Aye, they are young yet, but it will come to them, my friend, for they are English. Did you not, just last month, tell me that even after all your journeys, all your time in Malaga, that you now long to feel English soil beneath your feet?"

Ransdell could not deny his words and Agnes nodded in agreement.

"Thomas, 'tis true for me as well. We have been at this long enough."

"Lady Margaret has malice for me, Lady Agnes, not for you nor for your family. You must return. And I must decide whether to join you and risk everything or stay on here as I know I must."

Agnes laughed aloud.

"Old man, what think you, that I would leave the other half of my family, you and the Lady Elizabeth, here whilst I traipse home to Coudenoure? You are older and more senile that I suspected if 'tis the case."

"And Elizabeth?" asked Ransdell. "What is to become of Elizabeth?"

Silence fell across them like a shadow on a sunny day. Elizabeth.

Chapter Twenty-Six

She pulled on her cotton leggings and her breeches, being careful to tuck her underdress into its waist. Over the thin garment she layered first a man's shirt, gathered at the wrists and neck, and then an oversized vest. Finally, a heavy scarf around her throat and a cap given her by Roberto completed the outfit. Pulling on her boots, she quietly opened her bedroom door and joined Roberto on the landing. He playfully pulled her hat low on her forehead as they went in search of Michelangelo.

Elizabeth was unrecognizable from the days when they had first arrived in Rome. Then, she had been a thin, timid woman-child, unable to cope with the sorrow of her broken engagement and frightened at what the future might hold for a creature such as herself. For in her eyes, that was just what she was at that moment. Not a woman, not a man, but a being caught between the two. Over and over again in her mind, she ran down the list of her differences. First, there was her education. She was now fluent in six languages.

Her fluency, however, did not stop at the written page - she could converse in the vernacular of each tongue like a native speaker. Her aptitude for language seemed to know no bounds, and she had recently begun to consider the study of the Moor's tongue, Araby. Its rough gutturals, combined with its strange cadence, had become familiar to her as she wandered the district of city where it was spoken at will, soaking in all it had to offer.

Wandering at will. She sighed at the second point. In the early days, once the numbness of Henry's rejection had begun to fade, she had searched for something, anything, to occupy her time and her mind. Initially, she had accompanied Thomas to his afternoon meetings with his bibliophile friends. But her presence was felt, and conversations became awkward when she appeared. After all, there were registers of language - those differences in speech reflected in everyday conversation but dependent upon audience. She knew enough about language to realize that the speech used when with friends or perhaps among women, the speech of men when with women or only amongst themselves, with strangers or children - these conversations inevitably held patterns specific to the parlance of that group. And when she was amongst the men who were her father's confidants, an air of restraint became immediately apparent. Months later, she gave up and began looking elsewhere. And it was then that she discovered how Roberto was occupying his time and passion. As he had hurriedly grabbed a small loaf of bread one morning before running out, she had followed him.

"Where are you going, brother?" she had asked.

Roberto laughed.

"To the studio, of course."

"The studio? Michelangelo's workshop?"

"Yes, I have been going there since we arrived and you know this. And you? What will you do with the day? Will you wash and mend and cook with Agnes and Consuelo?"

Now it was Elizabeth's turn to laugh.

"They seem to do a fine job without me. I have no calling, it seems, for household husbandry."

Roberto stopped and looked at her for a moment.

"I see," was all he said.

"You see what?" Elizabeth ran to keep up with him as he bounded up the steps to the studio. "What?"

"I see that you are lost."

With that, he opened the heavy door and disappeared inside.

"Lost?" Elizabeth spoke the word aloud. "I am not lost, you nit!"

She opened the door, continuing her diatribe against Roberto as she did so, hoping he could hear her disdain.

"Who do you think is lost, brother? Eh? Surely not me!"

She stopped, horrified. Michelangelo was already in the studio and had paused to listen to the exchange. But as she attempted to back out the way she came in, two young men threw open the door and inadvertently pushed against her, causing her to lose her balance. Quick as lightening, the artist was at her side.

"Child, each time I see you, it seems you are in trouble! Now, what is this business about you being lost?"

As always, Elizabeth found herself tongue-tied around the great man. But this time she was happy, for at least a mindless giggle had not escaped her lips. Seeing that she had lost the power of speech, Roberto spoke for her.

"Her heart is mending but she is lost. She has no calling."

"No calling?" Michelangelo stroked his beard thoughtfully. "'Tis a terrible state, is it not, Roberto?"

His student nodded vigorously.

"Tell me, daughter," Michelangelo began. It was at that moment Elizabeth found her voice.

"'Tis easy for you," she waved her hand in the air to indicate the studio and everyone in it, "'Tis easy, for you are men. For my kind 'tis not, let me assure you."

"You think men find life easier than women? Do you find they deal with broken hearts more easily? Are you sure?" Michelangelo's eyes twinkled. Elizabeth gave him an assured nod.

"Well, 'tis a question certainly worth exploring. Why not work with us for a while here, in the studio, and then tell me if you still feel the same?"

"Here?"

He nodded and threw her a smock.

"Umberto, fetch the woman an easel, some paints and a brush."

"M, m, me?" Elizabeth stuttered. "I should paint?"

Michelangelo nodded.

"But Agnes, my father. What will they think?"

"Madame, I could not care less what your kin might think. Now, there sits these students' work for the day, that bowl of fruit."

"What should I do?"

Michelangelo laughed.

"I suggest you paint."

It was there, in the early afternoon, that Agnes had found her, happily chatting with the young men around her and working assiduously at her canvas. A stormy look appeared on the older woman's face.

"Lady Elizabeth! Stop that at once!"

Elizabeth looked at Michelangelo, but the man refused to speak a word. You must decide for yourself, his shrug seemed to say, if you will live in the shadow of your family or be choose to be yourself.

Elizabeth stepped tactfully to Agnes' side.

"I am happy, and I have Roberto here, and Michelangelo, should anything unseemly be said or done."

Agnes was torn. She could see for herself that Elizabeth's countenance seemed more relaxed. For the first time in months, a tiny bit of rose could be seen in her cheeks. She wavered.

"You, sir," she spoke sharply to Michelangelo, "You must know that our Elizabeth is no common girl, and she is not accustomed to the rough language and ways of these artists." She looked around at the young men who were scattered about the studio.

"I agree, Madame, she is no common *woman*, and she will be well-respected here in my studio, as all women are. You live a mere fifty feet from this very place should your services be required. I assure you, it will do her good to explore her own creativity."

"Nonsense," Agnes replied, "But she is enjoying the day, and so I will leave her."

As the door closed behind her, Elizabeth grinned at Michelangelo before returning to her canvas.

With each passing month Elizabeth had grown more confident, more at ease with herself and who she was. Her paintings slowly began to improve, and the men and boys around her grew more accustomed to having a woman in their midst. But beyond the walls of the studio, her sex was still an impediment to her learning artistry and craft. One day, she said as much to Michelangelo.

"Yes," he was busy sketching and did not stop as they spoke, "I see your point, Leezie, but what do you suggest?"

"I do not know," she said bluntly.

"So you come to me with a problem and no solution? No, you must always think things through and come up with an answer."

Elizabeth had gone back to her work, left alone that afternoon for her male colleagues had gone to another studio to compare works with the artists there. As she sulked, a sudden idea came to her.

"I will be back, signore!"

She had skipped happily out of the studio and raced home. Once there, she had locked herself in Roberto's room while she transformed herself. Looking in the mirror, she was what she had hoped to see: a young man with an artistic flair in his manner of dress. The only stumbling point was her hair. Without thinking, she rummaged through the wardrobe which sat against one wall and then returned to the mirror. Pulling her long braid up and under a cap of Roberto's, she spoke softly to herself.

"Well now, we shall truly see how the other half do live."

Tucking her dress under her arm, she snuck quietly out the back door of the house onto the alley. Adjusting the hat so that it half covered her face, she began walking down the alley. After a moment, she adjusted her stride to a longer length and accompanied it with a small swagger. Two women carrying market baskets approached and ignored her as they passed by chatting about the cost of figs that day. Emboldened, she turned onto the main street and hands in pockets strolled to the studio. Michelangelo glanced up from his work as she entered.

"Go away," he called out, "We have no vacancies."

"But signore, I am not looking for a vacancy."

Michelangelo looked up, startled, and began chuckling.

"Well, Leezie, when I said you must seek a solution to each problem I had no idea this would be your answer!"

She laughed and took off her cap, bowing to him as she did so.

"So our experiment continues, does it not?"

"Which one is that?" he asked.

"Do men have an easier time moving through life than women do. I shall dress like this until we have an answer!"

"Tell me," Michelangelo asked, "Have you shared your solution with Agnes?"

"No, but since it is a temporary arrangement, she will not mind."

Michelangelo roared with laughter.

"You think so? I will pay you quite handsomely if I may observe that conversation."

"Perhaps I should change into my other clothes before returning," she said thoughtfully.

Michelangelo said nothing, but smiled and went back to his work.

Elizabeth ignored him and returned to her canvas, happy and confident with her decision. It was the first time she had ever stepped beyond her role of daughter and companion. It would be an adventure. But before she went home that afternoon, she changed back into her own dress. Only she, Michelangelo and Roberto knew.

Since that day, she had alternated between women's clothing and donning those of a man when she wanted to move freely about the city. Roberto frequently accompanied her on these expeditions. She found them exhilarating and at the same time disorienting. Her sense of being rootless, of belonging neither here nor there, increased, but it was accompanied by a soaring self-confidence. In understanding men from such a perspective, she also began to understand herself more. It was a welcome change after the heartbreak of the past few years. A serenity settled upon her which bespoke a maturity beyond her years, an understanding that sorrow did indeed cause spiritual growth.

She was finally happy, and the sense of rejection she had felt dissipated. In its place grew a calm certainty that her life would go on, and go on quite happily. She shrunk from all talk of marriage and alliances, choosing instead to paint and read and lose herself in conversations with the other artists of Rome.

Chapter Twenty-Seven

She had forgotten her dress that morning as she and Roberto had gone on one of their city wanderings, and as she crept quietly up the stairs, she heard the concerned talk of the old people. Quickly, she changed and came back downstairs.

"Child, I did not hear you come in," Agnes exclaimed, flustered.

"Has something happened?"

Thomas looked at her with sad eyes and told her his news, that their way had been blocked, and that he should never return to England. Elizabeth remained thoughtful and quiet the entire evening, and went early to bed. The next morning, she was in the studio before the others and had lit the fire and cleaned the room by the time Michelangelo arrived.

"So, my lady, you have decided to stay with the womanly arts after all?" he asked, looking around at the clean studio.

"No."

A raised eyebrow.

"Sir, I have a problem."

"Indeed, as we all do from time to time. But tell me, have you considered an answer?"

"I have, and I believe it to be the only way through the bog."

"Here, we say, "the fog", but no matter. Talk to me."

She set out the conversation her father had related to her the previous evening, and told him of her solution. Silently, he took her face in his hands and kissed her forehead.

"My child should be as you are," he said. "Tell the apprentices to continue with yesterday's work. I must step out."

Michelangelo did not return that day. But the next, a strange letter arrived by post at the house next door.

"What does it say?" asked Ransdell as he sipped his ale contentedly before the fire.

"Holy Father!" exclaimed Thomas as he read.

"You must confess and repent for using his Holiness' name in such a manner."

"No, Lady Agnes, I mean the letter is from the Holy Father. I am to see him this afternoon!"

The house fell into a panic as each of them attempted to help Thomas ready himself for his appointment. By the time he and Ransdell had left, no energy remained and the afternoon was spent fretting at the windows and pointlessly cleaning or tatting. It was nightfall before they returned.

"My wife, bring us ale and quickly," called Ransdell as they walked through the door. "We have news!"

All gathered before the hearth. Thomas refreshed himself with the bitter drink before speaking his news.

"My family," he said jubilantly as he raised his mug, "We are going home."

Amid the wild joy and questions, Elizabeth smiled and slipped out.

She knocked loudly on the studio door. After a moment, Michelangelo answered, bowing silently to invite her in. Going to the small area in which water and ale were kept, she returned with two fine glasses filled to the brim.

"So, we have been successful," he said as he raised his glass. Elizabeth nodded and they drank in a comfortable silence for a moment.

"When shall you leave?"

"Soon, I suspect," she responded. "Father is old now, and I must see him home safely. I owe him everything."

Michelangelo refilled their drinks.

"Roberto must stay."

Elizabeth nodded in agreement.

"Yes, he should finish his apprenticeship - he is talented, is he not?"

"Very." A pause.

"And you? What will you do once you are back in that god-forsaken cold and lonely bog you call home?"

"I know not," Elizabeth answered candidly. "But I will be forever in your debt, signore."

"For today? 'Twas nothing - the Holy Father wants a ceiling in his chapel painted, and I wanted a favor. He saw the reasonableness of our proposal immediately."

Elizabeth laughed.

"I do indeed owe you for today, Michelangelo, but that was not the debt to which I referred."

He looked at her intently and lovingly, as a father upon a child.

"You saved me. I might have recovered my physical strength in time, but my spirit was broken and confused. You took me in, and gave me the tools to heal myself. Truly, you are a great, great man."

Michelangelo smiled and raised his glass once again.

"I cannot deny it."

They drank comfortably for a moment before he put his hand to the side of his head.

"I should give you it now, before the packing and such begins."

From beneath his own work table he pulled a small bundle of carefully tied canvas and held it out to her.

"Oh? A present? 'Tis good! There is nothing I like better!"

Carefully she untied the cord and let the canvas fall away. Her breath caught in her throat. After a moment, silent tears began to fall unchecked.

Before her on the table was a bust, ten inches in height. Carved from the most flawless white marble Elizabeth had ever seen was the face of a woman turned slightly away from the viewer. Her hair flowed out behind her in a great wave, and her right hand, so delicately carved that a single breath might cause it harm, reached gently out towards the viewer. Beneath the face was the signature of Michelangelo. But none of that caused the sobs which now engulfed Elizabeth. The beautiful face, carved in such exquisite detail as to be almost ephemeral, was her own.

Chapter Twenty-Eight

April 5, 1509

The wain creaked and groaned as the oxen struggled against the icy ruts which filled the roads. The weather had turned against them an hour outside Woolwich, and there was nothing for it but to hunker down amid the trunks and crates which occupied the rickety vehicle alongside of them. Thomas was carefully swaddled in layers of woolen blankets and tucked securely between two crates. A brightly colored scarf provided a hood against the constant wind and he drew it carefully across the lower part of his face each time he put his head up to ascertain their progress. It was never fast enough or far enough for him, and the man who drove the oxen had been told at least a dozen times to pick up the pace so that he, Thomas, might see Coudenoure before he froze to death.

Agnes was uncharacteristically quiet on the journey home. So much had changed since they had last been in England. Was Coudenoure still standing? What about the servants and laborers - how would they manage if the estate had been abandoned? After all, it was one thing to run a house in town with little or no assistance, but quite another to manage a manor house and its grounds all on one's own. It was impossible and Agnes had shared her concerns with Ransdell. But the captain was typically unconcerned.

"You survived a shipwreck, woman, and yet you continue to fret about such matters? What would it take, I do wonder, to make you happy and carefree?"

"An answer *not* like that one would be a fine place for you to begin to find out."

Consuelo smiled at their bickering, and looked into the adoring eyes of her husband. The voyage aboard the Deimos had been singularly uneventful save for one drama: Consuelo and the young man who captained the ship for Ransdell had fallen passionately in love. Unbeknownst to anyone in the family, the romance had begun months earlier. Ransdell's voyages at sea had become less frequent as he had gotten older and he had promoted an Englishman from Woolwich, Edward Golding, to take his place in these circumstances. Each time the Deimos made port in Ostia, Consuelo had accompanied her father to inspect its cargo and to see what fresh foods, spices and gossip had been procured on its voyage. At some juncture during one of these visits, Edward and Consuelo had met and each time thence the Deimos made port, Consuelo had a second reason for accompanying her father to the docks. By the time the voyage home to England had occurred, it was all but settled in their minds that they would one day marry. Agnes had been the first to notice the change in the young woman. A frank conversation had ensued and at Woolwich, in front of Edward's family and Consuelo's, they had been married by the local priest. The estate was close enough to Woolwich that Edward could continue working for Ransdell while Consuelo set up their home at Coudenoure, a situation which suited everyone. Consuelo knew the rhythms of life imposed by a living earned upon the sea - Edward's routine mirrored that of her father and felt intimately familiar and right to her.

Elizabeth rode next to Consuelo in the wagon, and constantly strained her eyes for a glimpse of familiarity with her surroundings. It had come as a shock to her how foreign England felt upon their return. The trip north, through the great Pillars of Hercules once again and along the rocky coast of Portugal then France, had filled her with surprise. She had been certain that she wanted to return to England, and equally certain of her memories of the place. But the disappearance of palm trees and sandy beaches as they tacked north left a melancholy stain upon her soul. How strange, she thought, that the very things which had struck her as so foreign seven years earlier now felt like home. How odd that she should feel a wrenching of her heart as the leagues between her and Rome grew from one to thousands.

As they had docked at Woolwich, she searched her memory for something reminiscent of the scene before her but found nothing. What had been a small port town upon the estuary of the Thames had become a bustling center of maritime commerce. A dreary, cold mist enveloped the entire city, and as they finally cleared the town proper and bounced slowly upon the rutted road towards Coudenoure, a heavy snow began to fall. Compared to Rome and Malaga, the atmosphere was heavy and dank. She closed her eyes and remembered the bright sun and gentle warm breezes of Malaga as they rustled through the branches of the palms. What would they find at Coudenoure, she wondered, and would it ever feel like home again?

Some time later, the driver turned to Thomas and spoke softly as he turned the oxen sharply off the main road and onto a narrow cobbled way. Was this home? Elizabeth scrambled upright and spoke.

"Father, are we there? 'Tis Coudenoure?"

Thomas nodded.

"Aye, daughter, this is the way before we turn onto the drive proper. It will not be long now."

Even as he spoke, the wagon cleared a bend in the road and before them lay the long straight drive of Coudenoure.

Agnes felt her heart beat faster and as Elizabeth jumped from the wagon, too impatient to wait for the oxen, Agnes did the same. They walked swiftly through the deepening snow, towards the great manor.

Yes! Elizabeth's heart sang out to her. Yes, this was home! She saw the familiar heavy doors with the familiar motto etched in Latin above them. Beside her, Agnes laughed and took her hand and they picked up their pace. Once upon the marble step of the house, Agnes banged the knocker heavily. There was no answer, but then, she was not sure there should be any.

"What shall we do, my lady?" She turned to Elizabeth.

"Bang again, my mother, and if no one should answer we shall go to the back."

Before she finished speaking, however, the door gave a familiar creak and opened inwards. Before them stood a small, very pregnant woman with an impish face. Elizabeth stared at her for a long moment.

"I know you!" she finally declared. "Agnes, 'Tis Prudence!"

"My word, so it is! And grown into a woman now indeed! Prudence, 'tis the Lady Elizabeth and me, Lady Agnes!"

Great tears filled Prudence's eyes and the three hugged as though their very lives depended upon it. The wagon pulled to a stop and a great clamor started up. Prudence rang a loud bell and within minutes men and women scurried through the door and from around the corner of the manor. Boxes, crates and trunks were off-loaded and settled into the hallway. Thomas beamed with joy as he and Ransdell stood to one side, watching the work.

"So this is your home, Thomas, eh?" Ransdell's voice was laden with his approval.

"'Tis my home, brother," Thomas responded, "And 'tis yours now as well. You will stay here until the main cottage is set as Agnes will certainly require."

Ransdell nodded.

"Where is the cottage?"

Thomas pointed to west side of the property. In the distance stood a fine, two story home with a thatched roof. Ransdell smiled in pleasure.

Consuelo shyly went forward and Elizabeth took her hand as the four women moved indoors.

"Joseph, light the fire in the library! You there, get kindling and Mary, start the kitchen fires for our master is home and will be in need of good food."

Elizabeth laughed for no other reason than pure happiness. She and her father each made their way from room to room, inspecting every piece of furniture, remembering every vase, looking at each painting with memories from the past and new impressions from the present. Servants began to gather and with hats in hands curtsied as the old master and his daughter smiled and reclaimed their home. At length, Thomas was settled into his favorite chair before the library hearth. A roaring fire lit the room, and Ransdell sat in the chair opposite as the women fussed round them. Edward and Joseph, Prudence's husband, stood nearby until Thomas waved to them to join in. Food arrived and laughter filled the great room. At length, the women congregated in the kitchen while the men stayed in the library. It was then that Elizabeth learned the story of Coudenoure in their absence.

"Tell me, good Prudence, what has been the fate of Coudenoure, and you, all these years?" Agnes settled back in her chair with her feet upon a stool and a heavy shawl around her shoulders. Prudence glanced at Elizabeth before beginning.

"My Lady Elizabeth, and Lady Agnes, would you not prefer to sit in the house proper? I will happily relate the tale whilst you do so."

Elizabeth realized instantly that the class boundaries which had played no part in their lives abroad were causing Prudence discomfort. Consuelo realized it too, and took her new friend's hand.

"Prudence, there is no need for such reticence, for our time abroad has taught us that family and friendship are far more important than any such rules as may pertain beyond this house and beyond our small group."

Elizabeth nodded.

"Besides," she added, "As I recall, when you were but a young girl, you took a great risk on my behalf. I can never repay such bravery and friendship."

Agnes grew tired of the sweet sentiments.

"The story, girl. Tell the tale."

Prudence laughed and began.

"The young prince came as you said he would, my lady, and was turned away with lies by the old couple hired by Lady Beaufort."

"Lady Margaret," Agnes corrected her, "But do continue."

"I stopped him and his friend as they rode by the river, and gave them your note. They thanked me and left forthwith. But only a small time later, they returned. The old couple were sent away and in their place our young Prince Henry put his own people, the honorable Francis and Bess, who came to Coudenoure from the estate of the Earl of Surrey's mother."

Elizabeth nodded, knowing that Henry had always depended upon the earl for support and discretion.

"'Tis years they were here, my lady, and times were good. The young prince came often with his friend Charles, and made a great many changes at the manor."

"I have noticed some of that already," Elizabeth concurred, "But tomorrow perhaps you would show me them all."

Prudence nodded and continued.

"But the sweating sickness passed through Greenwich, and we fell to it. Aye, a great many were taken away, including Francis and Bess."

She paused a moment.

"Prince Henry was away a long time then, but one day he came back, and stayed several weeks. He seemed very sad, my lady, for he had heard, as had we, that you were taken from us."

Elizabeth looked shocked and Agnes sat forward.

"What are you saying?" they both asked. Prudence looked fearful and it was not until Consuelo patted her hand that she continued.

"My lady, the news that you and the old master were killed in a shipwreck, of course. We hardly knew what to think, for your father and you were always so kind to us, so good. A great fear gripped us all, for our fates were bound up with those of Coudenoure, and without its proper owners, we had no certain future."

Elizabeth sat, dumbfounded by Prudence's story.

"But Prince Henry is a good man he is, my lady, and he saw our grief as we saw his. One day his friend, Charles Brandon, recognized me and later spoke to me. He told me of the prince's sorrow but also said not to fear, for I had done you, and therefore the prince, a great kindness the day I stopped them along the river. In return, Prince Henry would allow us all to stay here and take care of Coudenoure. Lord Charles said it held a special place in the prince's heart, and if we would continue to look after it, our good lord would continue to fund its needs. And indeed, my lady, to even now he returns betimes and speaks kindly to us all."

Elizabeth rose abruptly and left the room. Agnes spoke reassuringly to Prudence.

"Do not worry, child, you have told the truth and 'tis a necessary element of life. Now, tell me about yourself."

Prudence shrugged.

"Lady Agnes, I worked as an undercook for many years and learned my craft well. Prince Henry is fond of good food and for a time, a cook," she corrected herself, "...I mean a chef, stayed with us here and taught us many fine recipes and ways of cooking. He was cross and mean, but I learned my lessons well, and when Cook died, I took her place."

She stopped and crossed herself. Agnes nodded.

"Tell me, I heard the men talking just after we arrived that there are quarters behind the manor house now?"

"Oh indeed, my lady, indeed. Prince Henry hired an ark, arki," she hesitated, "...a *man* to change the grounds considerably. He built cottages, small but lovely, on a cobbled way just beyond the back area. It is where my Joseph and I live."

"Are any of them empty?"

"Aye, two of them are vacant, for Phyllis left to marry Hugh, and then the other was never occupied."

"Consuelo, this shall be your home, at least for now. Prudence, take my daughter and the two of you inspect these cottages. Choose one, and we shall begin tomorrow to make it a home for you and Edward."

Consuelo clapped her hands.

"My own house? My own hearth? Oh, my, I never thought! And here with you, mother, and with Prudence, who may show me, I hope, the ways of the estate."

Prudence nodded enthusiastically and Agnes rose.

"Now, go. I shall see the men. Prudence, help Consuelo with a room upstairs for the evening, please kindly."

Agnes went into the main hall and reached for the library door, but paused. Smiling to herself, she ran her fingers along the wall of the library, stopping when the familiar feel of the displaced mortar touched her fingers. She pulled it out and put her ear to the wall. The men were deep in conversation, and she heard an unknown voice, likely that of Prudence's husband she mused, telling the men the tale Prudence had just finished in the kitchen. Satisfied and tired, she replaced the mortar and made her way upstairs. As she reached her own door, she opened it and looked down the hall at that of Elizabeth and said a small prayer. Crossing herself she pulled it behind her.

Elizabeth lay like a lifeless rag doll beneath the covers on her childhood bed. How many nights had she lain awake under these very covers and dreamt of the life she would have with Henry as her husband? She was drowning in memories that she had locked away an entire life time ago. And it was not Coudenoure which had brought them back but Prudence's news. Many years earlier, in Rome, the rumors of a delay in Henry's marriage to Catherine had circulated broadly. Elizabeth had heard them, but they had not changed her situation. The rumors were not of a break between him and his betrothed, but of a delay due to considerations concerning Catherine's dowry. Elizabeth had packed all of it away - her feelings, her memories, her sorrow - and moved on. She had known full well that she would have to deal with some of those emotions when she touched English soil once again. After all, Henry was the heir apparent and would one day be her king. She had reckoned with that and made her peace with it.

But Prudence spoke of Henry's continued interest in Coudenoure even unto the point that he still visited the estate from time to time. To reckon with the weave of her life and make peace with it was one thing; to welcome him into her sanctuary and see him again was quite another. She threw off the covers and stoked the fire in the hearth. Flames of light lit the room and shadows flickered and loomed across it. Sitting on the rug before it with her knees drawn up to her chest, she struggled with emotions she thought had died years earlier. What was she to do? She thought of Michelangelo and his insistence that she not present a problem without also presenting a solution. So, what would she do? What would her answer be? As the moon waned and the sun began to light the eastern sky, Elizabeth returned to her bed and pulled the covers round about her. She would treat Henry as he deserved to be treated - with all the dignity and respect due not just to his station, but to him as a man. In return, she was certain she would receive the same. There was no other way to translate their lost love into a viable relationship. Knowing she had made the right decision, she slept peacefully until noon.

Chapter Twenty-Nine

Spring was late that year and its arrival was not piecemeal. The Lenten roses did not bloom in March followed in April by the monkshood and campanula giving way in May to primroses and daffodils. Instead, the grand meadow of Coudenoure lay deep under its mantle of winter brown day after day, month after month. Occasionally, a lacy frost would lay itself gently across the rising slope like sugar on porridge, but otherwise, all lay in the silent grip of Persephone. And then one day, it did not. From nowhere the meadow sprang fully formed and alive with color. The winter winds gave way to spring breezes and the air filled with the smells and scents of new life. The sun presided over its sublime creation and cheerfully lent its warmth as a shelter and talisman against the return of the deathly cold. From deep within its ancient walls, Coudenoure stirred to life once again.

Elizabeth spent the weeks unpacking and adjusting to the world she and Thomas and Agnes had once known. She had never given up painting, and when she was not busy hanging her work about the house - street scenes of Rome, the soft beaches of Malaga, the grand plazas of Italy - she watched the drive carefully, for before leaving Rome she had arranged for fresh supplies, brushes and canvases to be sent to her on a regular basis. She had another reason for keeping her eye upon it as well, but that one she kept to herself. In due time her art supplies arrived, and with the advent of spring she ventured further and further afield, capturing with her brush the gay colors and lazy flow of the Thames. One afternoon, she found herself high on a ridge overlooking Greenwich wood. She tramped happily along, searching for just the right spot to capture the ephemeral color which surrounded the forest as its trees began to awaken to life. A meadow ran before it and the tender, pastel colors of the wild flowers presented in sharp contrast to the looming darkness and shadowy dampness of the woods.

"Um, yes, this is it," she said softly to herself as she steadied her easel upon the soft ground and unfolded the small, leather stool Michelangelo had had made for her years earlier. A fresh breeze blew and the sun beat down upon her. She had left the manor early that day, not bothering to put her hair up and as the day wore on she shed the cloak which had seemed needful that morning.

"Now who do you suppose that is?" asked Charles, pulling up sharply. His quiver was slung carelessly over his shoulder and he shielded his eyes as he looked across the meadow and up the hill which lay beyond it. A distant figure sat at an artist's easel, back turned towards him.

"'Tis a maid?" asked his companion following Charles' pointing finger. They both rested their hands on the pommels of their saddles, squinting against the bright sun.

"'Tis too far, I cannot tell," came the reply.

"They are on the King's land, by God!"

"No, they are in truth on the estate of Coudenoure," Charles said, still looking at the figure. "But what are they doing? Painting?"

"Well, 'tis a fair scene with the meadow and the woods beyond," noted his friend. "But tell me, does anyone at Coudenoure paint? I think not, so 'tis disturbing - trespassing is a serious offense."

"Trespassing to piddle with paint?" Charles laughed. "I think you make too much of it."

"Shall we have an adventure? What say you?"

"Whatever you say, my Prince."

Henry dug his heels into the sides of his great black steed and they were off. They took the ridge near the river and galloped along its peaks and valleys until the figure once more came into sight. The furious sounds of the hooves alerted Elizabeth to their presence, and she turned, brush in hand, to confront whoever it was that was trespassing on her land.

The spring breeze blew her long dark hair about her face, and the bodice of her overdress was laced tightly beneath her breasts. The ties of a soft white cotton undergarment had been loosed against the heat, and the cleavage of her bosom was exposed clearly. She waited for the horsemen to approach. But they stopped some distance away.

"Henry, you look strange. Is there some problem, my liege?"

Henry was struggling for breath and could not take his eyes off the woman barely fifty feet in front of him.

"Henry, for God's sake speak, man, or I shall have to ride for help."

Henry raised his hand for silence and continued staring at the young woman before them.

Elizabeth grew impatient and took a step forward. Suddenly, her breath became labored and she fell to her knees before reaching her hand out towards them. Her black eyes widened intensely and she waited, her breath ragged, wondering if he knew who knelt before him.

"Stay here," Henry's voice was rough and low as he dismounted and threw the reins to Charles. Never looking away, he walked slowly to Elizabeth and held his hand out to her. She took it and rose, trembling. Gently, he put his hand beneath her chin and raised her face to his.

"You are not an apparition."

She continued to stare at him. Tears welled up in her eyes and she did not bother to wipe them away.

"You are real."

Henry looked upon her face, her lips soft and slightly open, and kissed them sweetly and gently. Elizabeth was transfixed and did not move.

"My Henry," she whispered.

"Elizabeth, you are home," he said, and the tears began to roll down his cheeks as well. He gathered her in his arms and they wept together on the lonely ridge.

Chapter Thirty

It was late that evening before the threesome rode together up the long drive of Coudenoure. Charles had intended to ride for Greenwich, alerting the palace to his Highness' desire to spend a few days at Coudenoure. A game warden had crossed his path, however and he had sent the man forward with the message. Returning to the ridge, he found Elizabeth and Henry deep in conversation, oblivious to the sounds of his horse as he approached and the gathering gloom.

"'Tis late." He announced. They ignored him.

"I say, 'tis late, and the Lady Elizabeth does not wish to have the household of her estate sent with torches and alarms, I think."

Henry stood and assisted Elizabeth with gathering her canvas and supplies. He placed her on his steed and mounted behind Charles on his. He held the reins of his horse as the animals picked their way down the hill and to the drive of Coudenoure. Lights blazed from every window and torches could be seen near the front door. A great shout went up as they arrived.

"The Prince! 'Tis Prince Henry! And the Lady Elizabeth rides with him!"

The words rang through the house even as Prudence tolled the bell, indicating guests. Thomas stood on the front step, and Henry made his way to the old man, bowing deeply before him.

"Thomas, we believed you to be dead all these years."

Thomas bowed as low he could, and Henry helped him steady himself and continued.

"Come, you must sit by the fire, and I with you if that is acceptable."

With his cane, Thomas waved away the young boys who tried to assist him.

"Can you not see that the King's son helps me now? Eh, you nits? Prudence, fetch ale, fetch cider, for young Henry is home."

Henry put his arm across the old man's shoulders and arranged him carefully before the library fire.

Charles helped Elizabeth down and with the briefest of nods she disappeared indoors and ran lightly up the steps to her room, closing the door securely behind her. The front hall was frantic with activity as fires were lit and the kitchen staff called in from their cottages behind the manor house.

Agnes stood in the shadowy depths of the great hall and watched the scene unfold. She caught a glimpse of Elizabeth's face as she fled upstairs.

"Madre de Dios," she said to no one in particular as she crossed herself and watched the door close on Henry and Thomas.

"Lady Agnes!" She jerked her mind back from its wanderings.

"Sir Charles."

"You are older," Charles grinned.

"And you are no wiser. Come, we will sup together in the kitchen and tell each other all we know."

"Madam, 'tis a good plan."

They walked arm in arm to the kitchen.

*****

In the Matins hour he came to her. She bolted the door behind him and followed him to the great hearth of her room. He reached slowly out and gently pulled the bow string of her nightdress. It fell around her feet and she stood naked and trembling before him. She watched as he undressed. His touch was fire upon her skin, and they fell together, deeper and deeper until the universe was only they two and the flames before which they lay. Gentle and soft, fierce and firm, they learned what it meant to truly love. At dawn, Henry crept back to his room. For seven days and seven nights 'twas thus.

Even that day upon the ridge their conversation had flowed naturally as if they had never been apart. As the week sped by, Henry found pockets of his early identity that he had long believed dead. Each evening, as he and Ransdell, Edward and Thomas, and Charles sat round the fire in the library, he composed light music on the lute he had left long ago at Coudenoure. Poetry flowed from his pen, and Thomas' talk of Michelangelo's workshop, of art and books and culture brought Henry to life. He had forgotten what it was to be creative, and while the lessons learned at the hands of his fathers' stewards would not leave him, he vowed never to let them take priority over what he now saw as his true vocation. He would be king, but he would also be philosopher, musician, and poet.

His days with Elizabeth were filled with learning and love. She had matured into a woman of such knowledge and grace as defied his common notion of what a true woman should be. Each moment seemed to provide him with fresh insight into the female sex and how severely he had underrated their intelligence and abilities. One morning, as he carried her easel and paints up the meadow for her, he said as much.

"Yes, 'tis a richer life for me than that enjoyed by my sisters," Elizabeth had said. "But those are my thoughts only. If you were to ask Prudence, as she manages her kitchen staff, or Consuelo as she manages the household, they would tell you 'tis they that are blessed."

She paused.

"Perhaps the blessings flow when one is happily ensconced in a safe, familial place and is given to practice a vocation."

Henry nodded.

"You are right, I think. But, my love, your sisters as you call them have husbands and will have children."

Elizabeth continued walking.

"You know I must marry Catherine now, for the kingdom depends upon it."

"You told me that when we first talked, that day upon the ridge." A slight irritation crept into Elizabeth's voice. Henry remained silent. After a moment, she turned to face him.

"Henry, you say that I am intelligent for my kind."

He laughed.

"More intelligent than my ministers and friends," he observed.

"Then what makes you think I surrendered myself to you on a whim? Or out of thoughtless passion? Regardless of how I arrived at this moment, I am mistress of my own estate and of my own heart. The love you have shown me these past few days would see any woman through a lifetime. This is what I ask: when you leave two days hence, that you remember Coudenoure kindly, see that no harm falls unto my father in his dotage with his library, and that no one be allowed to pressure me as a titled maid for my hand. I wish to spend my days as you see me now, here at Coudenoure amongst my family. That is what I need from you now, my Henry."

He bowed deeply.

"It shall be done."

"And thing one more." Elizabeth smiled. "That you shall paint today, my lord, not me, and I shall instruct you as you go."

Henry laughed, secretly satisfied with the conversation. As the week had progressed, he had worried more and more about Elizabeth's future. What would happen to her when he married Catherine? He could see to her financial needs and would always do so, but she insisted that once he was married she could no longer enjoy his company in her bed. They must then part, she had said, or risk the wrath of God.

Initially, Henry had agreed, but each night as he lay listening to her gentle breathing beside him, he cursed the fate which had decreed they must forever be apart. He would be king, and yet he was denied. He imagined his life upon the loom, the pattern always moving towards a predestined kingship and glory. But if that were true, then how had his love for Elizabeth come to such a pass? Were he and Elizabeth forcing the pattern to reflect their own feelings? He doubted it, for the past few days had taught them that they were powerless against their love for one another – it controlled them, and they did not control *it*. Their destiny was to be apart, but a single flame would always light their paths as they went their separate ways.

The week passed in a deeply familial and loving way, and on their last night together, as he lay with his head in Elizabeth's lap in front of the fire in her room, they seemed finally to have talked themselves out. Content just to be with one another, they listened to the crackling of the fire and felt its warmth upon their bare skins. Elizabeth stroked Henry's hair and smiled down at him.

"So, you should know that you leave a happy woman behind you at Coudenoure," she said quietly.

"And you send a satisfied man abroad into his kingdom," he laughed.

For some moments only the crackling of the fire was heard. Then Elizabeth spoke in a whisper.

"Will we see you again?"

He played with a strand of her hair.

"Yes, certainly, but I know not when."

Henry sat up.

"My father is ill, more so than the public knows."

He weighed his thoughts.

"When I leave here, I must travel to his palace at Richmond, and await the news which is sure to come."

"You will be king."

"Aye, I will be king. And some of what that means I like very much, and for some of it I care not at all."

Elizabeth smiled.

"'Tis so in every life."

"Indeed."

He looked at her with tender strength.

"You are the love of my life, Elizabeth."

She nodded.

"And you, mine."

They returned to her bed, and as morning broke he slipped away. Charles was waiting for him with his steed, and they rode in silence to Richmond.

Chapter Thirty-One

Consuelo could not stop eating. Each morning she appeared in the kitchen early, and Prudence would whip eggs for her, cooking them quickly in the frying pan on the spider at the edge of the hearth. No sooner had she finished those, however, than the family began appearing and she would eat again with them. Scones with fig marmalade, cheese, ham, great draughts of apple cider from the bounty of the orchard and plums as well. She seemed to be a bottomless well of hunger, and even Thomas began to wonder about her appetite. Dinner and supper were merely repeat performances of breakfast. As the months wore on, Edward began to beam with pride, and each time he returned home from a voyage he would bring her a trinket. This time a small bracelet of stones, now a fine piece of linen, once a small colorful bird in a tiny cage. She was pregnant, and in due course the midwife from Woolwich began paying routine visits. The woman had delivered Edward and confidence was high that Consuelo would be brought through the birth in fine condition. Agnes watched over the affair carefully, and made certain that Consuelo took rests frequently. She went about with a worried face and all assumed it was because of Consuelo's impending labor. It was true that Agnes felt great concern, but her faith had grown stronger over the years and she was sure that a healthy baby and mother would be the final result. No, it was not Consuelo about whom she worried: it was Elizabeth.

In the household's fixation on Consuelo, Elizabeth's frequent bouts with a morning stomach flu passed unnoticed, as did her loss of appetite. Only Prudence noticed the change, and morning after morning, she would quietly visit Elizabeth in her room, taking her broth, making sure she was warm and comfortable. Mid-morning, when the flu had passed, she would take her plain soda bread with a bit of cheese or boiled egg. Consuelo fell onto what was happening next, and she began accompanying Prudence on her trips upstairs. She would sit before the fire, doing the household's mending or looking at her account books while Prudence fussed about her patient. Elizabeth would eventually feel well enough to sit with them before the fire and nibble on the food Prudence brought her.

"My sisters, I would be lost without you."

The words were frequently on Elizabeth's lips.

"'Tis three ducks we are," Prudence would chime in happily. "Waddling about our pond."

"Aye, but I must tell my father and Agnes," Elizabeth once replied. "I know not how."

Consuelo patted her hand and giggled.

"Elizabeth, they will be onto it before much longer." She looked knowingly at Elizabeth's middle.

"Yes, well, 'tis done and I do not regret it. But we must keep it amongst the family, for a king's child would not be allowed to remain here for long, should it be found out. We must vow to keep it secret."

A vow was taken and as the months passed, the rest of the household gradually became aware of Elizabeth's condition.

"Tell me, child," her father asked one day as they sat alone in the library, "How shall we manage our new line? For I believe you are to give birth."

Elizabeth began to cry.

"Father, I know you must be embar..."

He waved her silent.

"'Tis not true, Elizabeth. If this had happened before we went on our journeys together, I would have been, oh, I know not what. Angry? Frightened? Truly, I know not. But now, having seen a bit of the world, 'tis a natural state. I am proud and happy and we must plan for our young charge's future, do you not agree?"

Elizabeth smiled in relief and her tears flowed freely.

"Thank you father, thank you."

He patted her hand.

"But child, you must tell Agnes, and I want no part of that conversation."

"How, father, am I to do that?"

"You will think of something. Shhh! I hear her coming. I will leave and you will tell her now."

They sat quietly in front of the fire. Agnes knew what was about to be said but was uncertain how to react.

"My Lady Agnes, my own mother, I must tell you that my relationship with Prince Henry was not chaste, and that I am with child and that is why I miss breakfast so many mornings and I know I should feel shame and confess but I am not ashamed and if I confess the good father might feel the need to spread the word abroad and that cannot happen and I know not what to do and so I tell you everything."

She literally gasped for breath.

Agnes remained silent.

"Lady Agnes, do not deprive me of your company and your wisdom, I beg you! You are my rock and I have great need of your counsel."

Still Agnes said nothing but stared into the fire.

Elizabeth began crying and Agnes gently passed a rag from her pocket to her. She leaned over and hugged her tightly. In turn, Elizabeth clung to her as if her very life depended upon it. Agnes finally spoke.

"My child, 'tis not what I would have wished for you, but 'tis done, and I love you as much as ever. Do not forget that. You can do nothing, now or ever, that would cause me to believe bad about you or lose faith in your goodness."

Elizabeth sobbed louder and Agnes sat her in the chair before closing the library door.

"Elizabeth, child, it was meant to be. I knew this would be your path, but I could not accept it. Now that it has happened, I am relieved, for we may plan. You know that the knowledge of the child's father must never leave this house. Otherwise, we will lose the babe. I am certain of this."

"Yes, Agnes, as am I. But how do we go about protecting the child, and our home?"

"We must think," Agnes told her. "And we must limit those who know of your condition."

"'Tis better if I stay indoors until I deliver," Elizabeth said, "And we limit the number of servants about the house."

Agnes nodded and called Prudence and Consuelo into the library, and the four women talked until nightfall formulating a proper scheme to protect them all.

One week later, Prudence gave birth to her second child, a girl she named Mary.

Elizabeth never left the house, and only Consuelo and Agnes were allowed to roam freely about the manor. It was put out that Elizabeth was having bouts of a mysterious malady and that no one save family should be exposed to such a risk. But rumors began regardless, and when Prudence began taking her baby Mary to the great manor with her each day despite the risk of the sweating sickness, the servants became curious. Agnes and Thomas would have none of it. Overhearing two scullery maids discussing Lady Elizabeth one day in the kitchen, they confronted them.

"So you treat the hand that feeds you in this manner, do you?" Agnes was almost screaming. They cowered before her and the old master.

"What is your name?" she asked the younger girl.

"Milly, my lady."

"Tell me Milly, do you like food in your mouth and a warm bed at night?"

Milly nodded, terrified. Her companion stood mute and still as stone.

"The Lady Elizabeth travelled far and wide. Did you not know that?"

Milly nodded.

"And tell me, you nits, do you not know that various and sundry maladies are contracted by maids when travelling thus? Their constitutions are not as strong as those of men, and you may be certain that is why young maids normally do not travel - else they would not survive. 'Tis a miracle that Lady Elizabeth did, and if you treat her poorly because of her foreign malady, I shall turn the two of you out of this house quicker than you can move. Do you hear me?"

Violent nodding from both girls ensued.

Thomas shook his cane.

"If I hear such nonsense in my home, Coudenoure will no longer be yours. Now go back to your work, and if you choose to huddle together again in some dark corner where you exchange lies, you will be turned out with no compassion."

Later that afternoon, Milly whispered to her friend.

So the lady doth have some frightful disease from a far away land."

Looking about in fear, her friend nodded.

"Perhaps she is disfigured and ashamed."

"That must be why. We must avoid her lest we catch the same. And do not mention such things again," whispered Milly as she crossed herself, "Lest God punish us with it for even knowing of it."

From then on, Elizabeth's name was never mentioned in the kitchen.

Six weeks later, as Agnes snuffed the candles, Edward appeared in the great hall with Consuelo.

"Lady Agnes, 'tis time."

The midwife was sent for, and Prudence knocked softly on Elizabeth's door.

"Consuelo is giving birth," she said simply. A frightened look crossed Elizabeth's face.

"Are we certain?"

Prudence nodded in the candlelight.

"My good lady and friend, we are. It may not work but it will do no harm either."

Elizabeth opened the door to let her in, bolting it behind her. From her pocket, Prudence pulled a large clove of garlic.

"So I am to eat this raw?"

Prudence nodded.

Elizabeth commenced eating, washing down the clove with copious amounts of cider.

A minute later she was done, and burped loudly.

"Well, Prudence, we shall see." She rubbed her belly and began pacing in front of the fire.

Whether it was the tension, the stress, the garlic or nature, Elizabeth went into labor one hour later.

Just before dawn, the word rang out across the estate.

"Consuelo, wife of Edward, has given birth to twins!"

Elizabeth lay exhausted with her child in her arms. Beside her, Prudence kept watch.

"And the name, my lady?"

Elizabeth smiled blissfully.

"Constance. Her name shall be Constance." She smiled at the tiny bundle in her arm.

"And Consuelo?"

Prudence smiled.

"'Tis a healthy girl as well, my lady, and she is to be called Agnes."

Chapter Thirty-Two

July 8, 1515

A lone figure rode slowly up the long drive of Coudenoure. Occasionally stopping, the man on the horse seemed to be inspecting various aspects of the great lawn which stretched forward to the meadow and the parterres which separated the house from the great lawn. From a distance, he heard the familiar tolling of the household bell, indicating the arrival of guests. Lady Elizabeth stepped through the front doors and waited patiently for him on the step.

"King Henry! You honor us with your presence."

The man before her was so much different from the boy she had once known.

She bowed deeply as Henry threw his reins to the servant boy.

"And where is our fine daughter?" his eyes twinkled merrily.

Before Elizabeth could speak, a wild band of tiny ruffians came screaming around the far corner of the house. A small boy, barefoot and with holes in his breeches, was being chased by three little girls. He held tightly to a butterfly net made of white linen looped to the end of a small stick. The boy sailed past, and Elizabeth grabbed the first girl.

"Young Agnes, do you not see who is visiting? You must curtsey, child, and show civility."

Henry bent over and smiled at the girl.

"And young Agnes, how are you this fine day?"

Agnes nodded, her blond curls bobbing. With a look at Elizabeth, she continued her chase.

"And let us see, um, next we have Mary."

The second little girl stepped forward and curtsied politely. Her large green eyes fixed on Henry while her wild brown hair blew in the breeze.

"Please, sir, if you do not mind, my brother must be taught a lesson and Agnes needs my help."

Without waiting for a reply, she too ran in hot pursuit of the brother. Only one small girl remained, and Henry and Elizabeth turned their attention to her. There was no mistaking whose child she was. Flaming, curly red hair fell in ribboned cascades down her back. Even at such a tender age, she was square-jawed, like her father, and when Henry looked into her eyes, it was if he was looking into his own. They were the color of a thousand blue gray oceans, deep, large and intelligent. His paternal pride was evident, and he held Constance in her arms.

"So tell me, have you been a good girl?"

She looked at Elizabeth, who nodded for her to talk to Henry.

"Well," she began, "*Mostly*, sire."

"I see," Henry laughed, "And why mostly?"

"The Lady Agnes caught me pilfering sweeties in the kitchen."

"Indeed."

"She said I must confess but I feel I only must confess to only one, Sire. I took the others because of my good and kind heart."

"Is that so?"

Constance nodded.

"They were for Mary and Agnes, sire, for I was the only one brave enough to snatch them."

Henry laughed and put the child down.

"I agree with you. Now go play."

The library was empty and Elizabeth closed the door behind them.

"So what brings my king to Coudenoure?"

"Ah, Elizabeth, 'tis a day, a week, I am having. I am on my way from Greenwich to Richmond and wanted to see you and Constance."

He sat in front of the fire and stretched forth his long legs. Elizabeth looked at him lovingly. Gone was the gawky and awkward teenager. In his place sat a king, one who wore his leadership carelessly as one born into it. His physique had filled out and his full beard and significant height gave presence to his bearing. She sat in the chair opposite and waited.

"My wife has miscarried again."

"My lord, you have my heartfelt sympathies, but you must be patient, for you will have the son you yearn for."

"Elizabeth," he spoke as though he had not even heard her, "I must have a son! I am the King of England and my line depends upon it. Why is this happening to me? What sign from God have I misread?"

Elizabeth shook her head.

"No sign have you misread," she reassured him, "But patience is a difficult virtue to learn, even for a king."

He nodded and remained silent.

"Tell me, have you had visitors of late?"

"'Tis an odd question."

"Well, there was an uprising in the north, which has been put down, but some of the villains escaped to the south."

Elizabeth smiled uncertainly.

"They would have no reason to know of Coudenoure."

"'Tis right you are, Elizabeth." Henry rose suddenly.

"I must go."

Through the library window she watched him depart as he rode away. He had been at Coudenoure no more than an hour. Why had he come? His visits were usually two to three days, carved out of his normal schedule and secreted within this or that progress from one palace to another. Coudenoure had grown accustomed to his random stays and Henry had grown dependent upon them. Elizabeth and he had transitioned gracefully from lovers to friends. Their connection was made stronger by their lack of physical intimacy, for it forced them back onto their common interests to sustain their relationship and their passion. While everything had changed, nothing had changed.

All afternoon, Elizabeth continued to puzzle over the brief visit. What had been Henry's purpose? He would normally travel from Greenwich to Richmond by barge, yet he came on horseback to Coudenoure. There had been some reason for his visit, for his questions about guests and the matter of a son, but she simply could not fathom what it might be. Henry had developed the habit, or some might say the knack, of burying his true interest amid idle talk. Had he needed reassurance about a son, or was there danger from some far away uprising? Unease settled in her breast as she went about the remainder of her day. She needed more information, and it soon came.

Towards sunset, a sweet and gentle rain began to fall. As Elizabeth hurried back to the manor house from Agnes' nearby cottage, another figure made its way up the drive. This one, however, rode hard, and she recognized Charles Brandon.

"Elizabeth, I must talk to you."

They hurried into the library and waited impatiently as a servant stoked the fire. Thomas stirred in his chair.

"Young Charles, is it? What brings you hence?"

As the servant pulled the door, Charles spoke in a quiet and concerned voice.

"Where is the king's child?"

Elizabeth felt her heart beat faster.

"Constance is about the estate somewhere with her friends. I imagine they are in the kitchen for it has begun to rain."

"You must find her now, Elizabeth."

Thomas was alert and standing.

"What is it?"

Charles looked at the two of them as if trying to decide how much to say. Elizabeth spoke hurriedly.

"King Henry was here earlier and asked about visitors - are you here on the same business?"

Charles nodded.

"A rumor started at court some months ago about Constance."

Elizabeth sucked in her breath.

"They say she is the king's daughter. King Henry ignores this rumor and rightfully so - it will fade like a morning fog if given no credence. But there are reports of some rebels about who escaped the king's wrath in the north. They may have heard these rumors at court as well. He means to send a proper guard, but it must be done with discretion lest he confirm the child's paternity thereby. Meantime, I am here."

"Speak quickly, son, for I hear horses upon the drive." Thomas hurried him along and moved to the mantel. As Charles spoke he reached high above it and grasped the sword he had proudly displayed there since the day of Bosworth Field.

"Those horses must belong to our enemies. They have come south after all and intend to take Constance. Their plan will be to assassinate Henry and put her on the throne in his place. They are here to abduct her without doubt!"

Elizabeth flew out the library door.

"Prudence!" she screamed. "Consuelo!"

"My lady, what is the matter?" Prudence came running from the kitchen and the three little girls stood in the doorway.

"They are here to take Constance. Help me!"

Before she had finished speaking Prudence had turned to the children and gathered them together. Charles and Thomas joined them as a great jostling was heard beyond the front door, followed by an incessant and urgent pounding. In his hand, Thomas held his sword. Grabbing up Constance, Charles he ran for the back door, screaming orders over his shoulder.

"Thomas, you must defend long enough for me to get away with Constance!"

Thomas followed him.

"Your horse will still be in the stable. Ride man, RIDE!"

As Charles disappeared, Thomas placed himself at the back door. Prudence grabbed hold of Mary and Agnes and half dragged, half carried them after Charles and Constance.

"We will hide in the forest!" She screamed to Elizabeth as she ran past Thomas.

Elizabeth composed herself and hastened to the front door. The rain was heavier now, and directly as she opened, a man with a drawn sword pushed past her into the hall.

"Where is the lord of this manor?" he spoke loudly as others followed behind him.

"My father is the Baron of Coudenoure, sir, and pray you..."

The man, unshaven and disheveled, moved closer to her, his armed companions, wet and equally unkempt, crowding in behind.

"Where is this "baron"?"

"He is not here. He had business today in Greenwich..."

"Wench! You lie, for not five minutes ago we saw him arrive here. Where is the child?"

"What child?"

He struck Elizabeth across the face sending her sprawling against the library wall.

"She will lie! We must search the house. Eldwin, upstairs. The rest of you with me. Quickly before they hide it away!"

Thomas was waiting for them at the back door.

"Old man, where is the child?"

Thomas swung his sword in silent reply.

"Did you not hear me?"

Baron Thomas de Gray of Coudenoure pulled himself upright and spit before answering.

"You will burn in hell this very night. Now, come get your justice."

Two of the rebels advanced with drawn swords. Thomas managed a deep slash on the leader's arm before he was cut down. Elizabeth screamed and ran at them brandishing a candlestick seized from a small table. They pushed her aside and trampled Thomas' body underfoot then raced across the yard.

"I hear a horse - they are taking the child away! Quickly! Quickly!"

Charles barreled forth from the stables with Constance clinging to his chest too frightened to scream. Looking towards the house, he saw Prudence running with the other girls trying to make the forest's edge. Farther beyond that, he saw Elizabeth standing in the door over her father's bleeding, still body, screaming. Just as his mount reared and he loosed the reins, the deep and somber notes of battle horns reached his ears. They blared out Henry's call to war, and the sound of fifty horsemen thundered beneath their warning cry. The rebels too heard the commotion and turned.

Charles galloped to Prudence and grabbing Constance by one arm swung her down off the horse to waiting arms.

"I must save the king!" Charles shouted. "Stay in the forest until you hear my voice. Go, woman, and hide! Hide you all!"

He pulled his sword and turned upon the traitors as Henry roared into sight at the head of a small squadron of cavalry and archers from the east corner of the manor. Elizabeth raced through the melee which followed, frantically calling Constance's name as she ran in Prudence's footsteps. She had almost cleared the battle scene when she heard, more than felt, a dull thud against her side. Henry's enraged howl echoed across the yard as he watched her go down. But his rage turned to horror as her assailant, the lead rebel, raised his sword high above his head and laughed as he looked back at Henry, helpless to reach her in time.

"You cannot save her, my *grace*," he shouted with evil glee.

From behind him, a woman's voice spoke shrilly.

"But *I* can."

As he turned in surprise, Agnes plunged Thomas' sword deep within his belly. He looked at her in shock, but there was no time to react further, as Elizabeth escaped, darting into the forest after her daughter. He lay there, helpless to follow. The last thing he ever looked upon in this world was Henry's sword as it sliced through the air towards his throat.

*****

The rain gave forth a steady drumbeat as she ran and stumbled through the forest.

"Prudence! Where are you?"

From behind a massive oak a hand reached out and pulled her down. Prudence.

"Shhh, we must wait for dark now. 'Tis our best chance. We will try and find a horse and make for Woolwich - Edward and Consuelo have friends there, do they not?"

Elizabeth nodded and lay on the wet ground, reaching out and touching the three tiny, petrified faces of the little girls. They were safe, and she turned a steady gaze in the direction of the manor house. Frightening sounds of a mighty clash still drifted through the rainy gloom of the forest from Coudenoure - the terrified screams of men and horses, metal against metal in heavy, loud bursts, sickening cries - the two women shielded Mary, little Agnes and Constance as best they could. Darkness came on faster now and the sounds of battle lessened little by little until nothing but a dreadful silence remained amidst the rain. Suddenly, they discerned the sounds of a single horse coming their way. It chose and picked its footing carefully through the undergrowth and were it not for its snorting at the occasional stumble they might not have heard it. They pressed the children beneath them and sent their prayers heavenward. A voice, no more than a whisper came to them.

"Elizabeth, where are you?"

They strained to hear its whispered cadence - was it familiar?

"Elizabeth! Prudence? 'Tis me, Henry."

She was almost certain.

"Stay here and do not move."

Prudence's answer came as no more than a soft note in her ear. Elizabeth crawled silently away from the group as the voice came closer.

"Elizabeth."

Sure that she had put adequate distance between their hiding place and where she now was, she stood and answered.

"What is our firstborn's name?"

Silence. She prepared to run deeper into the wood away from Prudence and the children.

"Bucephalus."

A great gasp escaped her lips and she ran towards the voice through the darkness.

"Henry, where are you? Help us!"

In a burst he was upon her, holding her, intoning her name. The rain fell in torrents, and he pressed her against a tree, kissing her over and over as she sobbed and called his name. Grasping his hair, she pulled his face upwards and kissed him with a passion borne of eternal fire.

A small cough some distance away froze them.

"My king, 'tis me, Charles. We must get back."

"Prudence," called Elizabeth softly, "'Tis safe, come quickly."

A rustling and the small sobs of tiny children came their way. Elizabeth suddenly froze.

"Henry, they left a man in the house! Consuelo may be there!" She was trembling.

He took her by the arms and shook her gently.

"Listen to me."

She nodded.

"Stay here with Charles a moment longer. We will find him." He mounted his horse.

Elizabeth never paused.

"No, my king. Charles, ride with him and protect him, do you hear my words?"

"You may depend upon it, Lady Elizabeth."

"You would disobey your King?" Henry asked.

"Aye, if it means his life I would indeed," came her trembling reply. "Now go, and hurry. We will hide once again and wait for your voice."

Chapter Thirty-Three

Through the long, dark weeks that followed, Elizabeth was sustained by one purpose. She told no one, instead moving in step with the others through the motions of grief and closure after the bloody battle which had occurred at Coudenoure. Thomas died as he had lived, in the service of King Henry at Bosworth, and now his son, King Henry, at Coudenoure. As the story unfolded, and Henry began to understand the sacrifice and bravery the old man had shown in the face of certain death, he wept openly and frequently on his trips to Coudenoure. Who had ever loved him thus?

The sacrifice took him back to his childhood, and each night in his dreams he and Elizabeth once more romped through Coudenoure under the loving gazes of Agnes and Thomas. The strong sense of belonging, of people who loved him deeply for himself, returned during these dreams, and a heavy depression now accompanied him during his waking hours. He had no one in his life now, save Elizabeth and Charles, no one else who knew him intimately and loved him unreservedly. Others most certainly vowed allegiance, but Henry realized that the love and adoration he felt whenever he entered a room of courtiers and ministers was skin deep, and would evaporate in an instant should he lose the crown. With a bitterness he never thought possible, he began to know the isolating nature of absolute power. The only antidote to the bitterness was time at Coudenoure or with Charles. His dependence upon their steady presence in his life became tantamount to that of a talisman against an evil foe.

In a strange turn of events, Agnes recovered from her mighty effort to save Elizabeth, but Ransdell did not. Even as he had realized that dire trouble was afoot at the manor, and had raced from his garden to assist, Agnes was already ahead of him and ignored his screams to slow down and let him handle whatever lay ahead. She had heard the horses upon the drive and as the rebels had forced their way through the front door, she began running, for she knew what they were after. It could only be. Elizabeth's screaming over Thomas' dead body had pulled her along, and Agnes had grabbed Thomas' sword and run after Elizabeth through the yard, thinking of nothing but defense of her loved ones, even unto death. Ransdell, in turn, had followed her at a run, but as he passed across the gruesome scene had stopped abruptly, clutching his chest and falling face down directly into the muck of battle, barely able to breathe, much less rise.

*****

Consuelo arrived home late that evening, having accompanied Edward part way down the Thames on his departure for his next voyage. She had hired a small wherry to take her home as he continued on to Woolwich. The frantic undercurrents which had driven the unholy events at Coudenoure had dissipated, and even as Henry's men loaded the rebels' bodies onto wagons for public display in London, an exhausted numbness had settled in. Even from the river the light from the sentries' torches lit the heavens. Concern became anxiety and by the time she reached the drive her breath was ragged.

"Who are you, and what do you want?"

A sentry stepped forward with an unsheathed sword and spoke harshly to her.

"I live here - I am Consuelo and this is my home. What manner of chaos is this?"

Another man heavily armored stepped forward.

"Madam, the rebels tried to take this estate earlier today. We believe they planned to use it as a base for an attack against our king."

Consuelo suspected otherwise.

"Kind sir, you may escort me if you wish, but I must get to the manor immediately."

He nodded and a sentry accompanied her up the long drive. Inside was deadened chaos as Henry directed his troops. Thomas' body lay stretched upon the main hall floor covered by a linen shroud. Henry saw her, and nodded knowingly to Charles. He pulled her into the empty kitchen, telling her of the day's events.

"But I do not understand," she began, "Where are the children, my mother? Where is Elizabeth? And where in God's name is my father?"

Charles had barely finished when Consuelo raced upstairs. The three girls sat swaddled in blankets in front of the fire in Elizabeth's room. To one side wrapped in multiple shawls sat old Agnes. She only stared at Consuelo and said nothing. In Elizabeth's bed was Ransdell, silent and white as snow. Elizabeth and Prudence paced between them, offering broth and wiping their brows. Upon seeing her, the children broke into fresh tears and sobs. The night was long, and the following weeks bore no resemblance to normalcy for any of them.

Dawn was breaking as Henry entered the room and took Elizabeth into the hallway. She trembled as she fell into his arms. Hugging her mercilessly, Henry dried her tears and looked steadily into her reddened eyes.

"I sent some of my men earlier to Greenwich, and they have returned now with staff and guards. You will need time, Elizabeth."

She could only nod.

"I will return as I can, but the people must see their king after such a shock - they must know that I am alive and well and that those who challenge England shall not survive."

She kissed him passionately.

"Go," she finally pushed him away, "I shall manage here, and you must *manage the kingdom,* my king. We will always be here for you."

He turned and left.

Thomas was buried in the small cemetery once reserved for the holy men of the monastery which Coudenoure had in time past been. One month later, the guards were reduced in number and the staff of Greenwich returned to their stations at the palace. Two months later, Henry ordered the building of an estate wall around Coudenoure. It would encompass the great yard and the orchards, the cottages behind the house and that of Agnes and Ransdell as well. But the great meadow now lay beyond the pale, and as the wall went up higher and higher each day, Elizabeth wondered whether it kept others out, or her within. Henry had become obsessive in his desire to protect her, and she became unaccustomed to the rigors of a guarded existence. In time she would adjust, but for now it weighed heavily upon her soul. But each time she saw Constance once again playing merrily with her two friends, each time she thought of what might have happened and what might happen yet if the wall did protect them, she had nothing but gratitude for the man she would love until her last breath.

She stepped into the great library and interrupted Constance as she sat reading with one of the tutors Henry provided for the children of the estate.

"Constance, are you ready?"

"Aunt Elizabeth, I am busy reading Homer, can you not see?"

The tutor saw the look on Elizabeth's face and excused himself from the room.

"Now, let us play our secret game. What is the word that must always begin it?"

Constance swung her legs as she sat in Elizabeth's lap.

"Bucephalus," she shouted happily.

"You are right, my little one!" Elizabeth smiled at the child and played with her hair as she asked the next question.

"And when Auntie Elizabeth says the word, what must you do?"

Constance did not hesitate.

"I must run quickly to the small stable at the edge of the great wall, near the farmland, behind our manor."

"You are very good!" Elizabeth produced a fig coated in powdered sugar and as Constance happily munched on the treat she continued.

"And then what?"

"I will ride to a place you shall tell me about."

"And what will you take with thee?"

"What you give me to take, Auntie. May I go play now?"

Elizabeth watched the child run from the room, satisfied with her beginnings.

The next time, she would be prepared.

Chapter Thirty-Four

January 5, 1524

Wolsey sat patiently waiting for King Henry to finish his morning dispatches. The winter this year was biting, and he rested his tiny feet on a small footstool covered in red velvet. He sat before the great hearth which formed the north wall of the King's study at Greenwich. Nearby sat a bowl of fruit and nuts which he adroitly reached past to get at the plate of sweets just beyond. He was dressed, as always, in the robes only he was allowed to wear as papal legate to the Court of Henry VIII: a rich, red cassock with a white satin overlay. A bejeweled cross hung low upon his chest from a substantial chain of solid gold. A small velvet cap, round, red and high-fitting, crowned his luxurious look. Only his hair, thick and dark, short and straight, refused to cooperate with his image of what a man of his importance should look like. It jutted from beneath his ecclesial cap like autumn hay from a stack, and regardless of oil and careful dressing each morning, by afternoon it did as it pleased.

He cut his eyes to where Henry sat engrossed in a papal bull concerning the latest ecclesiastical ruling on the heresy of the Calvinists. Resting his hands on his ample belly, he continued to enjoy the quiet of the morning, dreaming of the time two days hence when he would travel to Hampton Court, a palace which had recently become his own and one which he was renovating at great expense.

"Tell me," Henry interrupted his reverie, "What think you of the new Pope?"

Wolsey coughed.

"Your highness, I believe Clement to be a good man, but one held in the palm of King Charles' hand. We must be careful with that one. I hear he thinks too highly indeed of the French king."

Henry nodded in agreement and changed the subject.

"Catherine is here at Greenwich?" he inquired.

"The Queen is indeed here at Greenwich, my Grace, and might I say she is looking quite fetching in her new black velvet gown. Why, the sleeves alone must have cost..."

Henry held up his hand for silence.

"Stop! You are wasting your time. I am done with that woman. Years upon years of marriage and what do I have to show for it? Eh? A *daughter*."

Wolsey remained silent, for he knew the rant by heart and also knew that only the foolish or uninitiated interrupted it.

"I am King of England, the greatest of the great realms, and all I ask for is a son. Is that so much?"

Wolsey said nothing.

"No, 'tis nothing and yet I am denied the one thing my heart truly desires - an heir, a son to carry my name and my line forward!"

Henry frowned as he approached the fire and sat near Wolsey. He, too, ignored the fruit and toyed with a candied cake as he fretted on.

"I tell you, Wolsey, I have done something to displease God. It must be so. And yet what? I go to mass at least four times daily. I am an excellent sovereign who has only what is good for my kingdom in my heart. And yet, here I am, with an aged wife who cannot carry my son, who must, *must* I say be waiting to be born. I tell you, I can no longer be in her presence, so offensive do I find her and her barrenness. What have I done to displease my God?"

The question hung in the air for several minutes until Henry roused himself from the melancholy he felt creeping up upon his soul. He finished the cake and walked to the door as he spoke.

"I shall ride to Richmond, Wolsey. I may be some time getting there."

As he entered the great hall, a small group of young women, brightly dressed and giggling, stopped suddenly as he came into the room. All bowed deeply, but one, near the back of the group, did so more slowly than the others, revealing her face to him.

Henry gasped aloud.

"Elizabeth?" He reeled against a nearby wall. Before him stood a specter from ages past: Elizabeth in her youth. The woman who now stood frozen before him, not knowing what to say or do, was of such a close likeness to his beloved that he could hardly take it in. She had a dark complexion with pale rose cheeks. Her eyes, almond-shaped and large, were as dark as ebony and bespoke an intelligence far beyond what Henry normally saw in the women at his court. Her chin was sharp and well-defined as was Elizabeth's, and her hair, a rich velvety chestnut, fell to her waist.

Henry felt the years roll away as he continued to stare, entranced and amazed at the resemblance between the two women. For a split second, he was back in his youth, running after Elizabeth, hearing her laughter float back to him upon a cool spring breeze. The sensation passed, and after a moment, he approached the group.

"What is your name?" he asked softly.

The woman's eyes grew even larger and after a brief curtsey, she spoke.

"Anne, your Grace, my name is Anne Boleyn."

Henry bowed and exited through the great heavy doors. His horse had been readied for him, and a small wooden stool was placed just below the stirrup as an aid to him for mounting. As he wheeled away towards the guards' gate, he smiled for the first time that day.

*****

Smoke was rising from the chimneys at Coudenoure, and as always, Elizabeth awaited him beneath the doors' lintel. Yes, he thought as he dismounted, we are both older now. Her face, once unlined and soft as a rose petal, carried her history upon it: deep lines ran from her nose to the corners of her small mouth, and her brow was deeply furrowed. Her hair, once a delight to run one's fingers through, was now graying with touches of white. She habitually wore it in a tight knot upon the back of her head, drawn away from her face deliberately as if she were proud to let the viewer see her and what the years had wrought. Her style of dress had changed as well. Gone were the pleasing pastels and embroidered flowers which her youthful gowns had displayed. Instead, she dressed simply in garb that marked has as neither lady nor servant, neither girl nor woman. She smiled at him as if she knew and understood what he was thinking.

"Yes," she laughed with a slightly rueful tone, "We are older, are we not?"

Henry laughed.

"I tell you, Elizabeth, that horse grows taller each day. If I could demand that someone ride him for me, perhaps I would."

"You are here because of the anniversary?" she asked.

"Aye, I could not let you be alone on such a day. Thomas was a good man, perhaps the best, and we remember him together, my love."

She nodded and they began to walk towards the old friars' cemetery near the orchard. So much had changed since that day! Captain Ransdell had never recovered from the stroke he suffered trying to help Agnes and her, and had died only a few months later. Agnes nursed him until the very end, and he was laid to rest beneath the same trees as Thomas. Young Agnes had fallen to the sweating sickness three years earlier, and Constance and Mary were left to carry on without her. In time, Mary had married a young stable hand, and with encouragement from Henry and Elizabeth, his knowledge of horses had grown daily, but in the second year of their marriage he had died from the kick of a mare as she foaled. Mary's culinary skills now rivaled those of her mother.

Edward, Consuelo's husband, had come and gone with the tides for many years. But his times away grew longer, and his visits home shorter and shorter until one day they had simply ceased altogether. Consuelo was never certain if she missed him or not, for the change had been slow in coming, and over the years she had adjusted to being on her own. Occasionally she wondered what had happened to him, and sometimes mourned, but she was never certain if her sorrow was for the loss of Edward, or the loss of innocence about the ephemeral nature of some love. Roberto, left long ago in Rome, had never been a man of writing.

"How many we have lost, Henry." Elizabeth spoke softly.

"But we have each other, and we have Coudenoure, the manor we have built together."

"Indeed we do," she said, looking about her.

With Henry's will and money, and Elizabeth's passion and daily attendance, Coudenoure had grown from a hulk of an aged monastery to a true manor and home. The wall which had once made Elizabeth feel trapped now gave her a sense of security. The ghostly remains of the original great chapel now provided her with a sense of continuity.

Some years earlier she had considered taking them down but Janyns had caused such a ruckus about her plans that she had left them as they had stood for centuries. Soaring, arching windows, skeletal and empty, reached high into the peaceful rural sky. They were elemental and over time, Elizabeth had come to hear and appreciate the rhythm they provided to the paean of the landscape all round, never understanding it but always aware of it.

They stood silently over Thomas' grave, holding hands and saying prayers. Elizabeth had gathered berried branches and yew as they walked, and she placed them against the marble grave marker. She bent and kissed it and crossed herself before turning, giving Henry time to say his own prayers in peace. After a moment, they walked back indoors and Prudence prepared a lunch for them. Over cards, Henry remembered his morning.

"There is a young woman at court, one of the queen's ladies, who is the very image of you in your youth."

Elizabeth smiled and took the trick.

"Indeed! So she is beautiful then."

They both laughed.

"She is," Henry replied as he threw down what remained of his hand in disgust. Elizabeth shuffled the deck.

"I have only one thought these days, Elizabeth – I need to know why God has denied me an heir."

She counted cards for each and as they picked up their hands, she replied.

"I do not know the answer, my sovereign, and I cannot pretend to know the mind of God."

"Although there are those abroad now who do so," replied Henry. "I do not care for the pope, but neither do I care for those who would be a law unto themselves, answering only to God."

They played on. Henry won the hand, and it was Elizabeth's turn to throw down her cards in feigned unhappiness.

"No more!" she exclaimed and moved to the fire. "Come, play for me while I sew."

The afternoon sped by as they sat together just as they had done a thousand times before, Henry strumming his lute and Elizabeth intent upon her needlework. Sometimes she painted, as did Henry, but the sense of an old and true love, together with contentment, was always the same. Henry paused in his lute playing and a slight noise could be heard in the library wall. They both smiled.

"All things change, and yet they remain just as they always were," Elizabeth noted quietly.

Outside, in the main hall, Constance carefully replaced the small piece of mortar she had removed so that she and Mary could overhear Henry's conversation with Elizabeth.

"Shhh," Mary said fiercely, "Or they will tumble to our perch."

Constance and she moved quietly through the hall and back into the kitchen. Prudence ignored them as they picked up fruit from a bowl and tripped lightly back out into the main hall. Only when they were situated on a low stair together did Constance speak.

"'Tis astounding, is it not?"

Mary nodded in agreement.

"And yet they do not know! They believe us to be as ignorant as the day they first proclaimed it as the truth!"

Constance looked at her friend thoughtfully.

"Do you think they imagine that we never steal into Aunt Elizabeth's room and peer into the looking glass she brought from Rome? And that the likeness is not unmistakable? And yet..."

They sat in silence for a moment.

"I am the king's daughter. It must be so. And Elizabeth is my mother, not may aunt. Yet they continue to fob off on one and all this fiction about twins. But why?"

"Because, friend, you were born out of wedlock, and Auntie Elizabeth could not confess to you. And as the daughter of Henry, you must take care that you are not taken from us by those who might wish him ill."

Constance waved away her friend Mary's explanations.

"She is my mother, and just once, I would like to call her thus."

"She loves you more than anything, Constance."

"As I do her."

"Do not forget her diligence after the battle, when we were but children."

Constance sighed. Her long red hair, offset perfectly by her pale, alabaster skin and grey blue eyes, fell to her waist. As she had grown older, the resemblance to her father had grown more pronounced, until visitors to Coudenoure, should they have met the king, would stare at her in knowing wonder. Rumors at court abounded, but no one dared speak of the bastard child of Coudenoure openly for fear of retribution from King Henry.

Constance had grown to womanhood as her mother had before her unrestrained by court decorum or family considerations. As a result, her interests were those of a well-read noble, one versed in several languages, familiar with the cultural norms and mores of her status but standing beyond them. Constance had been indulged but not spoiled. She was more than a little artistic, and her painting skills had surpassed those of her mother years earlier. As they sat around the fire in the evenings, old Agnes would regale them all with tales of Malaga and Rome. Talk of the famous artist, Michelangelo, was frequently on her lips with dire warnings about what would happen should they not keep a safe distance from such heathens.

"But Auntie Agnes," Constance would tease, "How can he be a heathen and yet paint for the Pope at the Vatican?"

Agnes always ignored such comments, only wagging her finger in response.

Henry's visits to Coudenoure, while not predictable, always played out in the same, comforting fashion. After a walk with Elizabeth, one in which they could speak without worry about the listening post in the library wall, they would take a small meal, play cards and chat in the library. Sometimes it was music, sometimes, one would read to the other, but the routine had fossilized years earlier and neither desired the slightest change.

As always when he left Coudenoure, Henry felt refreshed riding down the long drive late that afternoon. His spirit had been soothed. He rode on to Richmond, and thence to Westminster Palace some days after that.

Elizabeth watched him leave, and went into the great kitchen to see Prudence.

"His Highness has left?" Prudence asked.

"Yes, but I fear he is becoming ever more troubled by his lack of male issue," Elizabeth replied. "'Tis ever harder to turn his thoughts to less frustrating fields."

Prudence nodded and dismissed the scullery maids who had been assisting her. She poured two cups of cider and sat down opposite her friend, looking at her keenly.

"Elizabeth, you are troubled today, and it is not just the anniversary of your father's death or the king's visit. You have been quiet for some days."

Elizabeth sighed.

"I am not sure what ails me," she replied ruefully, "…for I have everything any woman could ever want."

She waved her arm and looked about the kitchen.

"My estate is beautiful and well-run, and 'tis mine. I indulge myself in artistic endeavors and have a beautiful daughter."

Prudence stayed silent.

"I learn your cooking, I read my books, I stroll my grounds and ride my horses, and yet…"

After a moment, she spoke again.

"Perhaps 'tis purpose I lack? Constance is now a maid with a mind of her own. She has no need of her aging mother. And while I enjoy my simple days, I long for something, but I know not what."

Prudence did not even pretend to understand.

"You must be happy as I am," she began, "…and be not always looking for something beyond what you have. I wonder if the adventures you had as a child did not make it more difficult for you now."

"No," Elizabeth stated firmly, "They made me what I am, 'tis true, but I would not trade them. I believe I must find meaning in my days or I shall continue to be unhappy, for that is what it is becoming."

"What about the library?" asked Prudence. "Lord Thomas was always saying it should be organized and catalogued. And you have said the same many times. And yet it goes undone."

"Because 'tis a huge undertaking," Elizabeth explained, "One that would necessitate much time."

She paused and looked thoughtfully at Prudence.

"And then, of course, the gaps in the collections need be noted and acquisition of appropriate manuscripts sought to fill them."

Prudence smiled as she sensed Elizabeth warming to the task.

"And how to organize them – that is the question. It would be wise to find how others organize theirs, perhaps? It would have made my father so happy, and it honors him. And it came to you on the anniversary of him giving himself for Constance and Coudenoure. Prudence, once again, you have saved me!"

Elizabeth clapped her hands and rose. "That is exactly what I must do!"

Chapter Thirty-Five

Early the next morning, she appeared at breakfast with paper, quills, ink and determination. Constance had no interest in being drafted into the effort and Elizabeth began on her own. By noon the library air was heavy with dust and the musty smell usually associated with parchment mites and papyrus rolls. Elizabeth had directed the servants bring in every book, manuscript, codex and scrap of vellum the library had to offer and they lay in great heaps upon the tables. She hardly noticed when Constance tripped through the door and announced Robert Janyns.

Elizabeth turned, blew a strand of hair from her face and sneezed. Janyns, dressed from head to foot in royal blue velvet, including his stockings, scarf and hat, bowed deeply before making an exaggerated examination of the scene which lay before him.

"And was it amusing for you, my lady?" he asked sardonically as he perused the chaos.

Elizabeth, too, paused to take a look at her handiwork.

"Auntie, I believe you have lost your mind." With that, Constance turned towards the door. "I am going riding!" she offered over her shoulder as she disappeared into the great hall. The heels of her riding boots could be heard clicking lightly across the stone floor and Janyns let out a long sigh.

"Children, Madame, are barely to be tolerated - they are such rude little creatures, do you not agree?"

Elizabeth had to laugh at the petulant tone and eternal truth of her guest's words. Prudence appeared and as they settled themselves at the end of one of the long tables, Janyns spoke to her.

"Prudence, is that not correct?"

Prudence smiled shyly.

"Our good King Henry tells me constantly that he will bring me some of your divine cakes. Yet every time he comes to Coudenoure and returns to Richmond or Greenwich or London, he says he has forgotten them. I am beginning to believe that the cakes are consumed while en route to their rightful owner. I really should say something."

Prudence laughed as she replied, "Kind sir, I do on occasion send treats and special foods with the king when he departs, but I would never speak as to what happens to them once they are gone from Coudenoure."

Janyns sniffed. "Yes, well, you and I need to come to our *own* arrangement concerning the results of your culinary artistry. Indeed, I believe that those who can turn radishes and nuts, leaves and such into gastronomical delicacies are among our greatest artists!"

He paused.

"After architects, of course."

He reached for the nearest piece of spice cake, slathered fresh butter on it and listened as Elizabeth explained her purpose in the deconstruction of the library.

"So that is my doing," she finished and helped herself to another dried fig, "Now tell me what brings you to my small estate, my good Janyns."

"Ah, sadness, Elizabeth, 'tis sadness that brings me here."

Elizabeth waited while he buttered another piece of cake and drained his cup of cider.

"You know that last year, my beloved Bessie passed from this earth."

Elizabeth stifled a smile.

"I knew her not, but I have heard you speak of her often," she managed in a somber tone. She declined to speak of the usual contexts (screaming and throwing candlesticks) and the adjectives which accompanied the architect's mentioning of his beloved Bessie (vexatious, nonsensical, fickle, and her absolute favorites…pretentious and overly sensitive).

"I am sorry to hear of your loss."

Janyns nodded sadly.

"Yes, but you see, my sorrows do not end there! I have asked three maids since then to honor me with their hands in marriage, and yet all three have seen fit to deny me such eternal happiness!"

"No!" Elizabeth exclaimed dramatically.

Again Janyns nodded.

"And so I come here seeking solace in the peaceful halls of Coudenoure and the soothing flavors of Prudence's spice cakes and pickled herrings and …"

His hand paused mid-air and he looked up from the cake tray and into Elizabeth's inquiring eyes.

"Tell me," he said artfully as though her answer mattered not one whit to him - he was simply passing the afternoon in idle gossip with an old friend – "…the good lady Prudence, how is her husband these days?"

Elizabeth laughed aloud and Janyns blushed.

"Prudence's Joshua died some years ago," Elizabeth explained, "But would you really marry a woman for her spice cake?"

"Madame," replied Janyns with all the dignity the situation would allow, which was not much, "I am beyond wanting the pleasures of young flesh. I am in need of someone to keep my house and cook for me and warm me at night in my bed."

"And three maids turned down such a chivalrous offer? 'Tis hard to understand."

Janyns smiled ruefully.

"'Tis true that my blunt approach does not seem to captivate the ladies in the manner I was hoping it would."

Elizabeth stood.

"Why not stay at Coudenoure for a day or two and give your weary heart respite from its searching for a mate? Help me design a new scheme for the library, one that will enchant Henry and help me maintain it in an orderly fashion."

"I could do that," he said slowly as he eyed the room. "Henry and I have spoken often of a new scheme to organize his own libraries. Did you know that some of his collections are still kept in scribes' desks? Really, 'tis quite medieval, and Henry is such a forward-thinking king! Our idea, well, mine really, is that rather than piling the books and scrolls willy-nilly as they are now, we will make a showcase for them by having grand shelving cover entire walls. Each shelf would be made of the finest wood and each could hold a separate author's work, or epoch of thought…you understand. Very Roman."

He continued looking around before finishing.

"Yes, it will make all three of us quite happy – you, me and our sovereign. I shall begin at once. I was en route to Hampton Court but I shall stop here for a moment and begin the design work. Later, I will send my workmen."

"En route to Hampton Court?" Elizabeth asked.

"Indeed," came the reply, "Old Wolsey intends to hold a masked ball there to show off his wealth. I tell you, the man is insufferable. Why, he had the audacity to tell me that my apparel was not suitable for a man my age – he actually used the word "dandy", whatever that means. Really, quite impossible. Did you know…"

The afternoon was passed happily with chatter, drawings, and Prudence's cakes.

*****

Lord Chancellor Wolsey needed an excuse. Hampton Court, his beloved country estate, was finally complete. While he had made York Place, his London home, grand beyond measure, Hampton Court was truly his jewel. Courtiers, servants, nobles - all who sought his favors would pass through eight separate chambers before being admitted into his presence, a sure testament to his wealth and power. He had spared no expense, wanting his palace to rival those of the continental princes of the church with whom he so frequently dealt. Rich, huge tapestries, each more intricately woven than the last, graced the walls of the state rooms. The Story of Abraham, his favorite, had just been delivered from the low countries, and even Henry had remarked upon the fine weaving evident in the piece. Holbeins jostled miniatures by Hilliard, and dazzling displays of church jewels were on display along with ancient statuary and medieval scrolls.

But now that the architectural renovations were complete, now that the interior rooms were decorated with an eye towards ostentatious display of his wealth, now, to whom could he show this magnificent accomplishment? For Wolsey, it was not an idle question. Son of an Ipswich butcher, he knew and understood viscerally what it meant to live on the other side. Through sheer hard work and brilliance he had risen through the ranks of those serving Henry to his current position as Lord

Chancellor and Papal Legate, and yet, what did it all mean if there was no one he could lord it over? He had no desire to be quietly and discretely rich beyond measure – he wanted an audience. He needed an opportunity to light the candles, hang the walls with even more tapestries and further draperies of fine silks and satins, and hire musicians. He needed a party. And so he had decided upon a masked ball.

Yes, it would be grand.

It was the evening before the event, and even Wolsey had to admit the splendor of the great, storied room was a wonder to behold. At one end of the hall, magnificent tables were set and ready to be laden with fine meats and sweets. At the other, a small stage set had been put up in order to provide his guests with the evening's main entertainment: a short play in which young maids, in the guise of the virtues, would be assailed and ultimately won over by male ardor. Between the tables and the stage the floor had been cleared and a yet smaller stage erected in the corner for musicians. As he walked through the vast space, he began to feel uncomfortable. In fact, small nagging devils began to plague him and he approached Janyns, the King's architect who was overseeing the stage set production for him.

"My Lord Janyns, what think you? 'Tis very grand." Wolsey paused. "Indeed, is it *too* grand? After all, I am only the king's servant. This place, these hangings, are they not too grand for one in my position?"

Janyns shrugged and tossed a cobalt blue scarf over his shoulder.

"What you mean to say is will the king believe you to have overstepped?"

Wolsey smiled sourly, impressed as ever with the architect's utter lack of subtlety.

"I know not if you have gone too far, but I know that if you have, King Henry will not hide the matter from you."

His mind was still on the work he had finished only a few days earlier at Coudenoure. Henry had chanced by at the end of his stay there and was enchanted with the plans for the library. Janyns was thus happy. Whether Wolsey would have the same luck was not a matter of any concern to him whatsoever.

The master architect walked out, leaving Wolsey to worry and fret on his own. He was still perturbed as his guests began to arrive the following morning - most would stay at Hampton court with their entourages, ostensibly so that their attire would be perfect for the coming evening's events; in reality, Wolsey had offered just such extended invitations that his guests might have time to wander about his fabulous new halls and admire his spectacular new belongings. Silks and velvets of all colors were to be seen, carefully placed within the folds of protective linen, as the servants of various houses descended upon Hampton Court. The musicians with their cases and flamboyant attire were politely shifted to the side and back entrances used by the servants. The grand entry way was for the king and his noblemen only. Wolsey's own staff, dressed grandly in Henry's colors, stood stiffly at attention as though they, too, were part of the palace's decorations.

As the evening got under way, Wolsey continued to fuss with himself - after all, the grand hall was grander than the king's own, and the tapestries were finer than any other's in the entire kingdom. What would Henry think?

"So you fear I may feel you have gone too far?" It was Henry, and so intent had Wolsey been on his own woes he had not heard the king approach.

Wolsey thought back to his earlier conversation with Janyns - the man was nothing if not indiscreet.

"Your Majesty, all I have I owe to you. I am your most humble servant."

"Aye, you are my servant, but not such a humble one." Henry looked admiringly around the room before patting Wolsey on the back. "But do not worry. I am too happy this evening to worry about you and your wealth."

Wolsey followed Henry's eyes to a slim figure, dressed in deep burgundy and dancing merrily. She held a gold mask across her eyes, but sensing their gaze, she dropped it dramatically and deliberately as she turned her dark eyes upon them. They offered a glimpse into the sophisticated soul of one recently come from France. Henry could not stop staring and smiling at the young woman.

"Who is she, Majesty?"

"Anne."

Chapter Thirty-Six

November 5, 1529

Someone was knocking on her bedroom door. Without waiting for her response, Agnes shuffled into her room.

"Elizabeth, wake up, for young Brandon is here."

"Young Brandon? Agnes, we none of us have been young lately."

Agnes ignored her and snapped her fingers at the servant who was hurriedly stoking the fire in the hearth.

"Hurry up, girl! You are the slowest of the slowest, and I wonder how 'tis not nightfall before you finish dressing in the mornings!" The years had not dulled Agnes' tongue. As the young woman finally pulled the door behind her, Agnes shouted after her.

"And have someone bring us cider and bread and cheese, do you hear?"

Agnes rapped Elizabeth's covers sharply with her cane.

"Now up, for as I said, Charles is here and I believe he has news."

"Why do you think that?" Elizabeth stood in front of the fire with her back to it holding up her night dress so that the warmth from the flames could reach her. The thin shift filled with heat and billowed out behind her near the flames.

Agnes stamped her cane on the floor, reminding Elizabeth of Thomas.

"You will burn the place down with your nightdress if you do not quit that habit."

Agnes ignored her smile.

"I believe he has news because as ever, he cannot keep it from his face and his manner. He speaks more quickly and paces when he is anxious."

As Elizabeth dressed and ate, Agnes continued her chatter.

"Now, I believe Mary finally has a suitor - widowhood does not suit that young woman. Not at all. She becomes more wretchedly morose with each passing year."

"Who is this that would take our Mary from us?"

"He is from Woolwich, and seems to be a fine young man. I suspect she could remain here while he sails."

"And how did Mary meet a fine young man from Woolwich?"

Agnes' face darkened to the point that Elizabeth had to laugh as she spoke.

"Oh aye, 'twas ever thus - young men do find ways, do they not? Likely he was visiting the stables to see his friend Jonathon, or his friend the yardman Vincent or some other such person and then such person happened to introduce him to Mary."

"'Tis not right for a maid, or a widow, to meet her husband in that manner. The woman should wait until her mother and father have determined who the best suitor is, and only then should she be allowed to meet the man. At that point, they should have supervised meetings, and only in due time should they be allowed to court and eventually marry. I do not know what is happening in this world that the young people behave as they do in this day and age."

Elizabeth had heard the lecture many times before and gently guided Agnes back to Charles Brandon.

"If you would finish eating, then we might both find out why he is here," Agnes said testily.

Eventually, they made their way to the library. Charles stood by the window and as Agnes entered, he spoke merrily to her.

"What have you done with Agnes? Oh! Wait! You are Agnes! For a moment I mistook you for a young maid, as fair as when – "

Agnes cut him off with a snort before silently leaving the room. After a moment, Elizabeth heard a tiny grating sound in the wall.

"Charles, sit. What brings you to Coudenoure?"

"You do not want to have a small, idle gossip before we launch into meaningful conversation? At court, such abilities are considered essential for polite society."

Elizabeth countered.

"I will indeed force you to hear my small talk which shall be about this library and its many volumes, but first, we shall hear your news."

Charles leaned back in his chair, sighed, and closed his eyes, giving Elizabeth a chance to look upon him uninterrupted. Like them all, he had aged considerably. His hair was quite thin now with gray streaks throughout. His face stood as a testament to his service to Henry – in the battle of the Spurs, at the battle of Flodden Field, and at the Field of the Cloth of Gold. It was lined and weathered, but it suited him, like marble etched over time by wind and rain into a finer more nuanced stone. But his body stood in stark contrast to the maturity written across his countenance. Whether through serendipity or discipline, Charles had maintained the figure of a much younger man. His muscular calves showed through his silk hose, and despite the fullness of his sleeves the musculature of his arms was evident. Sinewy, long fingers bespoke a gentle man, despite his military service. After a moment, he opened his eyes.

"'Tis our majesty." He spoke simply and waited.

"Henry is fine?" Worry was evident in Elizabeth's voice. Charles waved it away with a weary hand.

"Our Majesty is fine, praise be to God." They both crossed themselves as he continued.

"No, 'tis not his Highness' health which brings me here today. 'Tis his desire."

"Anne?"

Charles nodded.

"It seems he cannot have a single conversation without saying her name." Charles pitched his voice slightly as he continued. "What does the Lady

Anne think? How is the Lady *Anne* today? Where is the Lady *Anne*? I think I shall visit the Lady *Anne*. I believe..."

Elizabeth giggled despite herself.

"You see my point."

She nodded.

"But Charles, you have known this for some time. It has been years since the King shared Queen Catherine's bed - if I know this in my home so far removed from court, then you must know it as well."

"We all know it, and Queen Catherine makes a great display of inviting him to her bed often and letting everyone know he declines. What is the woman thinking with that? That he will lust for her in the face of such rudeness? I know not."

Blushing, Elizabeth asked, "How would a woman invite a man thus without being forward?"

Now it was Charles' turn to giggle. "You truly are removed from the ways of the court, my good Elizabeth. Indeed."

Elizabeth stoked the fire to hide her embarrassment. She had never learned the rituals of courtship and when in the company of those who were fluent in them, she never ceased to feel somehow less, somehow ignorant in ways that made her slightly ashamed, as though she had missed a vital part of life even though she knew such feelings to be false. After a moment, she returned to her seat.

"The King longs for a son, and I believe he will not rest easy until he has one. 'Tis natural that he turn his eye, therefore, to the maids of the court."

"Elizabeth, that is not what this is. He is obsessed with the woman. If it were only the need for a son, then we all would understand that. But she seems to have seduced him, to have bewitched him."

"Well, perhaps he is truly in love with the maid. And what of it?"

"We come to my news."

It was his turn to stoke the fire restlessly.

"You know he asked the Pope to annul his marriage to Queen Catherine."

Elizabeth nodded.

"Everyone knows this - is that your news?"

Charles shook his head vigorously while she continued.

"And everyone also knows the Pope will never give him a Papal decree of such a nature, and not only because 'tis wrong. The Emperor Charles is Catherine's nephew, and Clement will never do such a thing because of it. Henry wants it because he feels he has misinterpreted God's plan for his life and he stands always ready to do God's bidding. If he believes his marriage was not within the Almighty's plan, then I understand why he would attempt to annul it so his life will be in accord with the wishes of Providence."

"Elizabeth, do not be naïve. He wants the annulment not to satisfy God and the saints, but in order to marry Anne."

Elizabeth looked at him in horror.

"What? 'Tis not true. You cannot put your wife away because you have no male issue, even if you are the king!"

Charles said nothing.

"You must not say such things, Charles. 'Tis sacrilegious heresy to speak of such sins."

"Elizabeth, I tell you the truth. I heard it from the King myself. And there is further news. That viperous woman has turned Henry against his most faithful minister, Wolsey. There is talk that she will have him arrested and tried for treason."

"Treason? Pray tell, what treason would that be? Managing the king's accounts and business for him?

'Tis treasonous now to honor and obey one's sovereign?"

"The Lady Anne has filled the King's head with noisy, silly ideas. She tells him that the Pope drags his feet about granting the annulment because Wolsey is in league with him and further, that Wolsey himself does not want to see the divorce happen because he hates her."

"What manner of woman is this?" Elizabeth asked incredulously. "What matters whom Wolsey likes or dislikes? He does the king's bidding and we all know him to be the king's man! 'Tis true he loves wealth and has been known to display his own riches in very coarse, vulgar and inappropriate shows of privilege, but, but, my God, so do most of the king's courtiers - am I not right?"

Charles nodded glumly.

"There seems to be no one who can stop the woman, so beguiled is Henry. And it may all be traced back to Catherine's inability to bear a son. And King Henry shall have one at all costs. He has an obsessive burning deep in his soul for a son and that is the beginning, and end, of the Boleyn woman's power over him."

The sun waxed long above Coudenoure and they walked the grounds in the afternoon, continuing their conversation.

"There is an element of the tale which I do not understand." Elizabeth's words died in the windless air of the sunny day. "If she has taken the king to her bed, and still there is no son, then..."

"Ah, that is where her witchery and cunning are elevated to that of the devil himself," Charles explained. "...for she refuses to sleep with him until he is free of his wife."

Elizabeth stopped dead in her tracks while she considered his words.

"'Tis clever, that," she conceded. "And I see the King agreeing, for should he have a son, then he will want it born in royal wedlock in his royal bed. And Anne Boleyn, how does she keep him in line?"

"Spells, evil craft, I do not know. Likely she assures him that she will bear him a son and he, in desperation, has come to believe that God intends it thus. And so he pursues the annulment. You see? 'Tis a perfect web the woman weaves."

They walked along the perimeter path in silence for some ways. The winter was come early that year, and the grass of the grand yard was a patchwork of green and brown as the cold slowly robbed it of life. The espaliers along the perimeter fence had lost their leaves, revealing their underlying structure and symmetry. Years earlier, when Elizabeth had felt entrapped by the immensity and monolithic quality of the wall, Henry had ordered a path built fifteen feet from it. The path followed the lines of the security wall around the entire manor proper. He had then employed more groundsmen whose sole purpose was to turn the fifteen feet between the wall and the path into a show of flowers and seasonal botanical delights. Over time, his plan had worked, and rather than a bulwark against enemies, the flowers turned the wall into a keeper of treasures within. They bespoke a somber beauty now, all turned to seed.

"Poor Wolsey," Elizabeth said at last. "What will become of him?"

Charles picked up a stick and threw it as he walked.

"I do not know, but 'twill not be good, for she hates him and his power over the king. Aye, I believe his days may be numbered."

"Then we are all at risk, for if she is of that nature, she will brook no one being close to Henry other than herself."

They completed their walk in silence. As Charles' horse was brought from the stable, he turned to her one last time.

"I came to tell you these things, but also to warn you."

She waited.

"The king plans to see you tomorrow. He is riding from Richmond to Greenwich to see Anne, and told me he plans to stop and visit you and Coudenoure. Likely, it is because he trusts your counsel and will tell you just what I have just told you now."

Elizabeth nodded.

"I will think upon how to approach the matter," she assured him, "But tell me, does the Lady Anne Boleyn know of Coudenoure and the King's attachment to it?"

Charles looked at her with a seriousness and a sadness she had never seen in him before.

"Let us hope not." He tipped his hat and was gone.

The front door of the manor was slightly ajar, and as Charles turned his steed, Agnes stepped out. She stood with Elizabeth watching the horse disappear into the falling night.

"I do not like this." She put her arm protectively around Elizabeth. In turn, Elizabeth wrapped her arm around Agnes' waist.

"I agree. But how to counter? Perhaps the king will show the way tomorrow."

"Perhaps." Agnes replied without feeling. "But whether he does or does not, we must plan - we must consider Constance."

Elizabeth nodded, and they turned and went inside.

*****

As promised, King Henry appeared mid-morning at the door of Coudenoure. Elizabeth welcomed him and indicated that she wished to walk.

"Ah, my Elizabeth I cannot," Henry exclaimed, "…for my leg is bothering me greatly and I do not have much time. Let us sit by the fire, can we not?"

As they settled into their routine chairs in the library, Prudence appeared with a tray of sweet cakes and glasses of cider. As the king eyed the delicacies, he spoke to her.

"Prudence, you will make us all fat if you keep this up!"

Prudence declined to state the obvious.

"I am glad your Highness likes my treats," she bowed deeply.

"Tell me," Henry asked, "How are you situated here at Coudenoure?"

"Majesty, if I were able to choose a life for myself and my children, I would choose Coudenoure over any other place."

She bowed again and left.

"You run a strange establishment, Elizabeth. Your servants are your friends, and they love you as family."

"They are my family, Henry. And yours as well."

She could almost see the tension leaving his body as he propped his foot on the ottoman.

"You know, she still remembers my favorites, even after all this time!"

He was like a child in a sweet shop, and he and Elizabeth spent some moments choosing which cakes to eat first. Once that decision had been made, they both leaned back in satisfied silence, until, licking his fingers, Henry finally spoke.

"Elizabeth, you know that I seek an annulment of my marriage with Catherine," he began.

"You wish to live your life according to the principles of our God and his Son."

Henry sighed with relief, as though Elizabeth's support and understanding were what he desperately needed.

"Exactly. I believe that by marrying Catherine I displeased God and I must set that aright for my life to be as He intends it. Does not Leviticus say if a man shall take his brother's wife they shall be childless?"

Elizabeth reached for a second cake.

"It does, Henry, and I believe you are right in your actions."

He also found a second sweet before continuing.

"I must talk to you, Elizabeth, about a very sensitive matter. It concerns God's plan for my life."

Elizabeth listened.

"'Tis not enough that I make amends for disobeying God by divorcing Catherine. I must also produce an heir, a son, to carry on the Tudor line."

Elizabeth remembered her conversation with Agnes the evening before.

"Henry, you must put your mind at ease. Coudenoure, and I stand with you absolutely. I believe you must remarry in order to secure the throne for your line."

Once again, Henry sighed with relief.

"Why do others not see this?" he asked petulantly. "It is as though the world is against me in this matter, and yet I stand for what God wants, not what I want."

Elizabeth nodded.

"I think, Sire, that you must stay your course if that is what your conscience dictates. Your heart will always follow if you lead with purity of thought and Christian actions."

"Elizabeth, I knew you would understand! You are of my heart, dearest, and give me the truest counsel possible."

"There are others, Henry, who love you too. I am thinking of Charles."

"Yes, dearest, he does love me, but of all those upon this earth, only the two of you seem to know me."

Elizabeth moved the conversation forward.

"I know that you have spoken fondly of one Anne Boleyn. Is it possible you could come to love her and perhaps sire a child with her? That perhaps might be much the easiest way."

He nodded enthusiastically.

"She is my sweetest love, Elizabeth, and will give me a son when my divorce is final. 'Tis God's will, I am certain."

"Then, Majesty, you must proceed along those lines, for to do otherwise would put you in grave danger of mortal sin."

Elizabeth listened intently as Henry rhapsodized about the beauty and intelligence of his lady love, Anne. Charles was right: he could barely utter a sentence or an opinion without her name attached to it.

"And would you believe, my dearest, that Wolsey has procrastinating shamelessly about securing the divorce? It is treasonous, and Anne agrees! I believe he would rather lose all than support me in this fundamental and Christian issue."

Elizabeth tsked, and Henry stayed silent.

"What will happen to him?" she asked.

"If he cannot secure my divorce, then it will be because he does not wish to, and to go against me in this matter is nothing but high treason."

"He manages many administrative details for your Highness," Elizabeth said. "Do you have anyone who can replace him?"

"He has a man, Cromwell, whom I believe can get me what God intends me to have."

Later, as Henry left, Agnes joined Elizabeth in the library.

"I could not hear everything - Constance was hovering in a most annoying manner. Did you tell him what we need him to believe?"

"I did Agnes," she responded, "And I believe Constance will remain safe, at least until Anne Boleyn sits upon the throne. But I also believe that it is impossible that she will not learn of Coudenoure."

"Perhaps she will not."

"Women like that do not leave fate to chance. You may be assured she will learn of us, and then our troubles begin."

Constance replaced the mortar in the wall.

Chapter Thirty-Seven

February 20, 1530

Thomas Cromwell waited patiently in the great hall of Cawood Castle. The dark paneled wood which lined the room spoke of its ancient beginnings under King Athelstan five centuries before. The stone floor with its wide mortar seams and huge limestone blocks bled the cold through Cromwell's shoes and stockings until his feet were almost frozen.

"Boy, light a fire." He spoke sharply to the small child who sat listlessly by the hearth. Only embers remained from the previous evening and they gave no heat to the room. Shuffling his burlap shoes along the floor, the urchin did as he was told and Cromwell continued to inspect his surroundings. He sat near a floor to ceiling window, the only light source in the hall. The chair he occupied was comfortable and worn, and clearly ecclesiastical in purpose. Its velvet cushions were papist red, and the chair itself was placed in front of a heavy desk carved with liturgical scenes from the Passion.

A creaking sound erupted into the great silence and Cromwell turned to find Thomas Wolsey standing in the doorway. He bowed as the old man came forward and took his seat behind the desk. The past few months had left their marks clearly upon the Archbishop's face. He still wore the luxurious velvets and satin allowed by his office of Papal Legate, and his zucchetto still sat jauntily upon his wayward hair, but beneath the majestic clothing was a frail man with a hollow chest. He coughed deeply.

"You are keeping warm?" Cromwell asked kindly.

"Indeed, but towards what end I know not," his companion's voice was the definition of melancholy. No one brought drinks or food, and when the boy had finished his work at the hearth Cromwell dismissed him. They sat in the huge space alone listening to the crackling of the wood in the fire. At last Wolsey spoke.

"You know, do you not, that I have been called back to London?"

"Well, sir, if this cold and dreary castle is all that is offered to you as the Archbishop of the land, then I think 'tis a good development." Cromwell's wry remark did not seem to register with Wolsey.

"Treason. I am charged with treason." He coughed and spit into a small pot on the desk.

Cromwell leaned forward and spoke in urgent tones.

"You must fight, man, or you are lost. That woman shall have your head, and she will be happy to have it."

Wolsey waved his hand to indicate he wished silence from his friend.

"Do you know, the King has taken Hampton Court? I knew even as I built upon its ruins that I was reaching beyond my station, but how could I not build it? 'Tis a beautiful palace, and it was mine."

He paused before adding, "Mine for a moment."

Cromwell said nothing.

"And did you know, the tapestries there are the finest weaves available? Flemish, all of them. And the paintings..."

It was Cromwell's turn to silence his friend.

"You are babbling on about riches, sir, when you need to turn your thoughts to your life and how to escape the clutches of that evil witch."

Wolsey smiled sadly.

"My life is gone," he coughed again, "...and all I have left are my things. I love them. Did you know that I am the son of a butcher? Indeed. And yet I own Hampton Court and all that is within its lovely walls."

Cromwell rose in disgust. He could not fathom what would make a man such as Wolsey give up and surrender. Perhaps he was more ill than the cough suggested, but even so.

"When do the king's men come?" he asked.

"Tomorrow."

"I came to tell you to fight, but you seem not to be interested."

"Go, friend, for I will see God shortly. And Thomas, take a care for your own head, for that witch will come for it too one day."

The fire had reached a roaring pitch, and Cromwell left his friend sitting at the desk, looking out the window, already waiting for the king's men.

Chapter Thirty-Eight

October 11, 1533

Elizabeth pulled the heavy wrap tighter around her shoulders and pulled the hood over her head. She wore a blue woolen cap, the type worn by sailors when the sea turned cold and damp. A matching scarf was wrapped warmly around her throat. Agnes had begun knitting such small things when her eyes could no longer discern the delicate embroidery patterns she had always loved and worked upon. Autumn was early this year, but Elizabeth was oblivious to its beauty and its unusual cold. She had other thoughts on her mind.

News had reached Coudenoure of Wolsey's fall from grace, and of Cromwell's subsequent rise. She had never known Wolsey but she had never feared him either. His reputation had captured the two elements of his brilliant nature: his administrative skills, and his love of luxury. Instinctively, she had known he posed no threat to her small world. The king's inventory of palaces was well above thirty, and the monies given to Coudenoure each year were small relative to the king's other households. The fact that Coudenoure was never used on progress nor even mentioned in official accounts of the king's households gave her a sense of security from the prying eyes of those who would know the king's business at such a small estate.

But a new man was now responsible for Henry's households, and Elizabeth knew almost nothing of him. Was he an ally of the new queen? Would he question the king about his support of Coudenoure? Or perhaps the king would alert Cromwell to the private nature of the arrangement. And the king's pronouncements on the new church and his role in it as supreme leader - would they be questioned upon these issues?

Life at Coudenoure had a dreamlike quality to it - the seasons rolled gently through the year, and events at the manor were of interest only to those who lived there. After the turmoil of her youth, Elizabeth had come to appreciate the never-changing atmosphere of her estate, and her management of it reflected her need for regularity in her daily affairs. She had raised Constance as her father had raised her, and Agnes was always there to insure a continuity of tradition and community. But suddenly the realm far and wide was being torn asunder by new ideas, new modes of thought. Would Coudenoure survive?

Some years earlier, Elizabeth had decided that her legacy to Constance would be not only the estate but even more importantly the library at Coudenoure. Constance was of the same ilk as her mother, and scholarly learning had, over time, become a critical component of her nature. She took Coudenoure and its timeless grace for granted. She bought and traded manuscripts with a wide range of bibliophiles just as Thomas had done before her, and her thrill with each new acquisition was almost humorous in its intensity. When Henry came to visit, the two of them frequently sat together examining these purchases and discussing the ideas contained within. The extension of the library's holdings was a consuming interest for both of them and until now Elizabeth had had no reason to worry about the cost of books and manuscripts bound for Coudenoure. But she knew that on occasion, their cost was more than a year's worth of maintenance for the entire estate. Would the king's new man, Cromwell, become curious about these purchases and trace them to her manor?

She wondered if the years of joyous isolation had made her unduly fearful about her situation, but she did not truly believe so. Frequently, she and Prudence and Agnes would look at the cost of running the estate and compare it to the revenue received from their few tenants and the farm produce sold in the city. The numbers were always close enough, giving a sense of security to the women. But the library. The books.

Beyond all the chatter about Coudenoure which went round and round in her mind, she knew that it was just a veil to cover for her true concern: Constance. The child was now the woman, and Elizabeth knew that despite the discipline of her subterfuge, she had long ago deduced her parentage for herself. Indeed, when she and Henry sat together the resemblance was breath-taking, even down to certain mannerisms they shared. How would her future unfold? With her startling likeness to Henry, placing her at court would have been difficult if not impossible under Catherine. But Anne? There was no question that Constance would be endangered should the new queen even lay eyes upon her.

The matter of Constance's future came up time and again in her conversations with Henry, but neither knew what the best course might be - and it never occurred to them to ask Constance herself.

As Elizabeth slowly walked the perimeter path, she saw Henry riding up the long drive. As she waved he dismounted and came to meet her.

"Henry, should you not be with Anne? She gives birth now any day!"

Henry laughed.

"By god, Elizabeth, you are right! She is retired to her chamber even now. I will have a son! An heir to whom I shall pass my kingdom! Truly, truly I am a happy man this day."

Elizabeth smiled at his jubilation. His marriage to Anne and his certainty of producing a son with her had rolled years away from him until he was once again had the bearing of a man whose life had purpose and meaning.

"I had to leave Greenwich to see you, if only for a moment."

Elizabeth waited.

"Agnes tells Charles that you are troubled by the future."

"Charles and Agnes are thick as thieves, your highness."

Henry laughed again.

"Indeed. But I come to tell you that your worries are for naught. Put them away, dear friend, for I have spoken to Cromwell about my special love for Coudenoure and he will see to it that our secret abode remains ever thus."

Elizabeth breathed deeply.

"Oh, Henry, thank you. I have been nervous, seeing the changes all about me and my little world. I am afraid I have come to depend upon you and Coudenoure for everything."

He looked at her lovingly.

"You may always depend upon me for everything, Elizabeth, for you are my love. And do not leave it to Charles and Agnes to tell me of your fears - you must share them with me so that I may alleviate them."

Elizabeth wept with relief.

"Henry, go to your new wife. You will soon have the son you deserve and I and all of Coudenoure with me will await the ringing of the church bells telling us the good news. Today is the seventh, an auspicious number indeed. I will pray for Queen Anne to be delivered safely of your son."

She gave him an impetuous hug and he laughed as he walked hurriedly back to his steed. In turn, she went quickly back into the house.

"The queen is in labor," she announced. "We must all pray that she delivers the king's son safely."

Evening came on, and still the church bells did not ring out the glorious news. The next morning, Elizabeth found Charles and Agnes seated in the kitchen, talking quietly. Prudence pretended to be busy kneading a shapeless mound of sticky flour on the nearby long table, and the scullery maids had been dismissed. The east light of the rising sun poured in through the swirled glass of the huge windows and gave the room a festive air. A low fire crackled merrily in the great hearth as if confirming the mood, but a plate of fruit sat untouched between Charles and Agnes, and their conversation was fretful.

"Dear God, tell me the queen is fine," she said anxiously.

"Lady Elizabeth, the queen is fine," Charles answered glumly, "And so is her daughter."

Elizabeth gasped.

"What? You are mistaken, surely!"

Agnes looked at her wryly as Charles spoke again.

"Ask the name of the child, my lady."

Elizabeth looked at him not knowing what he wanted.

"Elizabeth. He has named his daughter Elizabeth."

Chapter Thirty-Nine

March 1, 1536

Constance had left her hair braided the prior evening to facilitate her plan. Before her maid came to stoke the morning fire, she was up and dressed, quietly peeking out her bedroom door. The tallow candles which kept away the midnight dark in the hall were beginning to sputter and go dark themselves, a sure indication that dawn was well on the way. Turning back, she packed her small easel with her paints, a small clean canvas and her mother's tiny painting stool. With one last look at the room, she slipped out and tripped lightly down the main stairwell before turning through the kitchen and heading out a side door. The air was chilly, but her woolen cloak and hood protected her against the breeze.

The night before had been a painful one, and she wished to make it up to her mother. For years, the unspoken secret of her birth had danced around the edges of many conversations at Coudenoure. The reasons for keeping her in the dark had always seemed nonsensical to her, and she and Mary had discussed the situation many times. Was it out of fear of the king? That could not be, since he routinely stopped by Coudenoure and always insisted on speaking to her and asking her after her health. Perhaps, then, it was fear of another attack, like the one which had occurred when she was just a small child? But that could not be the reason either - clearly, her paternity, if not known for certain was suspected by those at court and beyond. Indeed, she had often wondered if the occasional visitor her mother received from King Henry's court was there to inquire about Coudenoure or her mother, or if they were actually there to catch a glimpse of the child whom, so it was rumored, could be no one else's but Henry's.

But then again, perhaps those were only superficial reasons for keeping the details of her birth safely hidden from the world. Time and again, Mary returned to the fact that Constance had been born out of wedlock, and for the circumstances to be known and bruited about was tantamount to calling Elizabeth the lowest of whores. Remember, Mary always told her, that the plan may not have been to remain so secluded at Coudenoure. Perhaps Elizabeth had been intended to marry or attend court. Her reclusive lifestyle at Coudenoure had not been a choice so much as a gradual accretion of circumstance and fear over and around her until, like a pearl grown from a tiny grain of sand, she had embraced what her life had become.

The evening before had begun as usual, with Agnes, Elizabeth, Constance and Prudence sewing happily before the fire in the kitchen. Mary was at her own cottage putting her three children to bed. In the years to come, Constance was never certain what made her choose that evening above all others to force the issue. Agnes was railing about the king trying to replace the pope, Elizabeth was telling her he was not, and Prudence was planning the feast she intended to cook for Shrove Sunday. It was no different from any other evening. Perhaps that simple fact, more than any other, was responsible. Constance was frustrated with the lack of answers and the constant wall of silence encountered whenever it seemed the conversation might head in the direction of her birth. That night, she decided she had had enough and she looked up from her hoop.

"Auntie Elizabeth, you are not my aunt. You are my mother."

Three needles stopped mid-air, but no one looked up, and so she pressed on.

"I know this because I sometimes slip into your bedroom and peer into the looking glass you have there. I can only be the daughter of King Henry, for I am his female counterpart in every way. Consuelo never lay with the king, and young Agnes and I were not sisters. I am your daughter and I need to hear you say it."

Elizabeth sighed, realizing that Constance would not be put off. She put her embroidery down and looked at her.

"Child, 'tis true. You are my daughter and your father is the king."

And just like that, the secrets were at an end. Elizabeth lay a hand on her daughter's sleeve but Constance was suddenly, inexplicably angry and shook it off.

"Why, mother? Why did you lie?"

"Constance, you will not be calling your mother a liar in this house!" Agnes looked up in anger at the young woman. "We all did what we thought was best."

"Best for whom, Agnes? 'Twas not *best*, 'twas only *convenient*."

"That is not true," Elizabeth began, "There are dangers associated with being the king's child, Constance, and you are not old enough…"

"I am older than you were when you welcomed him into your bed!"

A gasp went round the small circle and Constance rose as she threw her embroidery aside.

"I have spent my life as another's child, and you seem to believe that is fine. Do you not see what pain you have caused me?"

She was crying now and could not stop herself.

"I wish you were not my mother! That is what I wish! Consuelo would never have kept me in the dark if you had not forced her to do so!"

She ran from the room, leaving her companions open-mouthed and alarmed. Elizabeth rose to follow her but Agnes put a strong hand on her arm forcing her back into her seat.

"Shhh, no, she will need to be alone for a moment. What she has known for many a year if finally confirmed for her."

"But she says she wishes I were not her mother!"

Prudence finally spoke.

"She says what she says in anger, Elizabeth, that is all. She has a wonderful life and she knows it, but she is young, and wishes to rebel. Her birth is all she has to rebel against. And so she does. Agnes is right - by morning she will be fine."

They continued speaking in low tones until the fire was almost gone, and they made their way together up the stairs. The servants had lit the night tallows, and Elizabeth hesitated outside Constance's room. Agnes gave her a look and she ignored it, opening Constance's door quietly. There was no movement and Elizabeth moved to the bed, listening to the quiet breathing of her child. She pulled and adjusted the covers around her, and smoothed her cheek before leaving as quietly as she had come. Constance waited until she was gone to turn over and stare at the ceiling.

She knew she had no right to accuse her mother, and that in every way she had wronged her by shouting at her and screaming such frightful things at her. And so she decided to make it up to her by giving her a painting. When Elizabeth was younger, she would take Constance to the ridge which separated Greenwich Palace from Coudenoure. It was her favorite place to paint and provided a commanding view of the estate. But years earlier the older woman had ceased making the journey, for her knees would no longer accept the climbing. She frequently expressed remorse that she had never captured a morning's frost upon the great landscape, and Constance determined that she would give her just that to express remorse over her outbreak.

The morning was clear and cold, and a white lacy frost covered the ground. Constance loved this walk, for it changed with each season. In the winter, the naked forms of nature were evident all around her. The trees stood naked with their great arching branches; wild roses exposed their brambled interiors while wheat grass and the decaying forms of echinacea and lavender covered the ground with soft and gentle cloak of brown. But spring would arrive shortly, and hazy color would begin to float upon the meadow. The trees would become clouds of lime green and crocuses would appear from nowhere. The brilliant colors of spring were slowly replaced by the mature greens and soft colors of summer, which in turn gave way to the breezy softness of autumn reds and yellows. Yes, each season different in its turn.

She had studied her mother's own work painted upon the ridge and knew the perspective and the place from which she loved to paint. She soon settled down and opening her small travelling palette, she began to paint. Many hours later, she was startled to hear hooves upon the ridge. Turning, she saw a solitary figure on a horse which hesitated and slowly picked its way across the rising ground behind her. But no sooner had she turned than the horse was pulled up short, and the figure on its back sat perfectly still, gazing at her intently. After some moments, spurs were put to its flanks, and it was not until the animal was almost upon her that Constance realized the heavily cloaked rider was a woman. She dismounted and threw back her hood.

"Tell me, young woman, do you always paint upon the King's land?"

Constance smiled unsteadily, wondering to whom she spoke.

"Oh, 'tis not the king's estate, my lady, but my own. It is called Coudenoure, and its boundary with Greenwich is at the base of this hill."

Constance nodded to indicate the property line. As she did so the hood fell from away from her face. The woman looked at her sharply before a jagged whisper escaped her lips.

"So the rumor is true."

Constance said nothing, but began to feel uneasy.

"Coudenoure." She spit the word out. "And tell me, what is thy name?"

"I am Lady Constance de Gray."

"A lady? Dressed like that?" The woman laughed and Constance's uneasiness became tinged with intense dislike. Over the years, her mother and Agnes had told her of tales of the royal court, where some women judged others of their sex based upon the fineness of their clothing. Coudenoure was utterly lacking in such ways, and Constance was quick to come to its defense.

"Aye, indeed, my lady, I am. This is my painting frock, and I am sure you will agree that keeping one's hair braided and up is the best way to avoid getting paint in it. 'Tis a shabby look, but I assure you, 'tis very workable." She paused deliberately before adding, "But I do confess that my usual garb is not much finer. At Coudenoure, we do not set store by such things. Do you not agree 'tis the best way?"

The woman's eyes narrowed and Constance continued.

"Your dress is fine indeed, my lady, and I would wager that you ride forth from Court, at Greenwich?"

The woman laughed.

"Is that what you would guess, eh?"

"Indeed," was Constance's only response. It did not please the woman, which in turn pleased Constance.

"Tell me, what is thy mother's name?"

With the certainty that the previous evening's conversation had brought her, she said it proudly and simply.

"Elizabeth. My mother is the Lady Elizabeth."

A hissing sound came from the stranger and Constance almost backed away.

"And tell me, thy father? Who is thy father, *child*?"

Constance panicked for a moment, realizing suddenly why her mother had kept her secret for so many years. If she were to tell the truth, there would be trouble, of that she was certain. So she stood straight, looked the stranger squarely in the face, and lied.

"Thomas, my lady. My father is Thomas of Coudenoure."

The woman continued to stare at her in silence. Finally, she remounted her steed and without a word, turned and trotted away. Constance was not certain of her feelings. She had certainly acquitted herself well for Coudenoure and felt a deep satisfaction and pride for having done so, but at the same time, she was deeply suspicious of what had just occurred. What was a woman doing riding out alone on the king's property? Who was she? Some errant maid accidentally separated from her party? That was the most likely explanation, and yet the woman did not conduct herself as a maid. She was shrill, demanding and seemed shocked by Constance's lack of awe. Whatever the truth, Constance knew it deserved to be reported quickly back to the manor.

She waited until the sound of the hooves had died away and the figure had disappeared back down the hillside. Quickly, she packed up and took the more direct, but difficult, path back to Coudenoure. She was covered in dirt and brambles by the time she ran up the drive and threw open the door, calling for her mother.

"Elizabeth! *Mother*!"

Agnes stomped heavily from the library while Prudence and Elizabeth ran from the kitchen.

"What is it, Constance?"

"A woman on a fine steed and beautifully dressed was on the ridge just now. I was already there painting, and she questioned me closely but I stood my ground." Despite her brave words she was trembling.

Elizabeth hugged her tightly.

"'Tis nothing, Constance, just a woman from Greenwich Palace, likely. Come sit, and tell us the conversation."

Constance did as she was told, and an ominous cloud seemed to descend upon the foursome as she spoke. When she had finished, Elizabeth asked, "What did this woman look like? 'Tis possible we know her?"

"That is the strangest thing of all, mother."

"Why?" asked Prudence.

Constance looked at Elizabeth.

"She looked just like you, mother. *Just like you*."

Agnes left the others to pick apart the conversation. She made her way to the back of the manor to the stable, and rapped sharply on the door with her cane. A sleepy stable boy appeared.

"You, wake up! 'Tis true that Lord Brandon keeps you informed of his whereabouts?"

"Why, my lady, you know 'tis true."

Agnes shook her head.

"'Tis a manner of speech, boy. Now tell me, where is the lord?"

The dark haired young man rubbed his chin and thought for a moment.

"I think he is at Westhorpe Hall, ma'am, for I believe he intends to ride to London shortly and then on to Greenwich to hunt with the king."

"So you know not where he is?" Agnes snorted and thought for a moment.

He shook his head.

"You must find him. Begin at Westminster in London, and if his lordship is not present, then return south to Greenwich and wait for him there. Do you understand?"

The lad nodded.

"I need you to ride the fastest horse in the stable…" she used her cane to point at a huge, black destrier in the first stall.

He shook his head vehemently.

"I cannot ride that horse for it is the king's mount as you know well."

Agnes whacked him on the leg with her cane.

"Do as I say, you nit, and when you find him, tell him I must see him at once on the most urgent business."

"If he is not at leisure, to whom do I give this news?"

"No one." Agnes put her face very close to his. "And if you dare tell anyone else where you are from or why you ride so hard to see lord Brandon, I shall make sure the king knows you took his horse."

"Wait…" he began puzzling it out.

"Just GO!" screamed Agnes.

Within five minutes he was on his way.

Agnes turned back towards the manor trying to ascertain its defensibility. Constance's recounting of her conversation on the ridge, and her description of the woman to whom she spoke, left no doubt in Agnes' mind that Queen Anne was now aware of Coudenoure. For reasons which she could not fathom, she felt threatened. She did not attempt to parse the deeper wells of her flawless intuition, but reacted in a practical manner. If a threat were abroad, then Coudenoure, and its hidden treasure, must be defended. But how? She realized that no one at Coudenoure knew how to reach out to King Henry. He appeared when he appeared and left when he left. There was never any rhyme nor reason, and over the years his visits had become routine and yet remained unpredictable. Never could Agnes remember a time when anyone from the estate had actually gone to court to seek him out.

Only Charles Brandon had recognized the situation and only he understood the intricacies of both the King's relationship to Coudenoure and to the court. After the last attempt to take Constance and use her with malicious intent against Henry, Charles had quietly begun keeping Agnes informed of his own whereabouts, knowing full well that as a nobleman but not the king, he would be infinitely easier to approach successfully in time of need. So many layers of yeomen, guards, courtiers, walls, palaces and supplicants surrounded Henry that it would be almost impossible for anyone to navigate them all, particularly if time were critical.

Agnes wondered how long Coudenoure would be vulnerable to the Queen's whims: how long before Charles and the King realized they were desperately needed at Coudenoure? Should Queen Anne be successful in whatever scheme she might devise, their only hope lay with the king's protection. The manor was staffed adequately for their needs, but it was a tiny operation. She listened to distant sounds of the old smithy's hammer upon some piece of farm equipment. O'Connor was a good man, but aged like herself. Beyond that, she heard the shouts of the miller at the small wheel which produced flour from the grain of their own fields. The stable bustled with men, but many of them were very young, and their skills beyond their immediate jobs unknown and untested. They had no one upon whom to rely in a trice. But it had always been thus.

She spat as she intoned the queen's name and went back inside.

Chapter Forty

Anne threw herself off her mount and hurried past the bowing and curtseying courtiers and ladies. She ran lightly up the stairs and down a long hallway at the end of which lay her own quarters. Musicians strummed quietly in the large room while several of her ladies practiced their dance steps.

"Where is the King?" she demanded of no one and everyone.

"My Queen, he is inspecting his new fortifications on the coast, and I believe afterwards he will ride here to Greenwich for hunting. We have been worried about you, for we knew not why you went alone into the woods."

"I am the Queen, am I not? I ride as I please?"

She did not say that rumors of the king's latest dalliance, coupled with her recent miscarriage, had caused her to seek peace in the solitude of a quiet ride through the forest, to find a place where her nerves were not constantly jangled by considerations of the court. She needed to lay out a plan to secure her own future and that of her child and she had always been one to think when riding in solitude. This time, however, her plan was thwarted and her anxiety was evident to everyone in the room. The king kept a long-time mistress and her bastard daughter at a neighboring estate. This could only be because he placed them higher than her own daughter. It could not stand.

There was no answer to her question and she continued.

"And Cromwell? Where is the Master of the Purse?"

"At Whitehall, Majesty."

She nodded with satisfaction and dismissed all but one of the women.

"Help me. I must change and leave quickly."

The woman began unlacing the Queen's sleeves but mid-point, Anne stopped her.

"No, no, I must think. I can do this and you must go and tell my brother I ride to Whitehall. Tell him he is to meet me there. Tell him alone and no one else."

The young woman bowed and hurried from the room. Anne continued with stripping off her own clothes until finally, she stood in only a chemise and breeches. She darted into a long room which opened off the main one and served as her wardrobe, then quickly selected an older riding habit. By the time the maid returned, she was dressed and anxious to leave.

"You have told him?"

The woman nodded.

"Now, whenever the king should arrive, tell him I decided to go to London and inspect the plans for my new wing at Whitehall. Tell him I return in one day."

Again, the woman nodded and Anne pushed her aside as she strode purposefully from the room. She slipped out a side door and after a short directive to the groomsmen, waited impatiently until he reappeared with two horses, one for himself and one for the Queen. With no further words, they galloped towards London. She had not been at Greenwich more than half an hour's time.

The noon day sun belied the cold, and the blue sky was crisp with frost. Anne rode hard, driven by her thoughts of the morning's events.

So he has a daughter at Coudenoure - all was just as had always been rumored. After the birth of Elizabeth, in the back hallways and darkened corners of the palaces, she had heard the whispers as she walked proudly past with her royal child in arm. Initially, she had not understood - who was this other child who was more of the king than her own royal-born offspring? Her ladies had ferreted out the answer for her. There was, they said, a child bastard born on a nearby estate. At first, she had let it go from her mind. After all, the king likely had many such bastards. But they continued to bring her tidbits of information and detail about this particular child, and most disturbing of all was what she had seen and felt for herself that very morning.

The woman on the hilltop was Henry in female form - flaming red hair, square jaw and blue-gray eyes. Anne's steed settled into a steady gallop and she found other details coming to mind. The woman was tall, as was Henry, and had the slimness of youth yet. But there was something more, something ill-defined yet just as tangible as the horse upon which she rode which defined their similarity. She had heard others speak of this quality of personality over the years, and had noted that they too found it a mysterious force, one almost impossible to name. Whatever it was, they possessed it together as father and daughter and it was undeniable. Beyond that, however, was another quality which Henry did not possess - an air of kind intelligence. If he had ever possessed such a trait, it had long since been buried beneath necessities of state. The combination provided the bastard woman a presence beyond what was normally found in anyone, much less a young maid. She had, and here Anne spit as her steed roared on, a certain gravitas, given to those who were in all ways a cut above her own station.

What did this mean for her own child, Elizabeth? Anne had been in difficult positions before and as always, she was confident that if she marshaled her anger and her anxiety, she would find a way through it, one which would put her on the winning side. Her decisions so far confirmed this confidence. They were made with the long game in mind, and there was only one outcome which would satisfy her: this young Constance woman must go, for she posed a threat to her own dynastic plans. Most certainly if she were blessed with another pregnancy she would bear the King a son, but as the years began to slip by that was becoming less and less of a certainty. Even as she rode, she remembered the last in a line of lost pregnancies – it had been a son, and afterwards, for the first time, she found it difficult to keep the king's attention.

At first, it had meant nothing to her. But as the weeks had progressed, and as Henry had shown no further inclination to come to her bed, she began to feel an anxiety rising up in her chest. It was coupled with the knowledge that Henry's health was not as it should be. Routinely there appeared on his legs ulcerations which refused to heal and which seemed to sap him of any desire but to dull the pain through eating. His weight increased sharply until it was difficult for him to hunt and joust as he once had, a situation which only exacerbated his problems and his foul moods.

Even if he were to come to her, would there be issue? She was no longer certain, and so her dependence upon her daughter Elizabeth's position became pivotal to her own security as queen. This Constance must go. But how?

She finally arrived at Whitehall and tiredly dismounted, throwing the reins to the groomsman who had ridden behind her. She went inside and screeched for her maids in waiting to attend her. These were not her most trusted - they did not make progresses with her - but they would have to do.

A long bath and clean clothes helped settle her mind, and she finally sat down at her desk, writing a note for her brother to deliver for her to Hever Castle once he arrived. That done, she dismissed her retinue and went alone to Cromwell's chambers.

The passageway to his quarters was cold and only dimly lit. There were no rugs upon the cold stone floors, and no tapestries adorned the heavy stone walls. She walked on in silence and the yeomen bowed in deep obeisance as she passed each one. Their Tudor uniforms, red and black with gold braid trim, provided the only color and regalia to her solemn progress through the inmost chambers of Whitehall. Finally, she reached a wooden door guarded by two squires. They looked straight ahead as though not seeing her but bowed as though on cue.

"Where is Cromwell?" She dispensed with his usual title.

"He is not within, Majesty," came the reply from one of the men.

"When do you expect him back?"

They shook their heads to indicate they were not privy to such matters. Anne spoke in frustration.

"When did he leave?"

"He has been gone only a very short time, Majesty, and he left with a considerable number of account books and rolls."

So he would be gone sometime, she surmised. With a wave of her hand she ordered them to step aside. As she entered the room, she pulled the door behind her.

What the hallways leading to his chambers had lacked, Cromwell made up for in this, his own private working space. Deep pile carpets, huge and deeply hued in colors of burgundy and blue stretched from wall to wall. There were no tallow candles with their smoke and smell. Instead, beeswax candles with as many as three wicks burned all round and with the fire roaring in the fireplace the room was as bright as day. Leaded windows gave onto one of the many courtyards of the new palace, built onto York Place, Wolsey's previous London show place. If her intuition was correct, she would find what she was looking for here.

Thomas Cromwell was the king's great administrator, having supplanted Wolsey in the king's affections when the latter could not achieve a divorce from Pope Clement. But Cromwell had not stopped with that act of loyalty. It was he who had shuttered the monasteries and channeled their riches into Henry's coffers. As a result, Henry had more resources, more wealth, than any king before him. And such wealth translated into great power. But regardless of the monies which poured into Henry's accounts, Cromwell continued to keep the king's books down to the penny. He had watched good men come and go over issues as simple as a failure to collect the even minute fines and taxes for chasing down some poacher on the king's lands. Such would not be his fate.

Anne made her way to the huge, leather-bound volumes which lined the wall behind Cromwell's massive desk. As she suspected, he kept the accounts by estate, and she hurriedly pulled volume after volume from the shelves, looking for one particular account she was certain must exist. Half an hour passed, and she stomped the hard floor in frustration - it was not here. She sat in Cromwell's over-sized chair, considering the situation. Then, in but a moment, she laughed aloud, rose and pulled down from the shelf once again the final volume she had just replaced. She lay the heavy tome upon its front cover, and opened it from the back. Five pages in, she found what she was looking for. Across the top of the page was a single, underlined word: Coudenoure. So he had indeed been true to his suspicious nature and kept an account of the place. Undoubtedly, he did so surreptitiously in the very back of a volume of miscellaneous records of no great importance because he wanted it to remain as the king surely must have ordered - unknown and unaccounted for, secreted away just as his mistress was. But Cromwell could not risk himself and so here lay the account, open before her.

She perused the pages and her anger grew with each entry. Henry had supported Coudenoure for as long as he had been king. Here were books ordered by the hundreds, improvements upon the estate, horses for the stables and kitchen stock equal to or better than that of her own hearths.

"So the mistress Elizabeth is learned," Anne observed as she read the lists of books purchased or traded. "And she has a taste for rare manuscripts."

"And here, she must be artistic, for how many canvases and paints! And from Italy yet! Who is this woman who lives higher than the Queen of England?"

But one thing was missing from the inventory - clothes for Elizabeth, Constance and their ladies. She poured over each page carefully, but there was no indication of any such finery purchased for those on the estate. Instead, there was a yearly notation of plain linen brought from France. That was all. There were wages, but only for minimal staff: stable hands, yardsmen, farm workers and smithies, but very little else. There were no charges for guards, and none for yeomen or squires. Anne leaned back and thought. So this Elizabeth, whoever she was, was a learned, yet simple creature. She obviously had no need for trappings, so how then, Anne wondered, had she kept the king dancing attendance and paying for Coudenoure all these years? Her anger and jealousy grew with each entry she read.

So absorbed was she in her work she did not hear the door open and close.

"Queen Anne, and how are you today?" Cromwell had entered the room. Dressed in his customary dark mantle, he looked at her quietly, warily.

She glanced at him deliberately, turned her attention back at the account book with even greater deliberation, then slowly, methodically, tore each page pertaining to Coudenoure from the volume. Looking back at him, she folded the pages and tucked them into her bosom. The vindictive fury evident on her face could have scorched a thousand lands.

"So you know of Coudenoure?"

Cromwell met her gaze and said nothing.

"Your queen has asked a question and you must answer."

"Yes, Majesty, I know of Coudenoure. 'Tis one of King Henry's smallest estates. It brings in no revenue to speak of."

She shook with silent rage.

"It is the *estate* of his *mistress* and his *bastard child*!" She flung a large china vase into the fire. Still Cromwell held his silence.

"And did you know of the king's bastard, Constance?"

Cromwell gave her a small, deferential smile.

"Majesty, there may have been many before you, but you know that only you did he make queen."

Anne was not mollified.

"If the King provides another coin - even a single one - to that place, I order you to tell me of it. *Do you understand?*"

Cromwell bowed but said nothing. Furious at his lack of responsiveness, Anne struck out and swiped her hand across his desk, creating chaos as his work. His ink, his whatnots, all fell to the floor in a giant splintering crash. She swept out and slammed the door behind her. She careened down the hallway, stopping only when she caught sight of her brother. Pulling him into a nearby chamber, she spoke hoarsely to him.

"My lady's maid has a note for you. You are to take it and ride to Hever Castle. I need three bowmen loyal to the Boleyn's and not to Henry, do you hear?"

George Boleyn looked at her in alarm.

"Anne, you cannot strip the king from the throne and put yourself upon it! 'Tis treason to even ..."

"Do not be *stupid*." She hit him on the side of the head before continuing. "I have this day found out that the king has a great mistress and a daughter who might one day replace our own Elizabeth in his line. Do you understand now? I must pull the bastard from the shadows along with its mother and expose them at court. Only then will our line, born of a *royal* marriage, be truly secure."

He nodded an immediate understanding.

"Where shall they go?"

"Tell them to take a barge, and not one of the king's, to the bend in the river just before Greenwich Palace. I shall look for them there should their services be required."

"And you? What is your next move?"

There was no hesitation in her response.

"I shall return to Greenwich, by barge, immediately, and await the king."

*****

Henry passed under the great arch of the Greenwich Wall at sunset. The day had worn on him badly, and the gentle snow which had begun to fall earlier in the afternoon chilled him to the marrow. He ignored the hordes of mendicants and vendors who pleaded with him to buy this or give aid for that. The saddest simply sat in the mud and dirt, wrapped in filthy rags with their dirty hands extended, as though a small display of alms might change their desperate situations. Surrounded by his men of arms, he was isolated to the extent that he wanted to be from these lost creatures, but Elizabeth always implored him to remember them, and almost without fail, he would pause at Greenwich Gate and throw a handful of sovereigns toward the waiting masses. He did so now before turning away and entering the regally quiet and ordered grounds of his favorite palace. Two beefy guards waited at the main palace entrance to assist him from his steed, and without a word he passed on through the heavy doors. A chorus of musicians and song pealed out from the main hall but he ignored it, as he did the myriad calls from maids and courtiers for the king to join them. Not today. His leg ached and as he moved step by slow step up the central stairway, he shouted for his doctor. It seemed an eternity before his men completed his disrobe and eased him into his new copper tub before the fire. One end of the bath abutted an interior wall and two faucets extended from it - one for hot water and one for cold. The hot water was fed from a hearth on the floor above, and Henry was thrilled with this particular renovation of his. As the water filled the tub around him, the aroma of medicinal herbs began to float upon the air. He sat with his leg on the edge of the bath and his doctor examined it as Henry drank the first of many glasses of wine.

"Well, Dr. Butts?" he asked. "And what do you find? Will the medicinals you put in my bath water be of help?"

"Let us hope so, Majesty." He looked up at Henry. "You have a recurring ulcer, and you must take care that it not become infected again as it did last year."

"And how much are you paid for such sage advice?" Henry smiled at the man, for he knew well there was no cure for the pustulating sores which afflicted his lower extremities. "And bleeding? Should we bleed them?"

The doctor shook his head.

"No, I think the problem lies not with the king's diet but with the king's mood."

Henry listened intently as the steward refilled his glass and the doctor continued.

"You must get out more and enjoy the fine air of the county," he began, "...and you must engage in sporting diversions, for we all know the salubrious benefits of exercise to your person."

"'Tis difficult, doctor, at my size," Henry observed.

"Well, to a lesser man, perhaps, but not to the King of England. Now, enjoy your bath and let your mind wander to pleasing thoughts, for anxiety is the devil of the flesh."

A loud knock on the door interrupted the sermon Henry was about to receive, and without warning, Anne appeared. The men present bowed and scraped their way from the room, and Henry pulled a cotton throw over the top of the tub.

"You did not ask permission."

"Nor did you."

He looked at his queen sharply. She was about to pounce but he was ignorant about what. Henry realized, however, that she was angry enough to ignore the sanctity of a man's bath in order to claw at him. Her dress was of an older style, the type she usually reserved for days when she would not be out and abroad, and her look was disheveled – the hem of her gown was muddied and still damp from some adventure unknown to Henry. He wondered idly what was coming his way, what was so important that she could not robe herself appropriately nor soothe her own anger.

"Nor did YOU!" Anne repeated her previous statement but with an ominous tone.

"I ask permission from no man, and certainly not my wife, for anything. What is it on your mind then?"

She looked at him with smoldering eyes.

"Coudenoure."

Henry cocked his head. So the Queen had learned his secret. Even though she said nothing more than the name, Henry noticed that her breath was hard, shallow and rapid. He was tired and had no desire to engage in the discussion she was apparently determined to have with him. His voice was weary with fatigue.

"What do you want, Anne?"

She threw back her head and gave a dramatic laugh.

"What do I want? Why, Henry, I want many things."

"List them."

"First, I would like to know why you have kept Coudenoure a secret all these many years." She pulled the pages from the account book from her bosom and threw them towards him.

"I told Cromwell to keep no record." Henry observed blandly.

"Well, you must take that up with the great Cromwell, for he did, and this afternoon, I found them."

"Apparently you did."

She was getting nowhere. She wanted him to feel her anxiety and rage - to engage with the matter at the level she now felt it. But Henry parried her at every opening, and rather than leaving to retrench and reconsider her strategy, she continued on relentlessly, seeking a crack in his armor in which to pour her rage.

"I believe I shall go and meet this Constance. I hear much about her."

Finally, she had his attention.

"I hear she is you, Henry, every inch your bastard child. And I am ordering her to court so that the world will judge her not as your royal offspring, but as your bastard issue. There will be no question as to which child was born in wedlock, and which was not."

"She does not come to court because I have not decreed that she may do so, and I will not. She is a learned woman, unusual, and will not be sullied by serving you or Catherine before you as a mere maid." He held her eyes and she knew instantly that this was a battle lost unless great care were to be taken.

"What hold does the mother have over you?" she almost spit the words. "Does she have some secret of yours that you wish to remain untold? Does she bewitch you with her womanly charms? What is it, Henry? Why do you persist in your relationship with this whore?"

Henry ignored the vulgarity of Anne's language and thought for a moment before closing his eyes and answering slowly.

"Only the hold the sky has on the sun, only the grasp of the gentlest of spring breezes upon a sprig of lavender, only…"

Anne interrupted him.

"You need give no more poetic responses. I have it now." She left quickly and he listened morosely as her footsteps faded away beyond the door.

"No good will come of this." He drained his glass. "Steward," he shouted, "…more wine. And guard…"

A yeoman stepped into the chamber from the shadowy hallway.

"Majesty?"

"Keep post outside Queen Anne's chambers this evening." Henry paused. "We have had a warning from a local knight, and we must ensure our persons are safe. She is not restricted in movement, but should she choose to leave her rooms, you must notify me at once."

The man bowed and disappeared.

"And I will deal with all of this tomorrow," Henry finished in a mumble to himself.

Chapter Forty-One

The day broke cold and promised rain. Anne was up before dawn, pacing in front of the window in her chamber. The fire needed stoking but she seemed not to notice the chill in the room. Instead, her lips moved silently as though she were rehearsing some great scene yet to be played. She ignored her maids' attempts to engage her. Confused and sleepy, they ordered a fire and a small repast from the kitchen, but nothing they did seemed to calm Anne's anger and anxiety.

The King had played another card last evening by posting a guard outside her door. Upon questioning, the man assured her he was there because of a minor threat to the palace revealed by a local knight. Anne had thanked him profusely and pretended both to him and her maids that she would be mindful of the threat and was grateful to the king for his concern. Nothing could have been further from her mind.

So he would block her from taking action by posting a guard? At her door, the Queen of all of England's, door? There was no fear in her, only anger and a rising sense of vindictive self-righteousness. Obviously, this woman, this witch at Coudenoure, had a power over the king that only a queen should have or exercise. It was her duty to the realm and to her husband to expose the evil which lay within the walls of that small manor. Before the sun was fully over the horizon, she had slipped away through the interior chambers assigned to her ladies. The rooms were interconnected and if one were familiar with their layout, one could easily avoid the main entrance to the Queen's wing and enter, or exit it, from some other, less grand entrance. Clearly, the king knew this and was using the guard's presence at the main door to send her a message. She would ignore it for his own sake.

She was dressed in riding gear, and had seen to it that her horse was ready. A groomsman and several guards waited patiently on their mounts for her arrival at the stable but she dismissed them all.

"I have a need for silence in which to think," was the only reason she gave for riding out alone. It was the second time in as many days and her escort thought nothing of it; she would, after all, be on the king's own property.

Not daring to use the main gate, she walked the horse through the servant's areas to a lesser known entrance used by tradesmen. Very few were about in the cold dawning of the day, and with her plain hood and dark cloak covering her garments she passed unnoticed. Once free of the palace, she rode north and crossed the main road well above the guard station. Looking behind to assure herself she had not been followed, she clicked her heels against the side of her horse and began to ride hard.

Stray remnants of the somber gray of the pre-dawn mixed with a heavy fog give her ride an eerie quality. She shook off the sense of foreboding it suggested to her and was glad to finally reach the bend where she had directed her own men await her arrival. A sigh of relief and power escaped her lips as the fog lifted to reveal a barge with her own heraldic crest on its side - a white falcon resting upon a clutch of red and white roses. These were her men and would do her bidding. No time was lost in traveling on to Coudenoure. By the time they turned onto the long straight drive a cold rain had begun to fall. Elizabeth was at the library window sipping her cider and called out for Agnes when she saw them.

"'Tis Queen Anne, I would imagine."

Elizabeth agreed just as Constance and Prudence entered the room. They needed no explanation.

"Did you send for Charles?" Elizabeth asked Agnes.

"Aye, but it may be a moment for our man must find his location first."

They sat, almost paralyzed by fear as the queen rode on and neared the door.

"Constance, you must go upstairs and hide."

"*Why*? Am I not the King's child? Mother, you are the best in every way, but you are not strong-hearted. You must not shrink from such a woman as this. If we stand together…"

"Constance," Elizabeth interrupted her harshly, "We can discuss my failings at a later date. That woman…" she nodded at the window, "…has bowmen with her who are not of King Henry's men. You see no Tudor rose on their livery."

"What does she want?" Constance asked. "Surely she understands that we are here at the king's good grace."

"I do not know what the lady wants, but it is not our health and the continued quiet of our lives, you may be sure," Elizabeth responded grimly.

Agnes hissed.

"You are right, Elizabeth, they are not the King's men - they wear her badge."

Elizabeth's breath quickened as the small procession continued its steady approach in the rain. The woman on the sole horse seemed oblivious to the weather and sat as though bolted to the great saddle of her mount.

"Daughter, quickly, go hide upstairs."

"No," Prudence interrupted. "No, you must go to my cottage. There is a small root cellar near the hearth - it is accessed by a door under the rug. Stay there, and we will come for you."

"Do not fret, mother, Agnes," Constance kissed them both before she and Prudence disappeared. Even as they slipped through into the kitchen a loud rapping came from the front hall. Elizabeth took a deep breath and got up to answer the door.

*****

"Majesty," Elizabeth repeated, bowing low, "My Queen you must know that the woman Constance you seek is not here."

Queen Anne's black eyes blazed as brightly as the fire. She had been stunned into deep silence when Elizabeth appeared at the door. Even her men had stepped back, aghast. They were looking at the queen's own shadow.

Elizabeth had bowed and was about to welcome Anne to Coudenoure when the queen brushed past her and into the hall. Seeing the door to the library open, she entered and found Agnes knitting doggedly before the fire. With aid from her cane, she rose and curtsied before sitting back down. As she did so, a small, almost imperceptible grating sound from the brickwork of the wall reached her ears, and she looked closely at her knitting to hide a satisfied smile: Constance was indeed her father's own daughter, recklessly brave in her support of those she loved.

With an imperious turn, Anne spoke her purpose.

"We are here for the Lady Constance."

"My good Queen, the Lady Constance is not here presently."

Anne's fury continued to rise as she looked upon Elizabeth. She understood Henry's ardor for her own self very clearly now. Indeed.

"The king desires her presence at his court."

Anne watched Elizabeth but could detect no sense of fear within the woman. She had no linking of how often Elizabeth had stared into the very gates of hell or that the pallor of the older woman's complexion was not her usual color. Elizabeth breathed steadily, knowing she must see them all through this moment despite her appalling fear. There was no question of Henry finding out and appearing, only a question of when. She must engage the queen and buy some precious time.

"My Queen Anne," Elizabeth began but Anne cut her off.

"Did you not hear me? I stated that I am here for the Lady Constance."

Elizabeth fought hard to maintain a deferential attitude. At her continued silence, the Queen changed tack and a treacly sweet tone covered her words.

"Lady Elizabeth, these bowmen are here to protect us as we ride back to Greenwich. Do not fear for your daughter's safety. She *is* your *daughter*, is she not?"

Anne could not stop herself so great was her jealousy and anger.

"And the *King's* daughter as well! Goodness, Madame, you must have a sorcerer's brew to have kept my husband enthralled so long."

Elizabeth began to tremble.

"Come, sit with me by the fire," Anne continued, "...and let us talk of Henry, and Constance, and of you yourself, Elizabeth. I wish to know what manner of woman you are. I am sure the King desires you to tell me all I wish to know."

One hour later, she had to admit a grudging yet furious admiration for the Lady Elizabeth. The woman had a spine of steel beneath her trembling presence and shortness of breath. Despite her wheedling, demanding, imploring, screeching, and ordering Elizabeth had refused to give up any detail about her relationship with the King, or about the bastard child Constance. Finally, Anne rose and stared down at Elizabeth, now almost crippled by her fear.

"Madame," she began, "Because I am sure the King would wish it, I shall give you one last chance to tell me where the Lady Constance is."

"Majesty," Elizabeth rose and bowed, "I tell you truly I do not know where she went or indeed, when she might return."

"You know 'tis treasonous to withhold information from your good and gracious Queen, do you not?"

Elizabeth said nothing, but again bowed deeply. Warming her hands before the fire, Anne spoke with an unnatural calmness.

"Since you do not trust your own Queen Anne, I fear I must leave these bowmen here to protect you from your very self. They do my bidding, and when the Lady Constance returns, they will escort her to Greenwich, where I will present her to the King and to the court. After all, why should such a bright flower, and the King's own blood, be hidden away here at this meaningless estate? Um? No, we shall show her to the world, and when we are done, we shall do the same with you."

She spoke sharply and quietly to her bowmen before leaving the room. Riding full tilt in what had become a driving rain, she returned to the barge which had delivered her men to Coudenoure. A canopy covered the seating, and she threw herself upon the cushions it protected as she pulled a nearby wrap around her. Even as her mind cautioned deliberation and thought her heart demanded action. There was no contest between the two.

"Greenwich," she ordered.

The boatsman turned southward.

Chapter Forty-Two

Henry woke with a blazing headache and an aching leg. He lay staring at the velvet tapestry which was draped over the tall frame of the bed. It depicted a hunting scene with him at its center as the hero. A great stag was being pursued through the woods and forest along the outer rim of the piece. As one's eyes were pulled into the center by ever increasing color and intricacy in the forest panoply, Henry was revealed in his finest hunting regalia. At his feet lay the princely beast, representing England and the realms of the Continent. Near the stag sat a small squirrel, denoting the obedience of the nations to Henry's will, and on one wrist sat a falcon as a symbol of his authority over both heavenly and earthly matters in his kingdom. He looked out from the tapestry boldly, as if questioning the beholder, and the old man in the bed sighed for his youth as he looked upon the great piece. A knock on the door provided welcomed respite from the melancholy he once again felt settling in upon his soul.

"My Liege! A fine stag has been seen recently near the Thames' edge - shall we bring him down?"

Henry laughed as Charles entered his bedchamber.

"I am laid up today, friend," Henry said with a great sadness in his voice, "And I may not hunt until my leg heals."

"Ah, well, even if we cannot hunt, let us ride, for I am in desperate need of fresh air. I understand there is a new maid at court and I wish to discuss her attributes in private."

He continued to cajole the king until Henry in mock frustration with him rose and dressed.

"Have them saddle my finest," he shouted to a guardsman in the hall, "...for I shall ride out with my annoying courtier here, Lord Charles."

A simple tray of fruit - dried figs, plums and apricots accompanied by bread and cheese appeared on a table. The steward left a jug of cider and bowed before leaving in silence. Charles looked at the tray as Henry continued to be dressed.

"What is this fare? 'Tis a woman's meal, it is. What are you thinking, my King?"

Henry grunted as the servant began lacing his great vest. In true frustration, he slapped at the servant's hands and dismissed him, tearing the heavy clothing off. Reaching to a nearby table he pulled a plain shirt over his head while responding to Charles.

"That," he pronounced, "Is what the good Physician Butts declares I must eat in order to allay the ulcerous festering which curses my leg."

"No meat?"

Henry said nothing but pulled on another shirt over the first for warmth and picked up a handful of the fruit along with a hunk of bread.

"Come, we will ride and afterwards I shall tell the good physician to look away while I eat a real dinner."

A stout cane was given Henry and they walked slowly down the hall and to the grand stairway.

"When will the architects be finished with your new chambers? Surely these stairs cannot be healthy for his Majesty."

"Aye, but 'twill be late in the spring of next year before my ground floor accommodations are complete. But I have ordered the tapestries. Perhaps when we return from our exercise I will show you the designs?"

"I should be honored."

They were mounted and riding slowly towards the perimeter wall when a loud argument just beyond the gatehouse reached them. Charles pulled up short and listened intently, cocking his head to catch the conversation.

"By God, that is Agnes' boy. Let us see what he wants."

"And you ride the King's own steed! Thief! You shall burn…" Two guards were dancing round the young stable boy from Coudenoure attempting in vain to pull him from his saddle.

"I must needs see Lord Charles Brandon. 'Tis urgent! 'Tis…quit clutching at me, man!" He beat at the guard with a switch he held in his hand.

Henry appeared through the gated archway and all activity ceased. The stable boy jumped from his mount and bowed quickly before running to the side of Charles.

"You must hear me in private," he said loudly.

"Can you speak louder? Lest anyone not hear you?" Charles laughed and indicated the boy should remount and follow the King and him to a quiet spot. Once aside, he spoke kindly to the young man.

"The guard speaks the truth," he observed. "For you ride the king's own horse."

The boy's eyes grew huge and he looked at Henry. Henry, in turn, said nothing, waiting to hear what urgent news came from Coudenoure. At last the boy spoke, his words pouring out in a torrential stream.

"'Tis Coudenoure, and the Lady Agnes says you must come at once!"

"Why? Tell us, lad!"

"I know not everything, but I do know that the young maid of the house, Lady Constance, did indeed see a woman upon the hill. But sire, I believe she saw a ghost, for the woman was like unto the great Lady Elizabeth! I hear she was dressed in finery and said many things to frighten..."

Henry knew all at once.

"Boy, ride through yonder gate and bring reinforcements to Coudenoure. Tell them you ride for the King."

The two horses cleared the road in two great strides before disappearing into the woods beyond.

Chapter Forty-Three

Elizabeth kept her eyes focused on the page in front of her. She sat before the fire in the library. Opposite her, Agnes knitted furiously. The Queen's two bowmen stood awkwardly at the window with their weapons by their sides. Not a word had been spoken in the hour or so which had elapsed since the Queen left. Only the fire crackling in the hearth gave evidence of activity in the room. Suddenly, the door from the great hall was thrown wide and back against its heavy hinges. Before them stood Prudence, drenched in sweat and pale as ice. She staggered into the doorway and leaned against its timbered frame. She spoke through a fit of violent coughing.

"My lady, 'tis the sweating sickness that took Adam yesterday. I fear I must have it for I am not well and can no longer stand." She collapsed in the door, effectively blocking passage in or out of the room.

"My God," Agnes was the first to react. She crossed herself before continuing and backing further away from Prudence. "'Tis true, my lady, for look at the sweat pouring from her. We are all in danger!"

The men backed themselves into a corner, a great fear written across their faces. Elizabeth turned to them.

"I must get cool water for the woman. Stay here, lest you be exposed by drawing nigh unto the poor creature!"

She picked up her skirts as she stepped over the fainting Prudence. As she ran into the kitchen, Constance caught her arm.

"Quickly, mother, we have no time!"

They ran together out the back of the kitchen to the stable. Its huge doors were thrown open and a giant steed stood saddled, ready to ride. The rain poured. Elizabeth hurried to a massive chest which sat nearby. She knelt and began clawing at its bottom. Beneath the hay and straw which covered the rough planks of the floor, she uncovered a small drawer. Reaching in her pocket, she found the key she had placed there earlier. Trembling, she opened the shallow drawer and pulled it out of the chest. Reaching behind it, she felt frantically for a hidden latch. Suddenly, the bottom side of the chest gave way, revealing a secret chamber. She ripped a heavy canvas bag from within it and rushed back to Constance, handing it to her daughter.

"Child, in here you will find all you need to make safe your escape."

"Mother, I long not to leave. 'Tis cowardly."

Elizabeth suddenly realized that Constance might not participate, thus endangering them all.

"Listen to me. Good Queen Anne is no *good* queen. I have been warned repeatedly by many that if she should find out you exist, she will stop at nothing to ensure your death, for your presence upon this earth is a shadow upon her own child's chances."

"Mother, the King has a legitimate daughter already, the Princess Mary! Even such a spiteful witch as Anne cannot deny that fact!"

"She intends not to deny it, but to bastardize the princess because of the annulment of Queen Catherine's marriage to Henry. And Mary is Catholic - and a Catholic will never again sit upon the throne of England. Constance, you are all that stands between that woman and her own dynasty and she will see to it that you do not long block her path. You must flee."

"And leave you? Mother?"

Elizabeth stroked her daughter's cheek and hugged her tightly as she whispered in her ear.

"Better I have a daughter who lives in a faraway land than a daughter who lives not at all."

Constance wiped tears from her own face and then from her mother's.

"What is in the bag?" she asked hurriedly, realizing that her mother's way was the only way.

"A bag of coin, for you will have to pay heavily for what you are about to do. Instructions there are within as well, which will see you through the worst of it - and a remembrance of me."

She wept as she pulled at the bodice of her dress. From around her neck she took a simple gold chain on which hung a ruby-encrusted cross. She pulled Constance closer and placed it around her slender, youthful neck.

"Do not forget me, my child, I pray of thee."

Constance hugged her firmly one last time before mounting the restless bay. She reached down and for a moment, their hands held tight. Then she was gone, racing out of the stable and through the muddied yard. Her mount easily took the low stone fence which defined the boundary between the farmlands of Coudenoure and the cottages of the servants. Elizabeth watched through the driving rain knowing that Constance would make for the hidden gate which lay within the great perimeter wall of the estate. Wiping her tears, she ran back to the house. She was met by shouting and screaming coming from the library. Running into the room, she was seized by a bowman.

"What manner of game is this?" he shouted in her face. "For I have seen you just now and you have sent the lady we seek away!"

Elizabeth screamed in pain as the bowman held her fast by her hair and hit her face.

"And this "creature"?" He pointed to Prudence's still figure lying on the floor by Agnes' feet. Agnes held her head in her lap, weeping.

"Was that the Lady Constance you put upon that steed?"

Before Elizabeth could answer, a thundering of hooves sounded from the drive. Both bowmen ran to the window.

"'No men of ours! She has called for help! We must prepare to hold them off until our queen's return!"

But even as they loaded their crossbows, two men jumped from their horses and ran through the open doors of Coudenoure. Their hair was soaked and their clothes bedraggled by mud and rain.

Elizabeth saw them and cried aloud while Agnes called out.

"Charles! You have come!"

But it was not Charles who entered the library first, but Henry. And as Elizabeth turned, she saw the bowman take aim.

"NO!"

Elizabeth screamed out the word and threw herself in front of Henry clutching his broad chest even as the deadly arrow flashed across the room. She felt its steel tip tear through her body and, gasping, looked up at her love as the blood began to flow.

Charles tackled the second bowman before he could launch his arrow. The King looked down at Elizabeth and gently sank to the floor, holding her tightly.

"Hold on, dearest, hold on! You must for I cannot live without you!"

Her eyes began to close but a whispered word caught his ear, and he leaned closer to her lips.

"I will leave a fire in the hearth for you, my Henry."

She was gone. Henry clutched Elizabeth's still body tightly. His tears began to flow, unchecked.

"No no no no no!" he screamed in anguish again and again. With a single arrow, his whole world had been destroyed, and he had been forced to watch her give her life for his. Gone now was his childhood, his love, his humanity. Charles knelt beside him, wrapping his sovereign in his arms.

*****

As the candles were lit against the dark evening, Henry finally stood, and Agnes and Prudence watched sobbing as Elizabeth's body was taken to her bedroom. Cromwell had arrived with troops, but not in time. He and Charles stood before the fire, waiting for Henry to return to them.

"Majesty." Cromwell bowed deeply.

Henry wiped away his final tears.

"This is her doing."

Neither Cromwell nor Charles Brandon responded. After a moment, the king spoke again, this time to Cromwell.

"She has written her own death warrant. Do you hear me?"

Cromwell nodded and bowed.

Henry walked from the room, knowing that his life had been torn to pieces and that not even he, the Great Henry, could ever put it back together again.

*****

Constance stood at the prow of the ship, feeling the salty sea air beat against her face. She held tightly to a heavy object with both hands, feeling her tears mix with the rain and the spray until she was one with the misty night. She held the object up and placed its bottom on the prow's railing in order to stabilize it and stare at it.

Carved from the most flawless white marble she had ever seen was the face of a woman turned slightly away from the viewer. Her hair flowed out behind her in a great wave, and her right hand, so delicately carved that a single breath might cause it harm, reached gently out towards the viewer. The beautiful face, carved in such exquisite detail as to be almost ephemeral, caused her tears to flow anew, for it was Elizabeth.

*****

[Continued by Royal Sagas 2: "The Other Elizabeth"]

Made in the USA
Las Vegas, NV
22 January 2021

16385413R00269